The Other Year

OTHER BOOKS BY REA FREY

Not Her Daughter

Because You're Mine

Until I Find You

Secrets of Our House

The Other Year

A Novel

Rea Frey

HARPER MUSE

The Other Year

© 2023 Rea Frey

Published by Harper Muse, an imprint of HarperCollins Focus LLC.

This book is a work of fiction. The characters, incidents, and dialogue are drawn from the author's imagination and are not to be construed as real. Any resemblance to actual events or persons, living or dead, is entirely coincidental.

Any internet addresses (websites, blogs, etc.) in this book are offered as a resource. They are not intended in any way to be or imply an endorsement by HarperCollins Focus LLC, nor does HarperCollins Focus LLC vouch for the content of these sites for the life of this book.

Library of Congress Cataloging-in-Publication Data

Names: Frey, Rea author.
Title: The other year : a novel / Rea Frey.
Description: [Nashville] : Harper Muse, [2023] | Summary: "In parallel timelines, mother Kate Baker lives a life where her 9-year-old daughter drowns and another life in which she survives. Can the entire course of our lives be traced back to a single moment?"--Provided by publisher.
Identifiers: LCCN 2023010755 (print) | LCCN 2023010756 (ebook) | ISBN 9781400243105 (paperback) | ISBN 9781400243112 (epub) | ISBN 9781400243129
Subjects: LCGFT: Novels.
Classification: LCC PS3606.R4885 O84 2023 (print) | LCC PS3606.R4885 (ebook) | DDC 813/.6--dc23/eng/20230309
LC record available at https://lccn.loc.gov/2023010755
LC ebook record available at https://lccn.loc.gov/2023010756

Printed in the United States of America

23 24 25 26 27 LBC 5 4 3 2 1

For my daughter
in every life

A NOTE FROM THE AUTHOR

A FEW YEARS AGO, I WAS STANDING ON THE BEACH IN SANTA Rosa, watching my daughter frolic in the ocean. Just like the protagonist of my book, Kate Baker, it was the first day of our yearly vacation, and my then-nine-year-old daughter was so eager to get into the waves, she didn't even consider the red flag whipping behind us.

As I paced back and forth along the stretch of sand, the entire premise of this book came to me in a single moment: one of those flashes of inspiration that are so rare, it makes you scramble to find paper so you can write it all down before you lose it forever.

This book was born from that single moment on the beach, and I am so very proud of the story you hold in your hands.

I wanted to share a few things, however. One is a hard truth about me as a mother, and one is a hard truth about this book *for* mothers.

Being a mother is one of the most difficult things I've ever done. I am not quiet about the fact that I never planned on having kids; in fact, I was vehemently "anti-kids" for most of my life. (When my daughter was young, I wrote a column for the *Nashville Scene* called "My Daughter, the A**hole." True story.) I figured I'd be terrible at motherhood. I was selfish and flawed and filled with wanderlust. I was sometimes critical and loved to do what I wanted to do. I was afraid of the changes it would cause to my body and relationships. Plus, I was not very nurturing. (By not very, I mean not at all. I actually laughed the first time my husband cried in front of me. I know that's terrible, but I am such a better human now.) How could I ever raise a tiny human to be a *good* human? How could I trust the world to take care of a child when I could not? It just didn't seem like the life meant for me.

When I met my husband, I sat him down early on and explained that I did not want kids and I needed to make sure he knew that. If he wanted to become a dad, he could get out before it was too late. He gripped my hand, looked me in the eye, and said, "I choose you." (Thirteen years later, this still remains true.)

Well, I always like to say our daughter chose us. *Ten days* after ovulation, I "accidentally" got pregnant. To say I struggled with the news of my pregnancy is an understatement. We were freelancers living in downtown Chicago. We had no stability, no clear direction, no health insurance, and it rocked me. None of it was easy. My fifty-two-hour labor wasn't easy. Being a new mom wasn't easy. Moving from downtown Chicago to Nashville to be closer to family wasn't easy. Living in suburbia wasn't easy. But loving her? That was the easiest thing I'd ever done. That was never a question. As we grew to know and love her even more, it seemed like it had always been just the three of us.

And as she continued to change, I often wondered, *What would my life look like if I had never become a mother?* And then, *What would my life look like if I lost her?*

This is not an easy question, and yet so many mothers lose their daughters. When a parent loses a child, it marks them. It *defines* them. But do we talk about it openly and honestly? Grief is not something we spend a lot of time on in books; it's easier to move around it, allude to it, but not go through it.

Dear readers, in this book we are going to take a hard look at grief, because grief often leads to beauty. Because grief is part of life. Because grief gets us to the other side, and life is not always about the good stuff (but don't worry, there's plenty of light and joy and fun and romance in this book too).

I can't imagine a life without my daughter in it; I can't imagine how I'd find the resolve to move on if something happened to her. And yet people do it every day. Here, on these pages, I used Kate's story to work out a bit of my own fears. To put myself in her shoes. (And yes, I shed a lot of tears while writing many scenes in this book.)

I have never written a story so deeply personal. I used a lot of my daughter's quirks to create Liv. Though she is not Liv, she is *in* Liv. Though I am not Kate, I can relate to Kate, because I am a mother to a daughter I so passionately treasure and am deeply afraid of losing. And yet I know my daughter is not mine. She came through me, but she is her own unique person, having her own unique experiences, and therein lies the rub of parenthood: Hold tight, but not too tightly. Help them grow, but then release them. Let them live, and then be there if they need you along the way.

I appreciate you taking the time to read *The Other Year*. I would love for you to ponder the question: Do we end up where we are supposed to no matter what, or does grief send us on a different path completely?

I will let you decide.

Summer

Prologue

THE RED FLAG RIPPLES IN THE WIND.

Olivia is all business, her body primed for the impending crush of waves. She squints up at me, as if to ask permission:

If I go in alone, will I be okay?

I nod. Olivia knows her boundaries. She passed her swimming test at the YMCA three years ago, and she will stay close to shore. Other adults and children dapple the ocean like buoys, towheaded, brunette, shaven—it's all one nation in the arms of the sea. Olivia glances down at a partially washed-away sandcastle, mildly curious, then retrains her focus on the ocean.

"The current is strong, Liv. Stay close, okay?"

We've talked extensively about how to swim parallel to shore if she is ever tugged out or gets spun up in a wave from the undertow. I gaze at her, toes flexing against the pliable sand, chest aimed at the water, her defiant chin angled toward a flawless sky. I love the way she announces herself to the ocean, the respect she has for its ruthless power. While she still makes occasional comments about the salty air, the stench of fish, or the way the coarse sand scrubs her ankles, she adores the water as much as I do.

Liv bobs her head, eyebrows scrunched, her mind already inside the thrashing waves that churn against the beach, receding in a froth of clotted white foam. I delight in her anticipation, wishing I'd worn my bathing suit too, but we'd come straight from the car instead of heading to the rental house first. She'd managed to wriggle into her suit in the back seat and had been so impatient to get to the water, she hadn't even closed the car door.

The first wave smacks her square in the chest. Her squeals send a swift punch of joy straight to my heart. It melts the tension from the overly long drive, the way we bickered about nothing. Mostly she'd stayed hunched over her iPod touch while we waited out a horrific accident, which resulted in an extra hour of travel time. When we'd passed the hunk of disfigured steel on the highway, like some god-awful modern art installation, I'd told Olivia to look away. But I hadn't. The image of the flattened truck was seared into my mind, the blood splatter along the pavement—still fresh—the endless ambulances and cop cars. I am still processing it, hoping whoever was in that truck is okay, but also knowing that almost no one could survive a crash like that.

Olivia waves. I wave back and take one picture too many as her limbs buck and dip in and out of the ocean. I send a quick photo to my best friend, Jason, who arrives tomorrow with his daughter, Ayana. He sends back a heart emoji and a quick line.

I can't wait to be there with you.

The sudden sexual tension between us floats through my mind—after one recent admission from Jason wondering what we would be like as more than just friends—and I begin to panic. We have never crossed any physical lines, and I haven't dated since my divorce, but something has definitely shifted, and I'm nervous to see what might happen when we are alone, on vacation.

I text the same photo of Liv to my mom, then post one on Instagram of my own sandy feet, which my ex-husband, Michael, insisted evolved from hobbits. I smile at the memory, all the ways he used to make me laugh. The smile vanishes as I think of his text message yesterday. He wants to talk.

We haven't seen each other for over a year—he's been in Israel on an archaeology dig—but I know that in typical Michael fashion, he's going to want to jump right back into Liv's life, even though his absence has left a painful residue for us both. Michael is either all in or completely wrapped up in his work. He's never been able to juggle being a full-time father and an archaeologist, something that has crushed me time and time again and disappointed Liv.

While he's been gone, I've been rethinking our coparenting arrangement; though we technically split custody, Liv lives with me. He's always on the road, always on a dig, something we used to embark on together before I became a mother and decided to take a steadier, more stable job in Nashville. Michael didn't want to move from our life in Virginia, didn't want anything to change, but he did it for me. However, once we moved, he was constantly on the road. It got to the point where I told him I didn't want a husband *sometimes*; I wanted him all the time, and he just couldn't make that promise to me. To Liv. To us. My body tenses as I replay that painful decision to separate, then eventually divorce. Becoming a single mother changed my life completely. For Michael, it has changed nothing.

Now, as the water rushes over my feet, tugging and receding, I toe a sand dollar free, rinse it clean, and wag it in the air at Liv.

"Hold on to it for me, Mama!" She wipes the salt from her eyes and dives under again.

I pocket the treasure and check the time. It's our yearly tradition to order pizza and salads for dinner on our first night of vacation, and the delivery is expected in less than an hour. I'm eager to get to the beach house, air it out, and unpack. I stalk the sand, watching Liv float, dive, and pivot.

Though this year has been tough, with demanding clients and huge projects that I must oversee, I've made a vow to be a more present parent. As an agricultural engineer, I've spent much of my career in the field, designing equipment, developing methods for land preparation, planting, and harvesting. With the promise of a promotion on the horizon, which would mean more computer work and less field work, I promised Liv I would be more available. I could sign up for PTA meetings. I could chaperone field trips and get to know the other moms at school. I could finally start the garden that Liv has been begging for but that hasn't happened yet because I'm always so busy with work.

My being more available means a lot to Liv, and I want to make her happy. I know that childhood is fleeting; soon she will be in fourth grade. There will be boys and hormones and battles between friends. I'm already witnessing her childlike traits disappear, her identity as my little girl transforming into someone else. I don't want time to pass us by.

She erupts from the waves every few seconds, her orange long-sleeved one-piece slightly too large. She is growing so fast and caught between sizes. Her crotch sags with collected sand, but surprisingly, she doesn't complain. After a year of no vacations due to my intense work demands, she isn't going to waste a second of this one.

When my phone dings in my pocket, I answer, one eye trained on Liv while scanning for shark fins, the other on the message. It's from Michael, as if by thinking about him I've conjured his text.

We really need to talk, K. Call me when you can, por favor, mi amor.

I sigh. *Mi amor.* Though we are divorced, there is still so much love between us. I miss him. I miss us. I miss being a family. I text back a reply that we are on vacation and I will connect with him when we're back in two weeks. Disgruntled, I return my focus to the ocean, back to Liv.

The waves climb and crash. Other children scream and play, tossing tiny footballs to each other or riding boogie boards on healthy waves. I search for Olivia's unruly brown curls, her bright bathing suit, that oversized rainbow on the chest. My heart seizes, and I take a step toward the water.

One moment she is there—*right there*.

The next, she is gone.

1

INSTEAD OF SCREAMING HER NAME, I SCAN THE SEA, SURE she's just drifted and will pop to the surface, algae braided through her hair like ropes.

After seconds of not seeing her, I step into the water until it drenches my pant legs, my eyes combing the sea from left to right.

As if on cue, Olivia explodes out of a wave, her limbs arched like a starfish. Her emergence sends an electric assault through my chest, followed by relief at her exuberance.

She is fine.

I motion for her to stay closer to shore. I stuff the phone into my fanny pack and delight in Liv's manic, practiced movements, wishing once again that I had my bathing suit. I glance behind me, suddenly aware of the few families still on the beach for the day. Under my jumpsuit, I wear a sports bra and boy shorts, both black, both luckily resembling a bathing suit. I step out of my clothes and crumple the jumpsuit on a nearby patch of dry sand, then wade in after her, the water an icy shock against my skin.

"Mama!" Olivia shrieks and slaps the top of the water with her tiny, open palms. "You're coming in?" She blinks and wipes water from her eyes, as we forgot her goggles back in the car.

In response, I dive under a wave and swim to her, my limbs jarring awake after so many hours in the car. I grip her middle. She loops her spindly legs around my waist. She is slippery and warm. We look so alike and nothing alike—Michael is Mexican, I am white, and Olivia is a perfect blend. She has pieces and parts of my family and his. She has my family's Eastern European cheekbones and strong chin; she has Michael's wavy dark hair, dark skin, chocolate eyes, and gap between her front teeth. I kiss her wet nose and smooth her unmanageable hair, now damp and flat, from her face. "*Hermosa,*" I say. *Beautiful.* Though Michael hasn't been as present in her life, I try to work in Spanish as much as I can.

"*Tú también, Mamá.*" *You too.*

I praise her flawless pronunciation, and she offers me a generous smile. Freckles trample her nose and cheeks. Another trait from me. A notched scar mars her right eyebrow from when she walked straight into our dining room table as a toddler, which resulted in two stitches above her eye. What used to embarrass her, she now embraces, as she's reached that age where scars are cool.

The water seems to pick up in its late-afternoon ferocity, and I keep an eye out for shark fins, always aware of whose territory we are really in. We swim and float, and then finally ride a wave all the way to shore. Olivia's bathing suit slides up to reveal a perfect half-moon of her butt cheek. I laugh and motion for her to fix it, emerging from the water refreshed, just as the flag changes to double red and lifeguards blow their whistles, commanding everyone out of the water. I gather my clothes and shimmy into my jumpsuit, and the two of us walk back to the car without towels.

Olivia chats a mile a minute on the short drive to the rental house. We pause at a four-way stop for an ambulance. It careens around us, siren blaring.

"I hope the people are okay," Liv says once it passes.

"Me too." I think again of the accident we saw on the way down, the dismantled truck, crushed like a flimsy toy.

Once we park, Olivia jumps out. "Look! A chicken!" She points to a beautiful rust-colored chicken waddling down the cobblestone path of our short block. "Can I pet it?"

I shrug, unsure if chickens carry diseases like birds. I once saw a documentary where people groomed their chickens and entered them into competitions for money. Olivia, who adores all living creatures, reaches out her hand, but the chicken ignores her and keeps clucking and walking in the opposite direction.

"So cute," she sighs. "Could we get a chicken for a pet?"

"I don't think so."

I catch her side profile, not for the first time registering just how much she's changed this past year. For starters, she's growing boobs. There will soon be locked doors, training bras, and a demand for privacy. No more joint baths or Liv running carelessly through the house in her underwear. That fleeting window of parent-child intimacy shrinks by the day, and Liv runs hot and cold—one minute treating me as someone she's always turned to, and the next, shutting me out completely. And Michael is missing it all. I loop an arm around her shoulder and squeeze tight.

"I need a pet, Mama. Every girl needs a pet. It's part of my hero's journey."

"Your hero's journey? What part would that be?"

"The call to adventure. Duh," she says. "Plus, if we got a chicken, it could lay fresh eggs, right?"

"True. But we also have coyotes and foxes that aren't too kind to chickens." I ruffle her damp hair. "Liv, I know having a pet sounds fun, but they're a lot of responsibility too."

She rolls her eyes and sighs. "You always say that."

"Because it's true."

At the door to Here Comes the Sun, I fiddle with the key, admiring the renovated rental. Inside, Olivia bolts upstairs, clearly annoyed with me about the pet conversation. This is the first time I've rented the house longer than a week, and while I initially had second thoughts about being gone so long, Jason and Ayana offered to keep us company (and pay for half, which helps). Plus, it's my fortieth birthday, so I figure it's worth the splurge.

When I hear the shower crank upstairs, I find a spare towel and pat myself dry while I assess the living room. A comfy sectional faces an oversized coffee table, fanned with local magazines. The open kitchen sits beyond, cut in an L shape with all new appliances. The twenty-foot dining table sits to the right, loaded with chairs for renters with large families. After making a quick grocery list and checking the app for the pizza delivery, I walk up to the third-floor primary suite and rinse off in the steam shower, then head back to the kitchen to chill a bottle of wine. I take the opportunity before Olivia comes back downstairs to slip onto the front porch and ease into a rocking chair without my phone.

Even though I am on vacation, I've already received at least twenty-five emails from my boss with the subject line, "Don't you dare respond until vacation is over, but . . ."

As if I won't read them. As if any workaholic unplugs enough to not constantly worry about the never-ending to-do list. I'm currently managing three big project builds, and my boss has implied that if all goes well, I could be looking at a promotion. While I've always been career-driven, once I became a single parent, it became mission critical. Though Michael helps with child support, most of the monetary responsibility falls on my shoulders, and I want to give Liv everything I can, everything I never had growing up.

It has taken me years to get where I am, and while no one is telling me I have to prove myself, the innate need is always there, especially working in a predominantly male field. Though most companies have gone remote since the pandemic—a wonderful gift for single parents everywhere—I still go into the office several days a week, just to have in-person meetings with my boss. I show up to project sites regularly, and I even work weekends if there's a client issue.

Much like Michael, I never established proper boundaries on my climb up the ladder, and I've paid for it in numerous ways: no time for romance, a shameful lack of presence with Liv, and various house projects and goals that never seem to get done because I'm too busy working.

And though I've carved out two entire weeks away—weeks that I've more than earned—there's always that nagging feeling that I'm not doing enough, that my team will drop the ball in my absence, or worse, that someone else might do a better job and my expertise will become obsolete. It's unnerving to try to maintain the balance of being a single parent and having a demanding career, and for once, I just want to tuck the deadlines away and enjoy a vacation. I've vowed that this will be the year that I strike the balance, that I stop trying to prove myself in the office and carve out more quality time with Liv.

Which starts now.

I blink into the waning sunlight, coughing as the neighbor next door lights up a cigarette. I close my eyes, bracing myself for the next two weeks. So much of this vacation hinges on how it all goes these first few days: Olivia not getting sunburned, not having irritated eyes from her goggles, not getting overly tired, not getting stung by a jellyfish, not getting homesick, not getting into a fight with Ayana . . . It seems all our trips hinge on her moods, and I often can't keep up with how savagely they swing.

I lose myself to the rhythmic push and pull of the chair, and my thoughts wander back to Jason. What he said to me as we sat out by the fire in my backyard a few nights ago. *"I've always wondered what life would have been like if we'd ended up together."* Twenty years of friendship rattled with one brazen sentence. And now? Now I can't stop thinking about the possibility of more.

The food delivery guy turns into the driveway, startling me from my thoughts, pizza boxes hot and fragrant in his outstretched arms. I take them and hustle inside, arranging the boxes on one end of the dining room table. The strong aroma of oregano and garlic makes my mouth water. I call for Olivia, who is already in her pajamas. The two of us sit at the dining room table with its fourteen metal chairs crammed around it. We are just a party of two. It amazes me how some families fill these rental homes completely.

We chew in silence before Olivia launches into the plot of a story she wants to write. I nod and swallow my wine, my mind working out how it's going to be to share a house with Jason, starting tomorrow. Finally, she loses herself to her food, and I ignore the itch to look at my phone, a typical distraction that keeps me from the present moment.

I tear off another slice of margherita pizza, which has grown cold, the cheese congealed, the crust hard. I eat it anyway, stabbing baby kale leaves and scooping some roasted brussels sprouts and cauliflower onto my plate. I barely say a word, but Olivia doesn't seem to notice.

Outside, a raucous family throws a football. Having been raised by a single mother, I always longed for a giant family, but after an extremely difficult labor with Olivia—and not getting pregnant until thirty—I took what I could get. I wanted more children, but after the divorce, the potential for a bigger family closed up like a box.

"What's wrong, Mama?" Olivia chews and stares thoughtfully at me.

"What do you mean?"

"You have your worried smile."

"I do?" I reach over and kiss her cheek. "You know me so well. I'm not worried, though, I promise. Just trying to go from work mode to vacation mode. Sometimes it takes Mama a minute."

"That makes sense." She plucks a glob of cheese from her pizza and abandons the crust. "Are you excited about your birthday?"

I smile. "You know me. Not much of a birthday person."

"I know. But maybe this year can be different."

I try to figure out how to explain why getting older isn't as awesome as celebrating birthdays when you're a kid. I don't dread aging; in fact, I'm looking forward to my forties, but I've also never been someone to throw big parties for myself. "I think sometimes it feels a little selfish to make a big fuss for just turning one year older."

She shakes her head. "That's not selfish. That's what people do."

"Which is why you always have the best birthday parties."

I admire Olivia as she launches into play with two tiny dolls and a pizza crust. Something rough roots around my heart. With every passing day, I worry that I'm not showing up as the role model I want to be. Yes, I am a hardworking single mother, and that's something. But when I look at all the other moms at her school, who constantly devote themselves to committees, fundraisers, and field trips, I feel like a fraud.

Doesn't she need more in her life than just me, my mom, Jason, and Ayana? Is she missing out on the great big family I always imagined for her? I chastise myself for going down the rabbit hole of *what is not* instead of *what is*, but that stab of worry needles its way in: What if it turns out that I've been failing her all this time?

But when Liv looks at me and smiles, a fleck of oregano stuck to her oversized front tooth, I begin to laugh, which makes her laugh. She chews a piece of kale, smearing it across her teeth with her tongue, and then asks, "What? Do I have something in my teeth?"

And just like that, the worry fades to a slight residue. Perhaps she has everything she needs . . . but do I?

Jason floats through my mind again. I haven't entertained the idea of bringing a man into my life since the divorce. I'm not one of those women who thinks her life is completed by a man. Quite the contrary, in fact, as my yearslong hiatus from dating has proven. At some point it became less about not wanting to date and more about not having time.

I'm also afraid of disrupting the dynamic between me and Liv. Even though she's creeping toward ten, I feel like I've finally gotten the hang of how to be a single parent. What would life look like if I added one more person to the mix? Would Liv feel left out? Would she feel as though she were competing with someone else for my attention?

Liv continues to goof around, and I hand her a napkin to smudge the greens from her teeth. I know the real question isn't necessarily just about what Liv needs. It's about what I need too. Sometimes I feel stuck in my past with Michael or too fully focused on the future.

When I really think about what I want for my life, what—or who—might I find waiting there?

ONE

INSTEAD OF SCREAMING LIV'S NAME, I HESITATE AND SCAN the sea, sure she's just drifted and will pop to the surface, algae braided through her hair like ropes.

I glance behind me at a large sandcastle. Is she there now, crouched in a ball as she sometimes is, inconspicuous enough to be trampled? *No.* The panic catches fire and spreads. One moment I am calm. The next, I howl her name with enough ferocity to quiet the remaining beachgoers.

I sprint down a stretch of beach, hunting for her bright suit. Children with buckets and spades startle as I hurry past them, examining both water and land. I turn in a hasty circle—check the dock, the packed parking lot behind me, the expanse of seagrass tall enough to conceal a body.

I jog to the right, my feet slapping the damp sand. I grip a sunburned man who's shading his eyes, staring into the ocean. "Have you seen my daughter? She's wearing an orange suit." He shakes his head, and I ask a few kids, rotating back toward the parking lot.

Did she go back to the car for her goggles or float?

Not knowing what else to do, I sprint forward into the ocean until the spray hits my calves and drenches my jumpsuit. My body is charged, my heart its frenetic leader. I wade deeper, scanning and talking myself out of my instinctive panic. *Olivia is a strong swimmer. Olivia knows to stay close to shore.* I watch for the orange bathing suit again and flap my arms toward the slightly tilted lifeguard tower. It sits vacant, thick with rust. There is no jet ski, no four-wheeler with a red emergency logo embossed on the side, no beach bodies clad in lifeguard apparel, tan and primed for rescue.

"My daughter!" I scream to no one and everyone. "She was just here!"

Barrel-chested men with deep tans and beers in ham fists join me; a few children smacked by waves stare, slack-jawed and unsteady. A little girl begins to wail. Her mother scoops her up and shoots me a concerned look. I press a hand to my chest in an attempt to calm myself. A child does not just disappear in the ocean. It is a clear day. She has to be on land somewhere. But then I think of the red flag violently whipping behind me, an obvious warning of a strong undertow.

"Olivia!" I call her name again, an eternity of nine years of worst-case scenarios and almost disasters frozen on my lips.

The crew divides. The current strengthens, and I am ripped to the left of where I just stood. I dive under, which is pointless, and choke on salty water. I emerge, coughing, my soggy clothes an extra weight. Waves pummel my back and knock me under. I grapple to find my footing and stand. Finally, a lifeguard high-steps into the water, a red buoy tucked under his arm.

I can hardly breathe as I utter the words, "My daughter was just here," and point to the endless depths of the Gulf. It seems to stretch forever. "Orange suit."

The lifeguard, who can't be older than twenty, whistles toward the beach and two more able bodies sprint from the shadows. I search the shoreline, praying that Olivia will suddenly reappear, wet and oblivious to the nightmare unfolding before me. We can apologize to the lifeguards, eat our pizza, and get on with our vacation. Nothing more than a terrifying false alarm.

"Please." I tent my hands in a mock prayer and wait, count, breathe. "Please find her."

My legs nearly buckle as the undertow tugs us sharply left.

"Riptide!" the main lifeguard exclaims before blowing a whistle and ushering people out of the water. The lifeguards dive in despite the danger, dipping and resurfacing empty-handed as I stand helpless, waiting for my maternal instincts to tell me exactly where she is. I clutch my wet phone in my hand, realizing I turned my attention away for just a second—*one second!*—and now she is lost at sea.

I think briefly of Michael, whose text is the very reason I looked away at the most critical second of my life. If she doesn't return, if she drowns . . . I will never forgive myself. Or him.

I advance deeper into the water, despite the dangerous undertow, and call her name, tears mingling with the salt on my cheeks. The beach was nearly barren when we arrived, in its pre-dinner wind-down, but an excitable crowd has grown and strengthened. Women grip their children while the professionals do their work. Somewhere far off, a siren sounds until an emergency vehicle speeds toward us, spitting white-gray sand under monstrous black tires. A female with sunbaked skin hops down. She radios something in as I'm wrenched again by the undertow.

A far-off whistle brings me back to my body. Something brushes against my leg and makes me instinctively jump. Hope springs. Liv? I scoop the object into my hand—just a mangled knot

19

of algae—and fling it back into the sea. I lunge toward the sound and spot a lifeguard, about thirty feet out, waving his hands. His head disappears and re-emerges, Olivia's limp body draped across his buoy. "Olivia!"

My voice cracks as I hurry out to meet him, but sets of waves gather strength and keep me from her. My body trembles and quiets as he nears the shore, slicing through the waves with one arm, dragging my daughter, head above water, behind him. I struggle to follow as the sea's impossible current yanks me backward. My phone slips from my fingers, then disappears into the churning surf.

Once out of the water, the lifeguard cradles Olivia on the sandy beach as others bark to give him room. Her body is all wrong. Bones loose and bendy. Mouth yawning open, jaw slack. Eyes half-open. Lacerations spatter across her cheek; she must have smashed into coral. Blood runs in thin pink lines down her face, mixed with the seawater. I catalog what I will need to fix her up: ice for the swelling, soap and water, ointment and bandages for the cuts.

"Liv!" I say her name and expect her to startle awake, as she sometimes does after a bad dream. I stand behind the lifeguard, then drop to my knees on the hard-packed sand, unblinking, in utter disbelief. Instinctively, I lunge toward her, hungry for contact. I scoop her hand in mine and squeeze.

"Come on, Liv. Wake up. *Please* wake up."

Her face is pale, lifeless, her limbs splayed like a starfish. I clutch her fingers again, willing life into her. Any moment she could spit up a gallon of water and suddenly come to.

The lifeguard asks my permission to give her CPR, checks for a pulse, and leans over my daughter, creating an airtight seal with his lips before giving her two rescue breaths. The shock of it consumes me—this grown man's mouth on my unconscious daughter's lips—and I'm suddenly struck with the idea of Olivia never growing old enough to be kissed.

He arranges his hands on her breastbone and begins chest compressions. Her hair sticks to her skin and wraps around her throat like black vines. He works diligently. Olivia's head makes sharp, jerky movements as beads of water drip onto her motionless face.

After a minute, another lifeguard steps in with a defibrillator. He rips her bathing suit down, exposing her bare chest, and towels her off before sticking the electrode pads on her skin. Voice prompts call out the directions in a robotic monotone, advising her to be shocked. Liv's tiny body jolts, then settles, lifeless, in the sand.

When nothing happens, the first lifeguard begins the ventilation cycle again with two breaths before compressing her ribs in the same spot between her nipples, aggressively pressing down again and again until my maternal instincts make me scream for him to stop.

"You're doing it too hard!"

I have no way of knowing that, other than what my eyes tell me. He ignores me. I fear the audible *crack* of her ribs, like kindling, and worry that, even if he doesn't break her ribs, she'll be sore in the morning. My mind floats above my body as I try to let hope override the fear.

There will be a tomorrow. This is just a scare. Olivia will be okay.

He works for another minute until the defibrillator administers its second shock. The first lifeguard sits back on his sandy heels, defeated and breathing hard as an ambulance arrives. EMTs spill out of the back, and he waves them over.

The first lifeguard resumes breath and chest compressions as the medics cluster around us, but I refuse to let go of Liv's hand. An indignant scream threatens to erupt as they huddle around my daughter with bags and boards, snapping commands, while continuing with the

CPR. I hold Liv's hand tighter, her wilted fingers laced through mine, floppy and wet.

"Wake up, baby. Please wake up. Olivia. *Please*. You have to wake up." I rattle her arm and pat the back of her hand.

Even as they prepare to usher her to the ambulance, I fear the worst. I assess the grim looks on the EMTs' faces, the weeping onlookers, the nervous whispers and solemn faces of the lifeguards.

An inhuman cry erupts from my mouth as I squeeze Liv's unresponsive hand in mine, begging her to *just wake up*. But her limbs are cold, shriveled. She smells of salt and fish—nothing like my Liv. The blue and red lights of the emergency vehicles explode around us in a kaleidoscopic halo. My senses shut off. The bystanders, horrified and hushed. The somber lifeguards, humbled by the unexpected turn of events. The bonfires canceled, empty chairs fanned in semicircles that will see no life or laughter tonight. The possible tragedy ricochets off this slice of beach, forever tainting it.

"Oh, my sweet Liv." I choke on the words and begin to sob all over again. I am not a woman who cries openly, but I let it all go— snot, tears, screams, agony. "This can't be happening."

I watch the paramedics slide Liv onto a stretcher and strap her down, her body relaxed and still unresponsive as they continue working on her.

My voice is raw, my legs rubbery, my throat sharp and dry. I command my legs to work and shuffle across the sand, wishing I could go back in time to change that one solitary moment—looking down instead of paying attention to my child. I pause at the back of the ambulance and watch as they hoist her up and in.

My mind is numb as I step up into the back of the mammoth vehicle, a witness to my motionless daughter on the stretcher. The female EMT hooks her up to a heart rate monitor, and I wait to hear signs of life. Maybe she's just unconscious. Maybe she will finally wake up. Maybe her body is still working, even though she's asleep. I search for the punch of an audible pulse, but the monitor is flat.

They push fluids and epinephrine and warn me they are going to intubate. I've seen this procedure on medical TV shows, but now that it's real, I can't watch. I squeeze my eyes shut just as they force a tube down her throat. The EMTs call out different commands, and once Liv is intubated, they continue to monitor her.

The siren blares as the ambulance cuts sharply around a corner. The EMTs are quiet as they fuss around Liv, working diligently. I sit, steadying myself amid the jostling equipment and cramped space, and fight the instinct to drape my body across hers. Streams of tears that seem to have no end leak down my cheeks and saturate my neck. I take an unsteady step forward to run my fingers along her arms and adjust the blanket they have draped around her bare legs. "Come on, baby. Wake up."

Olivia has so much life—she *is* life. She must wake up. I wait for an improbable flicker, a miracle that will help her spring back to life. It will be a story we tell, the time she almost drowned but didn't. That vacation she nearly scared me to death. The improbable moment she returned and everything, from that miraculous moment, was different.

"Ma'am, please. We need you to sit down." As if to illustrate their point, we fly over a bump and I lose my footing, my body cocked at an unnatural angle over the stretcher. I don't want to sit down, don't want to let go.

This is my child.

"Ma'am. Please, it's for your safety."

Reluctantly, I release her and take my seat. My eyes flicker to the screen again. More tears pepper my cheeks and slip onto my chest, mixed with incessant regret. If only I could go back. If only I hadn't looked at my phone. If only I would have gotten in the water.

If only I had one more chance.

2

THE NEXT MORNING I RISE EARLY AND TAKE A WALK BY THE beach while Liv's still sleeping.

I leave a cheery note next to her iPod so she can message me if she wakes. While most of my friends never leave their kids at home alone under any circumstances, no one I'm friends with is a single mom. Sometimes I have to run errands or make a quick stop and trust she is being safe and responsible.

I check the time. Jason and Ayana should be arriving later this afternoon. My heart quickens in my chest as I think about his admission. Will he simply pretend he never said it?

Though Jason has been single for years too, casually dating here and there, his circumstances are wildly different from my own. His wife, Shelby—my other best friend—died seven years ago from breast cancer. As they hadn't had children yet, five years ago, Jason decided to adopt a four-year-old from Ethiopia in honor of Shelby's heritage. He named her Ayana, which means "a pretty flower"; her middle name, Adia, means "returning." Over the years we have helped each other navigate every parenting challenge imaginable, and because of that, Olivia and Ayana are inseparable.

I walk across the cool sand. The waves break over my feet, revealing translucent crabs, shells, and half-broken sand dollars that I collect for Liv. Suntanned men hustle across creamy stretches of beach, timers set, past umbrellas expertly drilled into the earth for the crush of vacationers staying at overpriced condos.

This year we bought cheap umbrellas and backpack chairs to avoid the exorbitant rental costs. I walk for twenty minutes, then turn back, a light sweat working its way over my body. My phone dings.

Ayana just hugged me and said, "I love your stomach, Daddy. It feels like my pillow." WTF? #fatboy #over40 #dadbod

I laugh and type back a response. *Did you really just use hashtags like a MILLENNIAL? #officiallynotmybestfriendanymore*

Only an extremely old, out-of-touch person would use a hashtag so long, he replies. *#coolerthanyou*

At least my daughter doesn't refer to my stomach as a pillow.

You are not a nice human, Kate Baker.

I roll my eyes. Jason runs a functional-training wellness facility back in Nashville and is one of the fittest humans I know. We've been friends for half my life and have been through the wringer in every way. Shelby and Michael used to joke that in another life, we were probably meant for each other.

They aren't wrong. Jason and I have an unshakable bond. We are passionate in the ways we talk and argue, and we have similar interests. We met randomly when I was just out of college and took a trip to Nashville to visit my mother, who had decided to move from our hometown in Virginia. I was hunting for my first job and had gone on a hike to clear my head. We literally bumped into each other and have been friends ever since. Over the years our friendship always trumped any potential for romance. At least until last week.

I type back a hasty reply. *We'll do wind sprints on the beach every morning. Get ready, old man. #olympics2024*

Though Jason is a few years older than me, we were both prepared to step proudly into our forties, certain that we would avoid the same clichés as everyone else. Instead, we have succumbed to the typical tell-tale aches and pains and attempt to deny that we are, in fact, getting older and that, yes, everything hurts when we get out of bed in the morning.

Did you mean to send this to Michael?

Ooh, burn, I respond.

Jason first met Michael when we were dating, and they get along famously. But that's not surprising. Michael comes off as charming, affable, trustworthy, and passionate to almost everyone he encounters. It's being married to him that's the challenge.

Drive safe. Can't wait to see you both!

I can't wait to see you too, Kate.

A small spasm of pleasure hits me in the chest. I silence my phone and turn toward the sea. Over the years, I've definitely thought about dating Jason. Sometimes, when I'm lonely, I daydream about what life might have looked like if I'd married my best friend instead of Michael, but that fantasy never gets too far, because it means I wouldn't have Liv.

On the way back, I stop at Sunrise Coffee and order a large coffee and a chocolate peanut butter smoothie for Olivia. I cradle the carrier in my arms and walk past Gulf Place, with its boutique restaurants, overpriced shops, and antique ice cream parlor that Olivia and Ayana will most likely beg to go to daily.

At the door, my phone buzzes in my pocket, and I set the carrier on the front porch. I'm praying it's not a work emergency.

It can't wait until you get back to Nashville, mi amor. Please call me.

Annoyance pushes into my morning peace, because Michael knows exactly what he's doing.

Just tell me what this is about, I reply.

Olivia.

He never calls her Liv. It's always Olivia. I almost fire off a defensive response, but I take a breath and don't give in to the bait. *What about her?* I contemplate all the reasons he would suddenly reach out. Perhaps he wants her to go on a trip, which hasn't happened in years. He always comes to her, as he has yet to settle anywhere postdivorce. Michael is always traveling, always living out of a suitcase, ready for the next assignment.

It's not something to discuss via text, Kate. Por favor, mi amor.

I sigh and fire off a quick response that I will call him later and then pocket my phone. Of course he would do this to me at the start of vacation, which Liv must have told him about. How often is she talking to him? I try to push him from my mind and listen for her, but all is still quiet. I pop her smoothie into the fridge, tiptoe upstairs to make sure she's sleeping, and then drink my coffee in silence out on the front porch, staring at the house across the street, which is for sale.

I think about pulling it up on Zillow to see how much it's going for. How fun it might be to buy a beach house and have it as an investment property. Then we could come down whenever we want.

The fantasy subsides, and I find I am still rattled by the sudden intrusion of a man who appears and disappears like the wind. When we first divorced, he promised to visit often and stay involved. And he did. Then his frequent visits tapered as work ramped up, and during this past year especially, Liv has felt the sting of his absence. But if he's back in the country, Liv will want to know. She will want to see him. Despite the fact that he's not around often, he's still her favorite person in the world.

I re-read his text and wonder what he has up his sleeve. I pocket my phone and suck down my coffee too fast, eager to burn off some of this jittery energy. I glance at my watch and wonder if I have time for a quick workout before Liv wakes up.

Inside, I head up the three flights of stairs to change. My footsteps make the stairs groan, and Olivia, always a light sleeper, calls to me just as I pass her room. I open her door. She is sprawled on the lower bunk of one of the room's four bunk beds.

"Hey, monkey. How'd you sleep?"

She stretches and opens her arms wide. I fold into them, her sour breath sweeping across my face.

"Good."

I pepper her cheeks with kisses until she giggles. Her sleepy voice worms into my heart, and I cuddle with her, telling her she has a smoothie waiting downstairs. I think of Michael again, how the two of them used to snuggle for hours, how naturally and openly affectionate he is with her. Not being so physically affectionate myself, I sometimes feel like I have to work overtime so she feels just as loved. Just as safe.

"Ready to see Ayana today?"

Her face stretches into a smile, and she clutches her stuffed fox to her chest and nods. "I'm always ready to see Ayana."

I cradle her against my chest, her warm, compact body contained and safe. I wish I could keep her this size forever. "Hey, can I ask you a question?"

"That was a question."

"Okay, smarty-pants." I hesitate over how to frame it but decide to be direct. "You know how you can send messages to people on your iPod?"

"Uh-huh."

29

"Have you been sending messages to Papá?"

I expect her to wrinkle her nose and say no, but she's quiet. She picks at her stuffed animal.

"Is that a yes?"

She shrugs.

"Hey, Liv. It's okay if you have. I just didn't know." Normally all the communication with her father comes through my phone, but now that Liv can chat or message on her own, I'm sure she reaches out to him. I gave her Michael's number ages ago so that she could memorize it in case of emergencies.

"We talk sometimes," she finally says. "He's back in America, you know."

So she already knows. "That's exciting, right? We've missed him, haven't we?"

She nods again. *"Mucho."*

My initial reaction is to ask what they've been talking about, but it's her right to have her own private conversations. Sensing Liv is on the verge of a shutdown, I change tactics. "Want to go to the beach?"

She nods and then tells me about her dream of an evil cat that shrank itself and got stuck in her hair, and then she is up and getting ready for the day.

Upstairs, I change into my white one-piece and let Olivia rub sunscreen on my back. She promises not to miss a spot. I do the same for her, kissing the top of her head, which smells like bottled sunshine.

"Deliciosa," I say.

"Do you want to eat my head, Mama? You love that smell so much."

"I do," I say, play munching her hair. "It's my favorite smell in the whole world."

We gather our chairs, towels, and toys, walking the few minutes toward the beach for our first full day. Thoughts of Michael aside, I remind myself how lucky we are to be here for an entire two weeks.

When I was a little girl, I used to come to this very beach with my mother and imagine what it would be like to own a home here someday. To vacation every summer and have the ocean for an entire two months. That used to be one of my main goals when Michael and I got married, but now it feels like a pipe dream.

We claim a spot near the water, though the beach is already crowded. Olivia clutches her pink inner tube and goggles and runs toward the shore.

"Stay close, *belleza*," I call.

"*Voy a*," she assures me.

I erect the rainbow-colored umbrella and stab the pole into the ground, packing sand on all sides so it won't tip. I pull out my novel and my towel and toss them on my chair before walking down the beach to feel the water. It is still surprisingly cold but crystal clear. I wade in, inch by inch.

"Just do it!" Liv calls. "Don't be a wuss!"

"A wuss?" I call as a wave slaps my chest and drenches me. I let out a surprised cry, then plunge my shoulders beneath the water and swim to Olivia, who is already laughing in delight. Her pink goggles make her eyes bulge, and I ask where her hat is.

"I don't want my hat."

"But you don't want to get burned on the first day," I remind her.

"I'm going to go under anyway," she insists.

"How are you going to go under if you have your inner tube?"

She shrugs. "I just am."

I know what a fight this will be if I persist. I sigh, letting it go for now. Instead, I enjoy the feel of the waves on my skin, the ocean lulling us back and forth. We bob and weave with the current, which is weak today, thankfully. I glance back at the beach, at the families with multiple children to wrangle.

I smile and splash Olivia, who expertly ducks beneath a wave. Thoughts of Michael trample my brain again. If he were here, he'd get her to laugh and smile. He'd get her to put on her hat without a fight. He always knows just how to talk to her. I attempt to shake those thoughts away and choose to savor the moment, to focus on what matters most—Liv.

But I can't help but wonder what he and Liv have been talking about. Part of me knows I should call him and get it over with, but somewhere in the back of my mind, I feel there is only one reason he could be reaching out. He wants to be an active presence in Liv's life again, which might mean more travel and shuttling her back and forth to wherever he is living. It could also mean a new custody arrangement. But as I try on that scenario, I let it go. Michael would never ask to revisit custody. He could never take on more responsibility than he already has, especially with the nature of his work.

I'm grateful that part of life is over—lawyers' fees, paperwork, and the division of time. Liv splashes and ducks underwater, and I float next to her, my head tipped up to the clear sky.

But what if it's not?

TWO

IN THE EARLY HOURS OF THE MORNING, I SIT IN THE rental house, unable to move.

Snapshots from the hospital haunt my mind: moving out of the way as Liv was rolled into the emergency room, so many bags, bodies, and equipment fighting for space. They took her from me, and I was told she had chest X-rays. Then, at last, they found a pulse. The doctor worked on her for a full forty minutes. A flicker of hope, something to cling to. Then . . . nothing. All that effort defeated in one defining moment when the doctor stepped into the waiting room. He'd removed his mask, scrubbed a hand through his brown hair, and leveled me with a glance.

"I'm so sorry," he said. "She didn't make it."

I didn't believe him. I hadn't been in the room, hadn't seen their hands and instruments attempting to revive her. I hadn't witnessed her last breath. Because of that, I'd pushed past him, down the bland hallway and into her room. I lunged toward the hospital bed and gathered my daughter in my arms, a rag doll against my abdomen. I'd stroked her back, cradled her, as if she had simply fallen asleep after a hard day at the beach and I was going to carry her to bed.

I'd gripped her too tightly, unable to fathom putting her down for good. When I'd lowered her against the stiff sheets, I'd pressed my palm over her heart, rooting for what they must have missed: *life*. Her bathing suit was cold and wet, rolled down to her middle. I hunted for a pulse for a full five minutes, even as the doctor seemed on the brink of intervention. I waited, willing time to reverse and the thick pump of her heart to fill my hand.

Finally, I'd mashed my ear to her chest. I'd grown this heart in my body, this electric, lively organ that never stopped beating. How many times had I listened to her heartbeat in bed? It was always as fast as a hummingbird, as swift as her ever-shifting mind, so full of life. I kept my ear wedged against her chest, but there was no wild, consistent thump. No whooshing air running smoothly in and out of her lungs. Just the ruthless clutch of death.

The doctor had gently explained what would happen next. There would be an autopsy, which could take up to four hours. They would then move her to the morgue and await pickup from the funeral home, which could be sometime tomorrow. While I filled out paperwork, I was peppered with questions. *What do I want to do with her body? If she isn't cremated, can I transport her home? Can I make arrangements for that? Will there be a funeral? Is there someone they should call?*

Once a doctor got my information on where to mail the death certificate, I was free to go before I could even make sense of what had happened. But I didn't go. I sat and waited until the autopsy was performed, practically catatonic in one of the cold, plastic chairs. When there was nothing left for me to do, I'd paused at the elevator, turning back. How could I leave her body here? How could I not bring her home, tuck her into bed, kiss her good night, and begin again tomorrow?

The truth slices through my body now, eternal nicks that will never heal. My daughter is gone, and yet here I am, in her favorite place, still breathing, unable to quantify what this means.

I blink into the early morning light filling the living room. While other families are just arriving in Santa Rosa, eating a hearty breakfast before heading down to the beach for the day, I am contemplating how to handle my daughter's remains.

I've always been exceptionally calm in a crisis, wearing that ability like a badge. Not today. Maybe not ever again. I sniff, my nose clogged from so much crying. "What am I supposed to do now?" I ask no one. I can't stop shaking. I need to call Jason and my mother. I need to call Michael. *Oh, Michael. How will he ever deal with this?* But I can't seem to make myself move. Suddenly I look around. Where is my phone? Do I even have it?

I think of each emotional conversation, breaking such unbearable news. From there, there will be more people to call, more hearts to break. In nine years I have never known someone's child to die. Not in my circle, at least.

I need to shower. I'm freezing, but I feel rooted to the spot. I think of the stairs I must climb, the process to undress and stand under the spray. I glance at the mirror above the couch. Already the burden of Olivia's death mars my features, evidence of my eternal mistake. It's all my fault, and everyone will know it soon enough.

Uncertainly I stand, as if I've just learned to walk, and shuffle toward the stairs. I take them slowly, going over and over what the coroner said. Apparently Liv had either caught a riptide or been pulled out by the undertow and smashed into something that had knocked her unconscious, rendering her unable to swim. I think of the wounds on her face.

I shake my head. Olivia knows to swim parallel to shore, to roll and float, to not fight the current. She would have tried to get my attention if she were in trouble—popped up, waved her arms, made herself loud. I always joke that you can hear Olivia from a mile away. She is not a quiet child. She announces herself, wherever she is.

Was.

The coroner's report also stated she had water in her belly, which prevented her from screaming for help. I clench the blanket tightly in my fist and drop it on the second-floor landing. I can't stop imagining her panicked face, that feeling of running out of air, the fear as she drifted out and then lost consciousness.

Drowned.

I pass the bunk bed room, devoid of Olivia's belongings, which are still packed in her pink suitcase in the car: bathing suits, pajamas, shorts, flip-flops, brightly colored underwear. She'd brought the whole series of her Warriors chapter books and an armload of art supplies. Her stuffed animals that she would have arranged on the bed tonight. I stare into the cheery room, sobered by the stark realization that I'll never see her again. All I have are the reminders of her, mere possessions and toys.

She's gone.

My heart begins to pound, then ache, as though someone has stabbed me through the chest. This is too much; it's all too much. I back out of the room, closing the door firmly behind me, before winding my way up the last flight of stairs. The air is frigid, but I'm too tired to adjust the thermostat. Instead, I undress and turn on the shower, stepping into it before it's fully warm.

I move under the showerhead, thinking of all the bickering we did yesterday morning on the way down. Olivia got up late and insisted on swinging and listening to music for a full twenty minutes, which was part of her morning routine. She wouldn't eat breakfast and had already packed her toothbrush, so she didn't brush her teeth. Her hair was tangled. She didn't help load the car and instead buckled herself in and then complained about the iPod not working before we'd even hit the road. On the way she'd snacked endlessly, which dusted the back of the car in crumbs. I'd criticized her and accused her of not caring about the car. And then, just moments after we arrived, I'd lost sight of her because I was texting. Now she is dead.

The whirlwind thoughts cascade with the water, pounding my shoulders and chest. So many mistakes I've made as her mother, so much unfixable, permanent damage. My one child, my *one* chance at being a parent, and I've ruined it.

I don't even wash myself but instead stay under the spray until my skin burns and the water turns cold. Finally, I emerge and wrap a towel around my body, climbing into pajamas and then under the covers, even though there's so much to be done. I have to call Michael, then my mother. I must tell her teachers and friends, our friends. Jason floats through my mind but leaves again just as quickly. I can't talk to anyone right now. I don't even know what to say.

And where is my phone?

I pull the covers over my head. I don't expect sleep to come—I'm not sure I'll ever sleep again—but suddenly the weariness wins. I think, for just a foolish moment, that maybe Olivia will appear in my dreams. Maybe this is all a nightmare and I will wake up and everything will be different.

Before I know it, I'm slipping under. I let myself be taken, half hoping I'll die too. At least that way I can be with my daughter, my sweet baby girl.

My Liv.

Hot tears slither down my cheeks, and I take a shuddering breath. I imagine her here, in my arms. I can almost feel her, almost smell that favorite spot on the top of her head. Bottled sunshine.

Deliciosa.

Guilt materializes, agonizing and fast. I will myself to go under as the morning becomes shockingly bright. Thoughts grip and torture, but I allow them to come. I deserve them. I deserve all of this.

I have no idea how our vacation has turned into this nightmare, or what I'm supposed to do next.

3

BY TWO IN THE AFTERNOON, WE ARE SPENT AND CRISPED, ravenous from hours in the water.

I take a shower and throw on a dress, wearing my hair loose and wavy around my shoulders. *Mermaid hair*, as Olivia calls it. I normally don't wear makeup at the beach, but today I slick on some red lipstick for a little pop of color. I make my way downstairs. Olivia's shower blasts, and I hear her little voice making up songs. She has a beautiful voice but will only sing if she thinks no one is listening.

I round the last step and pour myself a glass of wine. It's a little early for a drink, but I'm on vacation. Jason texts that they are almost here, and I find myself irrationally excited for the days ahead.

I'm sitting on the front porch, nursing my glass of Syrah, when Jason lays on the horn in a quick succession of honks, announcing their arrival. I rise and wave as he parks their rental car in our wide driveway. Ayana explodes out of the car, searching behind me for Olivia.

Her hair has been neatly braided in cornrows and her beautiful skin glows from the strict skin regimen Jason has adopted after a few bouts of contact dermatitis. Before Shelby died, she was meticulous about Jason knowing how to care for Black hair and Black skin. She assumed they'd have a child one day and wanted Jason to be able to share her heritage: how to dress, how to celebrate her culture. It pains me to know she will never see what a good job Jason is doing, how he continues to honor Shelby through Ayana.

As if on cue, Olivia bursts from our front door, hair tangled and damp, clad in footed pajamas. I roll my eyes, as this is one of Olivia's quirks. She wears short sleeves in winter and sweaters in summer and insists it's "her thing" and that I leave her alone. I have learned to pick my battles. Ayana sprints into Liv's outstretched arms. Liv picks her up and Ayana yelps in protest before the two disappear inside our house. Jason exits and stretches his arms over his head, revealing a patch of flat—not pillowish—stomach.

"God, they really are useless, aren't they?"

I laugh. "When it comes to helping load or unload anything? Um, yeah, utterly."

I walk around the car to give Jason a hug. He pulls me tightly against his chest, and I inhale the sharp scent of palo santo and soap, standing on tiptoe to give his cheek a quick kiss. His heart beats against mine, and it feels strangely erotic, the mad thumping of blood and muscle, separated only by fabric. His hands linger on my lower back, and I step back, embarrassed, as I study him. He is impossibly tall and annoyingly handsome, a former basketball player whose career ended in a knee injury—hence his profession in functional training. I hold my breath as our eyes lock. His words burn through my mind again, a blinding sear of possibility. It is a weighty statement, much too heavy for now. To lighten the mood, I punch him on the shoulder and ask if he's ready to go for a morning run tomorrow.

"Only if you can keep up."

"You're on."

Jason and I are both morning people, and our spouses were not. I remember how I used to have coffee, go for a run, do a load of laundry and the dishes before Michael had even stumbled from bed. He often got inspired late at night and would spend hours out in his studio until the wee hours of the morning, researching or working. I used to tiptoe around our home in the mornings because he did not like to be woken up. Shelby was the same, often sleeping in until noon on the weekends or vacation. Now Jason and I can do what we like. Though I miss Shelby like a limb, we keep her memory alive by talking about her as often as we can.

He playfully pulls me into a headlock, and I finally escape.

"You remind me of the brother I never wanted," I say, winded.

"You remind me of my actual brother I never wanted." He rubs my head affectionately.

"Austin? Wow." I extricate myself and step around to help. "I'm calling him."

"Trust me. He knows."

I help Jason unload the car and tell him I've made reservations at Borago, one of our favorite Italian restaurants in Santa Rosa.

Inside, he whistles as he surveys the house and collapses on the couch, arms outstretched. "Thanks for having us," he says. "We really needed this."

"Us too."

We make conversation about their drive as the girls squeal upstairs before Olivia calls down to ask if they can watch a movie.

"You're at the beach!" I look at Jason. "What is with these kids and their screens?"

"So is that a yes?" Olivia asks.

"That's a definite no," I reply.

Jason eyes the open bottle of wine on the counter and pours

himself a glass and shakes his head. "They live in a world of technology, Kate. We have to find the balance."

"Well, if you find it, let me know." I have a bad habit of always telling Liv how things were when I was young: hours of playing outside, climbing trees, and so much wandering. It's rare to see kids outside doing the same these days.

The girls bound down the stairs. "Mama, can I help Ayana unpack?" Olivia has already changed into a bright yellow long-sleeved shirt and green pants. I nod.

"Sure, *cariño*. Just don't make a mess."

"I love that you still incorporate Spanish into her life," Jason says. "I've sucked so hardcore with Amharic."

"Yeah, but you're teaching her words like *hardcore*, so there's got to be a silver lining, right?"

"Har har." He tosses a pillow toward me, and I catch it with one hand and lob it back before refilling my glass.

"Are you still doing that Ethiopian group meetup?"

"Once a month, yes." After the adoption, Jason discovered there was a robust network of individuals in Nashville who'd also adopted from Ethiopia. He'd traded grief groups for adoption meetups, always keeping himself busy.

"I think that's great," I say. "I always worry that I'm not exposing Liv to more of her culture." While Michael's entire family lives in Mexico City—a family that always embraced me like I was one of their own—Liv has been there only a couple of times since the divorce. Michael's cryptic texts flit through my mind, but it's not the time to dissect them. "Now that she doesn't see Michael as much, I feel like those traditions are dying."

"Don't beat yourself up. You're doing the best you can. We all are."

I know he's right. Our girls are lovely, well-adjusted humans who've dealt—and will continue to deal—with diversity issues. Because I'm not Mexican and Jason isn't Black, we are often looped into the same camp, as strangers assume we aren't the biological parents of our children. Even though Nashville is diverse and our pocket of town is progressive, the amount of racism or ignorant questioning we receive makes me realize how much work we have yet to do.

"Is it bad I'm on my way to getting drunk after a glass of wine?"

"I think it's endearing," I say. Once Jason became a father, he cut way back on his drinking, wanting to present a good example for Ayana. I offer him a glass of water and get lost in easy conversation about our work. Upstairs, Liv bursts out laughing, followed closely by Ayana. My favorite sounds from my two favorite girls.

For the first time since we arrived, I begin to relax. And even though our conversation is light and easy, there's an undercurrent of something more—a charge that wasn't there before. I feel it and wonder if he feels it too. I sit beside him and my knee brushes his. He doesn't pull away and instead swirls his wine and smiles.

"You look gorgeous by the way," he says. "With your mermaid hair." He reaches out and tugs a strand of wavy hair, then tenderly tucks it behind my ear.

I swallow and search for what to say. "I'm wild at the beach," is all that slips out.

His eyes trail to my mouth, then back to my eyes. "Is that so?"

Is that so? What am I even saying? I shrug and stare into my glass. "I guess you'll have to wait and find out."

THREE

I DON'T WAKE UNTIL LATE AFTERNOON.

Somehow I slept most of the day. I am both relieved and appalled, unsure of how my body didn't stir. I sit up, head throbbing, groggy and fatigued. I feel like my mouth has been stuffed with cotton. I blink into the bright room. My throat is parched, and I reach for my bottle of water on my nightstand. I search for my phone, wondering if I have any missed calls from the hospital or funeral home, before remembering I've lost it. My eyes finally adjust to the harsh light. I feel like I've aged a decade overnight.

Her body.

I think of Olivia, cold and lifeless, left in the raw black of the morgue while I slept in our vacation rental without her. The guilt is a vise. Before I can think of who I need to call first, someone pounds on the door downstairs. Then the doorbell chimes, a high, shrill succession of notes that makes my headache worse. I look at the clock and balk when I see that it's three in the afternoon.

It must be Jason. I scrub a hand over my face, realizing how heart-wrenching it will be to tell Ayana the news. She was so excited to vacation with her best friend for the first time, and now she will never

44

see her best friend again. I bury my face in my hands, wanting to curl up and sleep forever. But I can't.

I throw back the covers as fists continue to pound the door, pull on shorts and a tank top, and walk downstairs. The house is too quiet. Whenever Olivia stayed with my mom overnight, I would revel in the silence. I always joked she was loud enough for at least five children, which made me happy to have just one. Now the silence is a reminder of all I've lost; her absence is the loudest thing in the room.

I open the front door. The sun is blinding. Jason and Ayana stare back, suitcases at their feet. Ayana is already wearing her bathing suit, a sunny hat shading her big, bold eyes. She holds a stuffed animal to her chest, and my spine stiffens as I look at them.

"Jesus, Kate, are you sick?" Jason asks.

"Where's Olivia?" Ayana asks at the same time. She peers behind me, smacking a huge wad of gum between her teeth.

Instead of answering, I stand, stoic and numb, and stare somewhere in the distance, at the house across the street, empty, waiting for someone to buy it. Somehow I channel the mother in me and tell Ayana to go upstairs for a second. She does as she's told, and I pull the door shut behind me, hoping I can get through this without collapsing.

"What's going on?" Jason steps forward and grips my elbow. "Is it Liv? Is she okay?"

I open my mouth to tell him what happened, but nothing comes out. I sink down on the front porch, and Jason gasps as though I've just fainted.

"Kate, please tell me what's going on. You're scaring me."

Jason's eyes are trained on mine, and I shake my head and begin to cry.

"Yesterday, when we got here, Liv wanted to swim in the ocean," I

45

say. I realize, as I begin this story, that this will set the stage for just how many times I will have to keep telling and retelling it. This horror—*my* horror. This will be my new narrative, one I can't unclaim. He remains silent and waits for me to finish. "The current was strong, but other kids were in the water, so I thought it was okay. I looked away for just a second, and when I looked back, she was gone." My voice is hoarse and barely above a hushed whisper in case Ayana can hear.

"My God," Jason says. He crouches down beside me. "Is she . . ." He glances back at the house, then to me.

I shake my head and curl into him, resting my head on his shoulder. "She drowned." It's the first time I've said the words out loud, and they are sticky in my mouth, a betrayal, a nightmare.

"Oh, Kate. Oh my God." Jason pulls me into his arms, and I cling tighter to him than I ever have to anyone in my whole life. I grip his back, claw at him, pound on his chest. I let it all out as he ushers me back inside, though I'm afraid my reaction will scare Ayana.

He leads me to the blue-and-white-checked couch and rubs soothing circles on my back. He knows me well enough to understand there's nothing you can say in a situation like this. It's unspeakable.

When I feel wrung of tears, I wipe my face and look at him. "I don't know what to do. I lost my phone in the ocean. I haven't called anyone." I let out a shaky breath. "I wish it had been me."

He moves closer and threads his fingers through mine. "Oh, Kate. I know. I know."

Of course he does. Before Shelby died, she was as healthy as a horse. They had been together forever and were still wildly in love. The cancer came out of nowhere. Two months after her stage four diagnosis, she was gone. He hadn't had time to prepare. None of us had.

Still, this fact brings me no comfort. There is no getting through this. There is only surviving and existing in a world without my child—a world I want no part of.

I lean into him, and together we breathe. After some time, my nervous system settles, and when I'm finally ready to speak, Ayana bounds down the stairs, wild eyed and tear streaked.

"Liv drowned?" Her chest bucks, and she heaves as if she might be sick.

I nod and open my arms, and she falls into them, crying hard. The only other time Ayana has cried in my arms was when she stepped on a spiky ball from our chestnut tree. She was inconsolable, and once I finally got her settled, I had to pluck out each of the tiny spikes with a pair of purple tweezers. It took an hour, and she has never gone barefoot in our backyard since.

I soothe her, my emotions cementing into place. I must be strong for Ayana, for my mother, for Michael, for everyone who is going to hear the shocking, horrible news of Olivia's death.

This is just the beginning, I think. A new normal, as unfair as it is. I have joined the club of other mothers who've lost their daughters. They exist all around me, cautionary tales that walk among us, in perpetual, everlasting pain.

I take a breath and stroke her hair. There is no going back. Whether or not I like it, I am here. I hold Ayana until she cries herself to sleep while Jason helps make arrangements back home. Since I don't have a phone, Jason lets me use his to call my mother. The conversation is brief because I'm too upset to talk. When she insists on coming down, I tell her to wait.

After the call, I step outside onto the primary suite balcony, where a sliver of ocean glistens like jewels in the distance, and dial Michael's cell.

"Jason?" Michael sounds perplexed.

"No, it's Kate."

He's quiet for a beat. "Thank you for finally calling, *cariño*. I've missed your voice."

His mother says something in Spanish in the background. I'm thrown by Lucia's voice, then realize Michael must be visiting home, in Mexico City. Lucia and I, though once close, have drifted apart the last few years with all of Michael's travels. We used to have monthly phone calls and would exchange the occasional handwritten letter, but all of that has evaporated as I've gotten busier with work and Michael has been overseas. She still sends cards to Liv on birthdays and holidays, but they haven't seen each other in so long.

I descend into a fresh wave of grief as I try to collect myself, but Michael can hear me crying. My silence extends long past comfortable, and finally, he clears his throat.

"Kate, my love, what is it? What happened?"

"When you texted me yesterday . . ." My voice is still hoarse and unsteady. I'm not sure how to continue. Answering his text is the reason Liv is not here. This tiny black seed, if not squashed, will continue to grow, so that in my darker moments, Michael will be the person I blame, not me. "Liv was in the water. She got pulled under." My heart beats loudly in my ears. "She drowned." The words sound hollow leaving my lips. Silence pounds between us, dark and unsteady.

Finally, there is a crack in the void as he inhales sharply. "Oh no, oh my sweet Olivia. *Mi niña*." He must have put the phone on speaker, as Lucia's deep, heavily accented voice asks me what's wrong. I deliver the news again, each time a brand-new death, and she begins to openly wail. In a matter of seconds, it is one great big cacophony of disbelief and ill-timed prayers for their sweet Olivia. Luckily they do not press me on exactly how this happened but instead ask what they can do to help. I tell Michael I will go to the funeral home later today or tomorrow and keep him updated on when I'm heading back to Nashville so they can meet me there. He insists on flying in to be with me here, but I tell him it will be easier to meet in Nashville.

It is an incomprehensible conversation, one with too many moving pieces and parts. It's not until I've hung up that I realize Michael never even told me why he wanted me to call him in the first place.

Does it really matter?

I grip the balcony and stare at the life pulsing around me. The other rental houses dappling the short street, the stretch of packed shops just two blocks away. I can hear the joyful shouts from the ocean as people bob in the gently breaking waves. Such a beautiful day to spend with family. I close my eyes and clench the railing until I fear my hands might break.

I step back inside, my eyes struggling to adjust to the dimmer light. I don't want to be here. I don't want to deal with this.

Hurriedly I take the stairs down to the main level and tell Jason I need some air. He asks if I need company, but I shake my head, pull on my shoes, and leave, barely shutting the door behind me.

On the way to the beach, I pass my car, still in the parking lot, and realize it hasn't even been unpacked. All our snacks and supplements have been roasted by the sun. Everything that took so much time to pack and gather now seems insignificant.

I just want my daughter back.

The crush of young, sunburned bodies scatters across the white beach. I glimpse several children that remind me of Olivia and almost turn back to the house. Will I ever again see a little girl and not think of her? How in the world can I go on as if everything is normal?

I step over meticulously built sandcastles, abandoned beach toys, and chairs that have tipped on their sides due to the rapidly changing tide. I force my feet to move, my lungs to breathe. I don't stop or slow, even when my legs tire. It's only when the sun sets and I glance at my watch that I realize I've been walking for over an hour.

The lights from Seaside twinkle ahead. My heart drops. It's always tradition that I take Liv to Seaside on the last day of vacation so she can go to Duckies toy store, then Sundog Books, then finally get two scoops of overpriced ice cream. The realization that I will never again treat her to *anything* buckles my legs. I collapse onto the sand before I can catch my breath, and an elderly couple rushes over to see if I'm okay.

"I'm fine. Just got dizzy for a second." I almost tell them the truth, but I don't want the sympathy of strangers. I don't want to be defined by a tragedy that is ultimately my fault.

Jason told me he'd call our friends and Olivia's school principal tonight, which I appreciate. One less thing to do, one less round of conversations to cry through. I drop my head on my bent knees and sob into them, thankful for the cover of night as it descends upon me, the bright white moon nearly full in the sky above. I ease onto my back and ogle the stars when they appear, wondering if Olivia is aware of me down here while her body awaits transportation to the funeral home. Though I have no idea what Liv would want, earlier Michael and I briefly discussed cremation. At the hospital they told me if I choose to cremate, it can take anywhere from four to fourteen days to get the ashes back, though they would rush the process, considering I don't live here.

I close my eyes and pray for a sign—something to tell me she's here. When nothing comes, I allow the lull of the ocean to settle over me. I'm nearly asleep when someone gently calls my name.

"Hey, Kate. You awake?"

I blink into the darkness as a warm hand clutches my elbow. Jason hovers over me in the dark.

I sit up and brush sand from my hair. "What are you doing here?"

He scratches his neck. "We followed you since there's no other way to reach you without your phone. We didn't think you should be alone." He attempts a joke. "However, I didn't think this would be a ten-mile round trip or I would have worn shoes." He points to his bare feet.

"Where's Ayana?"

He motions behind him, where Ayana offers a tentative wave. She's wearing her headlamp, and my heart kicks. She and Liv were excited to search for crabs at night. Besides the bright light, Ayana's dark skin blends into the night so that she becomes a part of it. I want to fold her in my arms and tell her how sorry I am for taking her best friend away. I attempt a smile or some simple offering, but my lips won't work. Instead, I lean against Jason as he situates closer to me. We could easily pass for a couple watching the stars and not two friends grieving the loss of an irreplaceable human.

"Kate, I know this goes without saying, but I am just so sorry. When Shelby died, everyone kept saying that, but this is different. This is your child."

I remember how deep the pain was when we lost Shelby. She was my closest female friend. I told her everything. When I moved to Nashville, our long-distance friendship became local. I loved having someone to have coffee with, go to yoga with, go shopping with. When she died, her absence nearly killed both of us. But Jason is right—this is a different loss entirely. It is deeper than any agony I could have imagined.

And while I've heard people say that they are sorry for someone's loss—I've even said that to people on occasion—now I know how it actually feels to be on the receiving end. How little it helps. "This is my fault."

"No, it isn't." He grips my forearm firmly. "It was an accident."

"Agree to disagree." I shake my arm loose, find Jason's eyes in the dark, and study the outline of his face: the strong jaw, the piercing eyes, the sturdy shoulders and thick neck. The brief thought about what might happen between us on vacation seems so insignificant now. My birthday. My plans. My life. All ruined.

I imagine reworking my life without Olivia; imagine walking into our home in Nashville, clearing out Olivia's room, boxing all her belongings, staring every day at her swing set, trampoline, climbing dome, and tree swing Michael built for her as a surprise years ago. It's just not possible.

"I can't do this, J. I feel like I'm dying."

"Hey, *shh.* I know. Come here." He tucks me back into his side, his limbs warm against mine. "Breathe with me. In for three, out for six. Slow."

Back when we first met, Jason was obsessed with breathing before it was trendy, and instead of pushing him away, I let him guide me. I breathe as he instructs until my heart rate slows and I feel calmer. I watch Ayana while I breathe as she stoops to collect seashells and search for tiny translucent crabs. Liv should be here with her, gathering a bucket of shells that they would then spread out on the monstrous dining room table to sort through. The image punctures the calm, and my heart breaks all over again.

Ayana approaches and, sensing the mood, drops down beside me and takes my hand in hers. She squeezes it and I squeeze back, a game Liv and I used to play. We'd make up codes for squeezes: one for *yes*, two for *no*, three for *I love you*. We shared the system with Ayana when she was nervous about her first day of school. She squeezes my hand three times, and I squeeze back.

"Thank you both for being here," I finally say. "You are my family too."

Ayana scoots in closer, and I breathe her in—the smell of Buttah Skin and remnants of sunscreen.

"We love you, Kate."

"I love you too." I remind myself that Jason survived losing Shelby. He's here now, with a daughter and a life. He rebuilt his entire world without the woman he loved.

"In my experience, it doesn't necessarily get better, but you will eventually adjust to the pain. You'll learn to walk with it, not against it."

We did learn to walk with the pain after Shelby's death, but this is my own flesh and blood. *My baby.* How do you ever walk in peace with that?

"I don't want to go back." I'm not sure if I'm talking about Nashville or the rental.

"Then let's keep walking."

I clap the sand from my clothes and let him tug me down the beach, his hand in my right, Ayana's in my left. We walk several miles toward Gulf Place. Ayana doesn't complain even once, and I am grateful for her grace. We dodge other kids hunting for crabs, bright flashlights and headlamps cocked at all angles, blinding us. My mind is numb, scrubbed of any true emotion other than this black hole of bottomless grief.

We walk almost the entire way in silence before he tells me to wait at the public beach entrance. He runs across the street to the liquor store. Jason knows I'm not much for spirits—wine is my vice—but tonight is an exception. I swing Ayana's hand in my own, and we stare at each other. There is so much depth to her, so much soul. She has been through so much too. Losing her own family at three due to a chemical raid on her village. She was badly injured, suffering from second-degree burns on her back and chest. She was buried beneath her mother, father, and baby brother, who all died. She was found days later, singed and barely breathing. She had become an orphan overnight.

While most people didn't want to adopt a four-year-old, Jason had already been on the list for a year, so he flew out to meet Ayana after she'd been put into the system. He's told the story so many times, I feel like I was there. Him, crossing the threshold of the foster home and waving hello. He'd learned a bit of the language so she'd feel more comfortable, though he'd prepared himself for her to be afraid. He didn't know if she'd ever even seen a white man before and figured some stranger coming to adopt her might be terrifying. Instead, she'd walked right up to him and put both hands on his face, which had immediately made him cry.

"Hello," she said in English, the only word she knew.

Jason said it was like they recognized something in each other—as though they knew each other from a different life. And it wasn't just him. Ayana had trusted him almost implicitly. It didn't matter that he was white, or that she didn't speak English, or that he knew so little Amharic. Together, they figured it out.

Years later, she continues to flex her bravery, facing a world that doesn't often reflect her own culture or people. Her *otherness* is always on display, much like Liv's. But they navigated it together. Now she will be alone, other than the kids in her support group and the Black and Brown friends that Jason offers up to her as some sort of consolation prize for not having any blood relatives in her life.

"We were going to have a sandcastle contest," she says. "And make forts in the bunk bed room."

I smooth her braids and cup her tiny face in my palm. "I'm so sorry that I couldn't save her." I begin to cry and take her in my arms. She stands rigid beneath me, accustomed to grief this close. She'd been forced to become acquainted with it because it had almost killed her too. She allows me to breathe her in, to hold her—a substitute for Liv—even though we both know she's not.

She doesn't tell me it's okay, because it isn't. But she doesn't pull away either. Jason returns, hesitating as he takes us in, and reluctantly I release her. She stumbles back in the sand. Was I holding her too tight? I pat her arm in an apology. Wordlessly, Jason offers me a bottle of Jameson. The liquid burns the back of my throat and lights my chest on fire.

"Let's talk about her," he finally says. He looks to Ayana for approval. "Yes?" She nods and sinks into the sand until we both follow suit. The grains are cool beneath my legs. "If there's one thing I've learned, it's that when people die, we stop talking about them. It's uncomfortable. It's too painful. It's too soon, blah, blah, blah. Before you know it, years have passed, and you walk around as though your loved one is a secret just for you. But they're not. Olivia is not. She's a *force*. Tell me your favorite thing about her."

He's right. Do all the lovable details about her disappear just because she's no longer here? I know it's not the big stuff that will be the starkest reminder of her loss. It's the little things. The sound of her toothbrush tapping against the sink after she brushes her teeth for exactly twenty-three seconds instead of the requisite two minutes. The heat from her body when she first wakes up. The slam of the door as she heads outside to swing and listen to music. The scratch of her markers on paper. Her voice, her laugh, the *greatness* of her, occupying every square inch of space. *Who am I without her, and how will I ever find my way?* I flounder for what to say, and recognizing the panic on my face, Jason butts in.

"Ayana, you first."

I'm grateful I don't yet have to speak. Already my throat is tight and dry, and I'm on the verge of tears.

"I have more than one," Ayana says, scooping up handfuls of sand and letting the grains sift through her fingers. The headlamp is beside her, and she absentmindedly clicks it off and on, illuminating a smooth patch of sea. She still has a network of scars on her left hand, where the flesh crisscrosses in a baby-pink web of skin. Liv used to rub lotion on it for her when it hurt. "She got me to try things. When I was afraid of the diving board, she went first. When I was afraid to ice skate, she got me a bucket."

I nod because it's true.

"And she's always there when I'm sad, to give me a hug or just to listen." Ayana continues to list all of Liv's best traits: how helpful she is, how she has always been willing to share or even give away her most prized possessions, how she can make anyone laugh . . .

"Her big heart," I finally say. "No matter what kind of day I'm having or if I snap at her, she always forgives me, always says she understands and asks me about my day. She gives me head massages and wants to talk about my problems. Just last week, after a stressful day, she made a pallet on the floor and put teddy bears on my belly and talked me through breathing before giving me a shoulder rub." I close my eyes and can feel her little hands on my shoulders, the sweep of her breath across my cheeks. "She's also the most loving person I've ever met." I don't talk about her in the past tense; I can't do that yet.

"What else?" Jason takes the bottle, and we pass it back and forth until my head is fuzzy and I am telling hilarious stories about Olivia: the time she spotted a woman she could swear was Captain Underpants and actually begged for her autograph; the time she was being chased by a boy named Kale and she stood up to him, telling him boys who were named after leafy greens really shouldn't be chasing anyone; the time I talked about a possible promotion at work and she looked at me and in a southern twang said, "Life changes, honey. Life changes"; how, in the mornings, when she made fried eggs and poked at the yolks, she would exclaim, "Mama! Mama! Look! Someone peed in the pool!"

As I talk, some of the pain shrinks. My relationship with my daughter goes so far beyond the physical; it's in my thoughts about her, the memories I have of her, the way I want to preserve her legacy.

Before long, I'm drunk. Jason helps me stand and walk the short way home. At the house, once Ayana is inside, I take his hand and pull him to me.

"I love you." This is something we say to each other, something we've said for years, but I mean the words now more than ever.

"I love you more, Kate." He sighs heavily into my neck before telling me to drink some water and get some sleep.

Inside, the beach house is cold and quiet. I can't walk up those stairs with Ayana and Jason, can't pass Liv's room, can't crawl into bed with my own grief, as crippling as a death sentence. Instead, I curl up on the couch and stare at the ceiling until the sun comes up, not wanting to face what comes next.

4

AFTER A CELEBRATORY BIRTHDAY DINNER, THE GIRLS settle upstairs with a movie, and Jason and I leave them with a phone and head for a quick walk on the beach.

Even though Ayana and Liv stay home on their own sometimes, it still makes me feel like an incompetent parent. *It's not the 1980s*, I'm constantly reminded. *Bad things happen*. I shake away the negative voices. They have a phone. And we are literally two minutes away if they need us.

I loop my arm through his as we head down toward the water. I grip my belly and moan. "Why did I eat all that bread?"

"Why does anyone eat all the bread? Because it's delicious." He hip checks me, and I laugh. "Plus, it's your birthday. You're allowed to indulge."

"You'd think after four decades of meals like this, I'd know my limits better."

"You'll work it off. I'll make sure of it."

I blush at the sexual undertone, but he corrects himself.

"With a morning workout, I mean. Get your mind out of the gutter, Baker."

"Hey, I'm all for other ways of burning off food if I could find someone to date who's not a total troll." I toss out the joke, but part of me is baiting him to see how he might respond. I haven't had sex in who knows how long, and Jason's admission last week has me evaluating my romantic life in an entirely new light. Plus, we're on vacation. What happens on vacation stays on vacation.

"See? There you go. Problem-solving already. I like it."

I sigh and stop to stare at the ocean, flinging my arms wide. "You know, I've been coming here every summer since I was three. My mother couldn't afford much as a single parent, but she always made sure we had a yearly vacation. Every summer I'd ask why we couldn't buy a place here like the other families, and she always said that she was working on it." I shake my head. "I had no idea how much anything cost, of course, but I remember wanting a beach house so badly and not understanding why we couldn't have one."

"Did you buy a beach house and not tell me?"

I playfully slap his arm. "No matter how many years passed, she'd always say the same thing when I asked her. 'I'm working on it.' She never bought a house, so eventually I stopped asking."

"I'm so lost," he says.

"I'm *saying*," I emphasize, "that dating is a bit like that. People ask me over and over why I don't just date. It's been years; I'm not hung up on my ex; I don't really need financial support. But, like with my mother, other priorities always seem to get in the way."

"Why do you think that is?"

"I don't know. I think I'm worried about ever having to rely on someone again. Or bringing someone else into Liv's life."

He nods. "Kind of like how your mom probably feels?"

My mother never dates, but she keeps herself busy with all sorts of interesting people and activities. I shrug. "You know, I'm not exactly sure how she feels."

"Lonely, most likely," he says.

I swat him and he leaps away, his tan quadriceps flexing as he cuts right. "What? I'm just saying she probably gets lonely sometimes."

Is she lonely? Though my mom prefers to live alone, she has a rich social life. She's also frequently available to help with Liv, and I'm so grateful to have the built-in help when work gets tricky.

"So what's your secret?" I ask as we continue walking. "It always seems like everything is so peaceful in your life. You don't seem lonely."

He scoffs. "Peaceful? It's all a facade," he whispers.

"But you're having regular sex at least, right?" My face warms as I say it.

"Define *regular*."

I glance at him. "Are you not?"

He shrugs. "It's not about sex for me anymore. I mean, don't get me wrong, of course I have needs like everyone else, but I want something deeper. It's hard to meet someone organically these days."

"We get a hundred new people moving to Nashville every single day. That's as organic as it gets."

"You know what I mean. Every time I meet someone . . ." He sighs.

"You compare her to Shelby," I finish for him. "I understand that."

He stares at the stars. "And no one compares to Shelby."

I smile, thinking of her. "Damn straight."

He pivots toward the ocean. The waves crash over our bare feet and cause our heels to sink into the dampened sand. "You know, I always thought you were still in love with Michael. That maybe, after some time, you'd find your way back to each other."

His admission catches me off guard. "And why would you think that?"

He tips his head back and sighs. "The way you are with each other. The way you talk to each other. Your chemistry." He continues staring at the stars and stuffs his hands deep in his pockets. "I've never seen two people have as much passion and respect for each other. And you're divorced." He laughs. "I guess I just always thought that maybe if his job settled down you two might give it another shot."

Of all the things he could have said, I wasn't expecting that. "No." I shake my head adamantly. "We are definitely better off divorced." Even as I say it, a little part doesn't quite ring true. The truth is, I *have* thought about being with Michael again, just like I've recently been contemplating my feelings for Jason. No one drives me crazier or makes me happier than Michael, but there isn't one without the other. With Michael, it would always be a life of extremes.

"You sure about that, birthday girl? I'm sensing some hesitation."

"I mean, of course I've thought about it. How great it would be for Liv."

"And you."

I shrug. "And me. But Michael is complicated. He's a true rebel. He goes where the wind takes him. When we were married, I used to think it was the most exciting thing in the world. But once I got pregnant, it just felt irresponsible."

"I get that. He's a great father, though, Kate. You have to give him that."

We walk a few paces. "When he's around, yes."

"I know the absence is hard on both of you." He nods his head, as if deciding something. "What you two had was real. What Shelby and I had was real. I think neither of us wants to settle."

"Ugh," I groan. "I don't even know what *real* is anymore. Do you?"

"Nope." He sinks into the sand, and I lower myself beside him, scooping a handful to sift through my fingers. The sun's last vibrant rays drain from the sky, and we are drenched in darkness. "But does that mean we should just give up on love? We're in our forties so—boom—we're done?"

"This is a depressing conversation."

Jason places a hand on my knee and squeezes. Grains of sand stick to his palm, rough against my skin. "In the past, you've avoided talking about relationships. You know that, right?"

His hand is large and hot, and desire charges up my thigh. "We should probably get back to the girls," I say. "I never leave Liv home at night."

He lets the conversation drop. "Sure thing. Let's head back."

We stand and both groan as various body parts pop. "Man, we're getting old," I say. "Remember when we used to be pain-free and fun?"

"Fun?" He cocks his head and smiles. "Were you fun?"

"I was fun!" I exclaim. *Right?* I try to think of the last fun thing I did where a nine-year-old wasn't involved.

"I don't think fun is high on the priority list these days," Jason says. "And that's fine. We're parents." He heads back the way we came.

His silhouette looms ahead of me, a shadow as familiar as my own. At this moment I don't want to be a parent. I don't want to be responsible. I don't want to worry about the girls. I want to be a woman on vacation on my birthday who doesn't get rattled by text messages or eating too much or talking about love. When I don't join, Jason turns back.

"You coming?"

Instead of responding, I take a breath and slip the straps of my sundress off my shoulders until I'm just in my bra and panties.

Jason inhales sharply, his eyes roaming appreciatively over my body, a body he helped sculpt. "Good God, woman. You look sensational."

A thrill works up my spine at that word. When was the last time I was called sensational? I close the gap between us, and my fingers linger at the hem of his shirt and lift. My nails brush against his bare flesh. I trace the large dragon tattoo on his entire left arm, the ink muted in the darkness. I realize how intimate this is, standing next to him, half naked, in the dark.

"What are we doing?" he whispers.

"Being fun," I say.

He wriggles out of his shorts until he's standing in only his briefs, his thick legs flexing in the moonlight.

"Come on." I run toward the water, my body slicing through the waves. The water is inky and cool, invisible against the black night. I've always been afraid to go into the ocean after dark, but I'm done being afraid. If my story ends with a shark attack in three feet of water in Santa Rosa, Florida, then so be it.

Jason whoops and jumps in after me, grabbing me around the waist and carrying me farther out. I squeal and break free, diving under the waves and bobbing to the surface, tipping to my back to float and stare at the stars, which fleck the sky like salt.

"Look," I say. The water carries us as we float. "Look how infinite it all is."

We admire the vastness in silence, until he finds my hand in the dark. His fingers thread through mine, and another seismic jolt travels my entire arm and settles between my legs. I let go and swim away a few paces, commanding my body to calm down.

We continue to swim until our limbs are exhausted and I have a cramp from how much food I ate. Refreshed, we emerge onshore, balling our clothes in our hands as we walk back toward the house.

"You're full of surprises, you know that?"

"Even after twenty years?"

He stops and stares at me. Water beads off his chiseled body as he rakes a hand through his damp hair. "Even after twenty years."

"That's something, right?"

"It is something." He opens his mouth to say more, but then I hear the girls screaming our names. I turn around and see the outlines of Olivia and Ayana standing on the long dock leading down to the public beach.

"Girls?" My heart hammers in my chest as I realize they left the house and walked the two blocks to the beach alone. "What are you doing?"

"It was our bravery test," Liv explains.

"Actually, it was a dare," Ayana says. "We were playing Truth or Dare."

"We told you to stay in the house," I insist.

Liv looks between our soaking-wet bodies. "Why are you two in your underwear? Did you not bring a bathing suit, Mama?"

That makes Ayana crack up, and they dissolve into a fit of giggles. I think of yesterday, when I also stripped down to my underwear. A bit of my anger slips. She has a point, but I won't let her distract me from how irresponsible they were. Though they are almost ten years old and the house is just two blocks away, they are still children.

Jason pulls Ayana aside to talk to her, and I do the same with Liv. "You cannot disobey me like that, Liv, or you won't be able to stay home alone at all, okay? Trust is very important."

"I know, but we knew exactly where to go."

"But it's dark."

"We used the phone's flashlight."

I prepare another rebuttal—there are strangers and kidnappers and it's Florida, land of the weirdos—but then refrain. She gets the point, and so do I. She looks at my wet body again as I tug on my clothes. "Why were you swimming naked?"

"I'm not naked."

"You're *mostly* naked."

"Will you just stop saying *naked*?" I say. "Come on, let's go."

"I wanna swim too," she whines.

"Not tonight," I say.

"Why? That's not fair. You did it."

"Because I'm an adult."

"So? I'm a better swimmer than you."

"There are sharks," I say.

"I love sharks," she replies.

"Can we just not argue tonight, please? Maybe we can all go for a swim tomorrow night."

"You'll forget. You *always* forget. Papá would let me swim."

The statement lands like a punch and stops me in my tracks. Liv never says things like that, never throws Michael in my face. She stalks ahead and whispers something to Ayana. I wearily fall into step with Jason, worried and irate, as the four of us head back, the girls already lost in a new conversation.

"Well, that was fun," Jason says.

I consider confiding in him, but I don't want to ruin his moment too. "It was," I say.

I pack away Liv's comment and instead replay that moment in the water—Jason's hands on my body, his fingers in mine. I haven't felt that alive or aware of a man in years. My damp hair wraps around my throat, and Jason sweeps a few strands over my shoulder. Chills cascade like a lightning bolt from my neck to my feet. I inhale sharply, and he looks at me. "You good, Baker?"

Am I good? My dormant vulva is feeling things for my oldest and dearest friend. That is most definitely not good. Is it?

"I'm great," I say. "Just cold."

He loops an arm around me, and the pressure of his body makes me shiver. "I make a good blanket."

"No, I'm really okay." I shrug him off, distracted and hurt by Liv's comment, and hurry to catch up to the girls.

FOUR

AT THE FUNERAL HOME I WAIT TO SEE LIV.

Time seems to exist on a cruel, endless loop, where I beg to rewind, and it mocks me with my current reality—a life without my daughter. I glance around the sad, sparse space. Because Liv could never sit still, much less live for eternity in some funeral plot in Nashville, Michael and I have decided on cremation. I want to take her with me, wherever I go.

"Ms. Baker? We're ready for you." A very gentle man in his late sixties with bushy eyebrows and a kind smile leads me to a private room where Liv lies under a sheet.

I come unglued the moment I step inside, now wishing Jason had come with me, though I insisted I do this alone.

"I'll just give you a moment." He pats my shoulder, offers me a box of tissues, and steps out.

I have opted to help prepare the body for cremation, and now I wish I hadn't. I don't want to remember Liv like this, lifeless under a sheet. I want to remember her full of life, splashing in the ocean, before I looked away for *one second* and ruined everything.

I take a steadying breath through my tears and walk closer to her.

"Hi, baby." I rest a trembling palm on her belly, instantly reliving the terror at the beach. I've now glimpsed her dead two times—as if fate is branding into my conscience that she really is gone—and no matter how much I hurt, her absence is permanent.

Slowly I roll the sheet back and drop to my knees, banging my elbow on the side of the table. I erupt into a full-blown wail as I see her, cold, pale, unmoving. Even though I know she is gone, half of me expects her to loop an arm around my shoulder and tell me not to cry. I sit there until I'm exhausted, then finally stand on shaky legs and flip the sheet back up.

I'm not sure I can do this.

A knock at the door severs my uncertainty and the man peeks in, taking in my tearstained face. "Do you need more time, dear?"

I shake my head no, but what I mean is yes. I need more time with my child, *alive*. I need more time to be her mother. I simply need more time.

"Olivia is such a beautiful name," the man begins in a soft tone I have to strain to hear. "Family name?"

I nod, though my throat is raw, and am thankful when he doesn't have a follow-up question.

He dips around me, gathering sponges and a bucket, and hums a lovely song under his breath. "Did she have any music she loved? I sometimes find that helps."

I almost laugh. "Yes," I say. "She loved electronica."

I expect him to ask what that is, but instead he stabs a wrinkled finger in the air and scrolls through his phone until he plays a song by Niviro Liv actually knew. I look at him, amazed. He waves a hand dismissively. "I have three granddaughters."

First, we bathe her. He shows me what to do and then steps out so I can have my privacy. Lovingly, I bathe every inch of my sweet girl, lingering on the unique quirks that make Liv Liv: The small red dot beneath her eye that Liv called her own built-in laser pointer. The brown bean-sized smudge of a birthmark on her left hip. Another on her right shin. Her second toe, so much longer than the first. Her crooked toenails. Her left ear, slightly larger than her right. The scar above her eye. The freckle by her top lip. I linger around the friendship bracelet Ayana made her, not wanting to remove it, as she's worn it religiously for the last two years. After a mental debate, I gently remove it and secure it around my own wrist.

I work silently, the music a stark contrast to my grief. Finally, once I'm done, I drape her in the sheet and tell the man—Charles—that he can come in.

He walks me through a few more details about the cremation, and then my time is up. I inhale sharply as I turn to look at the lump beneath the sheet—my child. This is the last time I will see her in this body, in this life.

"I know, dear." He sighs, as if reading my mind. "It seems like you're leaving her, but you have to remember that Olivia is not just a body. She's a soul, and she will always be with you."

It is a beautiful, unexpected reminder, and I ask him to step outside again so I can have a final moment alone. I drag the stool beside her and grip her cold, ashen hand in my own. Suddenly I am unable to move, breathe, or speak.

This is it.

Our last moment.

Cruel reminders pick at the scab of this new reality: I will never hold my little girl. I will never hear her silly laugh, listen to her incessant chatter, blot her tears, curl up beside her with a book, feel her small, sticky palm clutched so tightly in mine. I will never watch her grow into a young woman. I will never see myself or Michael in her expressions. All these thoughts click and shift in my brain, fighting for space.

"When you were born," I finally whisper, "I thought you would die." I wipe my nose with my free hand and continue. Liv has heard this story a thousand times, but she never tired of it. "You made me wait fifty-two long hours to meet you, and when you were finally born, they thought your collarbone was crushed. And your head was the shape of a Foster's can." I smile, as she always loved that detail. "You were blue, and you weren't crying, because you'd been stuck so long. But finally, your eyes shot open and you looked at me—*right* at me—and I swear to God, I remember thinking, *This little girl knows exactly what she's here to do.*" I smooth my thumb over her waxy skin and smile through my tears. "Olivia, when you were put into my arms, I remember feeling like you knew something I didn't. That you understood more about this life than I did. That you were really here to guide me instead of the other way around." I swallow, my throat burning. "And you have. You've always seemed to be on a mission, so impatient to move it along, so uninterested in the way other people do things, so eager to follow your own path."

I sigh and kiss the back of her hand and press it to my cheek. "You taught me more in nine years than I've learned in four decades." The tears begin to fall again, dripping onto her hand and into my lap. I recount all the lessons in my head: *Always be myself. Lead with kindness. Find a way to play. Remember that you are you.*

"It's my birthday today. You always said I didn't celebrate enough, and now I'm not sure who will be here to remind me of that." Every year she'd make sure to do something special: A handmade card or jewelry. A lopsided cake. A surprise painting or "spa" treatment where she'd soak my feet and paint my nails. "You were always the best birthday present," I say now. "I love you more than anything, Olivia."

My words dissolve into tears, and when I can no longer stand the agony of my own silence, I place her hand back by her stiff side and let my fingers trail down the sharp blade of her nose and dance across the freckles still evident from the harsh sun. I let my lips linger over hers in our final goodbye and sniff the top of her head—which always, until that moment, smelled like sunshine. Not now. Not ever again. Her entire short life plays itself out like a movie.

Here one minute, gone the next.

It is a moment I would never wish on any mother. I stare down at the body I brought into this world, a body I created, once so full of life. And now I have to let go of this body, this person. I have to step away and understand it will be for the very last time.

As I hug Charles goodbye, I feel drained of all life. I linger at the door but force my feet to keep moving forward. When I step outside, into the brilliant sunshine, the palm trees sway in the breeze and a few bikers whiz by. I blink, confused, as if I've stepped into an alternate reality. How can my child be dead in there, when there is so much life out here?

Jason and Ayana are waiting by the car, but I gasp when I see someone else standing beside them: Michael. His clothes are rumpled, but he is still as tall, dark, and handsome as I remember. He's lost weight, his muscles taut and lean from this last dig. I lose all stoicism the moment I see him, as he rushes forward and folds me into his arms.

"Oh, *mi amor*. I know." He kisses every inch of my hair, cradling me, holding me upright as I come completely undone. "I know, my love. I know."

"How did you get here so fast?" I smear away the tears and stare up into his large hazel eyes.

"I had to be here for you." His hands cup my face. "I'm so sorry, Kate."

"No, I'm the one who's sorry, Michael. It's my fault." I grip his arms, struggling to find a steady purchase.

"No." His hands tighten as he looks deeply into my eyes. "Do not do that, Kate. It is no one's fault. Do you hear me? You must release this guilt. Olivia wouldn't stand for it."

The tears leak down my cheeks. He's right. Liv would never blame me for what happened. I barely nod. He releases my face, his hands trailing to my shoulders. He nods toward the funeral home. "May I see her?" His voice cracks, and he begins to cry. I smooth a hand over his back and nod. It feels good to soothe him, to know that we are in this together and that I am not as alone as I feel.

"Of course. Take as much time as you need. I'll be here."

I can't go back in there, can't see her like that again. I watch Michael prepare himself at the door, saying a small prayer and kissing the tiny gold cross he wears around his neck. He disappears inside and the tears start up again. Jason rushes over and envelops me in a hug, and I cling to him, all the grief swelling once more, a fresh, gutting wave that never seems to end.

"She loved you so much," is all he says. "And we loved her too."

We stay like that until sweat trickles down my back and my tears make my face stick to his T-shirt. But I dare not move, dare not breathe.

Once Michael emerges and we leave this spot, I leave without Liv.

For the first time, my world and hers will separate, and no matter what I do or how much I pray, I can't make any of it different.

5

AFTER A WEEK, LIV IS READY TO GO HOME.

While I planned for this possibility, I thought having Ayana here would help. But Liv misses her other friends, her routine, her own canopy bed with the tower of stuffed animals and frayed purple curtains. She misses swinging and listening to music and is tired of the sun and sand. Luckily, I called my mother, who was happy to drop everything and come help with the girls for the last week.

"But you love the beach," I remind her as I braid her hair after lunch.

"I've only ever been to the beach for a week," she counters.

"We talked about this, remember? How we were going to be here for two weeks this year instead of one?"

"I want to go home." Her voice quivers, and I pull her into my arms and stroke her back. Her damp hair presses a wet spot into her pajamas.

"I understand," I say. "But we already paid for two weeks, and now that Grandma Nell is here, we can have even more fun, right?" I know that if anyone can pull her out of her funk, it is my mother, but I also know not to push too hard, too soon, unless I want her to shut down completely. I think of Ayana and what fun she's having. "Doesn't it help having Ayana here?"

She sniffs and swipes a hand across her nose. "It does, but she's leaving a few days before we do." Her voice wobbles again, and I begin to wonder if that's what this is really about. Her best friend is leaving soon, so she wants to go home too.

"But she's still here for a few more days, so why don't you try to enjoy it as much as possible, okay? You don't want to miss her while she's still here."

She burrows against me in response, her eyelids heavy. I trace her open palm in my own, the same way I did when she was a toddler, then pull an imaginary thread out of the middle.

"Do the egg," she begs.

I smile and gently crack a mock egg on her head before spreading my fingers to make it ooze over her skin. I repeat the process until her breath deepens. I lie with her, matching my breathing to hers, taking in the length of her. It seems like yesterday I could hold her in my arms, and now she drapes along my body like a second skin.

When she is deeply asleep, I extricate my arm from under her head and nearly step on her iPod. I falter. I am not a parent who snoops, and I know she has a right to privacy, but I want to know what's been going on with Michael. I slip out the door, unlock it with her easy-to-crack code, 4321, and find Michael's texts immediately. There are dozens of them. I scroll back to the top of their text chain. I'm pleased to see some are even in Spanish.

Michael has been sending her all kinds of findings from his digs, and Liv's GIF and emoji game is strong. The exchange is so tender, it touches my heart. Even though Michael hasn't been here physically, he is still connected to his daughter. Liv seems to text him most when she's alone—if I'm running errands, going on a quick walk, or working in the other room—and I'm sad she feels she needs to hide it from me.

As I am about to place her iPod back, I see the most recent conversation. Michael alludes to Liv that he has a surprise for her but needs to talk to me first. That's why he wants to talk. He's planning a surprise for Liv but wants my permission first. *Please don't let it be a puppy.* I set the iPod in her room and gently pull the door closed.

I check the time—just after one—and wonder how long she'll nap. Ayana and Jason are out for a daddy-daughter date. I'm eager to get back to the beach for the afternoon, though I already know Liv won't want to go. Downstairs, my mother is drinking iced tea and flipping through a magazine.

"Where's the little one?" she asks.

"Will you still be calling her 'little one' when she's fifteen?"

"Yes." My mother rattles a few ice cubes in her glass and takes a healthy sip.

"She's napping." I almost tell her about the texts from Michael, how often he's been staying in touch, but realize I need to process first, as my mother adores Michael and constantly wishes we would get back together. "Do you mind if I run into Seaside for a bit?"

"Sure thing." She eyes me. "You okay?"

I swipe my keys and hat. "I'm good. Need anything?"

"A million dollars." She is already lost in her magazine again.

I reapply sunscreen, check my fanny pack, scribble a note to Jason, and tape it to the front door. Outside, I grab one of the hybrid bikes from the back of the house, slip on a helmet, and almost think of waiting to see if Jason wants to join me, but don't.

We haven't gone out alone together, even with my mom here. I'm not sure why, but I'm suddenly avoiding being alone with my best friend after dark. I'm unwilling to cross any lines or mess up our friendship after all this time, but I still can't shake what I felt in that ocean, or the feelings that have crept up since he arrived.

I climb onto the bike seat, toss my fanny pack into the basket, and take off. The sun bakes everything beneath it, and by the time I turn left onto the main road, I am drenched in sweat. I bike down a narrow patch of grass until I loop onto the bike path that leads all the way to Seaside. At this time of day, I have the path mostly to myself, but I still make room for other cyclists, joggers, and Rollerbladers.

The hot wind rushes past my ears, and I welcome the white noise. No music. No podcast. Just me and my thoughts. My legs pump harder, already darkened and strengthened by a week at the beach. I pass the ice cream shop at the four-way stop, a few kids waiting eagerly for their afternoon scoops. A bike rental, a host of shops and restaurants, and then a smattering of houses on the lake whip by as I bump over a newly constructed wooden bridge. I take in the palm trees, the glittering water beneath the sun, and am smacked with a wave of gratitude that I am here.

I keep pedaling, nearing Seaside, where the million-dollar condos cluster closer together and the community becomes whiter and wealthier. It has always been one of my main gripes about this place—how Waspy it is—though it has thankfully grown in its diversity. I smell the salty ocean a hundred feet to my right as lunch goers are out on foot, casual and damp, in search of a quick food truck and local beer. I pedal past the throngs of people and stop when I get to the overpopulated bike patch. I lock up my bike next to a giant red beach cruiser and make sure it's secure before walking around the knot of shops. A large amphitheater spans the middle of the town square, along with restaurants, local boutiques, and my favorite bookstore, Sundog Books. I think of what book I could surprise Liv with.

I wipe the sweat from my face and fan myself with my tank top.

Every store has a memory for me here—this was the foundation of my childhood. Later, during one of our summer vacations, Michael proposed right on the beach, after we'd been dating only a year. He'd dropped to a knee, taking my left hand in his right. He didn't have a ring yet, but as we stood under hundreds of thousands of nature's own diamonds, I didn't care. I just wanted him. I loved how spontaneous he was, but I also believed that we really would stay together forever. I shake away the thought, its impact lingering like an old scar.

I decide to turn my phone on silent and help myself to lunch and a glass of Shiraz at the wine bar. I peruse the art galleries and head to the local market, where I buy some cheese, crackers, and olives for Liv. I pick up a bottle of red for my mom and save the bookstore for last.

Inside, I break into a smile as I glimpse the total disarray of their chaotic stocking method. Books are crammed on each shelf haphazardly, some vertical, some horizontal, in clusters and bunches, according to what the bookstore owners like. I shuffle over to the self-development space and then the kids' section, tucked back to the far left. I pick out the newest health book by one of Jason's favorite authors and then grab a puzzle for Ayana and a chapter book for Liv. Lastly, I tuck the latest Mary Kubica thriller novel onto my stack so I can have another guaranteed good beach read. I know my mom will fight me for it.

When I check out, I'm shocked by the price but tell myself it's for a good cause. Outside, arms loaded with bags, I don't feel ready to go back.

As I dump my bags into my basket, I look at my phone and am floored to find that it's already four. There's no text from my mom, but there is one from Jason.

Still at Seaside?

I smile and respond. *I've been hijacked by the wealthy.*

Tell them you're a hipster, and they will release you immediately.

I laugh and type back. *Except I am definitely NOT a hipster.*

Debatable, Baker. Your mom is taking the girls for pre-dinner ice cream. I'm at Taco Bar. Want to meet me for a beer?

What? I turn around and stare at Taco Bar. Jason leans against one of the white columns and waves.

Tucking my bags back into my arms, I carefully cross the street. "When did you get here?"

"A while ago." He smiles and easily takes one of the bags from me to lighten my load. "Hungry?"

"Nah. I'll have a beer, though."

We order two beers and two shots of tequila at the counter and then take them to the patio overlooking the beach. The breeze has picked up, and under the shade of the awning, it's nice. I drop my bag into the chair beside me and fish around until I find his book.

"You love this author, right?"

He takes a sip of his beer and yelps in surprise when he sees it. "Kate, are you kidding? Thank you! I've been dying to read this." He eagerly thumbs through the pages and presses it to his chest. "You know this is a direct way to my heart."

"Oh, well, we both know that's not true." I lift my eyebrows sug-gestively, because when we were younger, Jason was known for his sexual appetite. At one point, way before Shelby, he had a rotation of girls that could put any player to shame.

"I'm a dad now," he says. "So it's all about books." He wags the hardback in my direction.

"Uh-huh." I roll my eyes and clink my shot against his, then chase it with a sip of shockingly cold beer, feeling the acidic burn as I stare off toward the ocean. "Speaking of dads, I just found out that Michael and

Liv have been texting. You should have seen how sweet their messages were."

He swallows and gauges my face. "And you would know that how?"

I look away, embarrassed. "I checked her iPod. And before you give me a hard time, I just wanted to make sure that everything was okay."

"Has Liv not mentioned that they've been talking?"

I shrug. "Not really. But it makes me happy to know that he checks in on her so much." I pick at the label of my beer. "I'm hard on him sometimes, but I knew the deal going in. He's an archaeologist; his life is travel. I don't know why I thought that would change when I got pregnant."

"Because *you* changed when you got pregnant."

He's not wrong. Michael assured me we could maintain our careers and be parents. I didn't have to go on as many digs. As an agricultural engineer, I could take a million other positions that would be easier, but I panicked. I wanted stable and secure. We'd been living in a studio apartment in Virginia, living from paycheck to paycheck, and that suddenly felt reckless. When I got offered a job in Nashville, where my mom, Jason, and Shelby already lived, it was a no-brainer. But not for Michael. Michael loved our little life, and he wasn't ready to give it up without a fight.

"I never understood why he didn't stay," Jason says now, as if reading my mind. "I mean, the guy loves you more than anything. I always thought he'd follow you to the ends of the earth."

"He doesn't like to be tied down."

"He put a ring on your finger."

I glance down at my bare ring finger. "That was different. When we got married, it was us against the world. I think having a kid scared him at first. He wasn't ready."

Jason rolls his eyes. "No one is ever ready. But you do it anyway."

Not wanting to go down this painful path of what could have been different, I tap my fork against my beer bottle. "How about a change of subject?"

"Sure." He swigs the last of his beer and orders another. "What else is on your mind?"

Besides your naked, slippery skin in the ocean? "Well, I've realized that it might be good for me to, you know, get back out there and date."

Jason looks at me, both of us probably thinking the same thing. "Got anyone special in mind?"

Do I say it?

Jason slaps the table, startling the couple behind him. "Wait, are we going to sign you up for a dating app?"

I make a face, slightly disappointed that we may not be on the same page. "God, no. I'm not twenty. I want to meet someone the old-fashioned way."

"There is no old-fashioned way."

I eye him. "Then how do you date?"

"I told you already. I don't really."

"Well, *when* you do, how do you do it?"

"I always meet people at the gym."

"You mean you date your clients."

He laughs, and his whole face lights up. "No, I definitely do not date my clients." He shrugs. "I really haven't found anyone I click with, so I just stopped trying."

"Wow, amazing pep talk. You should take this act out on the road." I toss a balled-up napkin in his direction.

"What? It's true." He looks at my drained bottle. "You know I've only got eyes for one person these days." His eyes roam over my face. "Another?"

His words give me a tiny jolt of pleasure. So maybe we are on the same page. "Is that so?"

We stare at each other, neither one of us daring to say more. I'm tipsy from the alcohol and turn down his invitation for another. I want to be clearheaded when I get back to the girls. I down my ice water until I have a brain freeze. "Did you bike here too?"

"Yep."

We leave the table and navigate across the street. My phone buzzes in my pocket. My skin tingles at the sight of Michael's name.

May I call you? is all it says.

For some strange reason, my heart begins to pound as I text him back. *You are persistent. I'll call you when I get back to the house. Happy???*

He texts back only one line as my heart continues to bang against my ribs. *You always make me happy, Kate.*

I smile as I pocket my phone.

"Ooh, what's this? Do we have an admirer already?"

I wipe the smile from my face. "No."

Jason looks at me as he straddles his bike, mock annoyance on his face. "That's all I get?"

"Yep." I unlock my bike and saddle up, the weight of the bags tugging the basket to the left. I push off in a rush, willing my thoughts elsewhere. But all I can think about is what Jason just said and what Michael has to tell me. I know it's about Liv, but part of me wonders if Michael and I have more to discuss beyond parenting. I think of all the walls I've erected around myself over the years, all the ways I've kept myself from trusting him. Am I really ready to open myself up again?

Jason finally pulls up beside me when we're safely on the bike path, huffing dramatically. "Hey, Lance Armstrong. You in a hurry?"

"I don't think calling someone Lance Armstrong is a good thing anymore, is it?" I attempt to keep my voice light.

"He's still a great athlete," he says. "And he happens to be one of the only cyclists I can remember by name, so . . ." He drifts easily beside me, his T-shirt fluttering in the wind. His face is easy and open. Here is a man I know better than anyone. A man who is my best friend. A man who has been here through it all—childbirth, death, divorce. This man would never disappear on me. So why haven't Jason and I ever been more?

Michael.

I run over a pinecone, and the loud *crunch* brings me back to my body. I realize maybe nothing has happened because Jason didn't really mean what he said. Or it was simply a passing moment of curiosity. Or the real reason . . . because I am still hung up on my ex.

Michael's request to call him causes me to pedal faster. I want to know his news, what gift he's giving Liv.

Jason calls after me again, but this time I don't slow down, even as he attempts to catch me.

FIVE

A FEW DAYS LATER, JASON DRIVES US ALL BACK TO Nashville.

I can't stop replaying my last moments with Olivia at the funeral home. I've had nightmares about her cremation, that she wakes up in the middle of it, screaming for me. Even now, pulling into Nashville with Jason behind the wheel and Michael in the passenger seat beside him, I fear I've made the wrong decision and want to undo the process. Though the urn will take at least a few more days to arrive, I worry that somehow I've burned her spirit along with her bones. That she is less of a person as ashes than she was on that hard, cold slab of steel as flesh and bones. That I've abandoned her body, that I've abandoned *her*. I distract myself and glance at Ayana in the back seat beside me, fast asleep with her head at such a severe angle, I worry that she can't possibly be breathing.

Is this what life will be like? I wonder. Constant worry for other people's children because mine is now gone? All too soon, Jason pulls into my driveway. The crunch of tires pops over broken branches from our maple tree. I sigh as I look at the modest, renovated ranch, painted white with cedar shutters and a sloping acre backyard. It is a good home, a perfect place for Liv to grow up. It's walkable to school and her best friend lives right down the road. And now, the slate has been wiped clean and all those prerequisites don't seem to matter.

As I step outside, my eyes sweep over the unkempt grass and bushes I've let go. Michael eyes them and clears his throat once he removes my suitcase and Liv's. I stare at her little roller bag and begin to cry all over again as he folds me against his T-shirt. Finally, I pull back and face Jason, who looks awkwardly between us.

"Do you want me to come inside with you? Sit for a while?"

I shake my head no because I don't know what will happen when I step inside. "I'll call you later, though, okay?"

"Okay." He looks at me uncertainly.

"I promise I'll call you if I need you." Already the to-dos are invading my heartbreak—I need to figure out if we are having a funeral or memorial. There will be arrangements, invitations, food, and flowers. I glance at the house again. Am I supposed to host? I am itching to call my mother, who was kind enough to fly to Florida to be with us these last few days and drive my car home. She arrived back yesterday, and at the moment I wish she was here to help me face walking into my home without Liv.

"Tell Ayana I said bye, okay?" I remove the friendship bracelet and press it into Jason's palm. "And give her this, will you? Tell her Liv never, ever took it off. Even when it started to smell."

"I will." He stares into my eyes, piercing the most vulnerable places, but I look away and fiddle with my keys. "I'm here for you, Kate. For anything." He places a warm hand on my shoulder, claps Michael on the back, and returns to his car, to Ayana.

Michael puts our bags inside the front door. I breathe in the stagnant air and hastily open the dining room and kitchen windows, immediately throwing my own clothes from my suitcase into the wash. I pause as I turn from the laundry. My bedroom is right next to Liv's, the two of us so physically close we'd sometimes have entire conversations from our beds. Michael gives me space and opens a bottle of wine.

I stare down at Liv's bag, unsure what to do with her clothes. I glance again at her closed door, with the various wrinkled drawings and positive messages taped to it, and let out an involuntary cry. Michael rushes over, wrapping his arms around me.

I sink into him and tell him I can't go in there yet, can't face the rubble of her life. How am I to decide between throwing it all away and keeping it perfectly intact, like some untouched shrine? I'm not strong enough to stare at her toys and drawings; to clean out her closet of favorite outfits; to pick through her stuffed animals and decide what to do with them; to gather stray bits of Lego bricks that used to make me curse every time I stepped on them; to sort through her charms, jewelry, and journals that encapsulate her very essence.

"You don't have to know what to do," Michael says, stroking my hair. "No one knows what to do in a situation like this." After a while, my tears calm and he tugs my hand. "Come, let's sit."

He pours the wine and I stare into the backyard, at the over-sized wooden playset Jason helped me build a few years ago; at the rectangular trampoline that is on its last leg with its tattered safety net and well-worn padding; at the metal dome Liv so rarely climbs and the expanse of trees beyond. I think of all the tea parties and snowball fights we've had in this backyard; all the hours I've spent making dinner, gazing at Liv from the kitchen window bouncing on her trampoline, lost in animated conversation with herself or a doll. I think of the family Easter egg hunts, the hide-and-seek, the fires and hot cocoa, and the walks to her public school playground that is just a straight shot through our backyard. I remember all the fox and deer sightings, and the oversized groundhog that would often stop, drop, and roll around in our yard. The nights we would energize our crystals under the full moon and drag out our massive telescope to point out constellations, count craters, or search for other planets.

I slug down a gulp of wine and turn away from the window, my eyes settling on Michael. "Thank you for being here."

"Of course." He swirls his wine and stares moodily into his glass. "I should have been here all along. I'm so sorry, Kate. I will never forgive myself." He sits on the couch and drops his head in his hands. "I've been so selfish. I love you both so much, and I . . . I . . . What? I decided I'd rather spend time with fossils than with my two greatest loves?"

There's a break in the mood, and I laugh. "Yes, Michael. You chose fossils. Because fossils can't talk back or tell you what to do."

He breaks into a smile, showcasing that healthy gap between his front teeth. Liv's gap. "*Es verdad*, Katie. *Es cierto.*" *It's true.*

No one else calls me Katie, and it tugs me back to our old life, all those happy years. I study his face, greedily sucking in all the ways he reminds me of Liv, how much of him she carried with her. Michael and I haven't sat across from each other in so long, and I cannot believe it is this horrific situation that is bringing us together again.

My mother is coming over tomorrow. I need to let her know I have arrived safely, but I can't bring myself to call anyone from the landline tonight. The house already feels cold and horrifically silent without Liv.

"Let me run you a bath." Michael sets down his wineglass and fusses in the bathroom. I don't have to tell him to put in Epsom salt or bubbles, because he remembers. I close my eyes, and there's the memory of Liv.

She used to love to crash my baths, stealing bubbles, clapping them between her hands to make confetti, then slipping into the steamy water to ask me questions about my day or rub her soapy hands across the stubble on my legs and pretend she'd been jabbed by a porcupine. The loss grows heavier and more real. Liv won't ever take another bath with me. Liv won't ever burst in to recite a random fact. Instead, she will be in an urn in our living room, and no matter how much I want it to be different, how much I would give to change that fact, the truth is a blinding, everlasting reminder of all that I no longer have.

"Are you hungry? I'll make you something."

I tell Michael I'm fine, and when the bath is ready, I slip into the scalding water and make a mental list of all I need to do. I dread the days, weeks, and months to come; dread facing all my colleagues and friends. I close my eyes and think of sweet Ayana, and Shelby, and how Jason dealt with that loss, which still feels like a fading bruise. Through every loss comes something beautiful, I'm told, but right now it all feels tangled, untethered, and raw to the bone.

I lower myself under the water. Sometimes, when the bath was filling, Liv would lock the door and I would panic, pick the lock, and burst inside to find her sprawled on her back with a book in hand, ears completely submerged underwater. I do the same now, then go all the way under, closing my eyes against my pain and agony.

After the bath, Michael has already made me some chamomile tea.

"I'll sleep in the guest room, if that's okay?"

I nod and he kisses my forehead before closing the door behind him. I almost call to him, ask him to sleep beside me. I don't want to be alone tonight. Instead, I sip my tea and curl on the couch, staring into the black night out my front window. The hook of the moon perches over the maple tree and casts a white shadow on Olivia's swing. My heart pulls.

I sigh and call my mother, who I know will still be awake at this hour.

"Are you back?"

"Yes."

"Michael there with you?"

"Yes."

"Can't sleep?"

"No." I sip my tea and hear the stroke of a brush in the background, the *tap, tap, tap* of damp bristles on a glass.

"Painting?"

"Yes."

My mother has taken up painting in her free time, mostly portraits of kids and dogs.

"You better not bring over a portrait of Liv, Mom. Seriously. I'll lose it."

She's quiet, and I know that's exactly what she's painting. She's funneling all that pain into creating something beautiful.

"How does it feel to be home?" she asks. Her voice is raw and scratchy; she's been crying.

"Wrong," I say. "This doesn't feel like home without her." I tug a pillow against my chest and squeeze.

"I'm so sorry." She sniffs deeply and her voice breaks. It's the tenth time she's said those words.

"I know."

"Any more thoughts about the memorial?"

I groan. "I should have the urn in a day or two, and then we can decide. I told Michael he can take some of her ashes back to Mexico City."

"I'm so happy he's there with you," she says. I hear her paintbrush clatter against her table. "Do you want me to come over?"

"No, that's okay. You should get some rest."

She sighs. "Sweetheart, I rarely sleep. Welcome to postmenopause. Be there soon. Have a glass of red waiting." She disconnects the call, and I smile. In my mother's world, there's nothing a good glass of wine, a hard cry, and a hug won't fix.

I splash some water on my face and look in the mirror, not even recognizing the woman I see. All those days I spent judging myself, and now all I want to do is see Liv reflected back in that mirror—little bits of her made from me. I blot the tears and pour myself a glass of wine, grabbing an extra one for my mother.

I curl up on the couch again. The night is calm and quiet, the streetlamps highlighting our maple tree in a faint yellow glow. Liv's tree swing sits untouched, and I stand again, yank the curtains closed, and wait for my mother to come.

6

BY THE TIME WE GET BACK TO THE HOUSE, OLIVIA AND Ayana are doing crafts at the table.

"Have fun?" my mom asks, eyeing the two of us, sweaty and out of breath from our race back to the house. She washes her hands and pours herself a glass of wine.

"We did." *Except for thoughts of my ex-husband.*

"I'm going to rinse off in the shower," Jason says. He kisses Ayana hello and then dashes upstairs.

"Mama, I took a superlong nap," Olivia says. Her hair is a tangled knot at the back of her head. "And then we had ice cream before dinner."

I kiss her head. "So I heard." I bring the bag to my chest. "I've got a surprise for you." I glance at Ayana. "Both of you, actually."

Liv turns from her craft and stands, closing her eyes and holding out her hands. "Is it a pony? A unicorn? Is it that chicken outside?"

"Hate to disappoint," I say, softly plopping the book in her hand and the puzzle in Ayana's. They open their eyes and squeal.

"Puzzle time!" They both hug me tightly, and then Ayana spills the thousand pieces onto the dining room table.

Mom chops a few carrot sticks and scoops some hummus onto a plate. "How was Seaside?"

"Crowded." I drop my bags and take a seat at the bar, chewing on the corner of my lower lip. I need to call Michael. Before I do, I change tactics as I watch my mother chop and hum, her ample hips rocking to her own beat. "Should I start dating again?"

My mother lowers the knife and looks at me. "Yes!"

The girls stop what they are doing and look over.

"That was an encouraging yes," she clarifies, scooping up the knife and slicing it through the air in a tiny circle. "Carry on."

I laugh and grab her wineglass to steal a sip. "Tell me how you really feel."

"I just did." She motions upstairs with the blade, a smirk on her lips. "Are you starting there?"

"With Jason?" I whisper. *She knows.* "We're just friends."

My mother rolls her eyes, and the gesture is so innocent and endearing, it makes me laugh. "Precisely why he's the perfect person. You already know each other. You already love each other. Your girls are best friends."

"Those all sound like reasons why we shouldn't rock the boat," I remind her.

"No, rock the boat, literally and figuratively. You're both crazy about each other. It's always been obvious."

I blink at her. "What are you talking about? It is not."

"Honey, I know you better than anyone. The only other person who makes you light up like that is Michael. And you know how much I love him and pray you two will find your way back to each other. But if you don't, pick that one. Every time you two are together, there's this energy between you. It crackles, I swear." She pops a carrot in her mouth and chews. "Plus, you're both single and long past the rebound phase. There's literally nothing standing in your way. Go for it."

"Shh." I motion to the girls. "We could risk messing everything up. And honestly, I've never had feelings for him like that." Until recently.

"*Risk* being the operative word. You need to take a risk, honey. You are so predictable. I can literally tell where you're going to be and what you're going to be doing a month from now. You need to make fun more of a priority."

"And who are you to judge? You never dated."

My mother eyes me. "Exactly my point, Kate. But I still manage to have fun."

I always assumed my mother was happiest as a single woman, but perhaps I don't know the entire story. I think of the calendar on our refrigerator at home, marked with Liv's school events, my meetings, and any extracurricular activities. Granted, my part of the calendar, outside of work, is pretty bare. Most of my close girlfriends still live in Virginia. When we moved to Nashville, I had two built-in best friends with Jason and Shelby. Now that Shelby's gone, I haven't put as much stock in building my female friendships as I should have, outside of the few moms I see occasionally through Liv's school. "I have a job that keeps me busy, Mother."

"And?"

"And . . ." She has a point. And *what*?

"You just turned forty. If you're not careful, it's all a slippery slope straight into menopause."

I roll my eyes as Jason comes back downstairs, freshly showered and distractingly handsome. "What did I miss?"

My mother looks at me and I give her a death stare.

"Grandma Nell thinks you and Mama should date," Liv says.

I jerk my head toward her. "Olivia Baker Nuñez, do you have X-ray ears?"

"That's a line from a movie," she says. "And yes, I do."

My face turns the shade of a beet, but Jason takes it all in good stride. He loops an arm around my shoulder. "We're practically like an old married couple anyway," he says. "Except we actually like each other."

"Because we aren't dating," I say.

"Okay." He squeezes my shoulder and drops it.

My mother motions between us. "Well, you two should go on a nondate tonight then. I've been offering for days. The three of us are having a movie night anyway. Isn't that right?"

"With breakfast for dinner," Ayana says.

"Oh, so ice cream was just an appetizer?" Jason teases.

"Yep!" they both say.

"I could go for some food," Jason says. "You?"

I stand, rooted to the spot. *Is this a date?* "Sure. Just let me change."

"Mama's going on a date!" Liv singsongs. The girls erupt in a fit of giggles.

Upstairs, before I jump in the shower, I take a deep breath, steady myself, and call Michael.

"There she is," he says, sighing happily into the phone. "How are my girls?"

"Good." I sit on the edge of the bed. "What's so important it couldn't wait?"

My nerves are fried, part of me dying to know what's going on with Michael and part of me wondering why I'm risking my relationship with my best friend for the sake of a pseudodate.

"You sound like you're in a hurry."

"I am in a hurry. Spit it out, Mike."

He sighs again. "Okay. I have news, both good and bad." When I say nothing, he continues. "I've gotten a gig in Mexico City for the next six months, so I am finally home." He clears his throat. "The bad news is that Mamá has been ill, Kate. The diagnosis does not look good, so I was hoping that Liv could come spend the rest of the summer with us, here. I know it's a big request, but it's been too long since we were all together."

The news hits me like a freight train. Lucia is sick? Michael wants Liv to come live with him for the whole summer? That's the big surprise, I realize. He is going to invite Liv to Mexico City.

"When were you going to tell me?"

"I'm telling you now, *mi amor*. I've been trying to reach you."

I think of all the reasons Liv wouldn't be able to go, but I can't think of any that would stick. I haven't signed her up for any summer camps this year because my mom agreed to help out on the days I have to go into the office. "I'll think about it. And I'm so sorry about your mom, Mike."

"Me too." He's quiet as he composes his thoughts. "It's brain cancer. They give her less than a year."

My heart aches for both of them. Lucia adores Liv. I know she'd want to spend this valuable time with her. "I'll talk to Liv about it, okay? But I'd obviously have to come over with her, get her set up."

"Thank you, Katie. That's all I ask. Just talk to her about it."

"Anything else?"

He hesitates. "I've been thinking about us." He swallows heavily. "I miss us so much. I miss *you* so much. I've been an idiot, and I'm sorry."

Chills stud my skin from the sudden blast of the air-conditioning above me. "I miss you too." I don't know why I say it, other than the fact it's true.

"If you come too, can we sit and talk? Please?"

"We'll see."

We end the call. I shed my clothes and shower. As my soapy hands slide over my waist and thighs, I close my eyes and imagine sitting with Michael, listening to whatever he has to say. I've often thought about what I would do if he offered to move back to Nashville, for us to be a real family. Would I say yes?

I rinse my body and Jason pops into my mind. Before the call with Michael, I was contemplating something more with Jason. What would it feel like to share such intimacy with someone I know so well? I hurry through the rest of the shower and get dressed in a slip-on red dress that I decide to wear without a bra. Maybe I should throw myself at Jason, just to see what would happen. Would it feel like betraying Michael?

Downstairs, Liv and Ayana are curled on the couch, two empty plates with remnants of eggs and bacon on the coffee table. Liv has a small glob of egg on her cheek, and she is so lost in her book, she doesn't even register my entrance. I take a moment to admire her, browned, freckled, and so exquisitely unique it takes my breath away. Selfishly, I wish she could stay like this, innocent, exuberant, imaginative, lost in a book, without a care in the world. No worries about relationships, jobs, mortgages, sex, cancer, or all the other grown-up baggage that we all unconsciously sign up for. Why do we complicate our lives so completely? What's really so wonderful about being a grown-up?

As if sensing me watching her, Liv looks up and smiles. "You look beautiful, Mama."

"Doesn't she?" Jason's eyes travel the length of my body until my cheeks warm.

I realize I have an obligation to tell Liv about Michael and his request. Suddenly the idea of a date feels foolish, selfish even. I glance at Jason and then back to the girls.

"How about you girls skip the movie and we go search for crabs instead?"

The girls look at each other, then immediately run to grab their headlamps. My mother frowns at me, but Jason's eyes rest on my face, a spasm of hurt and confusion passing through them.

"Rain check?"

Jason hesitates, as if he's going to say something, but then removes his jacket and rolls up his sleeves. "Sure."

The tension in my gut unclenches. Part of me feels bad for not going on a date, but if I really search my heart, it's mostly relief I feel. The girls return, and my mom waves at us as she straightens the kitchen. "Have fun."

I grip each girl's hand as we practically run to the beach. Jason stays a few paces behind, and when I turn to make sure he's still there, his eyes catch mine. They flash with disappointment, but it's gone quickly as Ayana shouts for him to catch up.

He takes her hand, and the four of us jog the last few feet toward the beach. My mind whips wildly with all the new information, but for tonight I'm going to enjoy the moment. I squeeze Liv's hand three times and she squeezes back.

She glances up, her headlamp so loose it dips over one eye. She adjusts it and smiles. "I love you too, Mama."

The blackness meets us as the dark water roils against the shore. Jason and I watch the girls rush forward, voices pitched high as they search for crabs. I smile contentedly and tip my head to the stars. Jason runs ahead, pretending to be a monster in the night. They scream in delight and run in zigzags along the pearly white beach.

I imagine a whole summer without Liv, and my heart constricts. No sleepovers with Ayana. No family dinners. No time with Grandma. Then I imagine a different life, a life where we can all be a family again. A life where Michael comes home. A life where I have a true partner again, where the past is forgiven and we can try again.

I squeeze my eyes shut as one word pulses heavily through my brain.

Yes.

SIX

AFTER THE ARRIVAL OF THE URN, WHICH IS GOLD AND much smaller than I imagined, we decide to do the memorial in the backyard, because it is simple and one of Liv's favorite places.

Though I don't want people in our home, it's not really about me. I drink three cups of coffee, and without proper sleep, I am dizzy and buzzed.

Michael has gone to retrieve his family from the airport. After that first night, he got an Airbnb, though I insisted he could stay here. He wanted to give me my space, though my mother has hardly left my side.

She arrives before all the others and folds me into her arms, as she has for the last three days. She is a sturdy woman and is still so strikingly beautiful, I can only hope to age as gracefully as she has. Despite the heat, she wears an elegant cream blouse and black slacks. Her hair is swept up in a neat chignon.

"Is it wine time yet?"

I appreciate an attempt at a joke, but I shake my head.

She envelops me again, where I am at once comforted and destroyed, since I will never again comfort my own daughter. Olivia will never go through losses, heartache, or breakups. We will never struggle through the teenage years only to come out on the other side with battle wounds to share and a closer bond because of it. We will never have another mommy-daughter day, paint our toenails, or be sloths and watch movies on the couch. That part of my life is done.

I cling to these losses, to Olivia, to this mess of a day, and my mother holds me, stroking my hair, and allows me to settle. Finally, I pull away and wipe my eyes, thankful I didn't wear mascara.

"Look." She cups my face, and I stare into her large brown eyes. A strand of pearls hugs her clavicle, covering a dark blotch where a suspicious mole was removed. Her eyes are full of tears. "Tell me how I can help you get through today."

"Just be here."

My mother lost most of her family when she was young. She got pregnant after a one-night stand with an older man she never discusses. She was such a good parent, I've never had the tiniest urge to know who my father is. For me, she has always been enough.

One of our inside jokes is that because she's been so riddled by losses, she's as tough as an ox. I've seen my mother completely break down only a handful of times in my life. And even though she's become increasingly spiritual and believes that we don't really die, this is different. This is Liv.

I wish I could adopt that mentality now, if only for the belief that Olivia is perhaps already thriving in a new body somewhere. But when I think about never getting to see her again in *this* body . . . that's what I can't wrap my head around. I wish my last images of her weren't dead on the beach, cold in the funeral home, or ground to dust in an urn. It's the very thing that almost scared me away from becoming a parent in the first place. I never wanted to love someone so much and then lose them. I feared I wouldn't survive it. And now I'm here, put to the test, unsure that I will.

"I have something for you."

My mother shakes me from my mental spiral as she goes over to the coatrack and picks up a wrapped package I didn't notice her bring in. She hands it to me. "For you."

My fingers tremble as I unwrap it, but I know what it is before the butcher paper is even off. It is a portrait of Liv, captured on her tree swing, hair flying wild, smile wide and bright, so full of life. I slap one hand to my mouth. It is the essence of her. It *is* her.

"Mom, it's perfect. Thank you."

"You're welcome, my love."

We busy ourselves setting out casseroles that friends and neighbors have sent. There are so many dishes, there's barely any room left on the table. It is particularly hot out, and though I chose a sleeveless black dress, I am already sweating from busying myself in the kitchen.

My mother frets about and finally uncorks a bottle of white.

"It's ten in the morning," I say.

"Or," she says as she fills a glass nearly to the brim, "it's ten, and I'm in mourning." She shrugs as she lifts the glass to her lips. "It's all the same today."

"It's been nice to have Michael here," I finally blurt as I chew on my bottom lip. I glance at my mother. "I don't think I realized just how much I've missed him."

She sets down the glass. "Of course you have, sweetheart. You two belong together."

"Knock, knock." Jason steps inside. "Nell, you're looking stunning." He's wearing a suit, his hair is slicked back, and Ayana pushes in behind him, peering into our house as if she expects Liv to come running out to greet her as she almost always did.

"Hey, guys." I tell them to come in, and Ayana slips off her shoes and peeks down the hall toward Liv's room. I still haven't been able to go in. Ayana tugs at the neck of her dress and holds one of Liv's favorite stuffed animals against her chest. She fiddles with Liv's friendship bracelet and looks so out of her depth that I rush toward her, crouch down, and give her a hug.

"Liv would be so happy that you're here," I whisper. "And you're wearing her friendship bracelet?"

Ayana nods and sniffs. "I haven't taken it off."

I smile. "She'd be proud." I grip the fabric in my hand, remembering the funeral home, when I made the decision to slip it from her wrist.

"She said it would smell sometimes," Ayana says, shifting from foot to foot.

To my surprise, I laugh. "You know what else used to smell?" I say. "Her morning breath. I used to ask her if a stray cat crept into her bed in the middle of the night and used her mouth as a litter box." Liv used to giggle hysterically when I'd make that comment and then spend the next five minutes breathing heavily all over my face.

"And her cheesy feet," Ayana adds.

I laugh again. Liv did have cheesy feet, an unfortunate side effect of never wearing socks with her shoes.

I stand back up as Jason and my mother stare at me with pained expressions. Jason wrings his hands together. "What can I do?"

"Just rescue me if I need it."

I extend my pinkie toward him, an old habit we picked up once the girls started doing it. We link hands, like children, and then kiss our thumbs. Our eyes meet, and a flash of gratitude registers through all this pain. I still have my best friend, my mother, and Ayana. At least there's that.

"You'll get through today," he finally says.

"Debatable," I say. All of this—from getting dressed to hosting to waiting for the circus to arrive—feels automatic, unconscious, like I'm floating through some parallel universe. I don't feel anything except her absence. Everything else has grown numb.

Right before people start to trickle in, I panic and wish we had chosen somewhere other than our home. What if people want to go into her room? What if they want to hover and hang? Death is private. Why do we have to gather to display our grief in the first place? I grip Jason's shoulder and he turns, already damp in his suit jacket. I told him not to wear a suit—that Olivia wouldn't have expected him to wear a suit—but Jason is nothing if not traditional.

"I can't do this." The words fly out of my mouth. Once they're out, I find that I really mean them. *I can't do this.* I don't *want* to do this. I glance around my living room and kitchen.

"Which part exactly?" my mother asks.

I gesture around us, to the urn perched on the island. "This is private. Losing my daughter is private. This feels exploitative."

Jason nods. He understands; of course he does. "Do you want to cancel? We can cancel and do something with just us."

"Ayana, can you do me a favor?"

She springs to attention, happy to be of use. I grab a piece of paper and a Sharpie and ask her to write *private* on it and tape it to Liv's door. "If anyone tries to go in there, tell them no," I say. "You are the only one allowed in her room, okay?"

She nods, draws on the paper, tapes it to the door—the word *private* outlined with flowers and stars—and then she stands back to admire her work.

"Liv would approve," I say.

The doorbell rings, and I hear them before I see them, the coven of Michael's family, all here from Mexico City. Once upon a time, I embraced them fully as my own. I was so ecstatic to find a partner with a big family that I overlooked some of the red flags of our own relationship. But seeing them all now, so animated and passionate, reminds me of how long I stayed because I didn't want to lose them too.

My mother pushes her wineglass toward me, and I take a healthy gulp and steel myself. Once the crowd is gone, my grief will be my own again. But for the next few hours, it belongs to the collective.

Michael enters ahead of the rest. He looks handsome in a charcoal suit with no tie. He finds me and kisses me gently on the cheek.

"How are you?"

I shrug. "How are you?"

There are already tears in his eyes as he shakes his head and clears his throat. "Surviving."

Jason nods in his direction and the two clap each other on the back. My mother clears her throat and opens her arms. Michael pauses for a beat before they hug, the tragedy of the day passing, unwanted, between them.

His brothers, aunt, and cousins all spill into my tiny living room, their shoes scuffing my freshly scrubbed floors. Michael's mother, Lucia, presses forward in a lovely emerald dress—Olivia's favorite color. Did she know that? Her squat, curvy frame barrels toward me. Her skin has darkened from the sun, but her eyes are hollow and sad, marred by dark flesh that reminds me of death. She's put on weight and her jawline has stretched, like pizza dough left out to hang, no doubt from her own decadent cooking. She leans heavily on a cane, which is a new addition. Regardless, she opens her free arm and practically forces me into her, murmuring soothing words in Spanish.

"Kate, *cariño mio. Lo siento mucho.*" *My darling, I am so sorry.*

"*Gracias*, Lucia."

Lucia, though always fiercely protective of Michael, was like a second mother to me. She embraces me firmly and rocks me back and forth across her ample bosom. Liv used to love her hugs. She'd get lost in them. I squeeze her back and inhale butterscotch and lilacs. If I were to dig around in her pocket, I bet I would find crushed petals from her garden and a mountain of butterscotch candies wrapped in clear cellophane. When Liv was old enough not to choke, Lucia would sneak them to her when I wasn't looking.

I ask Lucia how her flight was, though does it matter? She is here. Michael is here. Olivia—my heart, *mi amor*—is not.

We make small talk, and then it is time. As we all gather on the front porch—friends, teachers, and kids—and prepare to walk around back, Olivia's swing catches the corner of my eye. The frayed ropes have long ago been duct-taped, the once bright yellow seat caked with mud and stripped of most of its paint. It was her favorite spot in the whole world. Every morning she would shake awake her limbs, flying impossibly high in the air, twisting, turning, and screaming the lyrics to her favorite songs blasting from her iPod. I hesitate on the front steps. I've been thinking about this all wrong. *This* is the place she would want to be honored. This is the place we should gather—not the backyard.

I make an announcement, and Jason catches my eye and gives me a nod. We push into the front yard, which has been brutalized by moles and rain, and I hear a few of Michael's family members complaining about the wonky earth. I approach her swing and place the urn directly on the bald wood, biting the inside of my cheek so hard, the sharp tang of blood fills my mouth. I hadn't planned on saying anything, but here we are. She would want me to.

I clear my throat. Silent tears are already carving tracks down my cheeks, and I unfold my sunglasses and put them on to avoid staring directly at anyone. "This was Olivia's favorite place in the entire world," I begin. "When we moved into this house, I thought, *We have this great big backyard. She'll never want to come inside.* Little did I know her favorite place would be so close to the street and fashioned from ten dollars of material from Home Depot." A ripple of laughter cascades through the crowd, and I find the strength to continue. "Michael made this swing for her. We wanted her to be able to come out to this tree and connect with nature. I couldn't possibly know what a ritual this would become or how many circus tricks she would learn. Literally. I can show you the videos." I press my hand against the maple tree's massive trunk and pat it gently. "She called it her morning meditation with Mable the Maple." My voice breaks, but I continue. "This is how she started her day. Wild, ratty hair; mismatched clothes; dirty feet; loud music; and her little body moving and waking up to the music she loved. Under the tree she loved. Near the house she loved. On the swing built by a father she loved."

Michael wipes the tears flowing down his cheeks. I take a shaky breath before continuing. "This is an unspeakable tragedy. I should have been in that ocean with her. It is something I have to live with, and that is my burden to bear. But Liv's spirit deserves to be celebrated. She may have been nine, but she had enough love to consume her and anyone she met for a thousand years." I touch the urn. "To my sweet Olivia. We love you and miss you and will remember you, always."

I step away from the tree, unsure if anyone else will say anything, and to my surprise, Ayana steps forward, lightly resting a hand on one of the ropes. There are several awkward beats of silence, but then she finally speaks.

"Liv was my best friend," she begins.

I press a hand to my heart and find Jason, who is openly crying in the crowd.

"This was supposed to be our first vacation together." She stares at the urn and then right at me. "We talked about it for weeks—what we would bring and which bunk bed we'd sleep in." She sighs, and in that sigh, I know the loss she is trying to contain. She has lost so many people in her life, and now this.

"I know that wherever she is, she is probably making everyone smile. Liv made me smile every day. I feel lucky that she was my best friend." She fiddles with her friendship bracelet and then steps away.

A few more people talk—her teachers, friends' parents, Michael, and my mother. Though I didn't ask, people stack mementos around the base of the tree: My Little Pony stuffed animals; Liv's favorite flower, daisies; pads of drawing paper; pictures of the Rowdyruff Boys, specifically Butch, as she had a massive crush on him; and even a pair of ice skates. With every object placed on the ground by the trunk, I take a step backward, unable to visually face all my daughter's favorite things.

Once it's clear no one else is going to speak, my mother ushers everyone back inside for food and alcohol. Not ready to face the crowd, I place the urn in my lap and shift on the swing, tapping my heels back and forth in the well-worn dirt rubbed free of grass. Jason sends Ayana back inside and approaches, staring at all the leave-behinds.

"Well, this is the worst," he says.

"Beyond."

Jason crouches in front of me and places his hands on the ropes. "Look. You've just experienced the absolute worst tragedy a human being can ever face. You know that, and I know that. It's awful. But from this day on, you will meet your pain and you will get through it. Or it will become part of you. But it won't always feel this bad."

"Is that what it's been like for you?"

"Yes."

"How'd you get through it?"

"Jack Daniel's."

"You know I don't love whiskey," I say.

He thumps my knee. "Wine works too." He sighs and stands again. "To be honest, I decided I wasn't going to avoid the pain. I wasn't going to run from it. Every day that I got up and wanted to do nothing but cry, I did. Every day I wanted to be alone, I was alone. But I gave myself a cutoff. I knew that to be okay, I had to figure out how to still live my own life—because all the grieving in the world couldn't bring Shelby back. I chose to be an active participant in my life, because isn't that the point? Every time someone dies, we learn how we need to live."

"Okay, Yoda," I say, wiping my nose. "I hear you."

"Don't hate, appreciate."

I offer a small laugh, then immediately feel bad for laughing. How can I laugh when my daughter is dead?

"It's okay to laugh," he says, noticing my discomfort. "In fact, it's one of the best things you can do. They call it *medicine* for a reason." He pulls me to my feet. "Let's go."

"I don't want to go inside," I moan.

"I know. That's why we're leaving."

I hesitate. I can't let my mother handle everything, leave all those people who came to support me. "I can't."

"Yes, you can. Rule number one of grief." He summons me to follow, and I find myself hurrying to catch up as we head to his Suburban.

"What's that?" I ask as he unlocks the passenger door and I climb in.

He starts the car and offers me a smile. "You can do whatever you want for a while. No social niceties. No playing by the rules." He puts the car into gear. "Because there aren't any." His words send an awful ache through my chest.

But he's right. I've set so many rules for my life; every bit of my daily routine has centered on being a reliable parent and taking care of another human being. Who am I if I don't follow those rules anymore? Though work has been understanding, I can feel my boss itching for me to come back. I am needed there, and that is something. But what would happen if I just woke up tomorrow and decided to live a different life?

I stab at the button to lower the window and suck in fresh air, feeling completely unhinged. We drive around the neighborhood and then head out onto the main road.

"Let it out!" Jason yells over the wind.

I look at him. "Let what out?"

"Everything." He opens the sunroof and motions for me to stand. "Get up there and scream."

I think of the looks I would get from the neighbors, but at this particular moment, I don't really care. All the emotions from the past few days are climbing my throat, and if I don't let them out, I'm going to suffocate. Before I know what I'm doing, I unhook my seat belt, steady myself by the console, and pull my torso through the sunroof. I'm reminded of how Liv and I would often drive around our neighborhood, music cranked, her head jutting from the sunroof, singing songs in absolute joy. I'd always had a death grip on her leg, certain she'd go flying out of the car if we hit a bump in the road. She never did, of course. All the things I feared never came true . . . and the one time I wasn't worried, she died.

I close my eyes against that harsh reality, the violent wind its own soundtrack in my ears. Jason takes the corner fast and then pulls onto the highway.

"Let it out!" he demands.

I wait until he cranks the music and goes so fast the tears thrash my cheeks and disappear in the wind. Finally, I suck in a breath, open my mouth, and scream.

7

I STARE OUT THE PLANE WINDOW AS WE BEGIN OUR DE-
scent into Mexico City.

Liv's hand is in mine, as flying makes her nervous. I ask, "Are you
excited, *changuita*?"

"I'm not a monkey. You're a monkey," she says. She squeezes my
hand once for yes, and I squeeze hers back.

"Me too."

Ever since Michael asked her to come, it's all I've been able to
focus on. Despite my feelings for Jason, I'm excited to see Michael,
excited to see what happens while I'm here. Jason definitely felt the
shift between us, however, and that slightly open door of "something
more" seemed to slam shut. We haven't talked about it, though I
assume we will when I return.

I plan to stay for only a few days, though work has given me the
green light if I want to stay longer, as my boss wants me to scope out
a few projects while I'm here.

Liv squeezes my hand again. "Can I ask you something?"

"Always."

"Do you ever miss Papito?"

I smile. "Of course I do. I miss him all the time."

"Why did you two split up if you miss each other?"

I glance out the window again as we slice through the clouds. "It's complicated."

She scratches her nose. "Why don't you ever date? Brady's mom got divorced and she dates constantly."

I don't ask who Brady is or how she even knows about dating. I think about rattling off the excuses I always give: *I don't have time. Dating sucks. I'm too old.* "Dating isn't as easy when you're a grown-up," I finally say.

"Well, of course it isn't easy if you never try."

I squint at her. "Are you sure you're nine?"

She giggles as I begin to tickle her. "I am, I am!" she insists. I shush her as people around us look our way.

I press a little more. "How would you feel if I started dating someone?"

She shrugs. "I'd be fine with it." Liv clutches one of her stuffed animals to her chest and smells it. "Does Fred smell dank to you? I think he smells dank."

"Dank?" I laugh and sniff him. "He's a little damp but not dank."

"No, he's dank." She stares at her stuffed bear. "Fred, do you need a bath?"

Fred is the first stuffed animal Michael bought her before she was born. Even after all these years, it's still her favorite. I remember how Michael and I set up her nursery, hanging her tiny clothes, assembling her crib. I assumed we'd be on the parenting journey together, that he'd love us enough to stay. I ignore those painful memories and tune back in to Liv, who is suddenly off in her own little world of stuffed animal banter. When the wheels touch down, she gives a little yelp of surprise as we skid to a stop on the tarmac.

The sun is fierce, and I shed my sweater the moment we step outside. Michael is driving us to the estate, though I insisted we could just take a car. He doesn't trust the drivers here, so I relent. I remember how overwhelming it was to visit when Liv was little, navigating the packed streets, fighting for space, scraping by with my basic Spanish, and lugging Liv to and from tourist attractions until she passed out from sugar and endless walking.

This will be a different trip, mainly because I am leaving her here. It makes me ache to even think about it. Plus, Liv hasn't seen any of her relatives on Michael's side in a few years. While she is excited, I worry that the crush of enthusiasm and strong personalities might overwhelm her, but she assures me she's fine.

We wait in the pickup lane. Liv has her blue headphones on, bobbing her head to her iPod, no doubt listening to some new electronica song that would make my head spin.

I think about seeing Michael after so long and my stomach flips. Chemistry was never our problem.

It is warm and dry, and cigarette smoke hangs pungent in the air. Finally, I see Michael's Jeep. He gives two sharp beeps and barely shoves the car into Park before hopping out and opening the back for our bags. He steps around the car and my heart skips a beat at seeing him. It has been too long.

He flings his arms wide. *"¡Tu aventón!" Your ride.* Liv smiles, and he smiles back, scooping her up in a massive hug. She giggles as he sets her down.

"You've grown a foot, *mija*."

Seeing them together with their large eyes and dark skin makes me feel like he owns a part of her that I do not.

He turns to me and swallows, his eyes sweeping my face. "Kate, you are a vision, as always." He leans in and kisses my cheek. His lips are warm, and I let him slip his arms around my waist. I breathe him in, pissed he's been gone so long but also relieved to see him.

Liv instantly tells him every detail of our flight as he stuffs our bags in the back. I'm happy to see she is so comfortable. Part of me wondered if she'd be more reserved, since he has been nothing more than an emoji string on the other end of her iPod for the last year, but the two of them pick up as if no time has passed at all.

I climb into the back seat and shoot Jason and my mother a text that we've arrived safely. Michael is overly talkative as Liv takes it all in: the jammed streets full of tourists and locals, the city center, the landmarks, the racetrack, and the field where he plays soccer on the weekends. Michael's family lives in a sprawling compound in Condesa, which is a relaxed, authentic neighborhood untouched by the mammoth tourist and party scene.

It's only a twenty-minute drive, and I marvel at how strange it is to be sitting here, staring at the back of Michael's head, our daughter beside him.

As we near his neighborhood, I admire the traditional Mexican houses and point out some of the different features to Liv. The stucco and adobe. The hacienda architecture. The flat roofs and sprawling patios.

"We're only five minutes from the park," Michael says. "Maybe we can play fútbol?"

Liv shakes her head, her headphones still on. "I don't play fútbol, remember?"

"I know, but you're in Mexico now, baby. Everyone plays fútbol." She shrugs. "I like to rollerblade and ice skate."

"And *siestas*, right?" he asks. "Who doesn't love to nap?"

Liv has already tuned him out. I can tell she's getting nervous as she gnaws on a fingernail and watches the houses whip by. Finally, we arrive at his house, situated behind a black iron gate. Anywhere else in the world, this would cost millions, but this house has been in his family for decades.

"*Tu casa*," he says. "Welcome."

Though Liv is not fluent in Spanish, being here will be great practice for her to speak what she does know and learn more. We roll slowly through the gate, where the garden is lush and untamed. Ropy green vines and jacaranda trees, with their bluish-purple flowers, grace the path on either side of the long, winding drive. Cacti, ferns, bromeliads, and orchids, all wild and vibrant, fight for space.

Lucia is an avid gardener, and the flowers are in full bloom, a violent explosion of ruby and violet. It is the garden of Olivia's dreams. She gasps when she sees the array of colors, and I feel guilty that we haven't planned for our garden yet, after I promised we would.

The terra-cotta mansion was built in the 1920s and still stands, crumbly in spots, but just as stunning. I glance at Liv and she perks in her seat. She loves big houses and always wishes we lived in a larger house like most of her friends.

"This is like a castle!" she exclaims.

Michael turns and beams in pride as he shuts off the ignition. "Just wait, *mi amor*."

We hop out of the car and grab our bags as a gaggle of Michael's family rushes to meet us in the circular drive. A giant fountain bubbles into algae-stained water, and Liv peeks in before freezing at the onslaught of excited arms reaching her way. I shoot Michael a look, but he is oblivious as he introduces Liv to everyone: Abuela Lucia, of course; Michael's aunt and uncle, Rita and Joseph; and about ten cousins I can never keep track of. I stand awkwardly to the side as Liv is passed from one person to the next, as they ooh and aah at how tall she is, how stunning, how beautiful. "Isn't she beautiful?" "She looks just like Michael!"

Lucia finally breaks free and ambles over to me, leaning heavily on a cane. "Kate, it's been too long." I fall into a firm hug. "Welcome home."

Sometimes I forget how fiercely these people loved me; how they invited me into their lives, and then when we got divorced, they slowly drained away. Now, with all the unruly energy and enthusiasm, I remember how much space they used to occupy in my life.

I take in Lucia now; she is more weathered, but she definitely doesn't look like someone with terminal cancer. Nothing makes her happier than having her family together, and it thrills me to bring her this gift. We are ushered inside as I say *hola* to everyone and then walk up the grand staircase to our room. Until my departure Liv and I will share the blue room, which has two queen canopy beds and a balcony overlooking the grounds.

"This place is insane, Mama," Liv says, placing her suitcase on her bed.

"Do you remember it at all?" I ask, sitting on the edge of the mattress.

"I think so."

"Everything good? I know this is a lot."

She nods. "I just can't believe all these people are my family."

Part of me feels guilty that she hasn't had more visits with Michael's family, that I didn't fight harder for them to remain in her life or choose to bring her here more often. Perhaps I got lazy or became too selfish, but I realize now that it will be up to Olivia if she wants these people in her life. What right do I have to deny her a chance to get to know her relatives?

"It's pretty cool, right? So many people."

We settle in and then prepare for a traditional Mexican dinner. As I help Lucia in the kitchen, pressing tortillas, chopping and prepping freshly grown peppers and cilantro, I watch outside the large bay window as some of the younger cousins kick a ball around, and to my astonishment, Liv is playing too. The scent of onions and beans sifts through the air, and my stomach growls. Michael passes by and winks.

"See? Everyone plays fútbol here."

"*Ya calmate, hijo.*" Lucia shoos him away, and he steals a chip, dunking it into the chunky guacamole, and leaves the room, hands in the air as if in surrender.

"*Extrañé tu cocina,*" I say. *I've missed your cooking.*

"*Gracias,* Kate." She winks and gives me another task. I relax into it—the music, the easy conversation—and keep my eye trained outside. Liv isn't the most coordinated kid, but I love that she is trying. Lucia asks me to help set the table, and I do, biting my tongue that the men are outside talking while the women are inside working. I know this is a perpetual fight I will never win.

Once the table is set, I call everyone in to eat. Liv sits beside Michael and digs into the tacos, moaning that they are the best tacos she has ever had. She even speaks a little Spanish and makes people laugh as they take her in. I sit back, a cautiously optimistic observer. There is a place for her here. When had I forgotten that?

After dinner, Lucia offers Liv a churro, and her eyes practically roll into the back of her head with delight. She dips it into a bowl of melted Mexican chocolate. Cinnamon and sugar dust her lips, and I resist the urge to wipe her mouth clean. She springs from room to room as Michael shows her different possessions—old family keepsakes, statues, globes, ancient books—and then she passes out at nine, which never happens at home.

Once she is asleep, I walk downstairs and out to the back patio, where it's just Michael and Lucia. He's smoking a cigar, and I see the gray curl of smoke like a halo above his head.

"Hello, Katie girl." He sucks on the cigar, his cheeks puffing in and out. He pats the chair next to him.

"That went better than expected," I say, sitting. I take the glass of scotch that's offered and sip. "I just wish we could have come here under different circumstances." I glance at Lucia. "I'm so sorry to hear about your diagnosis."

To my surprise, Lucia snorts. "Oh, please. It brought everyone together, did it not? That is a gift."

I smile affectionately at her. "Why do you think I stayed married to this one so long?" I jab a thumb in his direction. "Because I didn't want to lose you." I reach over and squeeze her soft hand.

We all laugh good-naturedly, and Michael looks at the stars. "I've made some big mistakes with us, Kate. I know that, and I'm sorry. But I want Olivia to know where she comes from. I want her to know us."

"I want her to know you too," I say. "But we also have a life in Nashville, Mike. I've been on my own. We've been on our own." The words are sharp and raw, and Michael takes them like a bullet.

He traces the rim of his own glass and knocks his scotch back, the end of his cigar a dancing red orb. "I know you have, and I will never forgive myself." I sense there's more that he wants to say, but he doesn't.

He crosses one ankle over the other and jiggles the leg on top. We all fall silent as we stare at the stars. The night is cool and quiet, and I soak it all in.

Suddenly Lucia waves her hand in the air, her large diamond catching the moonlight. She has never removed it, even though her husband has been dead for years. "You know where cancer really is?" She taps her gray-black curls. "Up here. If I can't beat it here, then I don't beat it at all." She smiles, and I see Liv in her too. "But I want to know my granddaughter. You bringing her here . . . it means the world to me."

Michael suddenly starts crying, and the sight is so startling, I stay frozen in my chair. Lucia tuts and scoots closer, rubbing a hand over his back.

"I swear, this has been harder on him than me," she murmurs. "I'm fine. I know my maker, and I am not afraid of death."

I press a hand to my heart, searching for words. "Thank you for inviting us here."

She reaches over to squeeze my hand and smiles. "Of course, *querida*." *Honey.* She struggles to stand and leans on her cane, staring between us. "None of us really know how much time we have left, do we? Best to spend it with those we love." She says good night, and an unexplained chill runs the length of my body as Liv pops into my head.

"Well, that was subtle, yes?" Michael wipes away his tears and sighs.

"Completely." I lean back in my chair and stare at the clear sky.

"Kate." Michael's voice is suddenly serious as he sits up and takes my hand. His palm is warm as his thumb traces the tips of my fingers. "I want to give this another shot."

"Mike . . ."

"No, I know. There are a million reasons you divorced me, but it's different now. *I'm* different now. I want us to be a family again."

Thoughts swirl in my head, all clashing for space. Before I can speak, he continues. "We don't have to figure any of it out tonight, but I just wanted to tell you how I feel."

"Okay."

"Tell me you'll at least think about it."

I give it some thought, sifting back through our relationship—all the highs and lows, all the joy and disappointment. Am I willing to risk it all again? Finally, I nod. "I will. I'll think about it."

"Bien." He squeezes my hand three times for *I love you.*

After a moment, I squeeze back. He's the one who taught me this, after all, and I passed it on to Liv. I close my eyes, suddenly more confused than ever.

But also more hopeful than I've been in some time.

SEVEN

ONCE MICHAEL AND HIS FAMILY HEAD BACK TO MEXICO City a few days later, I walk over to Jason's.

His house is a sprawling Victorian at the very end of our street. Even in my state of grief, I still marvel at the landscaped yard, the shrubs trimmed into flawless rectangles and domes, the potted vegetation along the periphery, the absolute order to a world that can turn to chaos in an instant. Even though our house is only a few doors down, it is smaller and more modest, always in a state of disarray.

I briefly think of going back home. Another night of pulling back the duvet, slipping under, and never wanting to get up again. *No.* I don't want to be alone tonight.

Inside, Jason pours me a glass of wine and tells me Ayana is having a sleepover with a friend. I immediately think of Liv, of how quickly she will be replaced in Ayana's life by other girls. How all Liv's young friends will continue to make friends as they grow and one day forget her.

I kick off my shoes in their oversized foyer and sink into their couch, which Jason reupholstered in Sunbrella fabric due to incessant stains from Ayana. The fabric is rough on the backs of my legs, but

I pull them underneath me and take a big gulp of wine. My eyes are glassy, my throat raw from so many days of crying.

I adjust on the couch, wine stem clutched lightly between my thumb and index finger. I don't say anything at first. We are the type of friends who don't need to constantly break the ice or fill gaps. This is a situation where no comment, large or small, can change the outcome. Talking seems futile. I relish the silence as Jason excuses himself to make some food. I stare into my wineglass, swirling the rich, dark cabernet, and let my eyes drift up toward the mantel with family photos lined up chronologically—Ayana as a curly-haired four-year-old; Ayana in the bathtub; Ayana on her first day of kindergarten; Ayana on skis. My breath catches at a photo of her and Liv, covered in mud, their dirty palms pressed toward the camera lens. They used to have their annual "mud pie" parties in Jason's backyard.

Jason tracks my gaze from the kitchen to the photo and sighs. "I'm sorry, K. I didn't think to take it down."

"Don't you dare," I snap. I sniff, then take a large gulp of my wine. "I'm not going to pretend I never had a daughter. I want to remember her."

I close my eyes and push away the grief, instead placating my nerves with the comforting sounds from the kitchen: the fridge door suctioning open and closed; bowls and plates being taken down and noisily stacked; the slice of a sharp blade against the cutting board; the rush of water from the sink; the *click-click-click* of the blue flame from the gas stove.

I stare again at the mantel, remembering so many Christmas parties here. The fireplace with its incessant roar, old-fashioned stockings, holiday tunes on a repetitive loop. Every year the girls would disappear to play dress-up. They'd toddle down the stairs in some of Shelby's old dresses, belts, and shiny high heels Jason could never part with, their small feet shuffling from one room to the next as they struggled for balance.

One time they got into one of Shelby's makeup kits he hadn't ditched, so proud of themselves for their work. Instead of reprimanding them, Jason arranged an impromptu photo shoot. I wanted to be that kind of parent, to roll with the punches, to always be kind and seize the opportunity to play. Instead, my first instinct was to shame Olivia for not respecting other people's belongings, especially those of the dead. But it hadn't even occurred to Jason to be mad. To him, it was a way to keep Shelby alive.

I begin to think of work. Returning to the regular rhythm of my days could be a welcome escape, but it also sounds too overwhelming to comprehend. The past few years I've worked hard at my job, and for what? I wasted so many nights with Liv, existing next to her but not really tuned in to her, always plugged into my computer or running off to check on project sites. I'd assumed I'd have a lifetime of nights to make up for working so much, and I'd often told her I'd play, or we'd plant a garden, or we'd go do some fun mother-daughter adventure, and then I'd get swept up in work. I'd been so caught up in making sure we were financially comfortable that I'd overlooked the only thing Olivia really needed from me: my time.

"God, I can't stop dissecting what type of mother I was," I say.

"*Are*," he corrects me. "You're still a mother, Kate." He enters with a tray much too loaded for just the two of us: brisket, an array of local cheeses, grilled bread, and salty, oily black and green olives. My stomach growls. I can't remember the last meal I've eaten. He fixes me a plate and thrusts it into my hands.

"Eat."

I do as I'm told. Jason flips on some music to drown the morose silence. "Okay, let's discuss your next steps." He wipes his hands on a napkin.

"Next steps for what?" I ask.

"Your healing."

"I didn't realize there was a specific protocol for healing." I stab into a piece of meat.

He lets the statement hang in the air as I bite down on an olive. "All I mean is, we push our grief aside; we don't deal with it; we go back to work and pretend. And then everything falls apart. You can't skip over this part, Kate. The sooner you meet it head-on, the better."

I stare at him, knowing he's right, but also knowing that regardless of how much work I do—how hard I work to "heal"—this pain will always be a part of me. *Always.* It will burrow into my marrow and never let me go.

"What if I don't want to heal?"

"Tough shit," he says. He bites into a mound of brisket. "You know what Shelby would say if she were here?"

"Shut up?" I joke.

"Probably." He clears his throat and tosses back his head, trying to channel Shelby's fabulousness. "But she'd also say something like, 'K, this is your *Eat, Pray, Love* moment.'"

"And I'd say, 'This isn't a book or a movie, Shel.'"

We chew silently for a few minutes. "What about work?"

"What about it?"

"Are you going to take some time off?"

I shrug. "I'm not sure that's really an option. I need the money." My head is fuzzy from the wine, and I bite into a piece of bread to soak up the alcohol.

"Maybe you could take a sabbatical. I'm sure you have vacation days stored up, right?"

All of them, I think. I rarely take time off. "What would that accomplish?" The thought of being alone with myself, my house, all the to-dos . . . that sounds like a recipe for disaster.

He sets his plate on the coffee table and wipes his hands. "You've wanted to travel for a while, right? Maybe this is a good time."

I think back to my former life, before Liv, where I would jump at the chance to just pick up and go. "This isn't some scenario where I go away and suddenly everything's okay." My next words are out of my mouth before I can stop them: "How would you feel if Ayana died?"

Jason visibly flinches, but I continue. "Would you just sail off into the sunset drinking mai tais, living your 'best life'?" I air-quote the term *best life* and immediately begin to sob. "No, you wouldn't! You'd be devastated, destroyed." I sigh, suddenly exhausted. "I know you're trying to help, but I have no idea what I'm going to do next. Olivia isn't someone I can just forget. She's in me. She's in *here*." I clutch my chest with trembling fingers. "So back off, okay?"

"I'm sorry, Kate." He moves over and loops an arm around my shoulder. "You're right. I was just trying to help."

I'm too tired to respond. I know he means well, but I don't want to *do* anything. It all seems like too much. "I need to lie down," I say. I nearly apologize for making a scene but refrain. I'm not sorry for speaking up. This isn't a time for apologies and he, more than anyone, understands that. The blanket puddles to the floor as I drag my heavy body upstairs to the guest room and fall onto the crisp, cool sheets. I don't want to be here, in a house that isn't mine, stripped of everything I love, but I can't go home tonight.

I roll to my side and tuck my knees into my chest. All those nights of cuddling Olivia, nights that have been ripped away . . . I try to cling to them now, try to conjure her smell, the essence of her, the joy that used to radiate out of every pore and crevice. I drag a pillow to my chest and weep until I'm empty.

After hours of staring at the ceiling, I know I need to get up. My mouth is dry, and my head throbs. Sunlight streams through the cracked curtains, and I wait as a fresh wave of grief accosts me. My harsh words to Jason re-enter my mind, and I groan into my pillow. I don't want there to be tension between us. I don't want to work. I don't want to face the world.

I sit up. A gnawing ache spreads inside my belly and chest, as if someone has scooped out the best parts of me. I close my eyes and think of Olivia, willing her to come bursting through the door, demanding that I take her out into the world she so fiercely loved. If I strain, I can almost hear her—at night, when the door creaks, or when I'm sitting and think I hear her voice. I know these phantom noises will stay with me for a while. I think briefly of going home to shower and change.

I drag a hand over my face and pad down the hall to the guest bathroom. On the sink is a note from Jason.

K,

I'm sorry about last night. I feel terrible. I had to run into work for a 5:00 a.m. client, but please stay as long as you like, and let me know what you need . . . even if that's to use me as a punching bag.

Yours,

J

I clutch the letter to my chest and fire off a thank-you-so-sorry-about-my-outburst text. I'm still not used to my new phone. Thank God all my photos were stored in the cloud or my entire life with Olivia would have been erased.

I rinse my face, brush my teeth, and tidy the space before heading downstairs. The house is immaculate. Jason has a weekly cleaner and somehow manages, despite being a man *and* having a child, to keep everything tidy during the week. Whereas I clean, and then it's destroyed by the same afternoon, and then I clean again and complain about how pointless it all is.

My breath catches as I think of all the times I gave Olivia such a hard time about not picking up after herself. She was a force—a living tornado that would leave paper scraps, endless pairs of scissors, balled-up clothes, orange peels, and toys in her wake, wherever she went. It's one of the reasons I never let her have a pet—because she wouldn't clean up her toys, and I was always afraid a dog or cat would choke. I'd accused her so many times of being messy, telling her that she would grow up to be a messy person, and those conversations had crushed her.

Now, I realize, blinking heavily, she won't grow up to be anything. I press a hand to my chest to steady myself and assess Jason's kitchen. I imagine living in this big, fancy house, waking to a life so different from my own. No messes to clean up. Everything in its rightful place.

As I find the coffee and make a giant pot, I glance at the saltwater pool beyond the patio doors. A cabana sits off to the left, and when my coffee finally spits into the pot, I pour myself a giant mug, stir some ghee into it, and take it outside. The morning is humid but not yet too hot, and I slip into the cabana and collapse against the pillows. The water beckons. I close my eyes and try to imagine myself somewhere else, like Jason suggested. The image feels wrong. I place myself back at the beach house and immediately feel sick. There's not enough sun, sand, or shopping to dull the edges of this pain or the memory of what happened there. I need to work.

My fingers itch for my laptop, but I know that work is merely a distraction. I need to do something—something physical, something mental, something wholly encompassing that leaves me so exhausted at the end of the day that all I want to do is go to sleep.

I close my eyes and sip my coffee. Just a week ago I would have reveled in a moment like this. I was always sneaking away, trying to find the silence and stillness I never got with work projects or raising Liv. Now a palpitating loneliness throbs throughout my entire being until I'm sobbing into my coffee. I place it on the side table and allow the sadness to wrap its arms around me. I cry so hard, my chest shudders inaudibly. I tilt forward, clinging to the fabric of the cabana's cushion. I want my daughter back. I can't imagine going one more second without her.

Finally, I sit up, emotionally spent, and realize I have yet to get back to the arsenal of people who have texted me since Jason bought me a new phone. There are countless messages from family, friends, and employees who've heard the news, but I know, from experience, that in another week or two, these messages will lessen. These lucky people will all return to the safety of their own lives, mostly unaffected, just as I have before. They will get bogged down with deadlines, bills, and to-dos, and sadly think of Liv only from time to time. I bristle at how insensitive I've been to families who've lost loved ones. You never know what it's like until it's you.

I walk back inside, pour another cup of coffee, and scald the roof of my mouth in pursuit of a quick jolt of energy. Back outside, phone in hand, I bypass the endless work emails. There are a few from my boss with a pressing request to talk, though I can't deal with that now. Instead, I start making a task list of what needs to be done: Pay bills. Sort through Olivia's belongings. Close her bank account. Cancel her insurance. Writing a list makes me feel calmer, despite some of the unbelievable tasks I must complete. Once that is out of the way, I pull up a search engine and pause.

Jason may have been off base about going somewhere, but he's right about one thing: I need to take action to deal with my grief. I can't bypass it. I can't work it away, and I most definitely can't run away from it. But what I can do is find something—a cause, counseling, or a grief group—to channel all these emotions into so that I can learn how to cope and move forward. I start to research grief retreats and volunteer opportunities near Nashville.

After a while, I rest my head on a cushion and soak in the sun.

I'm completely alone.

I sit with that realization as I sip my coffee and continue with my tasks, returning the slew of text messages and letting my mom know I'm okay. I know I can't hide out at Jason's forever and that when I return home, I must face Liv's room and all her belongings.

I picture myself opening the door and stepping inside, and emotion ripples through me.

No.

It's clear I'm not ready yet. I pull up my boss's email again and, clearing my throat, dial his cell. He picks up on the first ring.

"Kate. How are you? I'm so glad you called." A swirl of activity registers behind him: car horns and the sounds of foot traffic. He's probably out running errands with his family.

"You wanted to talk?" I ask. I prepare myself for a client update or a dropped ball.

He sighs. "Look, I wanted to put something on your radar. We've got a potential project in Serenbe, Georgia. Cool community that a few partners want to re-create in Nashville. We need someone to go, scope it out, meet with the founder, the builders, and report back."

"And you need me?" I filter through all the other agricultural engineers at our firm. He could take his pick.

"I thought it might be good for you to get away for a bit," he says.

"We don't need someone until the end of summer or early fall, but I wanted to give you advance notice. Maybe even stay for a while. Take some time off if you need it."

My boss isn't a fan of taking time off, so I appreciate the offer. I consider the request and calculate the timing.

"Send me the details. I can't make any promises right now, but I'll see what I can do." I disconnect the call before I retract the tentative offer and toss my phone to the side. I type *Serenbe* in a search engine and begin to research. Maybe it will kill two birds with one stone—a chance to get out of town and also help the firm.

But didn't I just say I wasn't going to lose myself to work? I know, deep down, I want to distract myself from the pain of what's ahead. I consider the alternative: more days and weeks at home, reminders of my loss on display at every turn.

I know if I continue to wallow in my grief, it's going to be even harder to climb my way out, so I lose myself to research and the possibility of something new . . . a possibility of escape.

Fall

8

LIV AND I FIND PARKING AT HIGH GARDEN.

She yanks open the thick glass door. The bells jingle as we step inside. "Let the mommy-daughter date begin!" she declares.

When we have time, Liv and I carve out a few hours to come to our favorite spot in Nashville—High Garden, an apothecary that carries medicinal teas and tinctures and has a kombucha bar in back.

Every time I step inside, I enter a magical forest. Dried herbs jut from the ceiling like broom bristles while clear jars of fresh tea, as well as tinctures and salves, line the walls. No phones are allowed. Handmade tables and benches carve out sacred sipping spots. Rickety shelving crammed with borrowed books and wilted board games are first come, first serve. I hand Liv some cash, and she escapes to the kombucha bar to buy herself a flight while I peruse the menu and decide on a delicious fall tea latte.

As I wait in line to order my own steamy drink, my mind drifts back to summer. After I left Liv in Mexico City, she made herself right at home. We FaceTimed daily, and Michael texted me regularly. Just like that, the door between us was open again, and while contemplating what a life together could look like after all this time, I mostly just missed Liv. Then, at the end of summer, Lucia passed away. As a result, Michael and I have been in closer contact than usual.

Once my drink is ordered, I snag our favorite booth while Liv grabs a puzzle and a board game. She munches on two shortbread cookies at our booth, licking the sugar dust from her fingers as she tosses back her kombuchas like shots.

Because Liv was there when Lucia passed, it's been hard on her emotionally. She's made it very clear that she misses the estate and Michael's side of the family. While Liv was gone, I threw myself into work with new abandon and nabbed the promotion I'd been working so hard for. Since then, the demands have been even heavier, and I'm struggling to maintain the balance. But now, as we eat and talk, I feel my muscles unclench, the tension of the last few weeks dissolving as it always does in this unique space.

I lick the cinnamon from my latte and take a warm sip. The turmeric and cayenne tickle my throat. Liv has already downed all four of her drinks and is begging for more.

"Must we go through this every time?" I say. "Pace yourself, child. Savor."

"Bor-ing," she says.

We put together a zoo puzzle and then play a million rounds of Candy Land—still her favorite game after so many years—and I think about how happy I am to have her home. Just this morning I watched her swing and listen to music, wondering if she was comparing our small, little lives to what she had this summer in Mexico City. As she rocketed up toward the sky, a smile plastered on her face, I thought, *Is she truly happy?*

Suddenly Ayana erupts into the shop. The two girls disappear into the back closet to make homemade bath salts and disturb the crystals. I warn Liv that she can make only one jar of bath salts and to be mindful of the fragile objects.

Jason slides into the booth across from me, smoothing his hair, and smiles. He smells like the cold, and the cozy sight of him, in my favorite place with my favorite girls, solidifies something deeper I've been questioning in my heart. We haven't seen each other much since our beach vacation, and our relationship feels a bit strained, awkward even. But I find, staring at him now, that I have deeply missed him.

"Sorry to interrupt. I didn't think you guys would still be here." He glances back toward the nook, where the girls are giggling conspiratorially. "Though I'm glad you are."

I glance at my watch, surprised at the time. We've been here for over two hours. "Time always seems to evaporate here."

"It does." He smiles and tilts his head. "You okay? I feel like I haven't seen you much."

My heart kicks. "I know. I've been so busy with work." Jason already knows I got the promotion, but he does not know that Michael has asked for a second chance. I don't want to bring it up until I'm sure of how I feel.

Finally, we pry the girls away to walk them across the street to the community center playground. Jason and I sit on the swings and chat about nothing important, each of us going higher until we're in a race to see who can make it the highest first. Finally, I fly out of my swing and land hard, the sharp sting of my ankles reminding me I'm not a kid anymore.

We race through the playground and then climb toward the netted dome. Surprisingly, I make it to the top first. "Victorious!" I shriek, startling a few younger kids on the slides. The sun is blinding, and I squint at Jason, who is staring at me.

"You really need a competitive outlet."

"I just got one. Beating you."

I climb down as fast as possible, but my foot gets caught in the last rope, and Jason catches me, steadying my fall.

"Easy there, Baker." He doesn't let go. His hands tighten around my waist, and when I look up, his mouth is inches from mine.

We haven't been this physically close since the beach, and I feel caught off guard by my desire. Neither of us makes an attempt to move. Our breath mingles until the girls come screaming toward us and break the spell. We wrench apart and chase them around, finally caving to play an endless game of hide-and-seek. Once the girls are spent and cold, we take them for an impromptu dinner at Cafe Roze and then for ice cream at Jeni's. It is one of those perfect Saturdays, where one spontaneous act leads to the next, and then we are at Jason's house. After the girls fall asleep watching a movie, we lie outside by the pool, staring up at the stars from the cabana.

I ogle the open, inky sky. "Do you ever feel like life just keeps going in the same circles and the same cycles, and you've just gotten caught in a comfort zone?"

He shifts beside me. "Sometimes. Why?"

"I've just been thinking about the life we've built here. Liv was so stuck in her daily routine, but this summer, with Michael, she did more in two months than she has in almost ten years here. I'm just wondering if we're in a rut."

"I believe they call that life with a child," he jokes. "Kids need structure and stability, right? A routine. She probably did so much because Michael is new; Mexico City is new. It was like a vacation."

I consider that, but I was always on the go as a kid. My mom and I moved a ton, and looking back, I don't regret it, though it has led to moments of feeling massively restless. It's why Michael and I worked so well in the beginning. We were both gripped by wanderlust and thankfully had jobs that took us to new, exotic places.

He props himself up on his elbows and smiles. "Want to do something crazy?"

I sit up. "Define *crazy*."

He motions to the pool. "Me, you, a swim."

I laugh. "Wow, super crazy to swim in your heated pool, Jason. Really stepping outside of the box."

"Naked?"

Though it's a question, it's really more of a challenge. Immediately I'm thrust right back to this summer, to our slippery, wet limbs in the ocean. To what he told me sitting in this very spot. My entire body begins to hum.

He stands and removes his shirt, and I have the strongest urge to rake my fingers down the bare skin of his well-defined chest.

"What about the girls?"

"Asleep." He unbuttons his jeans and steps out of them, his briefs illuminating a very perfect package and strong, thick thighs sculpted from years of heavy squats and dead lifts.

I don't move; in fact, I can barely breathe as he maintains eye contact.

"This doesn't seem like a good idea," I whisper.

He walks over to me and pulls me to standing. I lift my arms, and he removes my shirt, which is suddenly the most erotic act I've been a part of in years. He kneels and slides my pants over my hips and thighs, trailing hot fingers against my aching flesh. I don't think I've ever been more aroused in my entire life.

He pauses as he stands back up, just my bra and panties and his briefs separating us. My body throbs with longing, but he traces my jaw with his fingers and smiles.

135

"Ready?" Before I can respond, he removes his briefs and jumps in, and I shimmy out of my bra and underwear, lowering myself in behind him. The water is like a warm bath, the salt prickling my skin. My body is more awake than it's been in ages.

We wade in the water, smiling like idiots before beginning to drift toward each other. The water is a buffer between us, the pool lights illuminating our bare bodies in the cool night. When he's in range and I'm wondering what he will taste like, the sliding door squeaks open and out peers Liv. I yelp and swim to the edge of the pool. Jason does the same to hide his naked body. I drape my arms over the side and press against the inside of the pool, praying she doesn't walk any closer.

Liv rubs the sleep from her eyes and looks between us. "Can I swim too?"

"No, sweetie." I attempt to keep my voice calm. "We were just finishing up because the pool isn't that warm." There's nothing Liv hates more than cold water. "In fact, could you go grab us two towels from the downstairs closet? Then we can head home."

She nods and stumbles back inside. I look at Jason, who looks as pained as I feel. Our breath is audible, as if we've been swimming laps. I search for what to say, what to do. Michael flashes through my head, and for one irrational moment, I feel as though I've cheated.

"Rain check?" he finally asks.

I push all thoughts of my ex from my head. "Rain check," I say.

EIGHT

THE DOORBELL RINGS.

I startle awake and look at my phone: ten thirty on a Saturday morning. Until recently, I never would have slept so late. When I don't answer, I hear keys in the lock and then footsteps in my foyer.

"Kate? You here?"

It's my mother.

"No," I call and tug the covers over my head.

My mother's efficient steps head right toward me. The overhead light flicks on, the curtains snap open, and she yanks the duvet off my body with the force of ten men. "All right, it's time to get up."

I sit up to yank the covers back. "There, I was up. Happy?" I pull them over me and make myself small.

"Kate, I'm serious. Grief is fine. Sleeping all day is not. *Up.*"

Her tone reminds me of being scolded as a child. Knowing I will not win this battle, I sigh and sit up. The lights are harsh, and I blink. My stomach growls.

"You're not taking care of yourself."

"What an amazing observation," I say.

"Kate, I'm serious. It's fall. Punishing yourself for months will not bring Olivia back. You know that, right?"

"I'm not punishing myself." It's true. I'm not intentionally neglecting myself. It's just now that she's gone, nothing seems to matter.

"Then what are you doing?" She blinks at me, her makeup flawless, another immaculate, wrinkle-free outfit in place.

"I'm grieving."

She motions to herself. "So am I. You know the difference between us?"

"You've showered this month?"

"Yes." She blinks at me. "And I know that what you're doing will make you feel worse. You know how I know?"

"Because you've been through it," I mumble.

"I have. Not with a child, mind you, but I've been there." She sits on the bed and squeezes my knee. "Olivia was my favorite person too, you know. Not that you don't love your own children, because of course you do, but a grandparent's relationship to their grandchild . . ." She shakes her head. "That's a different ball game. I thought Liv and I would have years of mischief ahead, but we don't. And as much as I cry about it or try to undo what's been done, I can't. So I move on with my life. Do I think about her constantly? Yes. Do I grieve? Of course. But I also keep living."

"Good for you." I yawn, touched by her words but still unmotivated to do a damn thing.

"We're going into her room today, Kate. Face the dragon."

"No." My tone is firm, but I know she's right. The longer I go without cleaning out her room, the harder it's going to be. She waits for me to reconsider, and finally I grumble and stand. My head is thick, and I'm in dire need of coffee. Sensing it, my mother moves to the kitchen and begins to make a pot.

I take the time to shower and get dressed, even managing to slick on some mascara and lip gloss. Too tired to wash my hair, I pile it into a neat bun and return upstairs to a full cup of coffee. My mother motions to the bathroom by Liv's room.

"Are you not ever going to use that bathroom?"

"That one's hers," I say. When we bought this house, Liv chose the bedroom that connected to the bathroom and claimed it as her own. And though my room is next to hers on the main floor, I agreed to use the bathroom downstairs.

My mother does not fight me on it, so I slurp down my coffee, grab some black garbage bags, and hand one to her. "You're going to help, right?"

She gauges me. "Do you want me to help? Or would you rather be alone?"

I consider her question. I don't want to do this alone, but I also don't want my grief on display. "Alone, I think."

"That's what I thought. I'm going to run to the grocery, get you some food for this monstrosity of an empty fridge, and then I'll do the laundry and clean up a bit." She surveys the messy kitchen, the unwashed dishes. "A shame you used to blame the mess on Liv. I see the truth now." She winks and kisses me on the cheek before leaving.

I consider going back to bed, but I'm up, dressed, and caffeinated. And she's right. It's time to face Liv's room. I prepare myself as I approach the door. I run my fingers over the wrinkled papers she taped to the door and start with those. *"You are you and that's okay!" "Be yourself and you'll always succeed!"* It feels wrong to remove them. I notice the worn wood I always said I needed to repaint but never got around to. I trace my fingers over the dents and bumps—effects of a tossed toy or a hard kick in protest.

I stand outside the room for what feels like a century before I finally open it. She sometimes used to lock the door from the outside with a slim skeleton key she'd once used as an oar for one of her tiny figurines in a kayak she'd built from a banana peel. She'd misplaced the key years ago.

When I step inside, I can't breathe. It's only been a few months since she was last here, but the evidence of her messy, hurried life is everywhere. While she promised to clean before we left for vacation, she never got around to it, so everything seems like it's in the middle of being dismantled or put away. I stare at the mountain of stuffed animals on her unmade bed, the random clothes strewn across her polka-dotted carpet, the books, half on her shelves, half on the floor, her fifteen mostly empty journals, open or dog-eared, and her cardboard box houses stacked and lining the walls. All the mementos left over from her memorial piled in a sloppy heap.

I have no idea where to start. I was always hassling her to get rid of things because I didn't want her to become a pack rat. And now, every drawing, story, or book I want to hold on to forever, as if it will keep a little piece of her with me. But it won't.

I decide to start with her clothes. I can easily donate the newer ones to families in need. I put on some upbeat music and get to work, unpacking her dresser, clearing off entire shelves of random trinkets, broken crayons, and mismatched socks. I gather the coins, rubber bands, and outgrown swimsuits hidden at the back of her underwear drawer. I then organize the books and grab bins to load into my car to take to Goodwill. Once that's done, I cram most of her stuffed animals into a bag but keep a few of her favorites: Fred, Foxy, Princess Cupcake Mouth, and Mama Llama. I take off the small harness and leash she bought for Foxy so she could pretend he was her pet. I gather them in my hands. She wanted a dog so badly. Why didn't I ever get her one? I pocket the harness and leash. Then it's her Legos, toys, and artwork, all of which I decide to keep. Her diaries. I skim a few pages as tears blot the paper. How sweet and innocent she was, how enthusiastic.

Today I got to bake cookies with Mama! She even let me frost them. I snuck one when she wasn't looking. Ayana came over for a playdate and we drew. I told her I baked those cookies, but she didn't believe me!

I flip through other short entries, tracing my fingers over her neat handwriting. I'm so engrossed in my work, I barely register my mother calling to me when lunch is made. My eyes are glazed, and I feel as though I've physically run a marathon. She walks into the room and whistles.

"You really did it. How do you feel?"

How do I feel? The grief settles, heavy and black. I turn to look at my mother, and our eyes connect. Despite how well she's keeping it together, the pain is there, as evident as my own. "Hungry," I finally say. "I'm starving."

"Well, that's a start," she says. "Let's eat."

We eat in silence, until my phone dings with an incoming text. I read it and then place the phone facedown on the dining room table.

"Everything good?" my mother asks, blotting her cheek with a napkin.

"It's my boss. He wants me out on a bid. This summer I told him I'd go, and now it's time."

She chews thoughtfully and nods. "Are you considering it?"

I know what she really wants to ask is if I'm considering going back to work at the office. After the memorial, I planned on it, and then just found my way into bed and haven't been motivated to do much else besides working from the comfort of home. I shrug. "Maybe. It's out of town."

My mother's eyes light up. "Maybe that's a good thing."

It seems I'm right back here again, weighing my options. Do I stay put and wallow, or do I get back out into the world, just as my mother is suggesting? I swallow the sandwich, not really tasting it, already wanting to go back to bed.

"I think you should answer him. I think you should take it."

"You don't even know where it is."

My mother motions around me. "It's got to be better than this, doesn't it, Kate? A little less painful?"

I know she's right. I know I need to do something, to take action in my life. I flip over my phone and hesitate before responding, then tap out a quick text.

Count me in, it says.

9

LIV DOESN'T WANT TO COME WITH ME ON MY WORK TRIP.

My boss has asked me to go to a place called Serenbe in Georgia to check out a project bid. When I ask Liv if she'd like to come with me, she insists on flying to Mexico City to stay with Michael instead. The request catches me off guard, despite how frequently she and Michael have been talking.

"We can definitely talk about going to Mexico City again," I say. "But fall break is just a week, so it would be easier for you to come with me. We'll make a vacation out of it."

Olivia huffs and crosses her arms. "But I don't want to go with you. I want to stay with Papá."

I look at her, trying not to feel hurt. "I understand, sweetie. But plane tickets are expensive, and this would be a short trip. It'll be fun."

"Blah, blah, blah. You just don't want me to see him!" She rips the beautiful drawing she's been working on in two, a clean tear right down the middle. "You never do what you say you're going to do."

Her words are like a slap. "What's that supposed to mean?"

"You promised me we'd have a garden this year. You pinkie promised! And we didn't do it *again*."

"You were gone this summer," I remind her.

"So? I'm back now! And we still don't have a gar-den." She breaks the word into two distinct syllables, kicks a doll on the way to her room, and slams the door so hard the frame shakes.

I sigh, scoop the drawing from the floor, and wonder why she always destroys her own belongings when she's angry. I attempt to calm myself, trying to see things from Liv's perspective. She's right. I did say we'd have a garden, but per usual, I haven't made the time to do it. But I didn't say no to Mexico City—I just said no to her warp-speed timing.

I try the knob, but it's locked. "Open your door right now."

"No!"

I jiggle the knob again. "You have three seconds to open this door, Olivia. I'm not kidding."

"I don't want you in here."

"Too bad!" I yell. "Now!"

She emits a monumental scream and opens the door before throwing herself back on the bed. She shoves her iPod under her covers and flips through a comic book, shutting me out completely.

"What is the deal?" I ask. My eyes scan the detritus of her room, but I choose to pick my battles.

"What is the deal with *what*?" she spits.

"With your attitude. I told you we would talk about it. Do you expect me to jump up and down and scream yes? I have to go on a work trip, Olivia, which is only a four-hour road trip from here, not a seven-hour plane ride. If you think I'm going to spend money on a last-minute ticket and spring this on your father when he's dealing with his own issues and hectic work schedule, then you obviously haven't thought this through."

"He wants me to come," she blurts.

"What are you talking about?"

"He texted me to ask if I wanted to come for fall break."

I search my brain to see if Michael brought that up with me, but no, he didn't. "Look, Liv. I know you're excited that he's back in your life, but there are still things to figure out. I can't magically snap my fingers and have him appear."

She tosses her comic book on the bed. "I know that. That's why I asked to go there."

"Okay, how about this? Yes, Olivia. You can go to Mexico City. Just come up with enough money to buy your own plane ticket, book it, and figure out the details. Sound good?"

She scowls at me. "You know I don't have money."

"Then I guess you're going to have to be patient and let me figure it out."

"Get out of my room," she says. The words are a warning, and her tone infuriates me.

"Listen to me right now, little girl," I say, taking a step closer. A lump of clay flattens beneath my bare foot. "I don't know where this attitude is coming from or why you're acting like this, but it needs to stop right now. Do you understand me?"

Nothing.

With every second, my anger swells, until I step over the random items littering her floor and pierce the flesh of my heel with a sharp Lego. "Damn it!" I pluck the offending object from my foot and sling it across the room. "And clean up your room. You are no longer allowed to live like this." I kick random toys out of the way and slam her door on the way out.

"Real great parenting!" she screams. "Now do you see why I want to live with Papá?"

I open the door again. "What did you just say?"

"You heard me."

"You know what, Olivia? If you'd rather live with the man who only shows up when he feels like it, then go ahead and take that risk. But I am a good parent. I do the best I can. I've done the best I can for nine whole years. And do you know where your father has been all this time?"

She opens her mouth to respond, but I continue before she can. "He's been living his own life in other countries, that's where. He goes wherever his work takes him, which would mean that you would go wherever his work takes him. But sure, be my guest. Go live with him. See how long that lasts before you realize how good you had it here."

Her chin crumples, and I know I've gone too far, but the anger is a hot, sticky thing that matures in my chest. I should walk away, I should cool down, but my attention is yanked back to her room again. Printer paper buries the floor, failed drawings she refuses to toss. This week's clean clothes are mangled in a massive heap by her dollhouse, stacked up like a colorful mountain. Remnants of clay and crafts pepper her rug like confetti, some so smashed in, they will have to be shampooed out. Four coffee mugs, half-filled with water, cluster on her nightstand. There are dried orange peels stuck to crusty bowls, empty raisin boxes peeking from beneath her bed—snacks she sneaks when she thinks I'm not looking. "You think Papá will let you live like this? Do you even know how tough your abuela Lucia was? What order and respect she demanded in her house? You won't be able to get away with anything you do here, Olivia. Do you understand me?"

Her eyes fill with tears as she gauges her own mess, a mess we fight about every single week until I begrudgingly help her clean it up and she makes empty promises to keep it clean. "How do you live like this?" The rage is a blinding, well-built cocoon. I gesture to her hair, which resembles a bird's nest. Her clothes are rumpled and dirty, mismatched, and I happen to know for a fact she is not wearing clean underwear.

"It doesn't bother me," she says.

"Well, it bothers *me*," I say. "You need to take better care of yourself, Olivia. Brush your hair, wear clean clothes, and pick up your space." I glance around in disgust. "And because you live here and *not* with Papá, you either pick up your room, or everything is going into the trash, do you understand me?" I turn to go, then stop, looking deep into her eyes. "You're going to end up a hoarder if you're not careful."

She balls her fists and screams at the top of her lungs, "Get out!"

"Gladly!" I scream back before slamming her door as hard as I can on my way out. The anger coils and releases in my body, an electric, ugly spring. It has been months since we've had one of these all-out battles, and I instantly berate myself for the things I said. No matter how much I grow as a mother, sometimes hurtful words slip out. But words are damaging, and regardless of how frustrated I get, I must remember that *I'm* the parent. Except, I'm the mom *and* dad, and I can't always keep it together—clearly. I stalk through the house as the anger recedes, realizing I've given Liv even more ammunition for texting Michael. I burst back into her room and snatch her iPod from her nightstand.

"What are you doing?" she shrieks. "Give me that!"

"You've lost all your privileges, young lady. No iPod, no computer, no Switch. Now clean up this mess. Right now."

I close the door without slamming it, my body surging with adrenaline. It is so easy to blame the tech—it's the phone's fault, the iPod's fault, the computer's fault—for why she doesn't pay more attention. But when I search deeper, I'm afraid the only one at fault here is me.

147

As I stomp through the house, the anger shifts to shame. Some days we are great, and then something tiny happens: Ayana can't sleep over. Liv printed the wrong coloring page. I suggest we do some off-line math, and then she becomes destructive. Normally I keep my cool and the storm cloud passes. But not today. Not with Michael offering up his estate on a whim and her wanting to go to Mexico City permanently. However I look at it, it feels like a lose-lose situation. If I want to present a loving, stable home, then I need to lead by example.

Wanting to get rid of this negative energy, I scrub the house from top to bottom while Liv takes a painfully long time to clean her room. Every time I check on her, she's sitting in the same spot, playing with a Lego or doll. Finally, I stand there until she shoves heaps of papers and mismatched crafts into random totes and slides everything under her bed. She stacks her stuffed animals on her wrinkled sheets and takes all her clean clothes and rams them into her dresser drawers. The reprimands are on the tip of my tongue—my insistence she do it over, do it right—but I have no more energy to fight and I let it slide.

After a quick lunch, once we've both calmed down, I ask her if she wants to go for a walk.

"No," she says simply.

It is a beautiful, clear day, and I need to move my body. "I would like to go on a walk," I tell her again, leaning against her doorframe. "But if I go and you stay here, you cannot use your iPod, unless you need to text me. Okay?"

"Okay."

Begrudgingly I give her the iPod touch, change clothes, and lace up my shoes. "I'll make it quick."

I lock the front door and take off at a fast clip. My mind slips back to our fight, the hurtful comments about how messy she is. I've been told on numerous occasions that's how Geminis are, or that she's highly creative, or that she will grow out of it. Though Liv is many things, she is not a neat person and has never been incentivized by an allowance or a chore chart or shiny gold stars for a job well done. She sees right through all that crap and just wants to be who she is.

And isn't that my job, to encourage her?

As I'm rounding the entrance to the greenway, I let our earlier fight dissipate. Instead, I must figure out how I can convince Liv that right now is not an ideal time to visit Mexico City—for a whole host of reasons—and see whether my mom can watch her if I go on my work trip to Serenbe alone. In my brief research, Serenbe, a biophilic community, seems like an idyllic escape, a place where Liv could play, run free, and enjoy herself, though I'm not sure how free she could be if I'm drowning in work. As I'm lost in thought, a scruffy mutt joins me, prancing toward me seemingly out of nowhere.

I jump from the sudden distraction, then crouch down to make sure he's friendly and search for a collar. "Aw, hey, buddy. Are you lost?" I feel gently around his neck, but there's no collar. He doesn't look particularly malnourished, but he has that scrappy look of most stray dogs. I continue ahead, but he trots along. "Don't even think about it," I warn. I turn on some music and take off at a jog, but he keeps pace, tail wagging, tongue lolling.

Together we snake down past the river, over the bridge, and then I turn around at the two-mile mark, as I don't want to leave Liv alone for too long. The dog stays with me the whole time and follows me all the way home. He's surprisingly obedient and even knows commands when I tell him to stop or sit. I slow to a walk and pull up our neighborhood Facebook page, searching for any missing dogs on the thread, but there are none. I post a photo of him and think someone will likely claim him.

A block from our house, I tell him to go home, but he's clearly not listening. His eyes are covered by unruly black hair, and I reason that I can at least feed him and give him some water while I wait for his owner. "All right, come on."

When I come through the door, I call to Liv, who comes bounding out of her room looking guilty. Crumbs of at least three different snacks stick to her lips and shirt, but all is forgotten as she glimpses the dog. She drops to her knees and opens her arms with a scream. The dog comes to her immediately. She rolls to her back, and he flattens himself on top of her, licking her face as she giggles.

"Mama, where did he come from? Can we keep him?" She sits up, breathless, one hand shoved possessively in his fur.

I check Facebook again, but so far, no one has responded. "Probably not. I'm sure he belongs to someone."

"Please, oh, please? I've wanted a dog my whole entire life." She loops her other arm around his neck and squeezes. Surprisingly, he doesn't squirm or move away.

"Oh really? You've never mentioned that before," I joke. I call to the dog, and he comes, curling up in my lap right there on the floor. He pants heavily, and I ask Liv to get him a bowl of water. She brings it back, sloshing a bit on the floor, and he laps it up until the bowl is clean. Liv rummages in the fridge and cuts a few pieces of leftover steak, which he gobbles without swallowing.

"Geez. He sure is hungry." She pets him as he plops on our floor. "What should we call him?"

"He probably already has a name," I say.

She glances at his scruffy fur and cute face, already in love. "What about Sir Newton?"

"No." I laugh.

She taps a finger to her chin. "Prince King the Nefarious Farting Sparkles?"

"Not happening." I pet his head and stare into his rich brown eyes. "Who are you, boy? Do you have a name?"

"Oh my God, Mama! I've got it!" Liv screams and claps her hands, which makes the dog bark. "Waffles! We can name him Waffles!" He barks again, and she points to him. "Mama, he likes it! Did you hear? He just barked at the name!"

I roll my eyes. "Waffles? Really?"

She rubs his neck and gives him a kiss. "Can we give him a bath? He stinks, like corn chips and moldy cheese."

I look at his matted fur. "We should probably take him to a vet first."

"But what if they take him away?" She slings an arm around his neck again. "What if he has a microchip and he's returned to his owner?"

I pet his head fondly, already growing attached but knowing if he belongs to someone, then we must return him. I've never had a dog before, but I've secretly always wanted one too. My mom and I were always on the go too much to have a pet, and Michael refused every time I brought it up in the early days of our marriage because we traveled so much. "I don't think he has a microchip," I say. "He doesn't look very well cared for."

I look up the nearest vet, recheck my Facebook post, and head that way. Liv is so excited to be going to a vet, she doesn't stop talking the entire way. Waffles sits in her lap obediently and is a champ during his exam. Though he's got fleas and needs to take some medication to ward off parasites, he seems to be in relatively good health. As he doesn't have a microchip, we have to wait and see if anyone claims him. I let them run a battery of other tests and balk at the bill.

Liv and I stop by the pet store on the way home and load up on essentials: food, doggie bags, shampoo and conditioner, a brush, a bed, a crate, a leash, a collar, and some toys. We wash him in our bathtub, both of us getting wetter than him. It's the most fun we've had together in ages, and a small, terrible part of me wonders if having a dog will make her reconsider wanting to go to Mexico City. Is this a bone tossed my way directly from the universe?

After he's been fed and bathed, he looks like a real dog, and we are both smitten. "Ayana is going to freak that we got a dog," she squeals. "This is the best day ever!"

I think about our tense morning—how we both yelled, the awful things we said—and am grateful for the turn of events and Liv's short-term memory when it comes to holding a grudge. I snap a photo and text it to Jason.

So this happened today . . . he found me on my run. Liv is in love. She's named him Waffles.

Hmm. He looks more like a Pancake or French Toast to me. ☺ *Tell Liv he's perfect.*

He asks whether Ayana can FaceTime with Liv, and the two spend an exorbitant amount of time talking about things other than the dog. I make us both a snack and feel a wave of happiness. Despite the stress, today has turned out okay. We have a dog. Liv is happy.

But then I think about work. It's just a week. Can I figure out what's best for Liv? I convince myself I can and start making plans. In the back of my mind, I worry about Michael, a strange sense of foreboding pressing on my shoulders. Did he really text her to ask if she could come without my knowledge? Already his presence is changing the fabric of my relationship with Liv.

The doorbell rings, and I rush to answer it, wondering if Ayana decided to run down the street so she could see Waffles in real life.

Michael stands on my front porch. "Surprise," he says. He's wearing a Grateful Dead T-shirt and slim-cut jeans, sunglasses blocking his dark brown eyes.

Before I can utter a sentence, Liv rounds the corner and screams. Waffles bounds forward, jumping onto Michael, who drops down and takes his furry head in both hands. "And who is this?"

Liv jumps up and down and fills him in as I stand there, feeling like a stranger in my own home.

"What are you doing here, Michael?"

"Visiting my two greatest loves," he says, smiling warmly at Liv.

I should be happy he's here, but for one fleeting moment, it takes everything in me not to slam the door in his face.

NINE

"WAIT, I'M SORRY. YOU'RE GOING WHERE?" MY MOTHER blinks at me, her smooth, Botoxed forehead unmoving.

"Serenbe." I place my hands on my stomach, full of Indian food. I haven't eaten properly in weeks, and my stomach complains. Ayana is upstairs in her room while Jason, my mother, and I drink wine and eat dessert in his dining room. "An agrihood in Georgia."

"I don't know what that means."

"Are you going to get chopped up into little pieces and buried in a backyard?" Jason jokes.

My mother frowns. "Is it a cult? This isn't like a *Stepford Wives* situation where you get turned into a robot, is it?"

"Nell, have you seen *Get Out*? That movie is beyond creepy," Jason remarks.

I roll my eyes at their joking ping-pong match. "It's not a cult, and I'm not going to get lobotomized. It's basically utopia. And I'm going for work."

"At least that's what they're advertising *before* they murder you in your sleep," Jason offers.

I let them poke fun, but I know they are secretly relieved that I've

154

decided to do something after literally lying around all day and crying myself to sleep for months. I know it's time to get out of my bed and back into my real life.

My brief stint cleaning out Olivia's room sent me into a three-day tailspin of grief. While Jason insists I crash with him for a while, I can't. I don't want to be home, but I don't want to stay with anyone else either. And then, after talking with my boss again about the offer to check out Serenbe for work, I began to research the sustainable agrihood on the outskirts of Atlanta and promptly fell in love with the idea of a private, self-contained community that connects people to nature and each other. The residents produce year-round cultural events with outdoor arts, culinary workshops, music, films, lectures; the town is full of shopping, art, trail riding, and even has an artist-in-residence program.

Now, with the memorial behind me and with life moving on, I know a change of scenery is what I need, even if it doesn't guarantee healing.

"When do you go?" my mother asks.

"I'm leaving tomorrow."

"Tomorrow?" Jason whistles. "Wow, you're all in, kid."

I shrug. "It's just for work." I thumb the label on the wine bottle and glance at Jason and silently wonder, *Is it just for work?*

"Well, maybe it's as great as it sounds, and then Ayana and I can come for the weekend or something."

I scoff. "Now you're inviting yourself?"

"Duh, dude," he says.

"I'm going to miss you two," I say, immediately tearing up. "I can't tell you how much I appreciate you both and what you've done for me."

"Of course." Jason's voice is soft, his eyes tender as they lock with mine. I will miss his friendship the most, and this warm bubble of familiarity. But I can't stay in limbo forever. I must regain some semblance of stability for myself, and I can't do that if I'm stuck in bed.

My mother pours us all more wine. "Well, I'm proud of you, for what it's worth. Even if it is a cult, at least it's a change. It will be good for you. Maybe put yourself first for a while."

I haven't put myself first in well over a decade. While I would gladly put myself last for the rest of my life if that meant I could have Olivia back for even a day, I know that I can't wish my way into that scenario. I'm finally realizing I really have two choices: wither from anger and sadness, or use this grief as a lesson to learn and grow.

For the last few months, I've been withering from sadness, but I can't do it anymore. I must accept what happened without being a victim of my circumstances or blaming the world. The worst has happened, yes, but there's always something valuable to be learned. At least that's what I've been told.

"Thanks."

I help them clean up the dishes, and then my mother leaves. Before I go, I tiptoe upstairs to Ayana's room. I knock on her door and smile as she invites me in. School is in full swing, and she is gaining more closure around the fact that Olivia isn't coming back. Her room is neat and orderly, everything tucked into proper cubbies and containers. Her outfit for tomorrow is already hanging by her bed. I once again observe the differences between her and Liv. Where Ayana is tidy and quiet, Liv was wild and messy. Ayana used to love to come over and fret about Liv's room and help her organize without belittling her like I so often did. I knock away the bittersweet memory and slip inside and sit cross-legged on her rug.

"Are you ready to see what happens to the infamous Boxcar Children?" We've been flying through the entire Boxcar Children set, and we've reached the last in the series.

"Yeah, but I'm sad too." Ayana curls next to me, a nasty scab on one knee where she fell off her skateboard. "I don't want to be done."

"Me neither." Though we are talking only about a set of books, there's a finality here that cuts deeper. This is the end of something, period, and we both know it.

I ache for Olivia in these moments the most. I miss reading her stories, feeling the heft of her body against mine. While I assumed I wouldn't be able to handle being around Ayana as much, I find, recently, it brings me peace and love, not pain.

I absently stroke her hair and feel terrible that I'm going to be leaving her after tonight, but children are resilient. She will be fine, and eventually, someday, maybe so will I.

As I read the story, my mind wanders a bit. In all my years of knowing Ayana, I've never really spent this much one-on-one time with her, and I now understand why Liv was so taken with her. She is such a kind, gentle soul, and this solo time with her has been a gift.

Once we finish, I turn to her and clear my throat. "So I'm going to go on a little work trip."

"To that fairy-tale place?" She scratches the bridge of her nose with painted fingernails. I'd told Ayana about Serenbe when I first researched it, showing her the video.

"Yes, to that fairy-tale place. I'm going for work, but I also need to try to find my joy again."

"Do you think it's there?" She blinks up at me, and my heart constricts.

"I think it's actually in here." I tap my chest. "That's where Olivia lives."

Ayana extends a hand and lightly touches my chest. "Is she happy?" Her chin trembles, and I ache to keep it together for both of our sakes.

"I think she is very happy, making messes and bringing laughter to everyone she meets."

Ayana smiles and looks around her room. "I miss her." Her voice breaks. "I miss her so much."

"Oh, sweetheart, I know. I do too." I fold her into my arms and inhale deeply. She smells like almond oil and clementines. "But you know what? It's okay to miss her. We should miss her. She was someone to be missed."

She nods. "She is. I still talk to her."

"Good." This admission fills me with hope. "Does she talk back?"

She shakes her head. "Not yet."

"She will." I'm still waiting to dream about Liv, for her to come to me in a vision or a moment, but it hasn't happened yet. Part of me thinks she is angry with me, that she won't appear until I first forgive myself.

"I'm going to miss you, but I'll be back soon, okay?"

"Okay." She hugs me, and I tell her good night and call for Jason to tuck her in.

In the months before Olivia died, my nightly routine with her had shifted. I'd taken on a demanding project and had been so tired from each day of work that I'd pass out in bed, and she'd say good night to *me*, then stay up late into the night crafting or reading graphic novels. Why hadn't I tucked her in more, spent more time cuddling in her bed instead of being preoccupied with my own agenda?

Not quite ready to leave, I pad back downstairs to a darkened living room and pour myself another glass of wine before slipping outside by the pool. The night is cool and rich with crickets and frogs. The lights above the water illuminate a swarm of gnats. I dip my feet in and sit on the edge, lost in thought.

I don't even hear the sliding glass door, but suddenly Jason is behind me. "Mind if I join?" His face is open and kind, and I feel a fierce longing inside me.

"I mean, this is your house, so . . ." I pat the concrete beside me and offer him my glass once he sits.

He sips and smacks his lips together thoughtfully. "Like toe jam and aged oak."

"Or damp basement." I laugh. Over the years we've attended a lot of wine tastings. While everyone always makes comments on what they taste or smell, Jason would crack me up with his answers, such as Turkish armpit hair, pork rinds, or belly button lint.

"I have a serious question for you."

I swirl my wine. "Shoot."

"Are you going to turn into a white-wine drinker while you're in the land of the wealthy?"

I slap his arm. "Don't be ridiculous." I eye him. "And how do you know there are wealthy people there?"

"Because I've been researching where my best friend is going since Ayana showed it to me. I still think it could be some sort of weird cult."

"*You're* a weird cult." He hands me back my glass, and I stare into it thoughtfully. "I'm really going to miss you." My voice catches, and he curls an arm around my shoulder and pulls me close.

"Me too, but I'm so proud of you for taking this step."

I sigh. "What step is that?"

"The first step. That's the one that counts."

We sit quietly. His warm body draws me in automatically. I burrow closer to him until our breath synchronizes, and my body awakens as he rubs my back in gentle strokes. My mind quiets, my breath deepens, and my thoughts drift somewhere they shouldn't. His words from the start of summer blast through me: *I've always wondered what life would have been like if we'd ended up together."* I clear my throat and pull away.

"I should get home."

"Okay."

He walks me back inside until we are both standing in the dark. We are less than a foot apart, and neither of us speaks. We just stare at each other, and for some unexplained reason, I feel like asking him to come with me.

"I guess this is goodbye for now?"

I step into a hug. "Goodbye for now."

"Please don't get murdered," he whispers in my hair.

"Please don't put that in my head," I say back.

We separate, and his eyes drift down to my lips. I move a step closer. Slightly tipsy and unsure of what I'm doing, I bypass his mouth and kiss him on the cheek. His skin is hot under my lips, and I linger there, wondering if he might turn his head to meet me.

He doesn't.

"Sleep well," he says.

"You too."

I watch him go upstairs and take my time walking out the front door. I almost call him back, almost do something foolish like ask him to come over, but I know it's just a reaction—a distraction—to my grief.

This next period of my life isn't about a distraction or a man; it's about me.

10

ONCE WE'VE BOTH COME DOWN FROM THE SHOCK OF
Michael's appearance, I throw together a quick dinner.

After, Liv passes out with Waffles in her bed, and Michael and I
head to the back patio for a glass of wine.

"You've done a few upgrades since I've been here," Michael says.
"It's really lovely, Kate."

I take the compliment, but it's loaded, as it reminds me of the
choices Michael didn't make. He didn't stay here with us. He didn't
help make this house into a home. Instead, he chose his work. He
chose to travel. He chose to stay the same.

Though I've been sitting with his proposal of giving our relationship another shot, now that I have him here on my turf, I don't feel as
amicable as I thought I would.

"So why are you really here, Mike?"

He sighs and swirls his wine. "I needed to get away, if I'm being
honest. I'm honored Mamá left me the estate, but it's been a lot to
deal with. Relatives coming out of the woodwork, all trying to claim
their piece."

"It's a big responsibility," I say. "What are you going to do with it?"

"I'm figuring that out. But I wanted to see you first. I know Liv has her fall break coming up. I thought we could spend some time together. Reconnect." He reaches out and lightly squeezes my knee.

"She told me you invited her out there."

He gives me an apologetic look. "I know. I'm sorry, *mi amor*. I just wanted to see her, but I realize I should have checked with you first. You know how excited I get."

I did know. It was both an endearing and infuriating quality. Could things ever really be different?

"I have to go on a work trip. I invited Liv."

"Oh?" He perks up. "Could we both come?"

I open my mouth to say no but then shrug. "I mean, technically, sure. Might even be able to use your expert eye." Because Michael and I are in similar fields, there's a lot of crossover between our skill sets. We talked in the past about creating our own company, but when I got pregnant, that felt like too much of a risk. I fill him in on Serenbe and what my boss needs, and Michael is sold before I've even finished talking.

"I guess we'd need to bring the dog." I massage my temples. "God, we so aren't set up for a pet."

"Oh, but a girl should have a dog. *Un mejor amigo.*" A best friend. "She will take good care of him."

I close my eyes and tip back my head. The air is cool, and the leaves are just starting to change. We sit in silence for a few minutes, then I slowly come back to the moment. "Where are you staying?"

"An Airbnb in East Nashville. Wanted to be close."

I appreciate that he didn't assume he could stay here, but part of me wishes he was. If we are really going to explore anything between us, we need to spend real time together, which I realize will be nearly impossible while on a work trip.

"Yoo-hoo!" Jason emerges around back, a bottle of wine in hand. He lowers it when he sees Michael.

"Hey, you." I sit up too fast and slosh my wine. "What are you doing here?"

"I texted, but I guess you didn't get it." He saunters over, and Michael stands to give him a hug. "This is quite the surprise."

I glance down at my phone and see Jason's text. *Care to cash in on that rain check?*

Oh shit.

Michael claps him on the back. "Good to see you, man."

"You too." Jason stares at me, and something painful flickers in his eyes but is instantly wiped clean. He eyes the empty bottle on the table. "More wine?"

I retrieve another glass from inside. When I head back out, Michael has started a fire, so we move from the patio to the Adirondacks around the firepit. I sit between them. "Where's Ayana?"

"With my mom." Jason swirls his wine. "So what brings you to town, Mike?"

"She does." Michael looks at me and smiles.

Double shit. I still haven't told Jason about our conversation in Mexico City, how Michael wants to give our marriage another chance. I think about being in the pool with Jason, how primed my body was to kiss him. As far as he knows, that possibility is still on the table. Suddenly, I feel like I'm keeping secrets from both men.

"Oh?" Jason asks. He shoots a look my way.

I feel trapped and take a steadying breath. "When I was visiting this summer, Michael let me know he'd like to give our relationship another try. So . . ." The words drift off as I stare into the fire. I can feel Jason looking at me, and I fear I've hurt him.

"And you said?"

I finally meet his eyes. "I said I'd think about it." I assume Jason will let it drop, but he doesn't.

"And have you told Michael about *our* conversation?"

I suck my last sip of wine down wrong and let out a dry cough. I sit upright, shocked he would be so bold.

"What conversation would that be?" Now Michael is interested.

I don't say a word, but I can't imagine Jason would share what we've talked about in private. Our building flirtation. Our near-miss moments.

"Well, friend, it seems you have some healthy competition." Jason smiles, swirling his wine aggressively, but his eyes are serious. He sits forward and stares intently at Michael. "Kate and I have realized that maybe there's more to our friendship after all."

"Kate?" Michael is as surprised as I am as he looks between us. "Is this true?"

I don't know what to say. My head is spinning. It feels like something a teenager would have to answer. I regard both of them, my past and my present, unsure of how to respond. Finally, I shrug. "Technically? Yes. It's complicated."

Michael's jaw clenches, but then he relaxes and spreads his arms wide on the Adirondacks. "Complicated is fine." He winks at Jason. "I've waited this long. I'm in no rush. Kate will do what's best for her."

The sentiment is nice, and yet I don't like feeling as though I'm some sort of prize to win. "Can we change the subject?"

The men hesitate, but then Jason asks Michael about his latest dig. Michael lights up as he shares everything he unearthed in Israel and what he's working on now, back home. After a while, I excuse myself and say good night to both of them. Part of me thinks leaving them alone together is the worst idea in the world, but at this point, I'm too tired to care.

As I get ready for bed, I'm more confused than ever. I peek out the kitchen window and can still hear them talking heatedly.

How did I get here? What do I even want?

Michael and Jason have laid the truth bare. It's all out in the open. What happens next is up to me.

TEN

EARLY THE NEXT DAY, I MAKE MYSELF A QUICK CUP OF COF-
fee and hit the road.

I don't linger on the steps or stare longingly out the window as I drive out of Nashville. Instead, immense relief floods every cell as I move farther away from my old life, my familiar pain, and the reminders of an existence without my daughter.

The sharp agony seizes me for the millionth time, and for a moment, I am paralyzed by my spontaneity. Is this really what Olivia would want me to do? I let up on the gas, hesitate, and almost turn around. Am I simply running away?

I try to imagine going back into my home, to the container that held all our memories as a family—our wins, our losses, our frustrations, our joys. I can't face the absence of Olivia even one more day.

I step harder on the gas. This is what I am doing for work. This is what I must do to move on, to survive. Four hours pass quickly to a slew of clashing thoughts as I navigate the congested I-24 interstate and finally pull off the exit, bumping through farmland and briefly wondering if I should have created some sort of code word with Jason and my mother in case this does turn out to be a cult. Despite the

166

gorgeous trees and sprawling farmland, the surrounding area is over-shadowed by shoddy trailers, abandoned lots, and conservative signs with even more conservative candidates skewering front yards.

I double-check the directions to make sure I'm going the right way. Finally, at the end of a long, curvy road, I see a copper sign that reads Serenbe. I turn left, under an awning snaked with vines and bright leaves. A small gravel lot sits to the right. I pull in, park, and stretch my legs, eager to settle into my rental for the next two weeks. Once I've done what I need to do for work, I'll decide if I want to stay longer.

I walk down a lovely, landscaped path. An in-ground trampoline tosses a young boy and girl into the air. Up ahead, there's a wooden swing that reminds me of Liv's, a basketball hoop with a man and a woman engaging in competitive banter—which instantly makes me miss Jason—and the inn's outdoor pool, which glitters untouched in the cooler weather. Beyond, there's a sprawling farm and a petting zoo. White and orange pumpkins rest on stocky hay bales. I take it all in.

Olivia would love it here.

I enter the converted barn. The Farmhouse restaurant sits behind the main building, serving traditional American fare for breakfast, lunch, and dinner. I am greeted, checked in, and asked if I would like to reserve a golf cart for my stay. I say no, retrieve my skeleton key attached to a cowbell, and open the map to the Selborne neighbor-hood, one of three hamlets on the property.

In my research about Serenbe, I discovered that the creator, Steve Nygren, modeled this place after New York, though, upon arrival, it feels nothing like Manhattan. Steve wanted to make a thriving com-munity on a smaller, more insulated scale, surrounded by nature, so that everything the residents need would be within reach. Each hamlet represents a specific area: Selborne is Brooklyn, Mado is Manhattan, and Grange is based on the Hamptons.

I pass signs that say Slow Down! Children and Adults at Play! and absorb the quaintness as I cruise down a long, narrow road, past wildflower pastures bustling with grazing horses and a small lake with ducks, and then over a bridge that dumps me onto a road with some of the most gorgeous million-dollar homes I've ever seen. There are no aboveground power lines. No typical yards to mow, as they are all impeccably landscaped and rich with plants and flowers. Multicolored butterflies the size of baseballs flutter around my car. Kids run free through an architected forest behind one of the hamlets. Golf carts putz by, and everyone waves.

Where am I?

It feels like a movie set. I slow as I near my rental, the Brownstone, which is situated behind a café, the Blue Eyed Daisy. There, people sit lazily, dogs at their feet, sipping coffee and chatting happily. I pass a couple of other shops, their doors flung open. A bright mural sprawls along one side of the café's outer wall, yet another thing Olivia would comment on. She loved to paint.

I find street parking, grab my suitcase, and walk down a few steps near a fountain. A black cat with a collar greets me, and I bend down to pet it. "You better not be an omen."

I glance at the Brownstone, which—surprise—is a brownstone. I turn the key in the lock, fiddle with the stiff handle, and finally crank it open, feeling at once like I'm in a proper city. The interior is sparse, modern, and clean. A living room opens onto a dining room staged with modern, minimal furniture and oversized gold-and-white light fixtures. A smattering of trees takes up the entire view off the kitchen in the back. I step onto the patio by the stairs and suck in the fresh air of the forest. At once, I am stricken with loneliness.

Whenever we would travel, Olivia would fuss over everything, opening doors, exploring every nook and cranny, before arranging her clothes, books, and toys in their appropriate places and then urging me to unpack too. I close my eyes and imagine her infectious energy now and try to channel some of that for myself. But all I capture is an intense sadness, hot and heavy in my heart.

I drag my suitcase upstairs into the giant primary bedroom. Everything is white and calm. A king bed, draped in crisp cream linens, takes up the center of the room. I almost snap a photo to send to Jason but think better of it. I flop on the bed and try to conjure all those times I used to crave moments like this. Me, alone, to do whatever I pleased. Me, on a solo vacation to reconnect and recharge. In all those visions, I never thought my child wouldn't be alive. I squeeze my eyes shut as fresh, warm tears glide down my cheeks.

Rather than feel sorry for myself, I unpack my clothes, line my toiletries on one side of the double sinks, and set off in search of food. I am instantly taken with the friendliness of this place as people walk their dogs, sit on their oversized porches and chat with passersby, and dip in and out of cafés and shops with the ease of beachgoers. It actually reminds me of Santa Rosa, just without the ocean. I grab a turkey wrap at Blue Eyed Daisy and then visit some of the local shops. Within five minutes, I see at least ten items Olivia would have loved, and out of habit, I pick up each one, as if to turn to her and ask, "Isn't this cute?"

I clutch a stuffed cat to my chest and begin to cry in the middle of Hamlin, an overpriced boutique with a hip young salesclerk who looks horrified at my public display of grief.

A few shoppers turn to me, clearly concerned. Before I have to explain, I set down the cat and rush out, sucking in air and fanning my shirt to force cool air in. I set off down the block, past more rows of impressive homes. I keep walking, beyond the flower shop, the bike shop, and take a right toward the next hamlet, Grange. A sea of white buildings lurches into view, with a lovely horse farm on the right. I stop near the pavilion, slick with sweat, and collapse into one of three Adirondack chairs. My breath is shaky.

Across the street, the General Store and Acton Academy look like they belong in a modern-day Mayberry. The bookstore, Hills & Hamlets, juts out of a larger brick building directly behind me. Rather than feeling energized, I'm homesick, tired, and feel foolish to have thought I could do this in the first place.

I begin to mentally spiral and pull out my phone to text Jason. *Okay, maybe I rushed this decision. I want to come home.* I wait for him to give me the permission I didn't even realize I was seeking.

Buried bodies in backyards already? Bones in your apartment?

Despite my sadness, I laugh. *Worse. Everything seems perfect. TOO perfect. Help!*

BECAUSE THEY'VE BURIED ALL THE BODIES IN THEIR BACKYARDS!!!!!

There are no dead bodies, idiot, I type back.

Because they are BURIED, Kate. Have I taught you nothing?

I begin to type a response, then stop. I'm not sure what I want to say or what I'm after, but I try honesty. *It feels so strange to be somewhere this amazing without her, J.*

I know it does. I'm so sorry, Kate. Just focus on work.

I sigh and swipe away more tears. *How are you?*

Missing my best friend.

Not helping, I type back.

The text bubbles appear, then disappear. *You need this. Home is here when you need it. And I'm here if you need me.*

I know he's right. In a day or two I'll find my rhythm with work and feel better. I decide to buck up; I shoot off a thank-you text and head to the bookstore to stock up on some grief books. I then load up on essentials—water, wine, protein bars, fruit—at the General Store and trudge back to the Brownstone, thinking that a golf cart would have come in handy right about now. Once there, I draw a bath, light a candle, and slip inside the steamy heat with my new books and a glass of wine.

I begin to feel better almost immediately as I let my mind wander and get lost in my books. But I still can't come to terms with the fact that my child isn't here. She's gone. She will always be gone. She won't grow into a surly preteen—those phantom years I used to complain about before they'd even happened. She won't ever experience a first kiss or fall in love. We won't sit around braiding each other's hair and talking about her friends or boys. We won't have movie nights. I won't be able to help her with her period or help her navigate all the land mines of teenage life. I will never help her step into womanhood and the holy grail that is her body and teach her to be proud of it and not hide it. I will never again hear her heavy footsteps padding down the hall, smell that spot right on the top of her head, or hear her infectious giggle. I will never hold her in my arms or fight about brushing her hair. I will never yell at my daughter, or hug my daughter, or worry about my daughter. All those little moments that defined me as a mother have vanished, just like her.

I slip completely under the water and hold my breath. Liv's face flashes before me, and I sit up and begin to cry, wanting her to appear so badly, I practically will an apparition to come into the bathroom. I let the intensity pass, pressing my wet knees to my chest, so afraid that I'm going to somehow forget the details of her as time continues to tick cruelly by.

I take slow, deep breaths just as Jason has taught me—in for four, hold for seven, out for eight—then down the rest of my wine. As grief demands, I must take it one day at a time. My healing starts and restarts every time I agree to go through, not around.

I just hope my body, mind, and heart can keep up.

11

MY BOSS LETS ME KNOW THE SERENBE JOB HAS BEEN POST-poned and says we can revisit it next year.

I'm annoyed that Liv and I have fought about this trip for no reason. I'm also annoyed that the two men in my life are trying to one-up each other for my attention. The only bright spot is that Liv is solely focused on Waffles, and she's even helping out with his food, water, and the daily walking.

We are all meeting up at a pumpkin patch today at Lucky Ladd Farms: Michael, Liv, Waffles, Ayana, Jason, and me. Part of me thinks this is a terrible idea, and the other part thinks it's fine. It's been made clear that both men are open and interested, but they will not push me if I do not want to be pushed.

Once we climb out of the car and get Waffles's leash and harness situated, Liv and the dog take off running toward Ayana, who's waiting by a hay bale. The two hug and Ayana drops down and starts kissing and petting Waffles, who barks happily. Jason waves. Michael isn't here yet, and I take the opportunity to give him a hug and then punch him on the arm.

"Ow! What was that for?" He rubs his arm.

I place my hands on my hips. "Oh, I don't know. What do you think?"

He rolls his eyes. "Look, I'm sorry about the other night." He drops his voice. "I just can't believe you didn't tell me that Mike wants to get back together."

"I was trying to process first," I say. "But you're right. I should have told you."

He leans in and I can smell the clean, sharp scent of his soap. "Look, you and I have been dancing around whatever this is for months." He gestures between us. "There's something here, Kate. Don't you feel it too?"

I weigh my options: tell him that yes, I do feel it, of course I do, or shut it down before it's even started. The sun disappears behind a fat cloud, and I shiver from the sudden drop in temperature. This doesn't have to be awkward. Next to me is my closest friend in the world. Nothing has to change. Everything can stay exactly as it's always been.

But when his hand brushes mine and he threads his fingers through mine, my body springs to life. Our eyes meet and hold for a beat too long before I tug my hand away.

"Here's the thing," I say. "You and I have actually proven over the years that men and women *can* just be friends. Are we really willing to risk all that for . . ." I motion uncertainly between us.

He leans closer, and I continue before he can do something stupid like kiss me. "It just terrifies me to think about messing up our friendship, because it's one of the most important things in my life."

"It's important to me too. We won't ever lose that."

"How do you know that, though?" I think about all the things we assumed we wouldn't lose: I never thought I'd lose my marriage. He never thought he'd lose his wife. Life has surprised both of us. Even with good intentions, love rarely turns out the way you expect.

Before Jason can answer, Michael surprises me by slinging an arm around my waist, then kisses my cheek. *"Hola, preciosa."* He releases me, then scoops Liv into his arms and twirls her around before setting her down gently. "Are we ready to see some pumpkins?"

Because he doesn't have an immediate assignment, Michael has decided to extend his trip for a while. Ayana and Liv yell an emphatic yes and move ahead with Michael as the three of them—plus Waffles—skip toward the entrance. The sight warms my heart, but I try to pull my attention back to Jason, back to our conversation.

"Look." He glances over his shoulder to make sure Michael is out of earshot. "I don't want to pressure you, Kate. And I'm not bringing this up just because Michael is here. I feel it. I've felt it for a long time, and I think it's fair that we give this a real chance."

His words remind me of Michael's in Mexico City, sitting under that black starry night. I have so much to say, so much to think about. Jason has never disappointed me the way Michael has. He's always been here for me, but I know a piece of my heart will always be with Michael. Sensing my rising stress, Jason grips my hand again. "Take your time, Kate. But if you decide you want to open that door, I'm going to be standing on the other side, okay?"

I nod wordlessly as he drops my hand and jogs to catch up with Ayana.

As I walk behind them, all of my favorite people, I can't help but think that the truth is finally out. Jason and I *do* have feelings for each other. Maybe we always have. And with that simple admission, we are entering into unfamiliar territory. But where does that leave me with Michael?

And how can I possibly know what choice to make?

ELEVEN

I PUSH MYSELF UP IN BED AND TAKE IN THE SILENCE, struggling to remember where I am.

No footsteps running down the hall. No *Story Pirates* podcast blasting from Google Home. No glimpse of Olivia outside swinging and listening to music, twisting the frayed ropes, hair wild, lost in that coveted morning meditation. No pans scraped as Liv makes us a giant vat of salty eggs. I cover my face with my hands and then glance beside me, at the empty space. I run my fingers over the white duvet. No partner to turn to. No lover to hold.

I pepper off texts to my mom, friends, Michael, and then Jason, who checks in to make sure I wasn't butchered in my sleep. Though Michael and I had not spoken much since the memorial, he did let me know Lucia passed away. I've been communicating more with him to make sure he's okay. While I thought the loss of Liv would cause us to grow further apart, instead it's brought us closer.

I take a shower and decide to grab a coffee at Blue Eyed Daisy and explore the grounds, or maybe go for a hike through the woods behind my rental. I order an extra-large coffee, then circle to the back of the Brownstone and start down a gravel path toward a set of steps that dumps into the mouth of the forest. The temperature drops beneath the thicket of trees, and I begin walking, not really knowing where I'm headed.

As I navigate the path, weaving through patches of trees on the designated trail, I realize it's been so long since I've gone off the beaten path like this. Every decision I made with Liv was somewhat calculated: from buying a house to what type of job I chose to putting Olivia in a particular school that was well rated and close to where we lived. I'd often dreamed of selling everything and traveling the world, letting Olivia explore and expand—getting her education from other cultures and experiences. It's what Michael always wanted for her. Instead of following that instinct, I'd done what everyone did: I played it safe.

I battle through that guilt in my head, playing the what-if game again and again. *What if I'd made different choices? What if I hadn't looked at my phone? What if I'd gotten in the damn water with her instead of standing on the beach?* The answer is always the same: then she'd still be alive. I stop in my tracks, breathing hard, and let the guilt crest like a wave.

I walk faster and approach a sign where the path splits off toward different hamlets. I decide to head toward Mado and cross over a bridge that opens onto a treehouse standing in the middle of the forest. I gaze up at it and imagine Liv yelping with delight and hurrying up the ladder, flying down the slide with abandon, and then jumping on the wooden swing and immediately making comparisons to her own. I would sit on the wooden bench and watch her. We'd have a conversation. She'd convince me to go down the slide. I'd resist and then do it anyway. I stand here and imagine her little voice in my ear.

"Come on, Mama. Come play."

If I could, I would take her hand and never let go. The image recedes as I inhale the scent of earth and trees and come back to my body. I keep walking, my legs a bit sore from the lack of recent physical activity, and finally emerge at the back of the community pool that takes up an entire block. A tiny village of brightly colored homes and shops connects in a perfect half-moon. Feeling hungry, I approach Halsa, a small restaurant serving healthy breakfast fare, and sit outside.

I decide I need to do something with my time since I don't have to work until Monday, so I look up the local events calendar. There's goat yoga (no), a live theater performance later (maybe), and a farm tour this afternoon (definitely). I consider the spa but decide against it in case I burst out crying during a massage. I'm not ready for complete strangers to touch me or help me access my pain. I take a photo of the goat yoga and text Jason because he hates all this trendy crap.

He texts back immediately. *Don't. You. Dare. Those poor goats.*

I smile, pocket my phone, and dig into my omelet, my eyes landing on the play area across the street. It's a kid wonderland, and again, Olivia's absence rushes in. This place would be perfect for any child, but especially her. It's somewhere she could roam free and explore.

My appetite dies as I replay my countless parenting mistakes, all of them clashing for space in my head. When will the relentless self-punishment stop? All that time I spent feeling disappointed with Michael for not being a more involved father, when I could have just focused on being a better mother. Maybe that was the entire point. Maybe the universe knew she was going to be taken away and I needed to spend every minute with her that I could.

I grip my head and take a deep breath. *This has to stop.* I notice someone on their laptop at the table next to me, and I sigh. This is why I came here—to work and keep pushing forward. And yet, not one part of me wants to resume my normal activities. My life's work, everything I've worked so hard to achieve as an agricultural engineer, now seems so insignificant. My existence seems pointless without my child.

I finish my meal and begin to wander back through the forest, taking my time, until I miraculously land back at the Brownstone and realize the farm tour starts shortly. I take a quick shower, change, and walk over to Serenbe Farms, which is back in Grange. It has a lovely, ornate sign and a greenhouse to the left.

People are already congregating, and I'm surprised at how many tourists want to learn about the organic farm that supplies all the food to Serenbe's restaurants and others nearby. I wait for the tour to start, smacking away a few bugs, and then the farm manager saunters out.

My belly tightens as I take him in. He's tall and well built, with insanely blue eyes and a thick, well-trimmed beard. His name is Ian, and I can tell, from the moment he begins to speak, that he loves what he does. He takes us through each area—rows of tomatoes that have gone off and rows of tomatoes that were a success. We pluck them straight from the vine, sorting through the varieties, and bite into them, some as crunchy as apples. I am instantly transported somewhere else, back to my own childhood, in my mother's modest but flourishing garden at the edge of our backyard, where we would grow squash, tomatoes, corn, and even kale. I forget about my sadness, about the state of my life, and simply listen and observe.

I crouch down to inspect the rows of onions—four thousand, to be exact—that need to be pulled to make room for the fall crops. We pass the kids' garden, which is wildly untamed. We trample soil that needs to be tilled by hand and a sprawling pumpkin patch. As we walk, I absorb it all like a sponge. Though I spent most of my childhood in the garden, I never built one for Liv. Every year she would beg to have a flower garden or a vegetable garden, and every year I said that we would. And then I'd get so busy with work, it was easier to just go to the farmers market instead.

At the end of the hour, people begin to drift away, but not before Ian makes an announcement: "So every quarter I hire a couple of apprentices to help with the farm." He smiles. "I'm not going to lie. It's the hardest work you'll ever do. We start at six thirty in the morning and go until three thirty. We do everything by hand. There is a stipend, and you get free room and board. If anyone is interested, just let me know. The next apprenticeship starts in a week and goes through the end of April. Thanks, y'all!"

I watch people disperse, but I stay rooted to the spot. I feel like I'm being swallowed by the earth. Before I can think too much about it, I approach Ian.

"Tell me more about this apprenticeship." It's not a question—it's a demand. I have no idea why I'm bothering. I have a full-time job that will keep me chained to the computer or in meetings for the next two weeks before I head back home.

He sizes me up as he wipes dirt from his hands. "Oh yeah?" He laughs. "I usually get college kids, not adults."

"Tell me." My voice is desperate, and he notices.

"Okay, well, like I said, it's a lot of physical work." He removes his hat, scratches his head with the thick palm of his hand, and then replaces his hat. "I started this farm a few years back, and I'm completely self-taught. I'm still learning as I go, so I'm always open to suggestions." He considers me for a moment. "You farm?"

"Growing up, yeah. My mother was a total green thumb, and she taught me well." I gauge his face. His eyes are startling, his skin darkened from the sun. His hands flex around the rake he's holding, and I notice his ring finger is bare. Again, something flutters in my chest, but I keep it at bay.

"Your tomatoes are a disaster," I blurt. "The way you set them up . . . the structure isn't right, which is why all of those collapsed." I point to the anemic fruit. "The trench is off."

He listens, impressed. "What would you suggest?"

I notice the whiteboard under his tent and walk over, drawing up a quick sketch. He nods, scratches his jaw, and seems to consider it. "What are you, an engineer?"

I cap the marker and hand it to him. "Yes. Agricultural, to be exact." I don't tell him that's why I'm here, to possibly shoplift this entire community to copy and take back to Nashville.

He smiles. "We could try it."

"And the stipend and room and board?"

"It's not much. Just a thousand a month."

"Well, that's not very incentivizing."

He chuckles. "Wait until I tell you about the room and board."

I wait for him to continue.

"It's a cabin."

"I love cabins."

"It's not a Serenbe cabin. It's very . . . *basic.*"

"Will you show me?"

"Sure. I can run you over there now if you like?"

I nod and follow him silently to a white truck with *Serenbe Farms* stenciled on the side. He chats about finding Serenbe a few years back. He never intended to stay, but he has because of the community. I half listen, feeling something strange blossoming inside me: A purpose. A message. A *meaning.* I might not be able to bring Olivia back, but I sure as hell can grow something. She was always complaining that I worked too hard, that I lived so much of my life behind a screen. The thought of being outside from sunup until afternoon, working with my hands, staying too busy to sit around and feel sorry for myself, too exhausted to keep my eyes open at night—it's exactly what I need. Hard work. Important work.

A distraction.

He bumps down a narrow path and turns into a gravel drive. "It's a cabin, all right," he says.

He pulls up to a small, nondescript cabin in the middle of the woods, just minutes from Grange. He grabs a ring of keys from his pocket and finds the right one. I assess the outside, which needs some repairs, but the woods encasing the cabin from the rest of the world make up for it.

"Central heat and air, so that's good. You get access to the gym and the pool for free. Some discounts at restaurants, things like that." He pushes open the door and makes room so I can step inside first. When I do, I'm instantly hit with the smell of mildew.

Dank.

Olivia's common word choice smacks me in the face, and I pause on the threshold as I take it all in. It's way worse than the outside. Crumbling paint, mismatched furniture, sloped floors. Mouse traps dot the perimeter of each room. A tiny bedroom with a fireplace sits off to the left. It opens onto the main room, which—with a little paint and the right furniture—might be cozy. Another bedroom branches back to the right, much bigger, with a decent closet.

"We're repainting this week," Ian offers.

I disappear into the kitchen, which is atrocious. An ancient fridge, portable dishwasher, and washer and dryer all lean, mismatched, next to each other. A stained farmhouse sink with a big window is the only saving grace. The bathroom is even worse. I peek in the shower and smell the mold before I see it lining the rim of the tub in fuzzy black rings. I come back and cross my arms. "Serenbe has a lot of money, right?"

He blinks, startled by my frankness. "Yes."

"Then this is what we're going to do. And by we, I mean *you*. You're going to go to the board—I assume there's a board?" He nods. "Ask them to get an inspection for this place. I'm pretty sure you've been poisoning your apprentices with mold. You can smell the moisture before you even step inside. After the inspection, have them take care of anything serious. Then you're going to have them paint, get rid of this god-awful furniture, and I'll handle the rest. And the stipend must be raised to at least twenty-five hundred a month. *Minimum*. It's why you're only getting college kids."

He stares at me as if I'm an alien. "You're a straight shooter then." He scratches his jaw. His nails contain a thick half-moon of dirt. "I can definitely talk to them, sure." He removes his hat and runs a hand through his hair again, which is thick, dark, and longer than expected. "Why do you want this job, Kate?" I'd told him my name on the drive over and that I'm from Nashville, but that's about it.

I think about telling him I just love gardening or need a change of pace. But if I'm going to be spending all day, every day with him, then I need to come clean. "My nine-year-old daughter drowned in June. I was a single mom. Most days I feel like I'm dying or drowning myself. When I stepped onto your farm, I felt like a human for the first time in months. I need this so I can survive, Ian," I say matter-of-factly. "That's why."

Ian's face changes from slightly amused to serious. "It's yours," he says. "I'll make sure the cabin is taken care of."

I nod and make my way outside and back into his truck. He drops me in Selborne and tells me he'll call me with next steps. He has a flip phone and hates technology. I like him already. Before I go, he stops me.

"I'm not sure if you believe in God, Kate, but I've been praying for someone like you. I think this is going to be good for both of us."

I nod. Tears fill my eyes as he drives away, and I take a deep breath. I glance to the sky, where some people believe there really is a heaven. I'm not sure I believe in all that, but if there's a chance that Liv is up there, looking down, then I'm going to do my best to make her proud.

And to start, I'm going to build the best damn garden this town has ever seen, and I'm going to do it all for her.

I just have to talk to my boss first.

12

AFTER MICHAEL PICKS LIV UP TO GO TO SUNDAY BRUNCH, I grab a coffee at The Well Coffeehouse and decide to stay and work.

It is a gorgeous day, unseasonably warm for fall, so I set up camp at an outdoor table and lose myself to a slew of emails and deadlines. When I look up again, it's noon. I stretch and check my phone to see I have three missed calls from Michael.

My stomach drops. Did something happen to Liv?

I put my headphones in, steady myself, and then dial his number. He picks up on the first ring.

"Hello, you," he says.

"Is Liv okay?"

"Oh yes, *mi amor*. I didn't mean to worry you. We're at the zoo."

"Okay." I wait for him to continue.

"I was going to take Liv to a movie after we finish here. Is that okay?"

"Of course." That will buy me a few more hours of work.

"Also." He clears his throat. "She wants to stay the night again. She can bring the dog too."

"Oh, okay." I thought I'd take Liv for pizza tonight, but because I don't know how long he'll stay, I reluctantly agree.

"Also, I'd love to take you to dinner. Can I arrange something?"

Though we've seen each other a lot since he's been in town, it's typically with Liv. I almost make a joke and ask if he even knows how to make reservations but refrain. When we were married, I planned everything. Michael loved to be spontaneous. I remind myself that this isn't ten years ago. People can change.

"That would be great."

"Okay, I'll have Liv call you tonight before bed, okay?"

We hang up, and I close my eyes, the sun beating down on my face. I feel like I'm losing my grasp. There's so much happening at the office, and despite how many hours I put in, the work never ends. I've practically ignored Jason these last few days, though the awareness of what's been going on between us is hard to ignore. And now Michael wants to take me on a date.

This should be a fun problem to have, but everything I do affects Liv. If I invite Michael back into our lives, I have to be sure. And if I explore a relationship with Jason, I also have to be sure. I would never want to put any tension on Liv and Ayana's friendship or make her feel like she's not the most important person in my life. I sigh, knowing I can't avoid this conundrum forever.

But contemplating romance feels like resurrecting a part of myself that I released a long time ago. If I search deep enough, there's a small part of me that would be happy for Liv to have a man in her life again. It would take some of the pressure off my shoulders and also give her someone else to rely on. But which man?

I bury the thoughts, step inside to order lunch to go, and shake away the indecision. I remind myself that Michael showing up now doesn't mean he's owed anything. And I don't owe Jason anything either.

My fingers tremble as I hand over my debit card to pay. Too

much caffeine. I think about Liv spending so much quality time with Michael, and a shallow, insecure thought tumbles through my head: *What if she loves being with Michael more? What if, the more time she spends with him, she decides that our little life is not enough? What if she really does want to move to Mexico City?* The realization stings. Everything we've built could crumble because of his re-entry into our lives.

I sign my receipt and wait for my food, but the anxiety pushes in. *What if I let Michael back in and he slowly takes Liv away from me?*

It's a ridiculous thought and I know it. My phone dings. It is just one line, from Jason.

Meet me in your backyard in twenty. Wear comfy clothes.

I reread the text, confused, but inside, I'm giddy. I love when Jason surprises me, yet another green check in the column of *reasons to go for your best friend.* I navigate afternoon traffic and pull into my driveway right on time. As I park in the back, I gasp when I see what Jason has done. I practically leap out of the car and step over the mole-hills toward the open patch by the fence with the newly constructed raised garden beds. "What did you do?"

"Surprise!" Dirt clings to his forearms and he wipes sweat from his forehead. "I know it's going to be winter soon, which isn't the best time to start a garden, but I also know you and Liv have wanted to do this forever. I thought we could put in the dirt, but you and Liv can plant the seeds. And look." He pulls at least twenty seed packets out of a small duffel bag on the grass. "I've got plenty to choose from."

I step around the boxes and fling my arms around his neck. I breathe him in. He smells like the earth. He smells like home. I lean back and stare up into his eyes. "This is the nicest thing anyone has ever done for me." Before I can think too much about it, my hands slip to his warm cheeks and I tug his face down to meet mine.

He lets out a tiny gasp of surprise as our mouths meet, but then hunger overrides the shock. His fingers wind down my spine and then he grips my sweater in his fist. He yanks my hips toward his. Our mouths open, tongues entwining, and I moan and grip him just as tightly. I haven't been kissed in so long, and everything goes into it: all the passion, desire, and uncertainty. All the flirting, conversation, and sexual tension. Our bodies meld together as our kisses deepen and all sense of time disappears.

A few minutes later, we break apart, breathless. I am dizzy and place a hand on my chest to steady my erratic heartbeat.

"That was easily the best thank-you of my life," he says. He's staring at me, primal and wild, his lips swollen, hair mussed. It is clear he wants me as badly as I want him. I press my fingers over my own lips. Whatever that just was, I want more.

"Take me on a date," I say. "Tonight." It feels like a betrayal to Michael, who just asked to take me out too. But at the same time, I have to know. I have to know which man is the right man, and if I'm going to do that, then I have to explore both options.

"Done." His voice is hoarse with desire, his eyes tracking my every movement.

I stare back down at the beds and smile. "Liv is going to be over the moon," I say. "Thank you so much."

"I'd do anything for you, Kate. You know that." He crouches down, and together we fill in the boxes with soil. The kiss plays over and over in my head.

We've crossed the line.

Might as well pay for the crime.

TWELVE

FINALLY, THE CABIN IS READY.

I've checked out of my rental and moved in. I've bought a few new outfits, toiletries, and the basics, but I've decided to stay as minimal as possible so I have less to take care of after a long day's work.

The community has donated some furniture—more modern than the cabin calls for, but I'm not complaining. When you walk in, there are white walls, a warm striped rug, a white couch with two blue armless chairs, a tree trunk coffee table, cut and sanded by Ian himself, and lovely bedroom sets—canopy beds, dressers, nightstands—in both rooms.

Already the people of Serenbe have become more familiar to me than my neighbors back home. There's Laurence, who owns all three restaurants; Josh, who runs the bike shop and sold me a vintage cruiser my first week here; Flynn, who lives above the flower shop. I run by there once a week to get fresh flowers and gab. Latrice and Hank own the Blue Eyed Daisy, and Steve's daughter, Monica, handles most of the real estate. They all pitched in with updating this cabin, and I am already beyond grateful.

I inspect the kitchen while I make coffee. It has a new fridge, a deeply scrubbed sink, and a set of dishes donated by a family who just moved back to Atlanta. There's fresh caulking around the tub, though the bathroom faucet still leaks. It has been professionally cleaned, and I revel in the fresh smell (there *was* mold, which they have taken care of) thanks to the Ecos paint that cleans the air.

I check the time. I need to be at the farm by 6:30 a.m. During an uncomfortable chat with my boss, where I agreed to meet with Serenbe's founders and get my boss the information he needed for a possible build in Nashville, I asked to take all of my unused paid vacation days, which amounted to a grand total of almost three months. With my poor performance since summer, he wasn't surprised by the request and acquiesced. My only agenda for the foreseeable future is taking care of a ten-acre farm.

As I collapse on the couch, my eyes drift to the mantel above the fireplace, where Liv's urn sits on full display. Finally, I tear my eyes away and call Jason.

"Find any dead bodies yet?"

"That joke never gets old."

"You know what does get old?"

I place the phone on the coffee table to tie my shoes, cranking up the volume on speaker. "What's that?"

"Farming."

I roll my eyes. "Man, you're really on a roll."

He laughs, and we fall into easy conversation as I fill him in on the cabin and Ian and text him the before and after pictures.

"They work fast there in Serenbe," he says in a country accent.

"That they do," I mimic back.

I've been able to find some sort of rhythm during the past week before the official start of the apprenticeship. I get up with the sun and walk down to the creek, which is hidden within the forest trails. I sit and breathe. Sometimes I cry or journal. I hike over to Mado, work out, and come back, then grab a coffee at Blue Eyed Daisy and chat with the locals. I pet dogs. I read. I think.

Though I've met a ton of community members, I've told only a few of them about my situation. However, I imagine word will get around about Olivia, and then I'll be the sad woman who lost her child. For now, I'm happy being the lonely transplant who floated in from Nashville and is going to be a farm apprentice. It smarts a bit that I am using all my paid vacation days only to be making a fraction of what I bring in every month, but I know that's just my ego talking.

In all my unraveling, it's been shocking to realize how little my job really matters to me. While I love the nature of my work, most of my position in Nashville has been grinding tirelessly. I'm beginning to question my entire life, every choice and decision I've made. I consistently wade back through them, as if on a timeline. I keep getting snagged around Olivia's death. There are so many choices I could have made differently—tiny, nothing choices—that would have resulted in her still being alive.

Living with that truth is what hurts the most. If I had just done one or two things differently, my daughter would be here. While time passes, I keep expecting the guilt to lessen, but it doesn't. It deepens.

I glance around the cabin as I drink my coffee and think how much Olivia would love it here.

"I've been going down the rabbit hole," I say to Jason. "Of how I could have saved her."

"Kate." Jason sighs. "Don't do that to yourself."

"I know." My voice cracks, and a few tears slip down my cheeks as I stare out the window. "But if I'd been paying attention, she'd still be here. Probably complaining about the mosquitoes and spiders." I begin to cry openly and press a hand to my mouth. "It just keeps getting worse," I say. "This longing for her."

Jason holds space for me. "Why don't I come visit?" he offers at last.

I stop crying and busy myself with filling my thermos with the remaining coffee. "What about work?"

"I'm the boss."

"What about Ayana's school?"

"Let me worry about that."

"Everything's good, right?" I realize the last few months have been all about me. I know almost nothing of what's going on in his daily life.

"Yeah, fine. Business is just a little hectic. You know how it is."

For some reason I feel like he's holding back, but I don't press. I glance around. "I do have two bedrooms. Want to come apprentice with me?"

"I said visit, not go to work."

"Hey, what's up? I can hear it in your voice." It feels good to turn the tables, to put myself in the role of listener.

"I just think I might need a break too," he says.

I pause. Jason never needs a break. "Well, my cabin door is open if you want to get away," I offer. "Mold not included."

"Seriously?"

"Of course." I wait for him to say more, but he's silent. "Anytime."

We chat about Ayana and work, and promise to touch base after my first day. I hang up, slightly unsettled. While I don't want to push Jason to open up, I realize our friendship has been focused on me, and though that's normal when someone is grieving, I don't want to miss anything critical. We usually tell each other everything.

I decide to momentarily shelve that worry and focus on the task ahead: surviving my first day at the farm. I round up my water, thermos, and lunch, toss it all into my bag, and make the quick walk to the farm.

The morning is brisk. Fall is here. It was Liv's favorite season—and mine. I think about how much she would adore this place and imagine her with me, chatting a million miles a minute. Sometimes she would talk so fast I literally couldn't understand what she was saying, her brain always a few steps ahead of her mouth. A few tears slip down my cheeks, but I wipe them away and steady myself for the workday.

The sun is just rising, and I stop to admire such a miraculous moment as the pink and orange rays burst over the quiet horizon. Instantly I am reminded of what's good about life. Even when things are hard, the sun always rises, and I can always stop to notice this one consistent beauty. I take a breath and sip from my thermos of coffee. Ian is already in front of his worktable under the farm tent, scribbling a schedule on the whiteboard.

He must sense I'm there because he turns and smiles. His bright eyes study my face and assess my clothes. He nods and turns back to what he's doing. "You ready?"

"Remains to be seen," I joke as I hoist my bag onto a spare edge of the table.

"You're here. That's a start."

"True." I am here and I do have my physical fitness, though it's waned over the last few months. I hope, after four or five months of this—if I make it that long—I will be what Jason refers to as farm strong. But for once, I don't care about my physique. I just want to lose myself to this type of work in hopes of reclaiming a sense of peace.

"So I've already opened up the tunnels and the greenhouse so the crops can air." He removes his cap and scratches his head before putting it back on, already a familiar gesture. "Haven't had much rain."

I nod and stare at the rest of the board. I notice the first thing is watering. I didn't see any sprinkling systems on the tour, so I assume we're doing it all by hand.

"Today you're going to be watering and weeding," he confirms. "I need to mow and then we can pull those onions you saw."

"All four thousand?"

"Good memory. And yes."

He runs down the rest of the timeline with me. We'll take a short break for lunch, then harvest for afternoon deliveries to the restaurants.

"You good?"

I adjust my own ball cap and nod. "I'm good."

He points me in the direction of the beds I will need to water, and I get to work. As I turn on the hose and fill the watering can, I'm transported back to working in the garden with my mother. She would occasionally turn the spray on me or set up sprinklers that we would both run through at the end of a hot day. I make sure to pay attention so I don't overwater. Though the sun creeps higher, it is a cool day, and I'm glad I'm wearing layers. It takes me an hour to water, and my wrist and forearm already ache with the effort.

Next is weeding. I grab a digging knife and Hoe Dag and get to work, not needing direction for this. As I begin to pull weeds, I wonder why I never did this with Olivia. It would have been so easy to expose her to the earth, to swap Minecraft or drawing for planting flowers. I dig harder into the earth, tugging clumpy roots free and tossing them behind me. Tears sting my eyes. I'm so tired of the guilt, but I let it wash over me now. There's no point in pretending this pain doesn't exist, that I won't replay all the shoulds a million times . . . probably for the rest of my life.

By noon, my shoulders are in knots, and I roll my neck around and shake out my joints, which are stiff from crouching. I meet Ian at the worktable, all the weeds disposed of.

"Nice work, Kate."

"Thanks." I take a sip of water and dig into my lunch. I'm starving. It's the first time I've had an appetite in weeks, and I'm thankful that, despite the grief, my body still knows it needs fuel.

"We've got five deliveries today, just so you know," he says. He ticks them off on his fingers and says we'll be making a special delivery to Acton Academy to surprise the kids.

"Oh, fun. Do you have kids?"

He hesitates. "A daughter."

I search the recesses of my mind for any mention of a daughter, but he hasn't said a word. "Does she go to Acton?"

"No."

"Is Acton the only school here?"

He nods. "Yep. A few private schools outside of town, though."

I take a bite of my sandwich and swallow. "Are you married?"

He offers a sad smile. "Not anymore."

"Amicable?"

He swipes his forehead with a handkerchief. "Is it ever?"

"Debatable," I say. "I got divorced years ago."

"I'm sorry." That's all he says, so we eat silently. I appreciate his sense of privacy. There's so much we don't hold tight to our vests these days, airing everything on social media for the world to see. It's nice to be here, in utter anonymity, with a stranger who doesn't lay it all out on the table at once.

"Ironically, I had just started to think about dating again when the accident happened." I briefly think of Jason, of his confession at the beginning of the summer. "Guess it's not in the cards for me."

"Give it time," he says gently, nodding. I watch his face, the heft of him, and my chest instantly warms. He's so different from Jason, who exudes energy and sex appeal, or Michael, who is exciting and full of passion. Instead, Ian is ruggedly handsome, safe, *grounded*. I glance at him again, in his plaid shirt, sleeves rolled up to reveal muscular forearms, slim jeans, and work boots. But he's also insanely hot.

After lunch, we get started on the onions. I find it methodic and meditative. We pull bulb after bulb and need to prepare the soil for the pumpkin patch. We load the onions in wheelbarrows and clean the dirt off for pickup.

I shadow Ian the rest of the day, make deliveries, and even ride on the tractor with him. I'm itching to drive it myself, but he tells me he'll show me in due time. By the end of the day, I'm physically spent but familiar enough with the land. My body aches in places I didn't even know existed, though I don't dare tell him that. I'm just glad I picked up some Epsom salt at the Typo Market a few days back.

He offers to drop me at home, and when he pulls up to my cabin, I hesitate before I get out of the cab. "Want to come in for a drink?"

Ian flexes his hands around the wheel in preparation to refuse. But then he surprises me and shoves the truck into Park. "Why not?"

He whistles as he steps across the threshold and removes his shoes. "Well, I'll be damned." Ian hasn't seen everything all put together. "How'd you get them to make it this nice?"

I kick off my shoes as well and grab us two beers from the fridge. "Monica put the word out."

"I'll say."

We toast, which reminds me of Jason for some reason, and walk to the living room. He glances down at himself and the white couch and decides to sit in one of the navy chairs instead.

"White might not have been the best option. But I'm just grateful

196

to have a couch." I'm itching for a shower, but I want to get to know Ian more, so I put on a record I found in the dusty crate by the fireplace and sit down across from him.

"I was hoping you'd keep that." He points the neck of his bottle toward the record player. "Never goes out of style."

"That it does not." I sit back and let the old jazz crackle through the room. "So how'd I do?" I cross my ankles and rest my dirty socks on the coffee table. "Grade me."

"Grade you?" He peers at me, dirt streaked and sun happy, and shrugs. "B minus, I'd say."

I sit up. "B minus? Seriously?" I filter through all my actions today. "I've never gotten a B minus in my entire life."

To my surprise, he lets out a sharp laugh that erupts across the room. It is a deliciously refreshing sound, which makes me think, in another setting, Ian might be the life of the party. "Straight A student, am I right?"

"Graduated salutatorian of high school and valedictorian of my college, as a matter of fact."

"Ugh, I knew it. You need some good Bs or Cs in your life, Kate. You'll learn so much more that way."

"Wow, spoken like a true subpar student."

He chuckles again, revealing white teeth and a charmingly crooked incisor. "That is technically true."

I glance around the cabin. "Do you have to pick up your daughter today? What's her name?"

He swallows and smiles. "Ella." He stares intently into the neck of his bottle. "She's not here anymore." Finally, he looks up. "It's complicated."

I don't press because I know how uncomfortable these conversations can be. I assume she lives with her mother somewhere. I think of Michael, how he slipped from Liv's life this last year and how much regret he will carry because of it. I don't say this now, can't imagine Ian would be the kind of father to just walk away. I don't know him well, but loyalty seems like one of his key traits. "Well, Ella is a beautiful name."

"So is Olivia."

My heart aches at the sound of her name and the fact that he remembered. "I mainly called her Liv. Or a million other nicknames that don't make any sense when I say them out loud."

He laughs. "Such as?"

I sigh and tick them off on my fingers. "Oh, let's see: Pop-Tart, Muffin, Bug, Little Chicken, Pepper, and the Spanish version of all those words."

He asks about Michael's family, and I give him the CliffsNotes version. I nod to his ring finger. "How long have you been divorced?"

He stares down at his hand and thumbs the spot where his wedding ring used to be. "A long time. We grew apart once Ella was born." He shrugs. "It happens, but I just didn't think it would happen to us."

"I can relate." I take another swig of beer. "Have you dated since?"

"Nah." His eyes flash with something deep and serious, and my heart begins to race. I lick my lips. "I'm not much interested in casual dating. Never have been. The farm keeps me busy enough."

I think of the similarities between us. His farm is to him what my career is to me. *Was.* I'd made excuses for years around why I couldn't let someone else in, but now it seems I'm out of excuses. "Can I tell you something?"

"Always." He leans in, the bottle dangling from his large hands.

"Today was the first day I didn't feel consumed by what happened." I pause, gathering my thoughts. "Instead, I thought of Liv out there

198

with me, imagined how excited she'd be. But it didn't paralyze me. It felt good to move, to work through that pain. It's exactly what I needed. It's exactly what I *need*, so thank you."

"You're welcome." He peers at me again, as if contemplating telling me something too. "You know, you're the first adult I've ever had work here."

"And apparently my work isn't up to a kid's standards." I raise my eyebrows.

He sits forward and rests his empty beer bottle on the coffee table he built. "Kate, you know I'm kidding. Today . . ." He shakes his head.

"Today what?"

"Today was the first day I felt truly in sync with someone on the farm. So much so that it didn't feel like work. It was unnerving."

"Unnerving? Don't you mean a relief?" I'm startled and pleased by the admission. "So why the B minus then?"

He rolls his eyes. "You and this B minus. You're an A plus, okay? Star student! Yay." He waves jazz hands, and I smile.

"Clearly my self-worth is not attached to praise *at all*." I stretch and glance toward the kitchen. "I'm not sure if you have plans tonight, but would you like to stay for dinner?"

He seems to consider the offer but then stands. "Thanks, but I should be getting on back."

"Okay." I clear both bottles and drop them in the recycling bin and then walk him to the door. "Hey, Ian."

He turns after putting on his shoes.

"Thank you for this opportunity. I'm really going to try my best."

"I know you are because you're a star."

"You just rhymed."

He winks and then disappears toward the truck. I shut the door, desperate for a shower and some hot food. Day one in the books. It is a small accomplishment but seems to signify something real. As I gaze around the room, I see Ian's touches everywhere: the selfless help he offered; all the pieces he made by hand; even the fresh produce lining the kitchen counter, plucked and bagged from the farm.

Though he has already left, it feels like parts of him are still here with me. Surprisingly, I find that I don't mind.

Winter

13

"WAFFLES, SLOW DOWN!"

I tug on his leash, but he is full speed ahead on a trail at Percy Warner Park. Liv giggles and adjusts her ball cap.

"He wants to run like the wind!" She whistles for him—a new talent she recently discovered with Michael while sucking in too fast. Now she whistles constantly.

"That he does." I walk up the rocks and breathe in the cool air. "We haven't done this in a long time, huh?"

"It's been freaking ages," she exclaims. "How come?"

I consider her question. Hiking used to be our thing. We'd talk about everything: life, work, ideas, places we wanted to travel, our crazy dreams. It was our version of talk therapy, and it set a solid foundation for our mother-daughter check-ins. But since an uptick in work and Michael deciding to stay in town indefinitely, regular hikes have vanished.

"You know, I think I just lost sight of what's most important," I finally say. "Sometimes adults get so busy working, we forget to take a deep breath, get outside, and appreciate nature."

"Papito hasn't worked the whole time he's been here."

203

I bite my tongue, wanting to remind her that he has a flexible job and family money, which means he doesn't have to worry so much about cash. Instead, he chooses when to work because he loves it. "It must be a nice break for him."

"He doesn't use his phone much either. I don't ever want a phone," she continues. "Rots your brain."

"That's my girl," I say. I don't remind her that her iPod touch is very similar to a phone, and if it wasn't for me putting it in a drawer every night, she'd be just as glued to that thing as adults are to their devices.

Waffles stops and lifts his leg to pee on the trunk of a spruce, then barks when he's ready to walk again. I've discovered, by talking to my dog-owner friends, that Waffles is incredibly smart. Luckily, over the past few months, no one has claimed him. I deleted my Facebook post and am praying to the heavens above that he is meant to stay with us, especially for Liv.

"I wish I could pee on trees," Olivia says. Often on our hikes she starts talking from the moment we step onto the trail until we have finished—about school, her friends, and what business she wants to start for her upcoming exhibition at school.

Last year she started an amazing soap company for kids called Sudzy Critters, which was promptly abandoned during summer.

Now she's on to a new idea. "A duck vet, Mama! There are no dedicated duck vets! Why? Did you know that some people keep ducks as pets but that they are very prone to botulism?"

"How do you know what botulism is?"

"Everybody knows what botulism is." She snorts. "Do you think chickens get botulism too?"

I think about summer, when Liv asked to have a chicken as a pet. "Probably." I try to keep up, but I'm fixated on keeping Waffles away from other dogs while listening to Liv's enthusiasm. We make the two-and-a-half-mile loop until we're both breathing hard and are back at the top of the park stairs. The air is crisp, but we've worked up a nice sweat. I snap a picture of the landscape below, the rolling hills spilling around us as far as the eye can see. Various people jog, walk, or sprint up the stairs, which seem endless from this vantage point. We are shaded by trees on either side, and the temperature drops even more beneath them. We stand silently, and I hook an arm around Liv's shoulders and tug her to me. "I love you so much, Olivia. I'm proud of you, you know."

"For what?" She scratches her nose.

"For just being you, because you are an exceptional human being. And you should know that being exceptional has nothing to do with accomplishment. It's just about being yourself."

"Like a duck vet." She laughs.

I bump her playfully with my hip. "Want to get lunch?"

"Yes, I'm starving!" She stares down at Waffles, who is very interested in gnawing on a nearby stick. "What will we do with Waffles, though?"

"We'll eat outside." I always promised that if I ever had a dog I would bring him everywhere, and so far, I'm sticking to my word.

"Can Papito come too?"

A bit of disappointment pushes in, but I swallow it. "I was thinking it could just be the two of us today, if that's okay?"

She shrugs, but I can see my refusal bothers her. My phone rings, interrupting the moment. It's Jason. I pause on our way down the steep stone steps and ask Liv to take Waffles the rest of the way and to wait for me at the bottom.

"Hey." I attempt to keep my voice light, but Liv's request still stings.

"Whatcha doing?"

"Hiking with Liv."

"Percy Warner, Radnor, or Beaman?"

"Percy Warner."

"Thanks for the invite," he pouts. "I'm actually right near there. Just finished training a client at their home gym."

"Where's A?"

"Swimming lessons."

"That kid and her endless extracurriculars." I sit on a rock as Liv takes Waffles to play in a grassy area near the bottom of the steps. "How are you?"

"I'm good. You?"

"Good."

"Good."

"Glad we got that out of the way."

Ever since Jason and I went out on a date, things have shifted between us. Our evening was lovely, and it was clear we wanted to jump each other's bones, but we ended the night with a steamy kiss instead. Then, a few days later, Michael took me out. It was warm and familiar, and as he kissed me good night, all those old feelings came flooding back. Ever since, I've been juggling the two, trying to decide between something old and something new. I feel like one of those ridiculous women on *The Bachelorette*. Neither one of them is putting pressure on me, but I feel it constantly. Liv has alluded to the fact that she wants us to be a family again, but I'm still not sure that's what's best for me in the long run.

"Want some company?" Jason asks.

I pluck some blades of grass from the ground and let them fall. "Maybe we can get together later? I was going to take Liv for lunch."

"Want to call me when you're done?"

I look to where Liv and Waffles should be, but they've disappeared. "Liv?" I stand, searching to see if they just went farther down the hill. "Jason, I need to call you right back."

I pocket my phone and attempt to stay calm. Olivia knows not to wander off, and she has the dog, who would bark if anything was wrong. I wonder if his leash slipped and she went after him, though she would most likely call for help. I cross over the rocks and down toward the creek. Dread begins to tighten its maternal fist. I scan the creek, but it's clear. I double back to where I was sitting.

"Olivia! Waffles!" A few people give me funny looks, but I push forward, in a full-on panic now. I climb up on one of the columns on the stairs and shield my eyes. Where could they have gone?

I call her name and sprint to the top of the steps to get a better view of the entire entrance. My legs burn from the strain and surge of adrenaline. They are nowhere. I don't know whether to go back on the trail or head to the bottom. The area is sprawling; she could have gone in any direction, as there are trailheads all over this park. I think about checking the car, which is parked on the west side of the golf course. Would she remember to go there if we got separated?

I practically sprint toward the car, but it's another dead end. I call Jason back and attempt to keep my voice steady. "Olivia and Waffles were right here, and now they're gone. I've been looking for ten minutes, Jason. I can't find them."

"I can be there in five. Where are you?"

I tell him to meet by the stone stairs and then rotate in a circle. If anything happens to Liv . . . I think of all the "almost" moments with her: scares at the zoo, in stores, or at parades, where I would lose sight of her for just a moment and then she would resurface seconds later, undisturbed, while my whole life was on the precipice of collapse. I think of that moment this summer when she disappeared under the waves for a split second before she re-emerged, unharmed.

Even as I convince myself that everything will be fine, a deep foreboding works its way up my spine. Olivia doesn't just wander off.

If she's gone, there's a reason.

THIRTEEN

I ARRIVE AT THE FARM BEFORE SUNRISE, COFFEE IN HAND.

Ian is there, as always, and I am comforted by the sight of him. He's scribbling a giant Welcome, Acton Eagles! on the board and turns to me, a glint in his eye.

"Are you ready for this?"

I swallow my coffee and nod. "One hundred and thirty kids on the farm? What's not to be ready for?"

Every year the Acton Academy students come out to learn about the farm as part of their studies. A few kids started their own farming business last year and even contribute to the weekly farmers markets with their own produce booth. I will be working the market on Saturday, which has become one of my favorite parts of the internship. The farm supplies produce at the weekly markets year-round, even if it's snowing.

At first it was odd to be behind the farm stand instead of the one purchasing goods; now I'm used to it. In the warmer months, Liv and I would go to the local market by our house. We'd get lemonade, pet all the dogs, and stock up on local produce, pasta, and freshly baked bread. Then we'd go home and make a big Italian feast.

But often, instead of eating together, I would go downstairs to watch Netflix, and Olivia would watch her own show on her computer, fisting noodles and making a mess on our couch. We had willingly zoned out from each other, so tired from the day that we couldn't even sit at the table like a family. The regret claims me quickly, hard and swift. Ian catches my sharp intake of breath and frowns in concern.

"You okay?"

I tell him what I was just thinking, knowing he can see right through any sort of lie. Over the past couple of months, Ian and I have found our professional rhythm, and while this is the hardest work I've ever done, part of me feels rooted in my own humanity in a way I've never known. When I'm outside, smeared in dirt, sweating and moving, I feel like I am coming home to that younger, wilder version of myself. I am doing the work of my ancestors, and it reminds me of all the ways I have become disconnected from what is truly my birthright.

He nods. "You know," he says, sitting on the edge of the table, "even if you'd had dinner with Olivia every single night, you'd feel guilty about something else. I've found that focusing on all the random, goofy moments you had together instead of those missed opportunities does your heart and soul a hell of a lot better."

Before I can respond, the first bus hisses to a stop at the edge of the farm. Dirt kicks up as chattering children spill onto the grass and charge directly toward us. It is in the fifties today—a Georgia December day—and some kids are even in T-shirts. They gather around Ian, a few giving him high fives and hugs.

My heart kicks as I glimpse each of them. I imagine Liv among them, arm linked through Ayana's as they stumble from crop to crop. Ian knows several children by name and instructs them to quiet down as he introduces me and then explains how the day will work. I stare out at their sweet faces, a smile plastered on my lips, but emotion swells hard and fast. This is the first group of kids I've seen since summer, and the shock of it is blinding. I shove away the grief.

Not now.

After introductions and instructions, we guide them through the various crops and toward the proper beds to help weed.

The sun is fierce today, and all the kids complain about the surprising boost in temperature. At noon, I inhale my own brown-bag lunch of peanut butter and jelly, which transports me back to field trips as a kid. Once everyone is fed and hydrated, I approach Ian.

"Want to come over for dinner tonight?"

He scratches his neck and bats a fly away. "What's the occasion?"

I stare at him and smile. "I've been in Serenbe for a few months now, and as far as I know, I haven't killed any crops, so I'd like to celebrate. Steaks, potatoes, salad, wine? What do you say?"

He grimaces, as if he's seriously having to make a hard decision, and then offers a tight-lipped smile. "Sure. I'll make it work."

I try not to take his hesitation personally. "Great. See you at six."

The rest of the day passes quickly, and I rush home with fresh lettuce, corn, cucumbers, potatoes, and grape tomatoes to toss together for a salad.

I think of the last few months and how quickly they've passed. Most days I don't even turn on my computer or look at my phone. While I was obsessive about checking in with work in the fall, I extended my sabbatical a few more months and am truly giving myself the time I've never had. At night, I am so exhausted, I grab a quick dinner at The Farmhouse with Monica, Serenbe's local real estate agent turned fast friend, go for a walk with Laurence or Hank, take a bath, and read until I pass out.

Though Jason is worried because I've been a bit more off the grid, and my mother sends me concerned voice mails, afraid I've been chopped into millions of little pieces and used as fertilizer on the farm, I am doing better. I stop what I'm doing and send Jason a text to show Ayana. I've been texting or FaceTiming with her more than anyone, and I've even sent her several postcards.

While I miss home and my community, I find that in all this work, I've been able to deal with a lot of my demons I've pushed away for years. I'm able to think, to move from point A to point B with a definitive purpose.

I take a shower, tidy the place, which has surprisingly grown on me, and throw on a skirt and sweater to go to the General Store for steaks, feta, and wine. My body has grown leaner, and I've developed muscles in places I didn't even know I had. My hands are rough and calloused, and my skin has darkened from all the time outside. Surprisingly, I've never felt physically better.

Right before six, Ian's tires crunch through the gravel and pop over twigs. The slam of the truck door is followed by a soft knock. He hasn't been by since our chat at the start of the apprenticeship, and I've been getting the strange feeling that outside of work, he's avoiding me.

He's freshly showered and offers me a bouquet of peonies. "These are beautiful," I say, searching for a mason jar to act as a vase. "They're also my favorite."

"Lucky guess," he says, ambling inside. He's such a tall, broad man, and I find myself a little nervous around him, without the plants and crops as a buffer.

"The steaks are just keeping warm, so we can eat whenever you're hungry."

"I'm always hungry."

We set the table silently. I sort through the new stack of records I bought at a vintage shop, choose something classic, and pour the wine. "I feel like we're in a movie," I say after a few minutes of awkward silence.

"Oh?" He drinks some wine and waits for me to continue. "Which one?"

I almost blurt *The Notebook* but think better of it. Instead, I attempt humor. "*The Godfather.*"

He laughs. "Now you're talking."

I steady a piece of steak with my fork and slice through it with my knife. "The kids seemed to have a great time today."

He smiles. "They did. They're good kids."

"That was really hard," I say, taking a sip of wine. "Seeing all of them."

He chews and wipes his mouth with a napkin. "I'm sure. Are you okay?" He reaches forward and covers my hand with his. The heat from his palm sends a jolt through my system. "I should have thought about that, Kate."

I don't dare move. The weight of his hand, his eyes, the presence of him, in this cabin that is becoming a home, is cracking open my heart in new ways. "It's not your fault." My voice is a whisper.

"I know, but I can relate." To my surprise, his eyes fill with tears, and he removes his hand to wipe them away. He clears his throat. "I'm sorry."

"Don't be sorry." I fiddle with my fork. "How can you relate?"

He waits a beat. "It's not something I love to talk about, for obvious reasons." I study Ian—with his kind face, his crow's-feet, deepened by the sun, and those eyes I could get lost in. He's probably wondering if he can truly trust me. He glances down at his plate again and then pushes away from the table slightly, sighing. "I don't know where to start."

Though I'm not sure what he's about to say, I proceed with caution. "You don't have to tell me, if you don't want to."

He looks at me, and something clicks. "No, I want to."

Before Ian can continue, there's a tentative knock on the door. At first I wonder if I've imagined it, but then a muffled voice calls from the other side. I rise to see who it could be, irritated by the timing. Only a few people have been over for coffee, and most of them have families and obligations after work. I push open the screen door and almost scream. Jason is standing there, looking sheepish, duffel bag in hand.

"Surprise?" He poses it as a question.

I glance behind me at Ian. Jason's eyes follow me toward the handsome, rugged man seated at the table, and he takes it all in: The candles. The wine. The flowers. The record crooning in the background. He deflates.

"Oh shit." He leans in and drops to a whisper. "Am I interrupting something?"

"Of course not." I motion behind me. "This is my boss from the farm."

Ian stands and offers his hand. "Not really her boss. More like her partner. Ian."

My face warms at the term *partner*. Jason looks between us and then offers his hand. "Jason, the best friend with terrible timing."

"Jason is one of my oldest friends from Nashville," I say, even though it doesn't explain his unannounced arrival. They shake hands and assess each other. My head swims with too much wine and an intense longing to hear what Ian was going to say. "Wait." I look behind him. "Where's Ayana?"

"With my mom for a few days."

"Why don't I let you two catch up?" Ian takes his plate, half-eaten, to the kitchen. He slips past me, his arm brushing mine, and desire seizes me again, deep and primal. He pauses on the threshold and turns. "Thank you for a lovely evening, Kate." He jogs down the steps toward his truck. I turn to a profusely apologizing Jason and pull him all the way inside.

"That guy is a total hunk," he says, dropping his bag by the door. "Like a beefier Tom Hardy with a beard."

I roll my eyes and pull him into a hug. He smells good, and I realize how much I've missed him, how long it's really been. He whistles as he steps back and takes me in.

"Jesus Christ, Kate. You've never looked better. Are you sure you weren't on a date? Because it sure looked like a date."

"I was not on a date." Though, for the first time, the thought doesn't make my stomach turn. I smooth my skirt and study his face. "You look a little rough."

Dark shadows linger beneath his eyes, and he looks like he's lost a bit of weight. The sudden thought of him being sick or telling me he has cancer crosses my mind, and I sit on the couch to steady myself.

"Gee, thanks." He rakes a hand through his hair and collapses beside me. "I'm sorry for just showing up here like this. I just . . . needed to get away."

"You never need to get away." I cross my arms and stare at him. "Why are you really here?"

"Can we at least eat while you grill me?"

I make Jason a fresh plate with Ian's half-eaten steak as he slides into the vacant chair. "I just wanted to see my best friend," he says between bites. "Is that a crime?"

"Depends on why you wanted to see me." I saw off a giant hunk of meat and down a gulp of wine. I can't stop thinking of Ian and what he was going to confide. It seemed like he was on the brink of telling me something crucial.

"My business is in trouble." Jason takes a sip of wine as if he has just admitted to infidelity.

"What?" All thoughts of Ian fly out of my head. "How?"

"I won't bore you with the details, but sales are down. More and more clients are working out remotely." He groans. "I'm freaking out."

"Don't freak out," I say. "We can figure it out."

"I left Sheri in charge of the gym and said I needed to clear my head. Ayana even told me to go, to stop moping."

"God, I miss that child."

"The texts really mean a lot to her, Kate. And the videos and postcards. Thank you for making such an effort to keep in touch."

"Don't be ridiculous. She's family."

"Speaking of, I'm thinking of taking her to Ethiopia next summer. We've never been, and I think it's important for her to see her roots."

"That's a great idea. I'm sure it would mean a lot to her."

He gestures around the cabin. "I have to say, the murder cabin isn't so murder-y in person."

"Thanks." I'm too tired to unpack what's happened to my best friend in my absence, but I know we will have plenty of time to talk. "Just so you know, as much as I'd love to stay up late chatting, tomorrow I have to work the farmers market."

"In winter?"

I laugh. "Um, global warming, first of all, and yes. They do their markets year-round."

He smiles and wraps his hands behind his head. "From agricultural engineer to farmer. This sounds like the premise of a good book."

"Ha." I saw through another piece of steak. "And what would the title be?"

"*Build It and Watch It Grow.*"

I give him a look.

"Can I help?"

"What, with the market? When have you ever sold produce?"

He stares at the ceiling. "I sell things all the time."

"Fitness and fruit aren't the same thing." I don't tell him that Ian and I have found our tempo and that I've become strangely possessive over our arrangement. I don't want anyone disrupting what we are creating. I prepare to explain but then glimpse his sad eyes and hopeful expression. "Ugh, fine. You can come."

He grins, his eyes landing on the urn and the portrait of Liv my mom sent me. He swallows hard, then slides his hand across the table, gripping my fingers. "I want to make sure you're really okay, Kate. I miss you. This is the longest we've ever been apart."

It is. "I miss you too."

We finish dinner, and I show him to the guest room, which luckily, with the new upgrades, is cozy and clean. The bedroom window stares directly into the cluster of thick pines.

"It's really pretty here," he says as he collapses on the bed. "I'm glad you haven't been lost to a cult."

"Cults have leaders. We have Steve Nygren," I say. I tell him good night and stand in the middle of my little sanctuary, suddenly rattled by someone else in it. While I selfishly want to remind him that I'm trying to focus on my recovery and grief, I also want to help him in any way I can.

I clean up the dishes, wash my face, and flop into bed. As I do so many nights, I picture Olivia's sweet face and I tell her good night too. It's only then that I can sink into sleep, hopeful that I will dream about my daughter.

But tonight I'm thinking of Ian, of what he was going to tell me, of what caused such emotion. I assume it has to do with Ella, how he doesn't see her, or maybe why. And yet that's not the only thing nagging at me.

I felt something else: a connection much deeper than friendship. I wanted to comfort Ian, to listen to him, to hold space for him. I bury the thoughts. He is technically my boss, and a romantic relationship is the last thing I need.

I readjust in bed and think of Jason and what he said last summer. Does he still feel that way? As I contemplate the possibility, I take deep breaths, willing my mind to clear and my body to relax.

But thoughts of Ian creep in again. I wonder if there's something between us for him too, or if it's all in my head.

14

TRUE TO HIS WORD, JASON IS HERE WITHIN MINUTES, BUT I'm too frazzled to even acknowledge him.

I've alerted a security guard who works at the golf course and told everyone within earshot that my daughter is missing. Men and women spread out to look, and someone has called the police. I try to think like Olivia would and know that she wouldn't have moved from her spot unless Waffles got loose.

People disperse on various trails and call out her name. I'm sweating despite the cold weather, and I feel sick. Once again, I wasn't paying close enough attention.

"What if she's gone, Jason? What if someone took her?"

"This is a safe area, Kate. I'm sure she just ran after the dog and got turned around."

The dog. Olivia has been practicing a high-pitched whistle that makes him come immediately, and though I suck at whistling, I give it a try now. Nothing. I try again, heading toward the trees and the line of cars that snakes beside the golf course. Jason joins me, not questioning what I'm doing.

"Did you hear that?" He grips my arm and stops, but all I can tune in to is my own panic.

I strain to hear, and sure enough, there's the echo of a distant bark. "That's him." I run toward the sound, which leads us parallel to the golf course and a walkway for pedestrians that cuts back into the woods. I jog across and Jason follows. The creek rushes below us, drowning out our footsteps. Suddenly, from the dense trees, Waffles emerges, wildly barking, soaked to the bone. "Waffles!" I grip him and inspect to see if he's hurt. "Where's Olivia?"

To my surprise, he turns and begins running back toward the woods. A sickening feeling grips my gut.

He's heading toward the river.

A million what-ifs play out in my head as I struggle to keep up. What if she drowned? What if she's seriously injured? What if she's gone?

We have to cross the creek to get to the mouth of the river, and Waffles is moving so fast, Jason and I have to sprint. Finally, when the creek spills to the left and rushes into the river, I hear whimpering.

"Liv?" My voice is strained, even to my own ears, as I splash through the water toward Waffles's maniacal barks.

"Mama?" Liv's voice is tiny, and then she's crying.

Oh, thank God. I round the corner, expecting her to fly into my arms, but then I see the problem and gasp. She has fallen, and her leg is bent backward from the knee down at a horrific angle, trapped under a huge log. She has vomited into the water, and the chunky foam floats around her. She's pale, freezing, and drenched. Jason examines her leg and looks at me, fear in his eyes. He runs to the road and yells for help, then dials 911.

"What happened?" I can tell by looking at the log that we won't be able to remove it.

"Waffles got away." She gasps, her teeth chatter, and I remove my jacket and drape it over her. "I was trying to catch him. The log fell." She looks at her leg and trembles uncontrollably. "My leg!"

"Shh, honey. It's okay. You're okay." I call to Jason, but I know we shouldn't try to move anything until the paramedics arrive.

Waffles tries to lick Olivia, but she's growing hysterical. She's never even had stitches.

"Hey, hey." Jason wades toward her. "You're going to be okay. Help is on the way."

She strains against the log, then lets out a piercing scream.

"Honey, I need you to stay still until help gets here, okay?" I attempt to keep her calm as Jason dashes back toward the street.

What feels like an hour later, Jason is waving his arms toward someone or something, and I pray it's an ambulance. Finally, sirens whine louder until Olivia squeezes her damp hands over her ears.

I move out of the way as firefighters and paramedics assess the situation. They have to cut the log away. The firefighters saw through it, hunks of wood flying through the air. The buzz of the blades makes Liv scream. Finally, the log gives way and her leg flops oddly into the water, the shin bone inverted. I look away as a wave of intense nausea nearly makes me vomit.

They strap her to a body board, covering her with shiny warming blankets, and hoist her into the ambulance. I climb inside after her. Jason says he'll meet me at the Children's Hospital at Vanderbilt. I hold her hand as the paramedics work, knowing I need to call Michael.

"Mama!" She attempts to sit up. "Waffles! Where is he?" She strains against the restraints while the paramedics insist she stay still.

Straining to see out the back windows, I catch a glimpse of Jason jogging back toward his car with Waffles cradled in his arms.

"Jason's got him, honey. He's fine."

She collapses back, looking older than nine. They've obviously given her something to manage the pain because she's calmed down enough that I can ask her what happened. "Do you know why Waffles ran off?"

"He saw a squirrel, Mama. I let go of the leash. I'm so sorry." She begins to cry again, and I smooth the hair off her forehead. "Can you call Papito?"

"Of course, honey." I assess her leg and look at the paramedics. This is all my fault. I shouldn't have been on the phone with Jason. I want to ask them how bad it is, but I know that will just freak out Olivia even more. They try to placate her by making jokes, but she's nearly asleep from the drugs.

We pull into the drop zone at the emergency room and I release her hand as they open the doors, but she grabs for me again, suddenly alert.

I entwine my fingers with hers. "I'm right here. I promise." When she's rushed inside, however, I must let go as they wheel her back for X-rays. I start to cry as she screams, bucking wildly, and then disappears behind double doors. I search for Jason and find him, Waffles in his arms. I crush him in a hug.

"How do I get back there?"

"Hold this." He hands me Waffles and I bury my face in his fur. He whimpers, as if he knows Liv is seriously hurt. A few minutes later, Jason comes back and reports the doctor will be out any minute. Because it's a bone and not a life-threatening emergency, I know "any minute" could be hours. After I hand over my insurance card and fill out incessant paperwork, Jason leads me to a chair and I sit, Waffles curled in my lap.

"I want to be with her," I say.

"You will. Just be patient."

I drop my head on top of Waffles. "I should have been paying closer attention."

"Hey, don't do that. Nobody pays close enough attention." He takes my hand in his, and I am grateful he's here—I wouldn't want anyone else by my side. But I know who Liv needs most.

"I need to call Michael."

Just then the doctor comes out, white jacket rumpled, hair neatly combed, eyes tired behind reading glasses. He explains she's fractured her tibia in two places and they may need to perform surgery, especially if her growth plate has been affected. I clutch Jason. Olivia is terrified of surgery. They tell us they'll know more shortly, and I ask to see her.

He jerks his head for me to follow him and ushers me toward a small room with a view of the park. I have to wait until she's done with her second round of X-rays. Finally, they wheel her in. Olivia bursts into tears and reaches for me from her hospital bed.

"Hey, it's okay, baby. Shh." The nurse gets her situated while I tentatively break the news. She glances at me, terrified.

"What if I don't wake up? What if it's like *Dr. Death*?"

I silently berate Jason for letting her watch even five minutes of *Dr. Death* last year. "Sweetie, it's not like *Dr. Death*. Look at me, okay?" I slide up a chair and grip her hand. "I can promise that it's like taking a big old nap. You go to sleep and when you wake up, your leg will feel better, okay? Plus, you might not even need surgery. I just want you to understand that it's a possibility."

She begins to hiccup. "Did you tell Papá yet?"

I smooth her hair back from her face. "Not yet, but I was just about to call him."

"Will I still be able to go to Mexico City with him? I have to be able to go!"

Liv has planned to fly back to Mexico City with Michael right after Christmas for a visit, while she is still on break. But there is no way she can do that now. "Let's not worry about that, okay? Let's just get you fixed first."

She hiccups. "I don't want to be fixed."

Jason knocks on the door and steps inside. "I'm not supposed to do this, but tough shit." He cradles Waffles inside his hoodie, his black furry face peeking out from Jason's stretched neckline. Olivia visibly perks up as he leans down to let Waffles lick her face.

"Oh, Waffles." Her voice shakes again. "Can he stay with me, Mama?"

"I wish he could," I say. "But he'll keep you company while you heal at home, okay?"

A nurse comes in, lowers her clipboard to her side, and shakes her head. "Uh-uh," she snaps. She points to Waffles and then to the door. "Out."

"Emotional support animal," Jason explains, cradling Waffles. "High anxiety." He winks at Olivia and actually gets the smallest hint of a smile.

"Well, take that 'anxiety' out of this hospital room, sir, before you get us all in trouble," the nurse warns.

Jason steps outside while the nurse fusses around Liv and then leaves, saying the doctor will be in shortly.

After an eternity, the doctor comes in and says he has good news. She doesn't need surgery, but she does need a cast.

I grip her hand. "See? A cast. How cool is that? All your friends can sign it."

He rattles off tons of information I will most likely forget. I tell her I'm going to call Michael while they prep her for the mold and that I will be right back. Jason walks me down the hall and I glance into other rooms, full of injured, sick, or dying individuals.

"I hate hospitals," I say.

"I think everybody hates hospitals." He slings an arm around my shoulder, adjusting Waffles in his other. "Thank God she doesn't need surgery, huh?"

I nod, but I'm already reviewing the task list in my head: call Michael first, then my mother. Outside the automatic doors, I suck in a cold breath. Jason lowers Waffles to the grass to let him pee while I steady myself and dial Mike's cell.

"Kate?" He sounds happy to hear from me.

"Don't freak out, but Liv had an accident. We were hiking. She let go of the dog's leash and then chased after him. She fractured her tibia in two places, but she doesn't need surgery. She's going to be fine." I spew the facts as fast as I can.

"Can I talk to her?" His tone is surprisingly clipped.

"They are prepping her for her cast. I can have her call you after."

"I don't understand how this happened," he says. "Were you not with her?"

"It was an accident. She's a kid. Kids get hurt." I know he could say something pompous like, *Not on my watch*, but luckily for both of us, he doesn't.

"Poor baby." He exhales loudly into the phone. "What hospital are you at? I'll come right now."

"Vanderbilt." I glance at Jason, wondering how this will go over, that he is here before Michael.

"*Bendito Dios*," he whispers. "I'm so sorry, Kate. I'll be right there." He hangs up, and I clutch my phone, gripping it much too tight.

Jason trots back over with Waffles in tow. "You good?"

"Mm-hmm." I'm already texting my mother.

Jason is quiet while I fire off the text. Then he gently places a hand on my arm. "You know that I'm always going to be here for you, right?"

I stop what I'm doing and really receive the words, feel their impact. There's been so much up in the air, so much uncertainty between us that now feels insignificant. I take a step, closing the gap between us to give him a hug. "I do know that," I say. "Thank you. And I'll always be here for you too."

We hold each other, and the build-up we've been experiencing since the summer seems to momentarily wane. There are so many other things to contend with: our children, our jobs, an ex-husband. I think about the ocean, the pool, the playground, my backyard, our date—all lovely memories to treasure. Then I think of all the other details that compose our friendship—that have nothing to do with romance—and I am comforted by the depth of our firm foundation.

Jason heads back inside while I handle Waffles and wait for Michael. In a matter of minutes, he's walking toward me, looking sad and exhausted.

He pulls me into a hug. "Are you okay?"

"Just a little shaken up," I say into his sweater. "And I hate it for her."

He releases me and drags a hand along his jaw. "Me too. Especially before the holidays."

"I know." I haven't even thought through all the ways this will hinder our normal plans.

"Maybe she could stay a little longer in Mexico City with me? Take a few days off from school? A change of pace might do her good. Help her heal."

"I don't think she's going to be able to go home with you, Mike. She's going to be in a cast."

"I'll talk to the doctors." He stares at his shoes, then into my eyes. "I hate to say this, but she's bored here, Kate."

His words are like a gut punch, hard and unexpected. I know I shouldn't take the bait, but I do. "Did she actually say that?"

"No, no. Look." He deflates. "I shouldn't have said that."

Jason walks through the automatic doors and glances between us. Sensing the tension, he addresses only me. "They're done." He flicks his eyes toward Michael and steps forward to take the leash. "I'll stay with Waffles. You good?"

No, I am not good. I hand off the leash and push past him, not even waiting to see if Michael follows. I'd forgotten all the ways he can subtly make me second-guess myself.

We walk silently side by side to check Michael in, and then we are ushered back. When we enter her room, Liv's eyes light up as she sees Michael.

"Papito, look at my cast!"

He rushes to her, and they embrace. He smothers her hair with kisses and tells her how cool her cast is. He asks if he can be the first to sign it, and she laughs as he wipes her tears away.

I stand near the door, feeling like an outsider, as if my entire world is somehow slipping away.

FOURTEEN

WHEN I SHOW UP WITH JASON THE NEXT MORNING AT THE market, Ian shoots me a curious look but acts pleasant enough.

Monica is there, chatting with our adjacent vendor, Ruth, who sells the best goat's milk I've ever had. When Monica sees Jason, she raises her eyebrows and mouths, *"Single?"*

I roll my eyes and give a small nod before turning back to Ian. He doesn't mention last night, so I don't either. Instead, I motion toward Jason. "Can he help out today?"

"Sure."

I show Jason how to take a payment with Square, and then Ian leaves us to it as we man our booth, arrange produce, and sip coffee while we wait for the market to open.

"You really like this place, huh?" Jason glances around at the open field.

I nod. "I do. It's been good for me."

"I can see that. You seem different."

I almost scoff. "Well, I am different, Jason. Permanently."

"No, no, I know that. I just meant . . . you seem more at peace. Like you've moved through some of the grief."

I consider that word, a word I've been reading so much about. I've gone through denial, anger, bargaining, depression, and am now swinging toward acceptance, though the first few stages of grief always seem to tug me back when I least expect it.

"Hey, Kate." Monica approaches our booth, flips her hair over her shoulder, thrusting her chest out, and offers Jason a dazzling smile. "Who's your friend?"

"This is Jason. My best friend from Nashville."

"You're Jason? We've heard so much about you." She extends her hand and he shakes it, tossing me a confused look.

"Oh?"

"She's exaggerating, but yes, I have told my friends here how much I miss my best friend."

"I can see why," Monica mutters under her breath.

"Real smooth, Monica." I laugh. "Are you going to buy something?"

"No, I'm just checking out the goods." She gives him a once-over again before waving goodbye.

"I feel dirty," Jason jokes. "But I'm glad you're making friends."

I place a bundle of squash in a basket and smile. "It's easier here. There's no pressure, no real plans. Everyone is just kind of available, but they don't take it personally if you're not around." As I say it, I realize how nice it's been. To have coffee or a glass of wine without the pressure of scheduling something months in advance on the calendar.

"Well, I'm glad." He places a hand on my shoulder and squeezes before motioning to the bounty of fall and winter vegetables. "So you grew all this?"

"Yep." I smile, realizing how proud that actually makes me.

Jason studies me as the market officially opens, and I busy myself bagging produce, taking payments, and ordering Jason around. He's amazingly sociable and is such a good salesperson, we run out of produce almost an hour ahead of the market's closing. Ian comes near the end and whistles.

"What happened here?"

I point to Jason and gather the email sign-up sheet. "He happened."

Jason shrugs. "Before I owned a gym, I was a regional sales manager."

"Are you looking for a job?"

I laugh and butt in. "He most certainly is *not*."

He elbows me. "Hey, you don't know that."

"Oh, I'm sorry. Are you selling your business and moving to Serenbe?"

"You never know." He shoots me a look, and I hand Ian the empty baskets.

"What now?"

"Now you go enjoy yourselves. Show Jason around town."

"You sure I can't help pack up?"

Ian places his hand lightly on my shoulder, just as Jason did earlier, but the warmth spreads through my body. "You deserve the day off. Go. Enjoy."

Jason hooks his arm through mine and ushers me away before I can protest. "Serenbe me," he says.

"How about we go shower first and then I'll give you the tour?"

"Even better."

We fall into a comfortable silence as we walk back to the cabin. I point out the local shops, and we wave at so many people, he gags. "Why is everyone so nice?"

"Because they choose to be here. No one is here by chance."

He shudders. "It's unnatural."

"That's what I thought at first. But it's grown on me."

He kicks at a rock and shoves his hands in his hoodie as we walk. "So how long are you staying?"

"I'm not sure. Technically, I'm still on sabbatical."

"Are you seeing a therapist yet?"

"No. I don't feel ready yet." I've thought about seeing a grief counselor, but every time I do, it makes me feel stuck. With my work on the farm, I'm moving through it and grieving in my own way.

At the cabin, I unlock the door and smile at the tidy space that has become all mine. "You can go first. Oh, just be warned the tub gets a little clogged."

"Got it!" He strips off his hoodie and T-shirt and tosses them on his bed. I glance at his lean torso and then avert my eyes.

I head to my bedroom and collapse on my bed. I stare at the exposed beams on the ceiling. What I told Jason is true. I am still on sabbatical, but the longer I take off from work, the less I want to return. I don't know what that means for the future. I can't work the same job and run in the same circles, as if I'm pretending everything's the same when nothing is. Without my role as mom, my entire world has changed. I run a finger over the quilt and think about how many years I've tried to make my life work in Nashville. And what's it all amounted to?

As it does so often when I stop working and get still enough to think, a gaping loneliness unfurls inside me. I worry that Liv would be disappointed if I just gave up on our life that took so many years to build.

Closing my eyes and imagining her sweet voice, I slide to the floor and wrap my arms around my knees and begin to cry. Once I start, I can't stop, even when the crank of the shower turns off and Jason runs into the room, dripping wet, a towel loosely clenched around his waist. "Kate?"

He kneels beside me and I roll into him, inhaling the fresh scent of soap.

"Oh, Kate. It's okay. Shh."

I cling to him. "I miss her so much, Jason."

"I know." He grips me tightly and rubs my back. I continue to sob, openly and loudly, but he just holds me. When I feel drained of tears, I stop crying, but Jason doesn't let go.

"Your balls are literally resting on my thigh," I finally whisper.

"I know," he whispers back. "And I'm so sorry."

I burst out laughing and push him away. The sound takes me by surprise. My abs tighten, and I swing from tears to incessant laughter in a millisecond. Jason laughs too, then tells me to hold on and runs to his room. I hear him curse as something crashes, and then he comes back in sweatpants and a sweatshirt, hair damp and messy.

I lie back on the floor, finally quieting. Jason lies beside me, rolling over and propping himself up on his elbow.

"I haven't laughed since June," I say. "What month is it?"

"December." He pushes some damp hair off my face and rests his hot palm over my heart. "It's okay to laugh."

I shake my head as more tears slip down my cheeks. "She would want me to laugh. I know that. She would want me to find the joy, but it's so hard without her."

"I know."

I grip his hand to my chest and squeeze his fist. "How did you do it with Shelby? All those quiet moments when her absence screamed at you."

He sighs. "Honestly, after a while, I tried to keep myself busy, which, looking back, wasn't always the best thing, but it helped." He rolls to his back and stares at the ceiling. "And then adopting Ayana. But those moments when I truly realized that she was never coming back . . . those were the times it really sank in. It's brutal."

"*Brutal* is the perfect word."

We lie with each other, my mind running its cyclical grief loop. Though I've been working and living in a new place, I know I'll never be able to outrun the pain.

He props himself back up on his elbow and stares at me, and his face changes. It looks . . . hungry. Something grips my stomach, and before I can make sense of it, Jason leans in. "May I kiss you?"

My mouth suddenly goes dry, and my heart beats wildly. *What?* There are a thousand and one reasons why *no, he most certainly cannot kiss me*, but it has been ages since I've been kissed by anyone. *Years.* Ian flashes through my mind, followed by Jason's words from last summer. I've been so disconnected from my body—only farming, showering, and sleeping—that I want to feel something else besides dirt beneath my fingernails or hot water on my back. I need human connection, a moment to be a woman seeking some sort of pleasure to kill the pain.

I close my eyes as he waits for an answer, and my head grows thick and dreamy. I give the smallest of nods, and then his lips are on mine. Desire catches fire and explodes. I rip at his clothes, bite his lips, and roll on top of him. His eyes are wild and appreciative as I take control, moving my hands over every inch of him. I lose myself to him, to us.

He grips my face in his hands and pauses to stare deeply into my eyes. "Kate."

"What?"

"How did I not know you were such a fantastic kisser?"

His words pierce that tiny, unwounded part of my heart, and I kiss him deeply in response. Though I think about taking it further, we don't. Instead, I revel in the sheer bliss of kissing my best friend, of giving in to this part of my femininity that I have been ignoring for years. No physical contact. No one to hug or kiss. No one to hold me. No one to hold.

Finally, I roll off him and we lie there, breathing hard.

"Holy shit," he says. He cranes his neck to look at me. "You're incredible."

I close my eyes and steady my breathing, ignoring the part of my brain still thinking of Ian. I open my eyes and look at him. "Prove it," I say.

He leans in to kiss me, as hungry as the first time. Everything quiets except our breathing, and I let him kiss me again.

And again.

15

LIV HATES HAVING A CAST.

As a child who has never broken a bone or been hurt physically in any major way, she is not an easy patient. I ply her with movies, books, and plenty of snuggly Waffles time, but all she wants to do is move and spend time with Michael. Luckily, she's on Christmas break.

"I can't believe I'm going to have a cast for Christmas," she pouts. "And I can't go on my trip. And we don't even have a tree yet! Worst Christmas ever."

Much to the disappointment of Michael, the doctor said it's not a good idea for her to travel and be up on her leg too much right now. We have tentatively rebooked her trip to Mexico City for spring break, but Liv isn't having any of it. Somehow her injury and the fact that she can't go with her dad are all my fault. And Michael hasn't done much to clarify otherwise. I've become the villain in my own household.

"Is it really the worst Christmas ever, though?" I ask. "You are healthy, you're alive, and you have a good story to tell."

"So I brought this on myself? Great." She folds her arms on the couch, leg propped up.

"That's not what I'm saying at all, Liv." I sigh, refill her water glass, and make her a snack. Work has been nearly impossible with her at home, and the stress of not being able to do my typical Christmas shopping is forcing me to buy everything online, which I usually avoid like the plague.

The doorbell rings, and I look out front to see my mother. "Thank God." I open the door and she rushes into the living room wearing her matching coat, hat, and gloves. She claps her hands and assesses Liv, in dirty pajamas, a clump of her curls easily passing for a dreadlock at the nape of her neck. Dried honey clings to her cheek from her breakfast this morning.

"Hi, Grandma Nell."

"Hi, yourself." She produces a Target bag. "Picked up a few things for you."

Liv brightens considerably as my mother pulls out a few new sweaters and pants in Liv's favorite color: green.

"I don't like green anymore." Liv sighs, chewing the ends of her hair.

"Since when?" I scoff.

"Since purple is my new favorite color," she says. "It's Papito's favorite too."

I swallow my rebuttal, making brief eye contact with my mother.

"Okay, Miss Purple, then I'll return these." She stuffs them back into the bag, unrattled by Liv's brattiness. "Get up. Go change. We're getting manicures."

True joy flashes across Liv's face for the first time in a week, and she struggles to sit up. I hand over her crutches and offer to help her get dressed.

"I've got it," she insists. "I'm not a baby." She wobbles off to her room and shuts the door.

I look at my mother and roll my eyes. "Be warned that the sass is on point. I've told her countless times that Santa is listening, but that doesn't seem to have the same effect as it did when she was six."

My mother glances around the house—at the messy coffee table, covered with printer paper and markers; the stray bits of paper Liv has been cutting for crafts, strewn across the rug; the plates of congealed food and endless cups half-filled with water; the dirty dishes in the sink; and the dog hair. So much dog hair.

Waffles circles around my mother's legs, and I almost remind her that he's a jumper, but she crouches down and cradles his face. My mother has always been good with animals.

The lovefest over, she stands and plucks the errant hairs from her trousers. "While I take her to get a manicure, why don't you get out of this house and go treat yourself to something?"

"I hate manicures."

"That's why I didn't invite you, Kate."

I have a huge deadline to meet, and having Liv out of the house will be the perfect excuse to get some much-needed work done. "It's fine. I've got a ton of work to do."

My mother sighs, one hand cocked on her hip. "Come on, Kate. All you ever do is work. Go out. Have some fun for once in your life. Remember our talk during the summer? You need to shake things up, and this is the perfect day to do it."

I do remember our talk during the summer, but that seems like a lifetime ago. When was the last time I went to do something just for fun? I haven't told her I've gone on dates with both Michael and Jason; I don't want to get her hopes up either way. Not until I'm sure. I think about seeing a movie, but it's a gorgeous day, and I want to be outside. The sun is shining, and it is bitingly cold. "Okay, fine. I'll find something to do."

Liv finally emerges with one of her pant legs cut to shorts to fit over her cast. She wears a wrinkled Christmas sweater and stuffs her good foot into a fuzzy boot. I don't bother to tell her to put on socks because she won't. She grabs her jacket and earmuffs, and they are off. I collapse on the couch and revel in the silence. It's the first time in weeks I've been alone.

I straighten the house, return a few emails, then get bundled up. I know Ayana is at sewing class today, so I text Jason and tell him to meet me at Opryland.

Did you get us a room?

You wish, I reply. I tell him to bring his ice skates.

He meets me in the parking lot, and we both grab our skates and walk to the side entrance of the massive hotel, where it feels like it's been transformed into a Hallmark movie. Fenced-in reindeer munch on carrots. A large ice rink, outlined with pines, takes center stage. Christmas music croons from a loudspeaker, and oversized decorations—giant candy canes, Christmas bows, and cardboard bells—eat up empty space around the ice bumper cars and sledding stations. We pay for our tickets, lace up our skates, and mount the ice. It's an off time, so it's not too crowded. I'm thankful for the open space as I pick up speed. Jason skates circles around me, turning backward and showing off his former ice hockey skills. I'm a decent skater, having dabbled in figure skating as a child, but I'm nowhere near as comfortable as he is. It makes me sad to think that Liv won't be able to skate for a while, as it's one of our favorite winter activities to do together.

I knock away those thoughts and instead focus on the present moment. Jason and I never skate without the girls, and I find it wildly satisfying to be here with him. My usual worries of Liv falling and arguments with her about wearing her helmet are replaced by an intense sense of freedom.

I spread my arms as one of my favorite Christmas songs, "Have Yourself a Merry Little Christmas," comes on. Judy Garland's voice hums across the ice. Jason skates toward me and loops my arm in his. We skate in large, lazy circles as I mouth the words. Slowly, Jason moves in front of me, smoothly transitioning to skate backward, and then tugs me to his chest as his arms encircle my waist.

We skate and stare into each other's eyes, our bodies glued tight. I'm used to being this close to him now, and the world shrinks to just the two of us until I am completely content.

"What are you thinking, Baker?" His icy breath billows in tiny white clouds between us.

"I'm thinking that I wouldn't rather be anywhere else in the world right now." It's the truth.

He leans in, even as we're moving, and I wait for the warmth of his lips. Instead, he bypasses my mouth and drags his lips across my ear. "Ditto." His breath tickles my earlobe and sends a shiver down my entire left side.

Suddenly he breaks away, leaving a physical ache when he takes off at a fast clip around the rink. All this teasing, talking, and testing boundaries makes me feel strangely detached, as if I'm floating outside my own body. It has been so very long since I've desired another person this much. Part of me wonders whether I'm enjoying the anticipation more than what will naturally unfold between us if we ever do take it further than a kiss.

We skate for an hour and then walk around the hotel, which is one of my favorite places to visit at Christmas. The indoor garden and hundreds of hotel rooms span miles, decked out in holiday cheer. We putz around through the Cascades and the Delta, across the various atriums, and then pause to take a selfie in front of the towering, decorated Christmas tree by the water. Jason kisses my cheek, and my entire face tingles as we pose and snap a few different shots to get the angle just right.

A holiday song kicks on as the red and green fountains erupt in a powerful spray. Liv loves watching the light show by the dancing fountain, and I realize she probably won't be able to navigate very well on crutches this year.

We walk and talk, and then it's time for him to pick up Ayana from sewing class. Back at our cars, we load up our skates.

"That was much needed," I say. "Thank you."

"No, thank you. It was a perfect day."

We stare at each other. There's been so much said between us, and even more unsaid. Though Jason is not pushing me in any direction, more and more I'm leaning toward the idea of really giving this a shot. Of finally going all in to see what's there. But I know I still have to talk to Michael, especially since our tense conversation at the hospital and Liv's subsequent icy behavior toward me. Jason's phone dings.

"It's work. I need to make this call before I pick up Ayana. Call you later?"

He gives me a quick wave, then gets in his car, already distracted. And just like that, the spell is broken. That's the thing about our new dynamic: while we must be careful not to disturb the friendship's balance, we also can't take anything too personally.

I get in my car and see my mom has sent me a slew of photos of her and Liv. She's smiling and waving her rainbow-colored nails at the camera. My mom asks if she can just keep her for the night, and I text back an emphatic *YES*.

A night to myself. I'm going to curl up with Waffles and watch a Christmas movie with a good bottle of wine. I drive the short distance home and pass Jason's house, thinking about texting to see if he'd like to get a sitter and come join later.

When I pull into the drive, Michael is sitting on my front porch. I shove the car into Park, wondering if he's here to see Liv. I stalk to the front porch, keys in hand. "Hey."

He wags a purple stuffed elephant in his hands. "Hi. Just came to see the patient," he says. "And apologize to you."

"Liv's with my mom. They're having a sleepover."

"Ah." He stands, eyeing the front beds that are full of leaves and weeds. "I wish I would have known."

"I wish you would have called first." I sigh and try again. "I'm sorry. I'm still upset about our interaction at the hospital. But come in."

I flip on the lights and pour us both a glass of wine as we head downstairs. I start a fire, and when it's good and crackling, I try to articulate what I want to say. "You really upset me, Mike. I felt like you were blaming me for Liv's accident."

"I know, *mi amor*. I'm sorry. I was stressed and I took it out on you. I shouldn't have."

"You know, Liv really looks up to you. Whatever we are doing here, we have to be careful."

"I know." He takes a healthy sip of wine and stares into the fire. "What are we doing here, Kate?"

I shrug. "I don't know. We have so much history between us, both good and bad. It's a lot to process."

"But history is also good, yes? We know each other. We love each other."

"Yes," I say carefully, "but it also brings a lot of baggage to the table."

"Baggage you don't have with Jason, right?"

I hesitate over how to answer. I shift and pull a pillow into my lap. "It's different. We've known each other a long time. We're best friends."

He looks wounded. "We were best friends too once."

241

Until you left us.

"I don't want to put pressure on you, Katie, but I'll be leaving soon, and I just want to know which life to prepare for: one with you or one without."

It's a blunt statement, but I know he's right. "I just need a little more time," I say. A little more time to figure it all out.

FIFTEEN

AFTER A COUPLE OF DAYS IN SERENBE, JASON HAS MADE friends with most of the locals.

Not wanting to step on my toes at the farm, he spends most of the day at the gym, then at Blue Eyed Daisy or the General Store as he plans ways to save his business. We meet for dinner and conversation, but we don't cross that physical line again. We both know that it was a heat-of-the-moment thing and nothing more.

"Hey, Kate! Need a ride?"

I'm knee-deep in pumpkins as I turn, my breath visible. Ian chugs forward on the tractor, and my heart kicks.

I shield my eyes. "When are you going to let me have a go at that thing?"

He pretends to consider his options. "How about now?"

"Really?" I wipe my hands on my pants and motion for him to scoot over.

He gives me a quick tutorial, and we're off. I take the corners slowly but love the feeling of sitting up so high. He points to a path much farther out than the perimeter of where we grow, and I revel in the umber leaves, the crunchy earth, and the breathtaking beauty of this land.

"What's all this going to be used for?"

He bounces in his seat as we tumble over a mound of dirt. "Hopefully for the farm. I have a vision."

"Oh?" I wait for him to say more, but in true Ian fashion, he keeps to himself.

"Do I get to be a part of that vision?"

"Depends. Do you want to be a part of that vision?"

I slow down and fidget with the steering wheel. I glance at him. "I'm not sure. Right now I'm focused on taking it one day at a time."

He nods and lets it drop. "So your friend Jason made quite the impression at the market. Several of the women were asking about him."

I roll my eyes and pick up the pace. "He's always been charming."

"How long have you two been friends?"

"Over twenty years. Our daughters were best friends." My breath catches, but I continue. "He lost his wife to breast cancer years ago. Ever since then, it's just been us."

He scratches his beard. "Yeah, I thought for sure you two were . . ." He motions between me and him.

"We were what?"

"You know." He shrugs. "You can just tell. He's crazy about you."

I laugh and brush off the words. I think about our intense make-out session and how I've now muddied the waters by crossing that physical line. In a lot of ways it would make perfect sense to explore a relationship now.

I contemplate how honest to be with Ian and decide that until I figure it out for myself, it's best to keep it simple. "We're just friends."

He nods, and I see a tiny smile prick the corner of his lips. "What about you?"

"What about me?" I take the long, lazy loop back to the farm entrance.

"What's next in the world of Kate Baker?"

"Well, right now . . . tractor driving?" I eye him, and he smiles.

"Do you miss your job?"

The question surprises me. We so rarely talk about my work or my life back in Nashville. Once upon a time, my career was my entire identity. While it's been nice to get paid time off, I know that once the break is over, I need to make some firm decisions. "Being an engineer is great, but I'm thinking of quitting. Might be time to move on."

"To?"

"Oh, I don't know. Maybe farming?" I smile, and he laughs. "In all seriousness, I really like working with my hands. It would be hard to go back."

He whistles in approval. "There really is nothing like it." He glances at me. "You seem good, Kate. Lighter."

Kissing until you can't breathe will do that to you, I almost blurt. "I'm getting there."

Back at the entrance, Jason is waiting with a bouquet of flowers, and I blush. Ian pokes me. "See? Smitten kitten. Better watch out, Kate. Don't want to break anyone's heart."

I swallow and hop down as Jason whistles. "That might be one of the hottest things I've ever seen."

"Me on a tractor? You need to up your fantasy factor." I point to the flowers. "What's this?"

"These are for you. I'm taking you on a proper date at The Hill."

"Why?"

"Because you deserve to be treated to a date." He turns to Ian and gives him a lazy smile as he tosses an arm around my shoulder. "Is that okay, boss? Can she leave a little early?"

Ian salutes and checks something on a clipboard. "You kids have fun."

I feel strange leaving the farm early, leaving Ian, but I grab my bag and walk back with Jason. "Have you talked to your business manager yet?" I ask.

"No. Have you talked to your boss yet?" he shoots back.

"Stop deflecting."

He sighs. "I'll talk to her, okay?"

"When?"

"Jesus, Kate." He slaps the bouquet against his thigh, and a few petals detach and flutter to the pavement. "Eventually, all right? I just want to enjoy myself."

I stop him. "Hey. I'm not trying to make you feel bad, I just . . . Look. If your business is in trouble, then you need to fix it. You've worked too hard to just run away. You have to face it."

He scrubs a hand over his face. "I know." He swats me with the bouquet. "You're right."

"I'm always right." I glance at the battered flowers. "Now give me those. You're ruining them."

He hands them over and then crushes me in a surprisingly tight hug. "Thank you, Kate. I came here for you, but it seems like you've really been here for me."

"That's because women are better at figuring things out than men," I whisper.

We fall into easy conversation the rest of the way home. It is a beautiful afternoon. The air is crisp and clean—not too cold—which is one of my favorite things about winters in the South. I let us into the cabin. We take turns showering and getting dressed. As I apply lipstick in the mirror, I think about what Ian said. I do feel lighter. I am making different choices, though I still have some decisions to make when it comes to career and love.

At dinner, the conversation flows easily. We drink too much wine and indulge in two desserts. Jason is flirty and happy, and I flirt back, letting myself feel freer than I have in months.

Back at the cabin, we sit by the firepit outside and reminisce about the old days: how we met; how we had massive crushes on each other, but both of us were too chickenshit to make a move. We only briefly talk about his business and my job, how we would both handle moving on to something new. After a while, he brings up Shelby and Ayana. I talk about Liv, and I'm discovering, as more time passes, that it's easier to talk about her with a smile on my face versus tears on my cheeks. Even in death, she is still such a revelation.

The flames slowly flicker out until there are just embers left. Jason finds my eyes in the dark. "Should we talk about what happened?"

I brace myself but only nod. "Sure."

"Look. I know I said what I said last summer, and then everything with Liv happened, so the timing was never right. But after the other night . . . I just know, Kate. I want to be with you. I want to give this a real try."

My heart hammers in my throat as he tells me how he really feels. I replay what happened in my head, how good it felt, how natural to kiss someone I've known and loved for so very long. But after it was over, it felt more like a completion than a beginning, and I don't know how to explain that.

"You don't have to say anything right now," he says. "I know you're considering a lot of big changes, and I don't want to confuse any of that. Take your time, but just know that I'm here if and when you're ready, okay?" He reaches out and threads his fingers through mine. I let him hold my hand and nod, more confused than ever.

Inside, he pauses before we separate to go to bed. He pulls me into a hug, then cradles my face and kisses me softly on the lips. My body is warm and buzzed from the wine, and his confession swirls in my heart. There are so many things I want to say: how grateful I am for his grace and understanding, for holding me when I needed it, for being there, for letting me rediscover desire, even if it might be short-lived.

But do I want more?

"Good night, Kate." His fingers trail down to my neck and linger around my collarbone.

I shiver and stare into his eyes. "Good night, Jason."

The next morning I wake later than usual, as I have the day off. Jason is leaving today, but I figure we can go for a morning hike and maybe get breakfast before he takes off. When I emerge from the bedroom, I don't hear him. I check his room, but it's devoid of his stuff. On the front table is a hastily scribbled note.

K,

I didn't want to wake you. My mom had a minor emergency, so I need to get back for Ayana. Thank you for letting me come into your new world. I am so happy that you are reclaiming yourself and that you have found such a safe space to do it in.

Seeing you here has made me realize that I, too, have been afraid of change. I'm holding so tightly to my business because I don't know what is on the other side of it. I've kept everything the same—the business, the house—because I keep thinking that's what Shelby would have wanted. But my life has changed, and so have I. You've reminded me of that, Kate.

Time has passed, and I am more than just a business owner and Ayana's father. What happened between us cracked open something inside me that I needed to see too. That I can feel things for someone besides Shelby, and that it's not a betrayal to her memory.

I have to believe that all these years later, she would want me to move on, to maybe have a partner someday and give Ayana a mother.

I've cherished these few days here with you, and I will always cherish what happened between us. I hope it's the start of something, Kate, but I want you to know that our friendship comes first. I will always be your best friend, I will always love you, and I will always be here for you, whether you live in Serenbe, Nashville, or Timbuktu. (But please don't move to Timbuktu. I can't afford the airfare.) Please don't forget how resilient you are.

I just want you to know that I choose you. I want a life with you, but I don't want you to feel any pressure to decide. I'll be at home, waiting. Take as long as you need.

PS: Tell Ian I said goodbye. He's a good one, Kate. I know you're in good hands as long as you're in Serenbe.

Yours,

J

I fold the note in half and tuck it into my nightstand drawer, a few tears splashing my cheeks. I make a cup of coffee, start a fire, and curl up on the couch. I think about Jason and Ayana, about Olivia, about the choices I've made, some good, some bad. I think about all that I've built in Nashville. Then I think about Ian and what we are building together, here. Am I ready to give all that up?

As I sit, the questions come, one after another, questions I'm not sure I'm ready or able to answer. I close my eyes and cradle my coffee mug to my chest and let my thoughts linger on Liv. Being her mother was the privilege of my life, and like so many privileges, you don't realize how lucky you are until it's too late. All she ever wanted was for me to experience more fun and joy in my life, more play, more happiness.

Is it finally my time to do just that?

Though it's only been roughly six months since she passed, it feels like six years. When she died, I woke up—to my life, to what was working, and most definitely to what was not. While it would be so easy to give up on moving forward, to just stay in bed as I did those first few months and go dark, I know I have an obligation to find a new way to live.

I owe it to my daughter, yes. But really, I owe it to myself.

Yet when I search my soul and think about how I want to live or with whom, I'm not sure what—or who—I see on the other side.

And I'm not sure what I'm willing to risk to find out.

16

EVERY YEAR LIV AND I PICK OUT OUR TREE AT SECRET
Gardens, a nursery that transforms into a holiday wonderland during
the month of December.

Normally, Jason and Ayana come too, but they got their tree weeks
ago. Since Liv is mostly confined at home because of her cast, she's
been lost to a sea of video games, drawing, and time with Michael, so
it's nice to be out and about.

We grab food at Tennfold, our neighborhood pizza joint, and sit
outside under the heaters so Waffles can join. Liv keeps sneaking him
bits of crust and giggling, even when I remind her that he doesn't need
to eat human food.

When we pull into Secret Gardens, Liv chats to Waffles. "This
is the best place on earth to get a tree," she says. "You'll see." She
grips his leash before giving it to me, and we spill out of the car as I
hand her a single crutch—since she can now bear slight weight on her
cast—and we make our way toward the small scrap of space outlined
in outdoor globe string lights. Decorated wreaths hang among the
freshly cut Christmas tree selection, which, with just a couple of days
to go before Christmas, is slim. Two handmade benches surround a

small firepit so kids can roast marshmallows while their parents shop. Liv hobbles inside the tiny store that resembles a gingerbread house to claim her free cocoa. Waffles is overly excited and yaps and bounds around, and I pray he doesn't knock anything over.

While Liv gets her cocoa, I peruse the trees and, as always, balk at the high prices. I bypass the remaining normal trees and head toward the land of misfits. Liv meets me, cup of cocoa in one hand, crutch in the other. "Ooh, so many to choose from," she says. She slurps her cocoa, eyeing each tag, and then falls instantly in love with a scrawny tree named Bee Gee.

"Bee Gee!" she exclaims, mispronouncing Gee with a hard *G*.

"It's Bee *Gee*," I say. "Like a *J*. This tree is named after a band."

"No, it's Bee *G-G-Gee*."

"Fine. Pronounce it how you want, but let's look around a bit before we decide."

She stomps her crutch and stands firmly by her tree. "Mama, I feel a connection to this tree. I've never felt such a connection. She *needs* us."

I roll my eyes. "You realize you say that literally every single year."

"And every single year we have the best tree ever, right?" She downs her cocoa and crinkles the white paper cup in one fist. "So can we get her?"

"Fine," I sigh.

Waffles barks. I tell the workers which tree we want, and we head to the back of the tree lot to take a posed picture with props. Liv takes an exorbitant amount of time sorting through the box of holiday goods. I grab a large candy cane and put a hat on Waffles. Bee Gee stands between us as Liv hobbles out in a Santa coat, reindeer headband, and elf mask. She's wrapped her crutch in garland. We pose for our picture, and then I instruct them how much to cut off the end.

The worker saws off a thick ring of the trunk and spears it with a green hook to make our yearly ornament. Liv takes it and sniffs. "Heaven," she says.

We forgo the netting and drive home, stray needles flying, singing carols all the way. With the addition of Waffles, everything feels more festive this year. However, since Liv can't help me, I have to wrangle the tree inside the basement myself, and she begins laughing at her pathetic attempts to help.

"Don't make me laugh!" she says. "My muscles turn to noodles." She drops her end, unsteady on the crutch, and Waffles twists his leash as he runs around her in a circle.

"Waffles!" I set down my end and unwind Waffles before dragging the tree inside the door.

The next twenty minutes consist of untangling Christmas tree lights, getting the tree in the stand, and then letting Liv hang all her favorite ornaments. It's taken me a while to let go of my OCD as Liv places ornaments almost directly on top of each other, so that our tree always presents as a cluttered, jumbled mess, but it's come to be one of the things I love most.

After, as is our tradition, we make chocolate chip pecan cookies and eat them, still piping hot, while we watch *Elf.*

"Mama." Liv licks chocolate off her fingers, and I wipe a smear from her cheek.

"Yes, my love?" I've been so preoccupied with Michael, Jason, work, and even Waffles that it's taken me away from Liv and what's important—what I have now. I stroke her tangled, curly hair, and my fingers snag on a knot.

"Ow!" She pulls away, and Waffles snorts and burrows deeper into my side. "Could Papito come over and watch with us?"

"What?" I pause the movie before it starts. "But this is our tradition."

"I know, but it's Christmastime, and he's all alone." She glances guiltily at her iPod with a tiny frown.

"Did you text him that he could come over?" I gesture for her to give me the iPod so I can see the text exchange. Sure enough, she texted him when we got to Secret Gardens. I consider how to handle this. I don't want to scold her just because she wants her father here, but selfishly I want to carry on the tradition with just the two of us.

I know boundaries have been blurred since he's been in town, but she's right. He's in town, and he's alone. Before I can tell her it's okay, there's a tentative knock on the back door, as if the two of them have timed this entrance. Momentarily I consider how everything would change if Michael truly re-enters our lives, how all of our previous traditions with just the two of us will expand and shift.

She cranes her head around, motioning to me. "Don't let him stand out there! It's freezing."

I plaster a smile on my face—my annoyed smile, as Liv calls it—and open the door.

"Well, hello." I swing it wide so he can step through. He has a bottle of wine and smells of the cold. A tiny stuffed animal is tucked under his arm.

"How are my girls?"

"Papá! You're just in time for *Elf*!"

"*Mi favorito*," he says.

I roll my eyes and close the door. *Christmas Vacation* is actually his favorite, but I don't argue. I remind myself that I loved this man; I built a life with this man; I made a baby with this man. It's just what came after that still stings.

Liv squeezes the stuffed animal to her chest in appreciation and makes room for Michael on the couch. He takes my spot, and much to my horror, Waffles burrows in next to him, resting his furry face on his lap.

Traitor.

Liv explains the recipe for the cookies—*our* cookies—and Michael grabs a couple. I take the bottle of wine from him, open it, and hand him a glass. Michael and Liv snuggle, giggling, just like Liv and I were doing not five minutes ago.

Liv returns her attention to the movie. I glance behind the couch at the Christmas tree, its stark branches now loaded with ornaments, handmade green-and-red paper chains, silver beads, and way too many lights.

Beneath the tree, there's already one gift from Michael that he brought from Mexico City. Every year he sends a nutcracker hand-crafted by a local artisan. It's Liv's favorite present, and she looks forward to opening that sacred package, insisting that her nutcrackers will spring to life on Christmas Day. When she was little, I used to move them around the house and write little notes for her. I haven't even thought about Christmas Day this year, how we will share time, presents, and attention. At the end of the day, I know this is about Olivia and what is best for her, which is definitely having her father in her life, but it's like she's forgotten all those years he decided he was too busy.

As Will Ferrell ventures to New York, I lose myself to the movie, the cookies, the tree, Liv's giggles, and being exactly where I should be. But in the back of my mind, a nagging worry blunts the festive cheer.

What if Michael disappears and breaks her heart—and mine—all over again?

SIXTEEN

IAN DRIVES ME TO A CHRISTMAS TREE FARM TWENTY minutes outside of Serenbe.

I insist that I don't need a Christmas tree this year. Plus, decorating the tree with Liv was always such a fun tradition, I'm not sure I want to do it without her. It is already so close to Christmas, and personally, I'd love to skip the entire holiday and start fresh in the new year. Even though Serenbe is as festive as any cheesy holiday movie, I've decided to have a low-key Christmas Day at the cabin, though my mother and Jason want me to come home—Jason especially. He has been giving me space, but we talk almost daily, and I can hear the longing in his voice, the desire for something more.

As Ian bumps along the back roads, I admire all the open fields and aggressively decorated houses. Finally, we pull into a Christmas tree farm with a wooden sign nailed to a tree. Ian drives down a long stretch of dirt road and parks. He hops out of the truck, pulls on some gloves, and grabs his saw.

"You mean business," I comment as I tug my beanie over my ears.

"Yep," he replies.

The more Ian and I have been spending time together, the more

I'm coming to understand his demeanor. He's not as loud or boister-
ous as Jason, but he has a knowing about him that translates to quiet
confidence. It is beyond refreshing. Though he has yet to resume the
conversation we started at dinner weeks ago, I'm hoping with time
he'll feel safe enough to open up to me.

We walk through rows of robust emerald trees. The fresh, woody
aroma of pine reminds me of how much I've always loved this time of
year. When I was young, it was always just me and my mom, which
set a perfect foundation for a slew of Christmas traditions between
mother and daughter. It had thrilled me to pass our familial customs
down to Liv. The tree hunting, the baking, the ice skating, the festive
movies. It was always one of the happiest times of the year for us.

As I assess the different shapes and sizes, I stop at the six-foot trees
and tip my face toward the sky. The moon is colossal, buttery yellow,
and nearly full. It hangs, suspended like a plate, in the bone-chilling,
inky night. I marvel at its beauty, then turn back to the task at hand,
guided by the twinkle lights that outline the farm.

"Okay, you win. This is pretty magical," I say.

"Right?" Ian walks alongside me, tugging on branches to test
needle strength.

I pass the perfectly symmetrical trees and search for my misfit.
Every year Liv and I would find the most unloved tree in the bunch—a
bald spot in the back, wonky, wilting branches, a tilted trunk, or
a total Charlie Brown outcast—and we would give it a home. Liv
attached to the tree as if it were a friend, talking to it while we decorated, or when she fed it water and its Christmas tree cocktail. Finally,
I spot it off to the side. It's fat and far too short. Liv would love it.

"This one," I call.

Ian lumbers over and smirks. "You sure?" He gestures behind
him. "Plenty of better ones over there."

"I'm sure."

"Then do the honors." He hands me the saw.

I've never cut down my own Christmas tree. I grip the saw and Ian directs me where to cut. I hack into the wood, sawing back and forth, the metal teeth finding their rhythmic hum. It is strangely cathartic as I make progress, and eventually the blade flies cleanly through to the other side as wood chips spray the earth.

Ian steadies the bulk of the tree in his palm and drags it back to the checkout area. Two workers in Santa hats feed it through the netting machine, and then Ian drops it into the bed of his truck.

"Your turn," I say.

"Nah, I'm good this year," he says, removing his gloves. "This is about you."

I look at him. "Oh no. If I get a tree, you get a tree. Them's the rules."

He rolls his eyes and tugs his gloves back on. By now he knows there's no chance he's going to win. If I set my mind to something, I'll do anything to make it happen. Though I haven't been to Ian's cabin, he's told me his ceilings are vaulted, so we make our way to the ten-foot tree lot.

"That's a lot of tree," I say as I gauge the especially tall ones.

"Yep." He circles around each tree until we both spot the perfect one at the same time. It's full, sturdy, and screams, *Decorate me!* We glance at each other, and he nods. "She's a stunner."

I watch him crouch and saw expertly, wondering how many times he did this with his family before he and his wife divorced. All those years I took for granted—Christmas shopping, getting a tree, hanging the ornaments. I simply assumed I would have a lifetime of such memories with my girl.

After it's netted, we carry the tree to the truck, and then Ian insists on paying for both. We each down a cup of hot cocoa and stare at the stars, which are unobstructed and infinite. I sigh into the air. "Thank you for this," I say. "I wasn't feeling very festive, though I'm quickly learning that's going to have to change if I'm to survive December in Serenbe."

"You're catching on quick." Ian smiles. "And you're very welcome." His smile warms me to my core.

"I remember being shocked by the holiday cheer when I moved here," he says. "It all just seemed over the top. But now, I don't know. I almost look forward to it." He crumples his cup and then breathes into his cupped palms for warmth.

I might look forward to it too, if it wasn't a constant reminder of all I've lost. I adjust my coat, down the last of my cocoa, and then we wordlessly walk back to the truck. He blasts the heat, and we cruise back toward home, both of us lost in comfortable silence. He finds some old Christmas tunes on the radio, and I enjoy the moment, thinking maybe he's right. I can still love my favorite time of year, bask in memories with Liv, and perhaps create some new traditions . . . in time.

Back at the cabin, Ian helps unload the tree and gets it inside, where, to my surprise, there's a tree stand, a tree skirt, and a box of ornaments in the corner by the window. I stop and turn. "Where did those come from?"

His cheeks, ruddy from the cold, color even more. "Don't be mad, but I may have called in some reinforcements." He chuckles. "Mainly Monica. That woman would walk through fire for you."

My heart warms thinking of Monica barking commands to all our friends to pull this off for me. "How thoughtful," I say.

We balance the tree in the stand and adjust it a few times to get it straight. Lovingly, I sort through each ornament, clearly hand-me-downs from the community. "These are so beautiful." I think about my own ornaments tucked away in my garage. Liv had so many favorites: The delicate glass moon. The polar bear. The mini nutcracker. The peanut M&M. The Christmas tree made from Q-tips. Tears burn my eyes, but I blink them away. Deeper in the bucket, I find some white twinkle lights and hold them up. "Want to stay and help?"

He nods and asks for the lights. I put on an old Bing Crosby record, pour us each a glass of wine, start a fire, and then we work. One of my favorite things about Ian is how easy it is to be in his company. We can talk—even if I'm the one doing most of the talking—but we can also be quiet, and it's not awkward. Just peaceful.

He wraps the lights around the tree in record time. "Here goes nothing," he says. He plugs them in, and my short, wide tree sparkles to life.

"Perfect." I hang the first ornament, an antique glass ball with red, blue, and silver glitter, which flakes onto my palm. "I'd love to know the stories behind each of these. Where they came from and what they meant to each person who gave them to me."

"Well, let's see." He digs around. "Ah." He pulls out a half-moon made from delicate glass and glitter, and I gasp, as it is a near replica of my ornament back home.

I take it from him and trace the face. "I have one just like this. Maybe it's a long-lost twin." I can't help but wonder if it's a sign from Liv—if she somehow had a hand in bringing this ornament here to me as a reminder of some of our best memories together. I hang it on a sturdy branch, and we go back and forth telling fictitious stories about the ornaments. All too soon, the bucket of ornaments is empty. We stand back to admire our work.

"This might be one of my favorite trees," I say.

"So this was a good idea?" He strokes his beard.

"A great idea. I always wanted to take Liv to a real tree farm, but instead we went to a nursery right by our house."

We ran out of time.

Ian wraps an arm around my shoulder and pulls me tight. I rest my head on his chest and sigh. "I know," he says. "I know."

We stand like that, admiring the tree, the fire crackling, the record having long since stopped. Finally, I step back and look up. "Okay. Ready?"

"For what?" He stares down at me, his eyes twinkling, his face relaxed, and I feel a stirring of lust and something deeper.

"To decorate yours."

He shakes his head. "I don't know if I have it in me tonight, Kate."

"Nope." I shake my head. "It's happening."

He sighs dramatically. "Not going to win this one, am I?"

"Not a chance."

Ian motions to the fire. "We can't leave the fire going. Let's stay until it's out." He glances at his empty wine glass. "Another glass while we wait?"

A thrill wraps its way around my heart. It has been so long since I've felt so at home with a man besides Jason, though a tiny part of me feels as if I'm betraying something. Jason is back home, waiting patiently for me, and I'm here, eager for the possibility of something more with another man.

I uncork another bottle and curl up beside Ian on the couch. The windows are frosted from the cold, impending snow heavy in the air. The fire warms my back as we silently sip.

"So tell me something." Ian sets his wineglass on the coffee table and folds his hands across his stomach. "You and Jason. There's really nothing there?"

Can he read my mind? I open my mouth to say no, and then I

think about what happened between us and wonder how honest I should be. "Jason and I have always been just friends," I say.

He seems to consider my statement. "When he was here, it seemed like maybe it was something more."

I nod and weigh my options, wondering if I should tell him about Jason's feelings, about the kiss, but something tells me not to. "I get that. We're very close." I quickly change the subject. "I know you said you don't have time to date, but you're such a catch, Ian. You should put yourself back out there."

His cheeks redden. "It's not just that I don't have time," he finally says. "My wife cheated on me. Broke my damn heart. I've had a hard time trusting anyone since then, if I'm being honest."

I swallow a big gulp of my wine, grateful I didn't tell him about Jason. "I'm sorry. That must have been hard." I think about our conversation over dinner and wonder if he feels close enough to me to open up now. "You remember when you were here for dinner?"

"Of course."

"It felt like you were going to tell me something important."

He stares into his wine for a while, then gives the smallest of nods. "I was." He gestures around him. "But I don't want to spoil the mood."

"How could you spoil the mood?"

"Because what I have to say is . . . heavy. It's something I should have told you sooner, but I haven't wanted to bring it up."

"Okay." I wait patiently, though I can see the war he's waging in his head. "Well, now you have to tell me."

Ian opens his mouth, closes it, as the seconds tick by. The fire dwindles into a glowing collection of embers and ash. "I really do want to confide in you, Kate. But tonight's not the night. Can we leave it at that?"

I attempt to keep my face passive, but the lack of trust really hurts. "Okay." I sit up. "Your turn now?"

He looks at his phone and yawns. "Maybe a rain check? I don't even know where my lights and ornaments are."

Once again I'm disappointed, but I don't want to push. "Fine, but promise you'll decorate it."

"I promise."

He groans as he stands, shaking out a stiff right knee. I take his wineglass and bring them both to the kitchen before walking him to the door.

"Thank you for tonight," I tell him. "I really needed it."

"My absolute pleasure. It's nice to see you smile."

"It's nice *to* smile," I say. Our eyes lock, and slowly I step into a hug. It takes him by surprise, but he puts his arms around me, and I feel completely at home. I fit snugly against his broad chest and my body aches for more. I step back, startled at how good he feels.

"Have a good night, Kate."

"You too, Ian." I close the door and turn to gaze at my tree, feeling strangely content but missing him the moment he's gone.

17

JASON'S ANNUAL CHRISTMAS PARTY IS IN FULL SWING BY the time I arrive.

The gym is strung with twinkle lights outside and in. Mistletoe hangs in vibrant green clumps every few feet so that couples constantly stop and kiss. Helium balloons dance along the ceiling, jostling each other for space. Their shiny gold strings drift down, tickling the tops of people's heads. It's hard to see through all the Santa hats, trays of Christmas cookies, flutes of champagne, and endless bodies crammed into Jason's modest space.

Liv and Ayana are with Michael tonight at my house. When I get inside, Jason's nowhere to be found. I shuffle through all the fit bodies he helped create, wondering if I should have worn something more casual. I glance down at my sequined jumpsuit and bright pink heels. Finally, I find Jason in his office, furiously signing what looks like a contract.

"Knock, knock."

He jumps and turns in his chair, a Santa hat askew on his head. "Jesus, Baker. You scared me to death." His eyes travel over my outfit appreciatively. "You look festive."

I fix his hat. "So do you." I glance at the contract. "What's that?"

He flips it over and pushes it aside. "Just work stuff."

"At your party?"

"The work of a business owner never ends."

I don't press him on it. Recently he confided his business hasn't been as profitable and he's thinking of selling. Part of me hates the idea of Jason selling his business, but the other part thinks it would open new doors of possibility for him.

He folds his hands behind his head. His cheeks are flushed and he's looking at me as if I'm something to be devoured. That familiar spark of desire reminds me why I'm here.

"Your gym looks like Santa threw up in it."

"Just the look I was going for." He stands and tucks an errant hair behind my ear, and I shiver.

"Cold?"

"No." My heart is beating much too fast. We gaze at each other as the energy crackles between us. I step closer, this time looping my arms around his neck.

He lets out a small moan and places his hands on my waist. His large, warm fingers dance across the expanse of my lower back, traveling up and then around to cup the back of my neck and tug me toward him.

"May I?" His lips hover near mine, and everything quiets. The music blaring beyond the door. The sharp peals of laughter. The incessant Christmas jingles that people belt on a repetitive loop. The possibility of making a monumental mess of our friendship or unleashing the start of something spectacular.

"Yes." I close my eyes, leaning in as his lips find mine.

Someone knocks on the door, and I quickly step back.

"Jase, we need you out here for the raffle." A young blonde with a mistletoe headband smiles adoringly at him and turns the wattage down a bit when she assesses me. "They're getting a little rowdy out there."

"Cool, be out in a sec." He lifts and drops his hand quickly and then aggressively scratches the back of his head beneath his Santa hat. "Great timing."

"What's with the cute nickname, *Jase*?" I tease once she's gone. "Who is she?"

"Marilyn. Working to be assistant manager." He rubs the back of his neck.

I press into his shoulder. "Ooh, does she like you? You're rubbing the back of your neck. That's a tell of yours, you know."

He immediately drops his hand. "I do not have any tells."

I tick them off on my fingers. "Clearing your throat, averting your eyes, rubbing the back of your neck. All tells."

He relents. "Fine. She did ask me out, yes."

A spasm of jealousy seizes me so unexpectedly that I suck in too sharply and begin to cough. Jason claps me on the back until my throat is clear. My eyes water, and I rub my chest a few times.

"Tell me how you really feel."

I grapple with what to say. Do I tell him that it bothers me, that I don't want him to date anyone else? "What did you say?"

"I said I'm interested in someone else." He gives me that look again before collapsing back in his desk chair. He removes the hat to reveal hair mussed and adorable. Deciding that *this is happening now*, I turn, lock his office door, and lean against it, looking at him intently.

"She means business," he whispers. I stride over to his chair and straddle him, but my heel gets caught in the corner of the chair, and we almost topple over as I wrench my knee at an unnatural angle.

"My knee!" I yelp. He rights us, and I take a breath and smooth my hands through his hair.

"Ow, ow!"

My ring gets tangled in a clump of his hair, and we spend two minutes getting it out. His jeans are rough on my thin jumpsuit, and I adjust to find a comfortable spot.

"This is off to a great start," I whisper.

"Just go with it," he whispers back.

Carefully, I lean in. The pressure of my body sends him catapulting backward in the chair, and I press into him harder, loving the feeling of my chest against his. My hands slide up to his face as he is nearly horizontal.

"Oh shit!" He reaches for his desk, but we are already toppling backward and go crashing to the floor. His head thuds on the carpet, and I land on top of him, my torso smothering half his face.

I roll off him. He rubs his nose as I examine my sore knee. We make eye contact, then laugh until tears stream down our faces. There's another sharp bang on the door, and we both sit up, the chemistry dissolving between us.

"That went well," he says, helping me up.

I wipe the tears from my eyes and he tugs me into a hug. We stay like that for a few moments. His heart thuds against my ear. He pulls back and kisses me on the forehead, and I readjust his Santa hat. "Let's get out there," he says.

I nod. He unlocks the door and we spill into the crowd. I grab a drink and step outside to get some fresh air and perspective. I pull out my phone, which has been on silent, and find I have an urgent text from Michael.

When you can, please come home. It's urgent.

Panicked, I call Michael, but it goes straight to voice mail. Now I'm alert and worried. Immediately I think of the girls.

I text him back and tell him I'm on my way. Dread tramples my body and floods me with adrenaline. I head back inside to find Jason. I attempt to keep myself calm as I fight through the happy, oblivious crowd. He sees me coming and offers a smile until he recognizes the serious look on my face.

"We have to go," I say. "It's the girls." He follows me wordlessly into the night. My phone buzzes in my hand, but it's not Michael, just a friend with a holiday text.

I climb into Jason's car, just wanting to get home, wanting to see Liv.

We pull up to the house less than twenty minutes later, and from the outside, everything looks fine.

I jog up to the door and stick my key in the lock, Jason right behind me. I step inside to a dark living room, and a sick feeling spreads through my gut. A moment later, the lights come on, and Ayana and Liv scream, "Surprise!" at the top of their lungs. I slap a hand to my chest as I look at all the paper decorations. The girls are wearing fancy headbands and dresses.

It takes a moment to go from scared to relieved, but I stare between them. "What is going on? Where is Michael?" They look at each other and giggle, smashing their fingers to their mouths to keep whatever secret this is.

"Follow me, madam," Liv says in a grown-up voice. She extends her arm and I take it. She hobbles toward the stairs carefully, and we navigate down to the basement. Jason follows uncertainly behind me.

I can hear Billie Holiday crooning from the TV downstairs. When I hit the bottom step, I see the Christmas tree, candles, and wine on the coffee table. Michael is in a suit, and he's looking at me in a way I haven't seen in years.

"Before you say anything . . ."

He rushes to me, and I'm so confused, I don't even register what he's about to do. He drops to one knee, and I audibly gasp. The girls take that as a good sign, though I see Jason visibly stiffen beside me. I glance between these two men and then focus solely on Michael. Michael, my first husband. Michael, my ex-husband. Michael, who is about to propose again.

"I know this seems crazy," he begins, staring earnestly into my eyes, "but marrying you was the smartest decision I ever made, Kate. Letting you go was the worst."

The girls are practically hopping up and down on the couch cushions, waiting for me to scream *yes*.

"I promise to love you, to be here for you, to be a family with you, for as long as I live. It's you, Kate. You are the one I want, the one I love. It's always been you."

I am floored by the bold move. We haven't talked enough to decide something like this, have we?

I stand trapped between two men, one who is offering me my old life back and one who is offering me something new. Michael grips my hand and finally asks, "Katherine Anne Baker, will you marry me . . . again?"

"Say yes, Mama! Say yes!" Liv is bouncing up and down so excitedly, careful of her leg, her cheeks stretched back in the biggest smile I've ever seen. I don't want to disappoint her; I don't want to ruin anything. Jason stares at his shoes, and I know, in that moment, I am going to hurt someone.

But the one person I'm not willing to hurt anymore is myself. I search my heart, listen to my intuition, and steady myself to respond.

I open my mouth to say one simple word, and I know it will change everything.

"No."

Michael's face visibly crumples and his eyes flick to Liv. I look her way too, and she immediately frowns. He grips my hand. "Just think about it, *mi amor*. Think about how great we could be again, if only we could try."

"Jason, could you take the girls upstairs for a second so I can talk to Michael privately?"

Jason springs out of whatever horrified trance he was in and claps his hands. "Come on, girls! Let's go upstairs."

Liv rips one of the decorations she made and hobbles toward the stairs. "You always ruin everything!" she screams. She struggles up the stairs, and Ayana is deathly silent behind her. She knows that when Liv is in a mood, it's best to give her time.

Michael finally gets up off his knee and shakes it out. "I'm sorry. I shouldn't have done this in front of Olivia. I just thought . . ."

"You thought I'd say yes."

He looks sheepish but stares at his shoes. "I did, Kate. Am I wrong?"

I gesture to the couch and we both sit. "Mike, we've been on one date since you've been here, and most of that time we just talked about Liv."

"I know, but it's me. It's you. We don't need to go on a bunch of dates to know that we love each other."

I grip his hand. "I do love you, Michael. I will always love you, but I feel like you made this decision without even talking to me about it. I mean, *marriage*? We aren't anywhere near that."

He scrubs a hand over his face and lets it drop heavily into his lap. "I've ruined this again, haven't I?"

"You haven't ruined anything, Michael. I just think you're doing what you always do when you get passionate."

He scoots closer to me. "But we're so good together, Kate. What I'm offering is a life, a *real* life, a chance for us to be a family again."

"I have a real life," I say.

"Oh, my love, I know you have a real life. But imagine being together, what that life would look like."

"Tell me what that would look like, Mike. Do you expect us to move to Mexico City?"

His uncomfortable silence says that yes, he does expect that. "They have some great jobs there, Katie. I've already looked into some positions and . . ." He trails off when he sees the look on my face.

"This is what I'm talking about, Mike. *You* thought it would be best to live in Mexico City. *You* looked into jobs for me, but you never talked to me or Liv about how that might affect us. You never even stopped to consider that what might be best for you is not what's best for us."

"Us being a family is what's best for us!" His voice thunders through the room, and the girls, who are chatting about something upstairs, suddenly go quiet.

I remember all the ways he used to make this very argument, always manipulating me into moving wherever the wind took him because it was *what was best*. His work, his needs, his desires were always more important than mine. But not this time. I was always capable of standing on my own two feet, but somehow he made me feel like I couldn't. I think I'd forgotten that.

"I know this isn't what you want to hear, Mike, but maybe I don't want to stay stuck in the past."

The devastation sweeps across his face, dark and dramatic. "Kate, please don't do this. Not again. Liv needs me."

"So be there for her," I say. "Be the best father you can possibly be."

I study his face, one I used to kiss and touch. I thought letting him back into my life might be the right thing, but I realize now it isn't. Not romantically. That chapter is done.

I grab his hand again. "I think it's time for us to write a new story."

He traces my hand with his thumb for a long time before meeting my gaze. "Okay, *mi amor*," he finally says. "Okay."

SEVENTEEN

THE SERENBE CHRISTMAS PARTY IS THE CULMINATION OF the holiday season.

Over the last few days, I've attended the holiday parade with a group of friends (where a not-so-chubby local played Santa), a beautiful rendering of *A Christmas Carol* at the Serenbe theater with Monica and her sister, Christmas caroling in every hamlet with Hank and Laurence, various house parties with all the locals, cookie drives with Ian, and the lighting of the Serenbe tree. Liv would be over the moon with all the festivities and traditions.

Now I'm at one of the locals' house parties—some hotshot movie producer whose home literally takes up an entire chunk of the street. By now everyone knows I've lost my daughter, that I'm an agricultural engineer, and that I've been playing farmer for the last few months.

Tonight I've tried to be more than just Farmer Kate, however, in a hunter-green velvet dress that shows off my hard-earned figure, paired with earrings handmade by women in Kenya. I feel good tonight, beautiful even. Plus, I've had an afternoon coffee to ensure I'm talkative, as the farm has been wearing me out lately.

Monica approaches with her friend Wendy, who runs a local

nonprofit. She hands me a flute of champagne. "You look sensational, Kate."

"Yes, dear. Those earrings are just divine," Wendy adds.

"Oh, thank you." I clutch one of the earrings and smile. "So do you two." I glance around the packed room, hoping to see Ian. "This is quite the party."

Monica snorts. "Every year this party moves to the home of someone richer with more toys to show off." She rolls her eyes and leans in, her ruby-red lips parting to whisper, "So what's the deal with you and Ian? I thought for sure you were getting it on with Jason, but now I'm not so sure."

I swallow my champagne too fast, the bubbles burning my throat. "What? Nothing is going on with me and Ian."

Wendy and Monica give each other a look. "Okay, whatever you say."

Monica waves to someone, her diamond ring twinkling in the light, and mouths hello.

Wendy leans in. "We'd really love to see you more outside the farm, Kate. I know you're an engineer, and Serenbe could really use your skill set. Especially with you being a woman and all." She rambles off a few jobs they need help with, and I bite my lip, not having the heart to explain the difference between an agricultural engineer and a civil engineer. "Anyway, we just love what you've done with the farm. And for Ian too," she adds. "He's been like himself again since you've been here."

I take another sip of the champagne as the bubbles pop and fizz in my throat, wondering if he's already here. "What do you mean?"

"Oh, I just mean he hasn't been himself since . . . well, *you know*. The two of you have so much in common. It's done him so much good to have you here."

Monica gives Wendy a sharp look, and she snaps her mouth closed.

I assume she means the divorce. "Well, I've really grown to care about him." As I say it, I realize just how much those words ring true. "As a friend," I add before they can get any ideas.

Wendy blinks at me with her large brown eyes while Monica chats with another local, Patsy. Wendy's fake lashes have come loose at her inner eyelid, and she quickly fingers them back into place. She glances over her shoulder to see if Monica is listening. "And he cares about you too, my dear. We all worried he'd never recover after the accident. But he's coming back to us, slowly but surely. And we have *you* to thank for that." She squeezes my arm and excuses herself to go talk to Steve Nygren, who just walked in. People flock to him like some sort of god. Suddenly I feel like I can't breathe.

Ian was in an accident? Everything shrinks as I try to figure out what she means. I rack my brain to remember if Ian ever mentioned an accident, but he hasn't.

I float through the rest of the party in a daze, making small talk with some of my friends and counting down the minutes until I can go home, throw on some comfy clothes, and drink a cup of tea. Usually this time of year I'd be at Jason's annual Christmas party or snuggled up with Liv.

When it seems the party is waning, I place my champagne flute on a table and find my way to the exit. I push past warm bodies until I'm outside. The arctic air stings my bare shoulders and I drape my wrap over my arms. A light snow has started to fall, and I tip my face to the sky, letting the snowflakes dance and melt across my skin. The streetlamps illuminate the way they swirl in the night.

I walk through the snow toward the cabin, past familiar streets and shops, until I get to the fork. I know Ian's cabin sits back to the left, tucked away on a private acre lot. My feet throb, almost numb. I don't want to show up unannounced, but I have to know what Wendy was talking about. Thoughts whip past me with the snow as I consider just going home.

But before I know it, I'm moving left, the sting of the cold making me walk faster. When I get to his door, I stomp the snow from my heels, suddenly self-conscious, and knock loudly, attempting to peer inside a window. Just when I'm about to try around back, he opens the large wooden door. His flannel shirt is unbuttoned, revealing an expanse of well-built chest. A glass of whiskey dangles from his fingers. His eyes are alive and sharp, as always. Music croons in the background next to a crackling fire and his large tree stands in the corner, decorated just as promised. I don't even ask if I can come in.

"Okay." He shuts the door and turns. "You okay?"

"I was just at a party," I say, my teeth chattering. "I had an interesting conversation with Wendy."

"Oh yeah?" He offers me a blanket and motions to sit by the fire. "About?"

"You."

He drops into the armchair across from me. "You'll have to be more specific."

I gather the words, again trying to make sense of something I might already know somewhere deep inside. "She said that you haven't been the same . . . since the accident. What accident?"

He goes completely still, his easy demeanor wiped away in an instant. He closes his eyes and drags a hand down his face. "I'm tired, Kate. I don't really want to talk about it now."

But I press on. "But you never want to talk about it, whatever *it* is. And I want to know. I think you owe me that, especially after all I've told you."

He fiddles with his whiskey glass and finally leans forward to set it on his wooden coffee table. "Okay."

I wait, sorting through what he might say next.

He closes his eyes and shakes his head. So much time passes, I figure he's going to decline the offer to talk, just as he did at the cabin, until finally, he speaks. "Three years ago, my ex-wife was bringing Ella to stay with me for the entire summer break. We'd been trying to figure out custody, and Ella wanted to stay longer than just a week or two." He swallows, and I watch his Adam's apple shift up, then down. "My ex, Marcy, she left late at night to get here. Thought she could hit less traffic. I told her she could come the next day, but she had plans in the morning so she wanted to drop off Ella and then get back. A drunk driver . . ." His voice tapers off and he closes his eyes.

My heart pounds as I fill in the gaps. All those silences. His solitude. His withholding. He isn't just a private person; he's been grieving too.

"Killed them both instantly." His voice catches, and he cries into his hand as he covers his mouth. His blue eyes are tortured, recognizable.

You are like me.

I swallow, leveled by this admission, but also confused. "I don't understand," I say. "I've been here for months and you never told me. Why?"

He sighs and wipes his eyes. "Because I didn't want to make it worse for you, Kate. You lost your daughter. I know what it's like. I didn't want to be another reminder."

"Worse for me?" I stand, my heart breaking. "How would you telling me your story have made it *worse* for me, Ian? We could have helped each other, been here for each other, but you lied to me. You let me believe your daughter and wife were still alive." A deep ache spreads through my heart as I realize I don't really know Ian at all.

He gauges me through thick, wet lashes, and I see everything: the pain and agony of losing not only his child but his ex-wife too. Carrying that truth with him every day and knowing that he can never, *ever* bring them back again. I'm sure he has played the what-if game a million times too, that he has blamed himself and the world just like I have. That he gets up every day and wonders if today will be the day he can move on, before realizing that he will never move on. That he will never feel better; he just has to deal with it because it's the hand he's been dealt.

"I didn't lie to you, Kate. I just don't like to talk about it. It's taken me a long time to get to a better place."

"And you think I like talking about it?" My voice booms throughout his living room, over the record. "All this time you've told me all the ways I can heal, and here you are, keeping this horrible secret to yourself?" I don't know why I'm so angry. Maybe it's because I feel like he doesn't trust me the way I trust him; that he can't show me the most vulnerable parts of himself, though he's seen me in my darkest despair. I look at his pained expression and feel a pang of regret. "I'm so sorry for what happened, Ian. But you can't shut me out. You could have confided in me, but you chose to keep me from knowing the most important thing about you."

He stares into his glass, contemplative, and I don't know what else to say. I grab my wrap and head back out into the night, more confused than ever.

The snow falls at a faster clip. The streets are a flurry of white as I fight my way through the flakes and let myself into my cabin. I think of my budding feelings for this man, a man who's been hiding the biggest part of himself. I stare at the small space with all its quirks, gifts, and imperfections, and for the first time in a long time, I miss Nashville. I miss Jason. I miss my mother.

I miss my home.

18

"MAMA, CAN WE WATCH SOMETHING ON OUR OWN?"

Liv calls down from upstairs as I'm setting out our buttery, salted popcorn and a dessert tray of chocolates, homemade cookies, brownies, and Jeni's ice cream with infinite toppings while flipping through Netflix. It is our New Year's Eve tradition—dessert before dinner—followed by pizza.

Jason ran out to pick up the pizzas, and Michael has flown back to Mexico City to ring in the new year with his extended family.

"We're watching a movie together, remember?" I respond. "It's tradition."

"But we want to watch something on our own," she insists. She smacks her crutch against the kitchen floor in protest.

"Too bad, so sad," I call. "You two get down here. These desserts wait for no one."

"Ugh, fine. Poison us with sugar." She makes a dramatic production of sitting on her butt and thumping down the stairs. Ayana walks slowly behind her. "I don't want to watch a movie, though," she adds.

"Tell it to the judge."

We all decide on a funny Christmas movie after watching fifteen previews, and five minutes in, Liv, per usual, is talking up a storm while Ayana quietly watches. I answer her questions and stab the volume up, but she keeps talking. Finally, I launch a piece of popcorn at her, which tumbles off the couch and ends up almost instantaneously in Waffles's mouth.

"Mama, stop! I'm trying to watch the movie." She swipes my reader glasses from the ottoman and puts them on. "I'm very serious. This is me, being serious." She puckers her mouth, squints her eyes, and makes a face as I lob more popcorn at her. Ayana laughs and returns her attention to the movie.

"You better not be impersonating me," I protest. "I do not look like that."

"Shh, you two, I'm trying to watch!" Ayana whispers.

We all get lost in easy banter and eating our dessert, the plot of the movie falling away as we enjoy each other's company. We're settling back into the movie when I hear the upstairs door open and Jason calls down, "Pizza's here!"

"Pizza!" Ayana runs upstairs to help as Liv calls, "Mama is holding me captive downstairs! Help!"

I pause the movie and look down at my cheetah pajamas, covered with popcorn. Is this really how I want to bring in the new year? I decide in an instant that, yes, it is.

After I told Michael no, he thought it was best to head home and get some space. While he was always great at the big, romantic gestures, where he fumbles is in thinking things through. Did he think I would give up my life and home to move to Mexico? I would never ask that of him. Which is why I know, without a doubt, that he's not the one for me.

Liv carefully climbs up the stairs to join Ayana. Waffles licks my hand and barks for more popcorn. Jason peers over the railing of the stairs and gives me a grin.

"Up or down?" he asks, motioning to the box of pizza.

"Down," I say. "Want a drink?"

"Sure." He comes downstairs and sets the pizza on the coffee table, then removes his coat, and I pour him a whiskey at my downstairs bar. I hand it over, and our fingers touch, a small sizzle of electricity racing to my heart. I clear my throat, and he motions to the ravaged dessert bar. "Dessert-before-pizza tradition still intact I see?"

"Yep." I take a bite of my pepperoni pizza and the cheese burns the roof of my mouth. "Thank you, by the way."

"For?" He swallows and wipes his face with a napkin.

"For giving up your New Year's Eve to be with us." I rub Waffles's head.

"Kate, please. Are you kidding? Where else would I be? I love being with you."

The word *love* slides between us, as sharp as a blade. He rattles the ice in his tumbler before knocking back the rest of his drink. "Holidays are always hard without Shelby."

"I know." I squeeze his forearm. "Never really gets easier, does it?"

"I'd like to say yes, but no, not really."

"I'm sorry, Jason." I wonder what that must be like, to still love someone who is no longer here—to live in the same house, carry on the same traditions, but without your other half.

I reach out and cover his hand. "We've been through a lot together. Losing Shelby. Divorce. Adoption. A new proposal, which you were witness to." That warrants a laugh. "I'm lucky to have you."

"Same."

Upstairs, Liv's bedroom door slams, and I sigh. "I've asked Liv a thousand times not to eat in her room."

"They're really growing up, huh?" he comments as he takes another slice of pizza.

"They are." I think of how much has changed since summer, how Michael has shifted the fabric of our relationship, and how nothing will ever be the same. Liv was furious with me when I said no to his proposal. She didn't talk to me for days. Finally, I sat her down and explained why marrying her father again wasn't the right decision for any of us, and she is coming back around. Michael and I are trying to organize a new arrangement where he sees her more, but where the boundaries are also clear.

"Sometimes I just want Liv to stay small and innocent forever. She's so wildly imaginative, so lost in her own world. I keep waiting for her to wake up one day and care what the world thinks of her tangled hair or mismatched clothes, but it hasn't happened yet."

"That's a good thing," Jason says.

I finish my pizza and pull my legs under me, studying my best friend. Though I am emotionally exhausted from turning Michael down, it has helped illuminate how I feel about Jason. "You really mean so much to me."

He is taken off guard by the change in subject, but he puts down his pizza and looks at me. "You mean so much to me too, Kate."

I move a pillow out of the way and scoot closer. "I've been giving this a lot of thought, what's happened these past few weeks . . . with us."

"And?"

And what? While I have been certain about my decision with Michael, I've wavered with Jason. If we were to work out as a couple, so many things would be easier. Our lives fit so seamlessly. However, I would also carry the guilt of dating Shelby's husband, of possibly tarnishing all that we've created if it didn't work out just right. And I could never, ever risk losing what we have.

"I've been thinking a lot about giving this a chance," I finally say. "About what that would mean. About how that would change things."

Upstairs, the staccato punch of Liv's crutch stomps across the kitchen floor as the girls go to get another slice. I look at him and grip his hand. Here is my dearest and oldest friend. He is a good father, a kind soul, the best friend, and everything I should want in a romantic partner. So what am I so scared of?

Before I can say anything else, Ayana and Liv come barreling down the stairs.

"To be continued?" Jason asks, a hopeful look on his face.

"To be continued," I say, patting the couch cushions next to me as the girls spread out to finish the movie.

EIGHTEEN

I'M RUNNING LATE FOR THE NEW YEAR'S EVE PARTY.

After I FaceTime with Ayana and Jason, who are giggly and wear top hats and festive glasses, I slick on some red lipstick, blot my lips, and pile my hair into a messy bun, but it won't stay. I search for bobby pins and remember there's a pile tucked away in my nightstand. I assess my outfit just as there's a knock on my door.

I open it to find Ian on the other side.

We haven't talked since the night of the Serenbe Christmas party. I've been replaying that night again and again, wondering if I was too harsh or insensitive. I lower my arms when he steps in, my hair tumbling around my shoulders. He looks insanely handsome in a traditional tux. His hair is slicked back, his beard freshly trimmed. He extends a bouquet of daffodils, which are my second favorite flower.

"Thank you." He respectfully removes his boots, and I glance at his fuzzy socks, which make me smile. I sink onto the couch. He sits beside me, and I can smell his intoxicating scent—like fir trees and woodsmoke.

"Kate, I wanted to talk to you sooner, but I thought I'd give you some time."

I wait for him to continue. Getting through Christmas was hard, but I made it with lots of tears and wine.

"You were right. I should have told you about the accident sooner, and I'm sorry that I didn't." He tugs on his beard. "After it happened, I talked about it all the time, and now . . . now I just find it's best to move forward as much as I can."

"I understand that, Ian; of course I do. But this is *me*." I reach out and grab his hand, which is warm and rough in mine. "I thought you trusted me."

He threads his fingers through mine, the most intimate act that's happened between us.

"I do trust you," he whispers. "So much." His mouth trembles as emotion fills his eyes. "That's what scares me, Kate. I can't go through it all again. I just can't."

I know exactly what he means. It's all so much. The thought of finding someone and losing them; once you've been through it, it seems easier to never open yourself up to love again.

I scoot closer and pull him against me as he cries. He sharply exhales as my arms encircle his neck. He turns his head and breathes into me, clutching me firmly against his chest, as if he wants me inside him. His whole body shakes as he cries, and I say nothing, just hold him until he's quiet.

I think of how long it's been since I've held a man, and I think of Jason, how many nights I held him after Shelby died, how many moments we shared like this.

As Ian pulls back, something loosens inside me too. Maybe this is why I feel so comfortable here. Why I have such a connection to him and this land. We are the same, he and I. I stare into his piercing eyes.

"I understand exactly what you're going through, Ian. Just let me be here for you. For all of it. Please."

He nods and sighs. "I'll try, Kate. I promise."

I get up and offer him some water, which he drinks in one large gulp. "Thank you." He wipes his eyes with his sleeve and laughs. "I guess I needed that, huh?"

"Yes, you did. Crying is cathartic. I should know. I've been crying for almost seven months straight."

He chuckles and shakes his head. "I guess I thought if I don't talk about it anymore, then I'll be okay. It's been three years, but when I think about it, it seems like it just happened yesterday."

"How old was she?" I ask, sitting beside him.

"Ten." He swallows. "She'd be a teenager now."

Liv will never turn ten. I place a hand on his shoulder. "I'm so sorry for your loss, Ian. Truly."

He sniffs, wipes his nose. "I know. And I'm sorry for yours too."

I reach my hand up and trace his beard, my fingers tickling his jaw. His eyes fall to my mouth, and he licks his full lips. Before I can breathe or decide if this is a good idea or a bad idea, he leans in, his hands gingerly cupping my face as he presses his lips to mine. A complicated emotional wound bursts open between us as he hungrily explores my mouth and neck and then trails kisses across my cheeks and forehead. We lie back on the couch, my body throbbing beneath him as our tongues entwine and our breath unites. It feels so far beyond a first kiss; I never want it to end.

I am breathless when we part. He sits back, almost embarrassed, breathing hard. I adjust my shirt, arrange my hair into a messy bun again, and gaze into his eyes. For some reason, I have been brought here, to this place, to find this man and to reclaim myself. To heal.

I grip his hand and pull him closer. We curl up together, wordlessly, and watch the flames.

"I really do trust you, Kate," he says after a while.

I turn to face him and kiss him softly on the lips, memorizing the taste of him, the perfect way he smells. "I trust you too."

A tingle runs down the length of my arm as I snuggle into him and close my eyes, feeling like this could be the start of something real.

"If we don't leave soon, I don't think we're going to make this party," he whispers.

I laugh and grip my quickly slipping bun. "Would you grab me a few bobby pins? They're in my nightstand. Meanwhile," I say, moon-walking toward the bathroom, "I need to fix my face."

"Look at those moves." He whistles. "Michael Jackson ain't got nothing on you."

I give myself a once-over and then smooth on some red lipstick as I walk back to the living room. "Did you get lost in there?" I call as I gather my hair again, rearranging it on top of my head.

He appears from the bedroom, eyes pensive. In one hand he clutches a small bouquet of bobby pins. In the other is a letter. Not just any letter—Jason's letter.

Oh no. I lower my hand and feign innocence. "What's that?"

"I wasn't snooping," he begins. "The bobby pins were right on top of it, and it wasn't folded." He swallows and looks down at the letter Jason left me, then painfully drags his gaze back to mine. "Anything you need to tell me, Kate?"

"That's not exactly what you think it is," I say, realizing what a horrible, clichéd statement that is. "Can we sit?"

Ian seems to hesitate but finally obliges, though his body language shifts. He sits stiffly next to me, guard up, walls erect.

"I know you asked me if Jason and I were more than friends, and the answer is no," I say. "That part is true."

He's quiet. "But something happened between you?"

I look to my lap and sigh. "It was one night. When he was here. I was upset. I was so tired of grieving, and I wasn't thinking. It was just a kiss," I rush to add. "But then he admitted that he wanted something more."

Ian winces, no doubt questioning what all this means. "And what did you say?"

"I didn't." I swallow. "I've realized that I don't have romantic feelings for Jason. But if that hadn't happened, I don't think I would have been ready for this," I say, gesturing between us. "This is what I want. You are what I want."

He's silent, and I know Ian well enough to know that he has to process things at his own speed. Finally, he speaks. "But I asked you," he says simply. "And you looked me straight in the eye and said no."

"Because I don't have feelings for him."

"But he has feelings for you, Kate. Even I could see that." He gets up, letter in hand, and paces back and forth. "I told you that my wife cheated on me." He stares at the letter. "How important trust is to me."

My stomach clenches. "I know it's important to you. But to be fair, this happened before us." I almost remind him that it's a similar situation; Ian omitted certain details from his life because he thought it would be easier for me—and I did the same for him.

He scans the letter again, folds it, and finally nods. Abandoning his wine, he moves toward the door. "I'm sorry, Kate. I need some air."

My heart crashes against my ribs. "What about the party?"

He won't even look at me. "You should go." He stares at me, his eyes painfully raking across my face. "I'm not really in the mood anymore. I'm sorry." Without another word, he leaves the cabin, and I collapse back against the couch, tears in my eyes. Why did I keep that letter? And why didn't I just tell Ian when he asked me that my relationship with Jason had gotten complicated?

I think about skipping the party altogether, but this night symbolizes too much. It is the end of the hardest year of my life, and I want to commemorate it, even if that means doing it alone. As much as Ian's reaction hurts, and as much as I want to convince him to come with me, I need to do this for myself.

When it's time, I put on my coat, lock the door, and walk the short distance to Mado, where the party is taking place. One of the large event spaces has been transformed into a winter wonderland. Silver and black balloons clog every empty space, and everyone is dressed in their finest. I quickly make the rounds to say hello to Monica, Wendy, Laurence, Patsy, Hank, Josh, Flynn, and Latrice.

Monica pulls me aside. "Where's your hot date?"

"I don't have a hot date," I say, grabbing a champagne flute from a passing tray.

"Ian was supposed to talk to you," she hisses. She lets out a moan. "God, why can't men get anything right?"

I don't tell her that he did show up, or that I blew it by not being honest in the first place. Instead, I exchange niceties with everyone and ask about their holiday. I keep watching the door, hoping maybe he will have a change of heart, but so far he's a no-show. I know texting is futile, as he checks his phone at most once a week.

As the clock nears midnight, I excuse myself and go up on the roof, surprised to see no one else. Everyone is inside, clustered around the oversized TV as the Times Square ball prepares to drop. I pull my wrap a little tighter and walk over to the rail, which gives me a view of Mado and the batch of thick, towering trees. I gaze at the community that's become my home in such a few short months, and I pray I haven't ruined my relationship with Ian. I think of Liv and close my eyes.

"Hi, baby girl," I say. A lump rises in my throat, but I force it down. "This is my first New Year's Eve without you, and I miss you so very much." A few cold tears carve trails down my cheeks. "I've been doing my best to live in a way you'd be proud of, but even so, I'm still making mistakes. I need you to keep me on track," I say. "You were always so good at knowing just what to say or do." I suck in a cold, shaky breath. "I just wish you could give me a sign that you're okay—that wherever you are, you're happy. Could you do that for me, Liv?" My eyes flutter closed again, and I wait—for what, I don't know.

I shiver again, clinging to the rail, and suddenly the sky seems to open up as fat white snowflakes drift down. At first it's just a few flakes, then an assault of white, and I spread my arms wide and twirl around. "My sweet girl." Only she would send me snow. It was my single biggest wish every December we spent in Nashville. I would pray for snow the way children wished for a toy at Christmas. And every year, without fail, it would be sixty-five degrees. But not tonight. At the exact moment I asked for a sign, she sent one.

I tilt my face up to the white, feeling cleansed and whole. I'm getting drenched in snow, blinded by white, but I dare not move. I can hear the rumbling of people inside, the countdown about to ensue. Suddenly, the door behind me bangs open. I turn, hoping for Ian, but I see a little person dashing straight toward me and realize it's Ayana. Jason waves from the door, laughing.

"What in the world?"

Ayana wraps her arms around my stomach and squeezes. "Are you surprised?"

I grip her tightly and drop down to smother her with kisses. "I am so surprised! I've missed you so much."

Jason walks over, hands shoved in his coat, a big smile on his face. "Hey, you."

My heart kicks at the sight of him. Maybe Ian isn't entirely wrong. Is there more here than I'm willing to admit?

"How are you here?" I ask. "I literally just talked to you guys."

"That's why we were laughing," Ayana says. "We were in our rental place here."

I smack Jason's arm and then pull him into a hug. "I'm so happy to see you."

"This is a big day," he says. "It signifies so much."

"It does." Liv used to love New Year's Eve more than Christmas Day. We would stay up late, eating desserts and pizza and watching movies, traveling through time from one year to the next. It always amazed her.

Inside, the countdown begins. "Ten, nine, eight . . ."

Jason links his arm through mine, and we stare at the sky full of snow. "I've missed you, Baker."

"Seven, six, five . . ."

I lean my head on his shoulder. "I've missed you too." The snow cascades over our skin and clothes. I smile and grab Ayana's hand, swinging it back and forth as we count with the crowd.

"Four, three, two . . ."

"Happy New Year!" Ayana screams into the empty air, blowing her kazoo. It honks and dies in the wind.

"Happy New Year, Kate," he whispers. The crowd inside goes wild.

"Happy New Year, Jason."

He leans in, looping an arm protectively around my shoulder, just as fireworks crackle across the sky. Down below, people fan out across the lawn, heads craned toward the sky, a few people dispersing on the roof around us. Breathless and cold, we watch the pops of color pierce through the dome of white.

Out of the corner of my eye, I see someone else dash onto the roof. I turn, clearing snowflakes from my eyes. It's Ian.

He freezes and takes in the scene in front of him—Jason and Ayana on either side of me, our arms entwined around each other—and even from a distance, I can see the hurt in his eyes.

He emits a sigh, stares at his boots, then gives the smallest of nods, as if deciding something. Before I can catch my breath or call out, he pushes back through the door and disappears from sight.

Spring

19

WHEN LIV RETURNS FROM MEXICO CITY AFTER SPRING break, I decide to treat her to a birthday surprise.

I take her to Restoration Hardware for brunch, where she freaks out over all the water fountains and the creamy eggs. Afterward I take her shopping for new clothes before we head to AromaG's for crystals and bath salts, and then we finish by having tea and scones at a local bakery. She is happy and full when we return home, and she hasn't stopped talking about Mexico City and how much she loves it there.

There's a question I don't ask—*would you rather live there?*—because I am so afraid of the answer. I'm coming to understand that with Michael back in our lives, there will be adjustments and compromises, and none of that means there is any sort of parental competition between us. There is room for both of us in Liv's life, and I need to remember that her enthusiasm for one parent doesn't always equate to preference.

After dropping our bags at home, we take Waffles for a walk. Liv is doing better without her cast, and the doctor said exercise is good for her, but not too much. We make a simple loop around the block, and she hums a song as she holds the leash. Her official tenth birthday is tomorrow, and she has decided this year that she just wants a sleepover with Ayana. No big party. No fuss. She and Michael celebrated with the entire family in Mexico City, and she said she's never felt more special in her entire life.

It breaks my heart that I wasn't there, but this is our life now: she will make memories with her father, and she will make memories with me. Unfortunately, I will miss things.

"Do you have any big goals or dreams this year?" I ask as I snap at Waffles to go when he stops to root around in someone's grass.

"Hmm." Liv flattens her tongue against her top lip, a tell that she's thinking hard about something. "I do, actually." She lists them off on her free hand. "I want to get better at Spanish. I maybe want to play soccer, because it isn't as bad as I thought. I want to read ten books. I want to travel to another country besides Mexico. Oh, and"—she looks at me, smiling—"I want you to find your happy ending." She adjusts the necklace Michael gave her from Lucia for her birthday.

My heart expands as I listen to my daughter. A year ago, she wouldn't have had such goals for herself, and I realize so much of that is thanks to Michael. "I think those are the most amazing goals I've ever heard," I say, trying to keep my emotions in check. "But I am happy. You know that, right?"

Liv shrugs. "Sometimes. You just seem to work so hard, and the only person you really ever have fun with is Jason."

My heart warms at the thought of Jason, of all that he's brought to my life, especially these past few months. "I really care about him," I say.

"Like a boyfriend, or a friend?"

I'm caught off guard by her blunt question, but I want to tell the truth. "I'm not sure yet. I'm still deciding."

"Well, don't take too long, Mama," she says as we loop back to our driveway. "Sometimes it's better to just go with how you feel than think so much." She unhooks Waffles's leash, and he darts around back.

From your lips to God's ears.

"Hey, before you go inside, I have one more surprise," I say. I lead her around back and dip inside to grab the seed packets. Miraculously, our garden survived the winter and now it's time to plant our spring vegetables. I hold up the seed packets for Liv and she hops up and down.

"Can we plant them now?"

"Yes, ma'am, we can." I hand her the packets and she darts off toward the raised beds. I've already prepared them for the seeds. I coach Liv on just what to do, and she follows each step, digging, pouring, and patting the soil on top as she goes. She begins to talk to each batch of seeds, and I smile.

I may not get it right most of the time, but this is a moment I don't want to forget.

"We are going to have so much food, Mama," she says, beaming up at me. She has a smear of dirt on her cheek. The sun hits her brown skin and highlights her freckles. In her face, Michael stares back. Lucia stares back. My mother stares back. A line of ancestors she carries in her DNA stares back, all mixing with mine.

"We are," I say. "Happy birthday, my sweet girl."

"Thank you, Mama." She continues to dig and plant, and I stand above, watching, grateful for this moment, grateful for how far we've come.

NINETEEN

MAY ARRIVES, AND MY APPRENTICESHIP IS OVER.

Liv's birthday came and went. Monica baked her a cake and we sat on my couch and looked back through baby pictures of her on my phone. After, I spiraled into a fresh wave of depression. It was one of the hardest days to get through, and I am still feeling the effects.

Though Ian and I have been cordial, he has been distant since seeing Jason and Ayana on New Year's Eve, and I haven't wanted to push. I've had a lot of time to think about what I want to do next: go back to Nashville, to my life and my job, or take a chance and move to Serenbe for something new.

Now I'm back in Nashville to talk to Jason and deal with my house. When I crunch over the random sticks and pinecones and see that the yard has been freshly mowed, I feel a little kick of gratitude for having such a good friend right down the road. My heart warms at the thought of Jason on his riding mower, diligently caring for my massive yard. Immediately, our time back in the cabin flashes through my mind, and his New Year's trip, where he, Ayana, and I felt like a family. Though nothing happened between us, it felt like a homecoming.

Inside, the air is hot and musty, and I open all the windows and spot a stack of mail a mile high on the kitchen island. I shuffle through it and find a letter from Michael. My heart jumps, but I tear it open and scan the contents.

Inside the envelope is a small gold necklace wrapped in tissue paper. Lucia wanted Liv to have it one day, but now he's passing it on to me. I clutch it to my chest and then fasten it around my neck.

The sorrow builds and squeezes, but I take a deep breath. *I can do this.* I'm not the same person I was last summer, and I know what I'm made of. I will call Michael and thank him for such a beautiful gesture.

I haven't told my mother, Jason, or even my boss that I'm back. As I assess the house, I steel myself to sort through the detritus of a life as a mother I can no longer claim and figure out what comes next.

I shoot Jason a quick text that I'm home, then get to work creating a punch list for the house. Regardless of whether I stay in Nashville or move, I can't be in this house anymore. There are too many reminders of a life once lived.

My phone dings. It's Jason's reply.

Welcome home, Kate. We've missed you so much, though Ayana can't wait to visit Serenbe again!

Guilt blossoms as I contemplate detangling my life from my friend of twenty years, from Ayana, from my mother, from work, from my yearslong support system.

I wish someone would tell me the right thing to do.

Doubt creeps in as I gather garbage bags and cleaning supplies. Now that I'm home, I'm afraid my old life is going to dig in its claws, remind me of my real roots, and keep me tethered out of obligation.

Ian flickers through my mind. I can't stop replaying what might have happened if Jason and Ayana hadn't shown up on New Year's

Eve, what he was going to tell me on that roof. As the months have passed, he's pulled further away, any thought of romance between us fizzling, though my heart still aches to try. I let out an audible sigh and focus on the work in front of me. There's plenty of time to figure out my relationship with Ian.

For the next two days, I get to work cleaning, caulking, painting, and sorting items into piles to sell, trash, or donate. Early on Saturday morning I ask Jason to come over after he drops Ayana at swim lessons.

I've brewed a pot of coffee and made some quick paleo banana bread that he loves. He knocks, and when I pull open the door, he yanks me into a tight hug and breathes me in. "Finally, she returns."

Over my shoulder, I can sense him taking in what's behind me: open cardboard boxes, furniture shoved against walls, various dishes wrapped delicately in crumpled newspaper. He steps back. "Kate, have you been robbed?"

"Let me caffeinate you, and then I'll explain."

I close the door, fix us both a cup of coffee and two slices of fresh banana bread slathered in grass-fed butter, then ask him to sit. Sun streams through the giant living room window. The leaves of the maple tree sway gently beyond the glass. Liv's swing still hangs, battered and unused, and the immediate punch of grief solidifies my decision: *It's time to move on.*

"Doing some spring cleaning?" Jason asks as he eyes me worriedly.

"If by spring cleaning you mean getting the house ready to sell, then yes," I offer.

"Ah." He's quiet as he stares into his coffee. "So you're really doing it?"

"I am selling, yes."

"Wow." He rests his head against the couch. "I guess I knew it was headed this way, but part of me hoped that maybe you'd decided to stay." He shakes his head. "Are you going to get a smaller place?"

"I'm not sure yet," I say. I glance around at my possessions, items that used to mean so much. "I've loved my life here and what I've built, but this was Liv's house. Without her, it doesn't feel like a home. I want to create something new."

He's quiet as he traces the rim of his cup. "Are you going to move to Serenbe?"

I shrug. "I don't know."

He exhales and gazes out the window. "Well, I'm proud of you, Kate. I know this isn't easy."

"It's definitely not, but it's the right next step."

He's silent as he sips his coffee and devours the banana bread in two easy bites. After wiping a few errant crumbs from his jeans, he speaks. "Can I say something unrelated?"

"I'll pay you."

"Ever since we visited Serenbe, I haven't been able to stop thinking about us." He swallows. "Like I said to you in my letter, after Shelby died, I figured the romantic part of my life was done. It was time to be a business owner and a father. To uphold a life she would have been proud of." He glances at me. "But then, what happened in your cabin, it shook something awake. It reminded me of what I want. And it gave me hope that maybe there's more than one person out there for me."

Ian flashes through my mind, but I nod and let him continue.

"It was so . . . *electric* but familiar. I haven't felt like that in years, Kate."

"I haven't either."

It's true. But what I've realized since then is that it wasn't about any sort of chemistry with Jason. It was about my need to release; to release the old Kate, the old baggage, the old anger, the old rage, hurt, grief, responsibilities, and ancient mistakes. It all culminated in one sensual, intense undoing, and Jason happened to be on the receiving end.

"So don't go. Stay. Let's give this thing between us a chance." His hand finds mine, and all it makes me think of is Ian. His warm hands. Those big, bright eyes. A connection that is so wildly different from the friendship I have with Jason. For a moment I don't know what to say—so caught between my future with Ian and my past with Jason.

"Our friendship is so important to me," I finally say. "I wouldn't want to risk it."

"We wouldn't have to." He shifts to look at me. "I've given this a lot of thought, Kate. Can you honestly say you haven't thought about us over the years?"

I nod. "Sure, there have been moments during our friendship where I've thought maybe there could be more, but the timing was never right, and I was always so grateful that you were such a constant in my life. Your friendship won out over any possible short-lived romance."

His fingers entwine with mine. "Who says it would be short-lived?"

"Jason." I gently remove my hand and look at him, realizing for the first time that this decision isn't about Ian or Jason. It's about me. "I want to start a new chapter in my life."

The statement pierces the air, and Jason's cheeks redden as he attempts a smile and retracts his hand. "I get it. Good for you." He rakes a hand through his hair and averts his eyes. "Shit. Now I feel like an idiot."

"No, don't." I scoot closer to him and rest my hand on his thigh. "I don't regret those kisses. I needed it. You needed it. But I know, in my gut, that you are my truest friend, and I am wildly protective of those boundaries. It's just not worth risking."

"No?" Hope lingers in his eyes.

"I don't think so. Not in this lifetime at least," I say. "Plus, I'm pretty sure Shelby would rise from the grave."

"She loved you so much," he says. "God, I miss her."

And I miss Liv. "I know you do. I do too."

He clutches my hand, and this time it's different. A bit of the tension has eased and in its place is acceptance. "So." He clears his throat and sits up. "How can I help you through this?"

"Know any good Realtors?" I ask.

"As a matter of fact, I do." He looks around the house and sighs. "We have so many memories here, don't we?"

I swallow the emotion and nod. "We do. But being here makes me feel stuck in the past, mourning a version of Liv I will never again be able to have. And being in Serenbe makes me feel better. I am better there, but that doesn't mean I don't appreciate everything I've gained here."

"So it sounds like you might stay in Serenbe after all? At least for a while?"

I nod as the answer cements into place. The community. The cabin that has become my home. Ian. "Yes, I think you're right."

He grips my shoulder. "I'm going to miss you, Baker."

"I'm going to miss you too. But I'm just a car ride away."

He fills me in on his business and tells me he's going to sell, which will open a new door for Ayana and their future. I tell him that I'm also going to meet with my boss and quit my job, a decision I've thought about a ton. During these past few months, it's been shocking to realize I haven't missed it. Not the people or the work. It didn't fill me up on a soul level anymore. And with the sale of the house, I will have a nice cushion if I decide I still want to be Farmer Kate.

"It seems we're both moving on, huh?" I say.

"Looks that way."

Suddenly, tears stream down my face, and he wipes them away, both of us reminiscing about what was and what could have been. We've both been through so much, together and apart, and I can only hope as we branch into our new lives that we will be better, braver versions of ourselves and dare to live the lives we both deserve.

20

I INVITE JASON TO EASTSIDE BOWL, A RETRO BOWLING alley meets diner meets bar meets music venue.

It is unpretentious and loud—two things we definitely need for this conversation. Plus, alcohol. I get there first and pay for our lane as Liv rubs her leg impatiently and asks when Ayana is going to arrive. As if on cue, Ayana runs through the door and sprints toward Liv, even though they just saw each other yesterday. I wave to Jason, who offers a tentative smile. I've already gotten our shoe sizes and hand over the stiff red, white, and blue shoes to Ayana and Jason.

"Lane 13. Prepare to lose."

He pops his knuckles. "You wish, Baker."

We walk past the hopping diner, the busy arcade, and the sprawling bar on the opposite side of the bowling alley. At our lane, the girls gush over the green leather banquettes, the brightly colored balls, and the large scoring screens. While Jason grabs us beers, the girls take an exorbitant amount of time making up fake bowling names and snapping candid bowler photos. I let them go first, as the bumpers rise and then lower when it's my and Jason's turn.

I bowl a strike right off the bat, closely followed by Jason.

"It's on," he warns. He points at me and then slides a finger across his throat.

"That's more creepy than scary."

The mood is light, and the girls take turns dropping their balls with a dramatic *thud* so that they barely roll down the lane. In between turns, they stuff the bowling balls under their shirts.

"Look, Mama! I'm having a baby!"

Jason and I snap pictures and take one of the four of us, all of us making goofy faces. I post it on Instagram with #family, and Jason gives me a hard time.

"I thought you hated social media."

"I do," I say, "but you guys are my family, and I want the world to know."

It's one of those spontaneous nights where everyone is in a good mood and reminds me of everything good about our friendship and the life we've built. Why would I ever want this to change? Why would he?

After an hour of bowling, the girls are bored and want to transition to the arcade. While they play games, Jason and I walk over to the diner to order dinner and watch the girls from our booth.

"So," I say, nursing another beer. "How are things?"

He pretends to scan his menu seriously and then finally looks up. "If you mean how have things been since I've been waiting to see if you want to become something more? Just peachy." He folds his menu and then his hands on top of the sticky plastic. "You?"

My heart aches for what we've put each other through—such unnecessary anticipation. I grapple for what to say and start with the most basic option.

I motion around us. "This has been nice. Feels like old times."

"It does feel like old times."

I fiddle with the ketchup bottle, not knowing what else to say. "Ever since I said no to Michael, I've realized that romantic relationships are somewhat overrated," I finally blurt.

He laughs. "Oh?"

"I mean, in the beginning, there's nothing better than falling in love, right? The butterflies. The consumption. The desire. The kissing." I drop my voice to a whisper. "The sex. But then it changes. Those early moments of ecstasy deepen into something familiar. Partners take each other for granted. Roles cement and harden. Resentment creeps in. We start worrying about money, or the dishes, or who's doing what or who's *not* doing what. Everything you treasured in the beginning fades away until you're looking for a way out . . . or trying to make yourself feel desired and new again with somebody else." I shake my head and close my menu. "It's a vicious cycle, and I'm not willing to do that to you—or to us," I say. "Before that kiss, we'd never crossed the line from friends to something else. There has to be a reason for that."

"Well, we were both married."

"Not for the last million years," I say.

He shrugs. "I don't think the timing was right."

"Or we just weren't supposed to be together." I gently clasp his hand. "I'd rather live with the thought of *what if* than ruin what we have. The thought of messing up our friendship is worse to me than any divorce."

"So in your fantasy, we're married?" he asks.

I slap him lightly and release his hand. "Seriously, with everything I just said, that's what you heard?"

"I don't know." He sighs. "I just told myself that we could be different."

I shrug. "Maybe we could. But I don't want to put that type of pressure on us—or the girls."

He's quiet as the waiter refills our drinks. "I get it. I do. But last summer and what came after . . . it was the first time in years I've felt remotely alive since Shelby died. You did that, Kate."

"And you did that for me too," I say.

He drums his fingers on the table and glances at the girls, who are arguing over a game. "So that's it, then?" he asks. "We just bury it?"

"Jason, you are my family," I say, leaning in again to grab his hand. "At the end of the day, it's really as simple as that."

He smooths his thumb over my bare ring finger. His eyes are sad, but there's a rumbling of mischief behind them. "How many times are you going to have to turn me down before I finally get it?"

"I'm not turning you down," I remind him. "I'm choosing to stay us."

He releases my hand, then tips his beer to mine in a toast. "Fine, you win, Baker. Here's to staying us."

"Can I get that in writing?"

He smirks. "No."

I watch the girls and smile. Liv is doing awkward one-leg dance moves while Ayana plays Zelda. Liv cheers her on, making funny faces that have Ayana folded over in laughter while she tries to concentrate on her game. We chat about Jason's selling prospects and how things are with Michael.

After my refusal of his marriage proposal, he's moved past the hurt, and in its place is the possibility of a truly functional relationship. Though I can't imagine parting with Liv on a regular basis, I know she needs it; she needs her entire family.

As we order shepherd's pies and turn to easier conversation, I sense it: Jason and I are going to be okay. We are going to find a way to enter a new phase of our friendship without compromising it. And I realize, without a doubt, that Jason is one of the greatest loves of my life.

But as I'm learning, not all great loves have to be romantic.

TWENTY

I LOOK AROUND MY HOUSE ONE LAST TIME.

The boxes have been cleared, the walls painted, the floors scrubbed. The house was artfully staged, and with the right Realtor, the house had ten offers in forty-eight hours. Just like that, after years of fussing over the house, of endless arguments on upkeep, outsourcing landscaping and mowing, painting and repainting, arranging and rearranging, and even planting two rows of trees to cover up the neighbor's chain-link fence—Liv and I promised we would watch the cypresses grow to thirty feet—it's all been handed to someone else.

I take my time walking from room to room. Because it was a cash buyer, we had a fifteen-day close. After sorting, discarding, and donating, I'm keeping just a few sacred objects from my life with Liv. I have some of her paintings, a journal, one of her favorite stuffed animals, and two books I've read to her a thousand times: *Watership Down* and *Where the Sidewalk Ends*. Though I know my memories aren't contained in materialistic items, it still soothes me to have little pieces of her. I also dismantled her swing and decided to take the wood with me; maybe I'll turn it into a piece of art in the cabin . . . that is, if I can work out the logistics of working at the farm for a more definite period of time.

I start downstairs, opening drawers, sweeping my eyes over every little place I could have missed in my cleaning frenzy. The house feels so cold without our belongings, as if it is a stranger's house. It has been stripped and sterilized. Every room I enter, I am reminded of how Liv would disturb the peace. The *thud* and *rattle* of the front door as she went out to swing and listen to music. The drone of Google Home as she listened to a podcast. The *pop* and *smack* of her bubble gum. The *bang* and *scrape* of a dining room chair being dragged over to the pantry to steal snacks. The *ping* of dropped marbles across our white-oak floors. The *thwack* of scissors across paper. The *squeak* of her markers on a blank page. The *slap* and *plop* of water sloshed in the bath. Everywhere she went had a soundtrack. Now, as I take it all in one last time, there is only the wounded hush of silence.

After I've looked through all the kitchen cabinets, bathrooms, and closets, I stop in Liv's room. I hired a painter, and now it's a boring white shell. Every nick and scrape, every bit of personalized detail has been scrubbed clean for the new family who will live here. Liv would hate it.

I step inside and my chest constricts. This white box once contained Liv's wild imagination, which was always full of color: glue and scissors and books and magic kits and dolls and clothes and stuffed animals all mingled to create her irreplaceable world. It was agony to sort through her remaining possessions, especially when I found the stack of cards Michael and Lucia sent her for Christmas every year. He'd given her his number again in one of them, encouraged her to reach out. All this time I thought it was Liv's idea to contact him, because she felt like she was missing something, but Michael had been the one who opened the door.

I open her closet and stare into it, expecting what, I don't know. As I'm about to shut off the light, I see that on the very end of her closet rack, to the left, hangs a gold necklace with an *O* for Olivia. I gasp. I gave her that necklace two Christmases ago, but she said she'd lost it. I grip it in my fingers, unknotting the chain and securing it around my neck with unsteady hands. It rests next to Lucia's necklace I now wear, two women who have greatly affected my life.

I readjust it and glance at myself in the mirror that hangs on the back of the door. Another small gift I can carry with me. I shut off the light and walk down the hall, survey the living room once more. A million recollections tumble through my brain—all those nothing moments I took for granted, all those memories I will treasure for the rest of my life. I made a home for us here, and that is no small thing. Liv loved our house and neighborhood. She loved her life.

I flip off the light and step onto the porch. The air is muggy and promises rain. I stare at the sky, the clouds low and menacing, which reminds me of the massive tornado that blew through two years ago, waking Liv and me from a dead sleep. We hurried downstairs, the neighborhood sirens blaring, trees whipping furiously, their bendable branches screaming against our windows. We'd crawled into the closet under the stairs. I'd never been more terrified, wondering if our house would get destroyed, if we'd be taken along with it. As I clutched her quivering body to my chest, I'd soothed her and told her it would be okay, secretly thinking, *If we go, at least we'll be together.* I'd never considered that just two years later, she'd be gone, and I'd still be here.

And now I will move on. I will start over, rebuilding a life in which I will always have the remains of this one in my bones. It will not be easy, and I will not always know the way forward, but Liv would want me to try. This much, I know.

I hurry down the steps and toward my car, which is packed to the brim. I already had dinner with my mother, Jason, and Ayana last night, all of us shedding tears and telling stories. They all promise to visit, and I know that soon enough, they will settle into a new rhythm where my absence won't scream so loudly. Where Liv's death will be a residue instead of a massive stain. Change is never easy, and leaving behind my support system, to most, seems foolish. But for me, for now, it's necessary.

Ian crosses my mind, and I smile. I think of the farm, my cozy cabin, and my new friends. While I can never replace my old life, I accept that I am stepping into the new, slowly and steadily moving forward.

I rub the *O* of the necklace as I start the car and put it in Reverse. I hesitate as I back onto the road beside the mailbox, the maple tree looking forlorn without that big yellow swing. A few tears slip down my cheeks, and my heart feels as though it might split in two. Part of me feels like walking away from this house is abandoning Liv, but I know that's just my brain trying to keep me safe. She would want this for me, to carry on, to find the light, even when the dark tugs me back.

I turn on one of Liv's favorite songs and stab at the button to lower the window. I knock away the tears, shift the car into gear, and drive.

When I pull into Serenbe four hours later, I feel like I've made the right decision. No more biding my time. No more waiting. I, more than anyone, know that life is much too short for that.

As I'm getting settled, unpacking some personal items to make it more like home, someone knocks on my door. "It's open!" I call.

Ian steps through. Just the sight of him comforts me. His eyes drink me in in that slow, delicious way of his. I don't ask how he knew to stop by. In a town this small, news really does travel fast.

"So you're back," he says.

"I'm back," I say, opening a box. "Come in."

I pat the couch next to me and he ambles over, situating himself to give me his full attention. That's one of the things I love most about Ian. When I talk, he's all in. There's so much I want to say, so much he has given me, and I fear I will never be able to repay him for his kindness and blind faith in me. He waits as I gather my thoughts, and when I do, he gives a little nod, encouraging me to speak.

"So, as you can see, I'm settling in."

He laughs. "I can see that, yes."

"Which leads me to an important question."

"Which is?"

"I know the internship is over, but I want to stay. I want to work on the farm and live here . . . at least for a while." I shift on the couch and pull a pillow into my lap. "Which is why I sold my house."

"You sold your house?" He swipes a hand over his beard. "I guess I need to tell the new interns, huh?"

I swat him with the pillow and suddenly panic. "Wait, are there really new interns?" I can't imagine handing this cabin over to anyone else.

He smiles, and his eyes crinkle. "No. I should have already started a new apprenticeship, but I wanted to wait." He looks me steadily in the eye. "You sure you want this, Kate?"

I've thought about this a lot—if I'm running away to start a new life, if I'm avoiding the hard things, but I don't think I am. Serenbe feels like the perfect place to grow roots and continue to heal. "I'm sure. Are *you* sure you want me here?"

He nods, just once. "Yes."

My heart hammers wickedly in my chest. I open my mouth to speak, then close it. I know he's talking about farming, but it feels personal, deeper. "Ian, when I came here, I was completely broken," I say. "You gave me an anchor—something to work toward, something to look forward to—and for that, I am forever grateful." I take a shaky breath. "I feel like I've really started to create a life here," I continue. "But part of me was still tethered to the past. On New Year's Eve, when Jason showed up, it solidified what I already knew. He is my dearest friend, and I love him, but I'm not *in* love with him. I've never been in love with him. Which is what I told him while I was in Nashville."

Relief floods Ian's face, but he stays quiet.

"It's important that you know that."

Instead of speaking, in one swift motion, he pulls me to him and kisses me until I'm breathless. He smooths the hair from my face and cups my cheeks in his large, rough palms. "I'm sorry for New Year's Eve. I'm sorry I had to work through my own stuff. I'm sorry I've been so distant and didn't come to you sooner, but I wanted to be sure. I wanted you to be sure." He releases me and sighs. "I know I said I didn't want to get hurt again, but damn it, Kate. You're worth the risk."

I nod, a few tears slipping down my cheeks. "You're worth the risk too."

I curl into him, and we sit like that, in silence. For the first time in months, I feel like I've come home.

Summer

21

LIV AND I ARE ON A QUICK WEEKEND TRIP BEFORE SHE leaves for Mexico City for the entire summer.

Once the Serenbe project was back in play, I promised my boss I would come, and true to my word, I'm finally here. Instead of our usual beach trip to celebrate my birthday, we are celebrating in a different place.

Unbeknownst to us, Serenbe is also having a yearly celebration, and Liv pretends it's all for me. The local parade is an onslaught of festive homemade floats and residents with adorable dogs—Waffles included—that feels like stepping back in time. In the evening we walk to the fireworks celebration down by the lake. It seems the whole town is spread out on checkered blankets, poking through gigantic picnic baskets and chatting. Dogs chase kids with sparklers that fizz and pop in a metallic burst across a quickly darkening sky. I spread out our blanket. Waffles obediently sits and wags his tail at all the potential distractions: dropped food, kids who love dogs, and the ability to run free. Liv massages her calf, her tell when she's been on it too long.

"Do you like your birthday now?" Liv asks, looking around. "It's like a huge party."

"I do," I say. I think back to last summer, how much we've both changed. "Want a sparkler?" I ask, motioning to the narrow dock jutting into the lake, where the DJ is manning the music and handing out sparklers by the fistful.

"Maybe in a sec." She wipes sweat from her nose and pushes into me, smacking a mosquito on her knee as she pats Waffles on the head. She smears the blood and leaves a tomato-red streak across her thigh. She reaches into her small bag and extracts a homemade card and a little box. "For you."

"Liv, how sweet." I read the card, which says,

Mama, birthdays really are the best. Remember that you deserve to be celebrated too. I love you to the moon and back.

Liv, a.k.a. Pepper

I clutch the card to my chest as tears spring to my eyes. "This is perfect, Liv. Thank you."

She gestures to the box. "Open it."

I open the tiny box to find a *K* necklace just like the *O* necklace I gave her a couple of years ago, which, of course, promptly went missing. "I've been saving money from chores so I could buy it. Do you like it?"

"Oh, Liv." I put it on and arrange the *K* on my collarbone. "I can't think of a more perfect gift."

I wrap an arm around her and take it all in: the endless joyful families, the crush of excitement at the impending fireworks show, the children running barefoot across thick patches of grass with their sparklers aimed high. A few dogs dash into the lake, doggy-paddling before bursting onto land and spraying droplets into the air. There is something timeless and strangely familiar about this place. Liv feels it too. She sighs and burrows in closer.

"I like it here, Mama."

"Me too, *cariño*. Me too."

I cannot fathom not seeing her for the whole summer, but I know it will be good for her, and this is what we have agreed to. Michael is going to meet us in Atlanta so Liv can fly from there while I stay here for a while and scope out the place for my boss. Already I have meetings lined up for the entire next week.

Plus, I know she needs more solo time with Michael, and it will expand her mind and her life in ways I cannot give her. I am coming to realize that it is not about choosing our family or Michael's family—she needs both.

We quiet as the DJ takes over once the sun sets, and then the fireworks show begins. Not knowing what to expect, we are amazed by the timed music and impressive display. The fireworks explode in multicolored starbursts across the inky sky. Their sparks rain down over the lake and disappear in a trail of thick white smoke. Waffles barks at the sky before cowering next to me. In twenty minutes, the crowd is on their feet, clapping after the finale, and I memorize Liv's innocent, happy face, tipped skyward.

It is one of those perfect nights I will never forget, and we chat about it long into the night and even the next day over pancakes. After breakfast, while Liv browses the bookstore and gets a lesson from the owner on how to choose the right book, I text Jason.

How's Ethiopia?

He immediately texts back a picture of him and Ayana in her village. *Healing. Incredible. Indescribable*, he types back. *Selling the business was the right thing to do. How's utopia?*

I smile. *Same.*

I'm so proud of Jason for taking Ayana back to her roots. She and Liv are growing up, becoming more independent and discovering who they are outside of us. I've also been pleased to find that once a potential romance was off the table with Jason, the sexual tension eased between us, and we've returned to being even better friends than before.

"Want to go to the farm?" I ask once we're back outside. Besides the fireworks celebration, we've visited the petting zoo, attempted horseback riding, eaten at the three restaurants, and even overpaid for stuffed animals and candles at one of the boutiques, Hamlin.

"Sure," Liv says.

We walk from the shops toward the farm. Waffles trots assuredly between us. I find my way easily, as if I know just where to go.

We arrive at the farm a little early, and I poke around the greenhouse, sniffing deeply at the perennials that surround it. I walk over to some of the beds to see what seeds have been sown: carrots, tomatoes, peppers, squash, sorrel, beans, greens, and various berries. I see another bed for okra and eggplants.

"Look, Liv. This is just like our garden back home, right?"

She runs over to inspect. "Yep, but this is way bigger." She commands Waffles to sit, and he obeys.

"Isn't this a cool farm?"

She nods. "It's like a fairy tale."

"It is, isn't it?" I wander back toward the greenhouse and see a flyer for a summer farm apprenticeship and a few summer rental houses. I quickly scan the details for both. What would it be like to work on a farm? Or to live here? To put away the computer and work with my hands for a few hot months? I almost laugh at the concept—me, taking time off as an engineer to be an apprentice on a farm—but something about it piques my interest.

Last year I swore I was going to strike a better balance between work and home. Have I even tried? Technically, I'll be done with my work obligations in Serenbe in a week or so. Liv will be with Michael. And I have about a million vacation days stored up.

This past year has taken its toll, both emotionally and physically. I've been going so hard so fast, I haven't really stopped to think about what I need. Now that I've turned down Michael's proposal, and Jason and I have agreed to stay just friends, what do I really have besides my work? I think of returning to Nashville, all alone for the entire summer. I know I will lose myself to a sea of deadlines and the usual routine.

Is that what I really want? I glance around again, at a place that oozes with a different quality and pace of life.

Maybe it's time for something new . . . at least while Liv's away.

Before people start to trickle in for the tour, a tall, broad man appears from the greenhouse, a few potted plants in his arms. My heart nearly stops as I'm hit with the strongest sense of déjà vu. He looks up, sensing me staring, and stops walking too. His boots scuff into the earth and a small plume of dirt floats up around us. Our eyes meet. The world blurs. I take a few steps forward.

After a few intense beats, I find my voice. "Need help?"

"Sure." He offers me a potted plant and points to a long wooden table under a tent. "Here for the farm tour?"

"I am. With my daughter." I point to Liv, who's chasing a butterfly and tentatively trying cartwheels, though she only lands on her good leg. "Say hi, Olivia!"

"Hi, Olivia!" she shouts midcartwheel.

"She seems shy," he jokes. He eyes Waffles. "And who's this?"

"Waffles." Even saying his name makes me smile.

"Maybe you can get him a brother named Syrup."

I laugh. "Maybe."

He eyes me and scratches his beard. "Have we met?"

"I don't think so." I extend my hand. "I'm Kate Baker. Visiting from Nashville."

"Ian Hunter." He slides his palm into mine, and the feeling is strangely erotic. He has a worker's hands, strong and rough. We both study our clasped palms and then each other, neither of us letting go at first. "You staying long?" he asks, clearing his throat and finally stepping back.

"I'm here for work," I say. "What can you tell me about this summer apprenticeship?"

He laughs as he arranges the pots. "Are you really interested?"

I scan the land, rich with crops and rolling hills. I turn back and study this stranger's face—a face that, for reasons I can't explain, I already know.

"Mama, look! Now there are three butterflies!" Liv and Waffles chase them as the butterflies dip and soar across the open field.

Olivia yelps and tries to catch one gingerly between her palms while Waffles barks and sprints in circles. Something releases in my chest as my heart fills with a strange kind of wonderful—that indescribable feeling of coming home.

I stare into Ian's warm eyes. Am I interested? After a beat, I nod. "I am," I say. "Definitely."

TWENTY-ONE

IT'S MY BIRTHDAY.

I wipe a clod of dirt from my cheek and tip my face to the sun. The warmth is a welcome reprieve from a surprisingly cold spring and mild start to summer.

"Kate, you slacking?"

I turn and smile at Ian, who saunters over with a hoe in his hand.

"I'm basking, not slacking."

"Is that so?" He slides his arms around my waist and pulls me to him. "How's the birthday girl feeling?"

"Older." I smile at him; his eyes are light and happy. We've just returned from the beach to commemorate Liv's passing. I wasn't sure I could ever go back to the place that took her from me, but it was one of Liv's favorite places in the world. I knew I couldn't avoid it forever, and I wanted to remember all the good times we'd had there too. Not just the tragedy.

On the beach, my people had gathered behind me, creating a human fortress: Ian, Jason, Ayana, Michael, and my mother. I'd waited until the sky performed its kaleidoscope of colors—orange, purple, and a vibrant splash of red—before I'd sifted some of Liv's ashes into the sea. The sea she loved, the sea we returned to every year, the sea that took her from me. Ian had looped an arm around my shoulders, heavy and protective. The others joined in, making contact with various parts of my body: my elbow, my lower back, my fingers.

No one said a word because there were no more words to say. We simply stood together, watching the last rays drain beyond the flat horizon, remembering my daughter, remembering Liv.

Now, a year after her passing, I'm still standing, but the circumstances have changed. I am not the same woman with the same worries. I have loved deeply and lost everything. I have slowly rebuilt my life and learned to open myself up again. I am learning day by day.

Though Ian and I are taking things slow, we have done a great deal of work on talking about our grief. Once he started sharing openly about Ella and his wife, something in him changed. Now we often compare details about our daughters and realize they most likely would have been fast friends. At least that's what we tell ourselves.

"You think it's going to be a good summer?" I ask, gazing at the land. It was a long, hard winter and dry spring, but we are hopeful for a strong summer growing season.

"I do." His fingers tighten around my waist. I lean against him and sigh. Though it has been the hardest and most tragic year of my life, it has also been the most transformative. Coming to this place, finding a new home, finding Ian . . .

It's a gift I won't ever take for granted. The light amid the dark.

"What do you say we get out of here and head to Atlanta for dinner?"

"Ooh, fancy." I slap him on the butt. "You buying?"

"Nope."

"Ha." We walk back to the farm entrance and hop in his truck. I am aching for a shower and a hot meal.

At the cabin, Ian jumps out first and runs around to open my door. I stare at him, perplexed. "That's unusually old-fashioned of you," I say. I hop down and feel his forehead. "You feeling okay?"

"You joke," he says, plucking my keys from my hand. "But I can be a gentleman." He unlocks the door and motions for me to step inside first.

"You're acting much stranger than usual," I comment as I walk inside. And that's when I see him: a scruffy black dog sitting in the middle of my living room. Not barking. Not chewing anything. Just sitting, as if someone commanded him to. He has a red bow around his neck. He scratches one floppy ear and yawns. "Ian?" I turn to find him grinning from ear to ear.

"Don't be mad, but a friend of mine couldn't keep him and asked if I knew anyone who wanted a dog. His name is Murphy. He's one year old, barely trained, and is a total handful, but he's loyal."

"Oh my God." I kneel, and he jumps into my arms. I look into his dark eyes and feel something familiar I can't quite place. It's like when people just look at pets and know a certain one is *their* pet. I feel that now. He barks and licks my face. He smells like corn chips, his fur is matted, and he looks like a combo of at least three different dogs. "He's perfect," I whisper. I begin to laugh, and Murphy knocks me back and climbs on top of me, flattening himself like a pancake.

"Love at first sight," Ian says.

I laugh and attempt to move Murphy off me, but he's surprisingly strong. I sit up and cradle him in my arms, thinking of Liv. "Is this really happening? I have a dog?"

"You have a dog." Ian kneels beside me and grips my hand in his. I look up, and his warm eyes glisten. "Kate." He runs his fingers over my own. "Ever since you came here . . ." He clears his throat. "You've brought me back to life. A life I didn't even know was still worth living. But it is. Thanks to you." He stares at me, and his eyes fill with tears. "I love you, Katherine Anne Baker. More than I've ever loved another woman."

My breath stalls as his words thrust deep. I never expected to love someone so quickly or to feel such joy amid such bone-deep pain. I search for what to say but can only think of one thing. "I love you too, Ian Eliot Hunter. More than I've ever loved another man."

Part of me thought that because Olivia died, I could never open my heart again. That I would be betraying her memory, or that Ian would be betraying his wife and daughter. But I've found that opening myself up again is exactly what I need. It's how I will continue to heal.

As I clutch Murphy against my chest and Ian scoots beside me, I feel complete in a way I haven't in so very long.

"Does this mean we're *not* going to Atlanta for dinner?" I ask, rubbing Murphy's head.

"Correct," he says. "I've ordered in. I thought we could have a cozy night with your new addition. Is that okay?"

I think of all the birthdays before this one, how they would come and go without much thought. This year I dreaded my birthday, but at this moment, I can't imagine anything better.

"It's perfect."

He threads his fingers through mine, and I notice the dirt caked under his nails—mirrors of my own. I think about those hands on my body. What his mouth can do. I've never had a physical connection with anyone the way I have with Ian. It is primal and deep. It is unshakable and unconditional. It is safe and warm. Any spark I've had in the past pales in comparison.

"Liv always wanted a dog," I say.

"So have you," he reminds me. "And you should have what you want, Kate. You deserve it."

Do I?

It's taken me such a long time to think about what I deserve, especially when it comes to my own happiness. But Liv would want me to be happy, and though I won't ever feel complete without her, I am learning to cope.

Slowly, achingly, I am learning to live.

EPILOGUE

THE GREEN LEAVES RIPPLE IN THE WIND.

I stand in front of Serenbe's lake. The water glistens, popping and shimmering with light. I tip my head back to an ocean of blue in the cloudless sky. Sunset is coming, my favorite part of the day. A multitude of trees reach toward the sky—pine, spruce, oak, maple—their leaves in constant motion.

I am the only one in the forest, as I am most days, and though sometimes I can't believe I'm in Georgia, part of me feels as though I have always belonged. Before, my life was on such a predictable track. Now, I don't know what's coming next.

But I'm here, and that's a start.

The heat is fierce. I smack away a few hungry mosquitoes and watch a hawk swoop down, nab a fish from the water, and rocket back into the sky. The dog barks beside me, arching up on his hind legs, ready to pounce.

"Sit," I command. He obeys, and I ruffle his fur. "You're such a good boy."

I never imagined having a dog. I never imagined farming. I never imagined my entire life not revolving completely around Liv. I shake my head, clearing the restless thoughts billowing through my mind like the leaves.

The dog barks at a squirrel that scurries into a small space beneath a boulder overgrown with moss. The tiny cave looks dank. I smile. One of Liv's favorite words.

I close my eyes, open them, absorbing all that's ahead and all that's vanished. I whistle for the dog to come and keep walking around the perimeter of the lake, then start back into the thicket of trees just as the sun begins its lazy descent beyond the horizon. It's not a long walk, but I want to keep moving while the pink light acts as a guide.

We walk in sync, my dog and I, heading back, heading out of the woods.

ACKNOWLEDGMENTS

ONCE IN A WHILE, AN AUTHOR WRITES A BOOK, AND THEY know it's a different kind of story before they've even finished the last line. For me, *The Other Year* is that book. When I wrote it, I was out of contract with my previous publisher. I was a suspense writer, and I had fallen a little bit out of love with writing and the publishing industry in general. I'd started a business for nonfiction authors that kept me tethered to my computer (and other people's dreams), and I was truly, deeply burned out.

I seriously contemplated leaving the writing world, because I was afraid: I was afraid of not ever reaching the goals I had set for myself or not telling the type of stories I wanted to tell. I was afraid that as long as I was an entrepreneur, I wouldn't ever make time for my own writing goals. Then, I got hit with an entire story in the span of a single moment.

And I knew I had to write it.

Since I was out of contract, this was the first book I had written in over four years where I wouldn't get paid for it ahead of time. Instead, I had to conjure the love I felt for the craft and create for the sake of creating. No deadlines. No publisher. Just me and the page.

I truly believe great things happen when you have the expansiveness to sit back and create. Though this story was hard to write, I felt its magic come through me, and when it finally landed at Harper Muse, I felt a different kind of energy than I'd ever felt in publishing. The closest thing I can compare it to is a sense of coming home.

The Harper Muse team has made me believe in publishing again. Their care, passion, and communicativeness blow me away. There's been a calm around this launch that I have never experienced before, and I think it's because I feel fully supported, in every way.

Thank you to my literary agent, Rachel Beck, who has been on this journey with me through all the highs and lows. In many ways, I feel we are just beginning, and I cannot wait to see what's next. Thank you to the most incredible, caring developmental editor, Kimberly Carlton, who has been my biggest champion. Your passion for this book has been clear since day one. I cannot wait to work together for the long haul. Julie Breihan, you are the most detail-oriented copy editor I have ever worked with, personally or in business. Thank you for making this book the best version of itself. Caitlin Halstead, Nekasha Pratt, Keri Potts, Taylor Ward, and Margaret Kercher, you are the best marketing, editorial, and PR team an author could ask for, and I mean that from the bottom of my heart. Thank you to the cover designer, the audio team and exceptional narrator, and publisher Amanda Bostic, who runs one heck of a business.

I also want to thank the writing group who helped me usher this baby into the world: Meredith Lyons, Melissa Collings, Emily Whitson, and Cheryl Rieger. This book could not have been published without your sharp eyes and insightful feedback. An intense thank-you to my own amazing freelance editor, Jackie Hritz, who worked on this book from the very beginning and helped give me the confidence to pitch it in the first place.

Thank you to all the authors I look up to in this genre—Josie Silver, Sophie Cousens, Rebecca Serle, and Taylor Jenkins Reid, just to name a few—and any author who plays with this little thing called time. Thank you to my dear writing friends (of which there are too many to name); my healers (yes, I am woo); my clients; my mom, dad, and brother; and anyone who has ever been brave enough to sit down and write a book. Thank you to Suzy Approved Books, for always putting on the best tours. Thank you to the readers, and book bloggers, and book clubbers who read and share. This is only ever possible because of you.

Thank you to my husband, Alex Holguin, who is the best partner I could ask for. There is a little bit of you in all the male characters in this book, and I know how lucky I am to build a life with my true best friend. Watching you step into your true passion as a breathwork facilitator and healer has allowed me to step more fully into my own dreams as an author. I know we've been around and around many lifetimes together, though I have to say: I'm really loving this one. Here's to us.

And lastly, thank you to my daughter, Sophie. Though I never planned on becoming a mother, I am thankful every day that I get to be one, and that you are who I get to be one for. You have been my greatest teacher and are so full of life, light, love, joy, and imagination. You continue to be exactly who you are and forge your own path in life, dear girl. It will take you far . . . and I will be there, cheering you on, every step of the way.

DISCUSSION QUESTIONS

1. In the book, Kate makes one fateful mistake. She looks at her phone while her daughter is in the ocean, and as a result, there are two very different outcomes. Is Kate responsible for what happens to Liv?

2. In one reality, Kate suffers a great loss. In the other, she lives life as she always has. Do you think it's possible to truly appreciate what we have while we have it, or do we only appreciate things once they're gone?

3. Which man do you like best for Kate, if any? Why or why not?

4. What was your overall takeaway from both of Kate's journeys?

5. Ian kept a big secret from Kate. Did this affect how you felt about him? Why or why not?

6. Kate is a single mother who is doing the best she can. If you are a mother, what do you think is the most important lesson to pass on to your children?

7. Kate is best friends with Jason, and they have maintained a platonic friendship for twenty years before they discuss the possibility of something romantic. Do you think men and women can just be friends?

8. In both storylines, Kate ends up with a dog and at the farm, meeting Ian. Do you believe we always end up exactly where we are supposed to no matter what, or does tragedy change our path completely?

9. Where do you see Kate in five years in both storylines?

10. If *The Other Year* were to be made into a movie, who would play all the major characters?

From the Publisher

GREEK BOOKS

ARE EVEN BETTER WHEN THEY'RE SHARED!

Help other readers find this one:

- Post a review at your favorite online bookseller

- Post a picture on a social media account and share why you enjoyed it

- Send a note to a friend who would also love it—or better yet, give them a copy

Thanks for reading!

ABOUT THE AUTHOR

Photo by Kate Gallaher

REA FREY IS THE AWARD-WINNING, BESTSELLING AUTHOR of several nonfiction books and four domestic suspense novels, *Not Her Daughter*, *Because You're Mine*, *Until I Find You*, and *Secrets of Our House*. As a book doula, she helps other writers birth their own stories into the world. Her weekly podcast, *The Book Doula*, demystifies the publishing industry for writers everywhere.

To learn more, visit reafrey.com